A WHISPER FROM OBLIVION

A WHISPER FROM OBLIVION

DECLAN O'ROURKE

GILL BOOKS

Gill Books
Hume Avenue
Park West
Dublin 12
www.gillbooks.ie

Gill Books is an imprint of M.H. Gill and Co.

© Declan O'Rourke 2023
Map on endpapers © Tailte Éireann/Government
of Ireland. Copyright Permit No. MP 003923

9780717194872

Edited by Conor Kostick
Printed and bound in Great Britain by CPI Group (UK) Ltd, Croydon, CR0 4YY
This book is typeset in 11 on 17pt, Minion Pro.

The paper used in this book comes from the wood pulp of sustainably managed forests.

All rights reserved.
No part of this publication may be copied, reproduced or transmitted in any form or by any means, without written permission of the publishers.

A CIP catalogue record for this book is available from the British Library.

5 4 3 2 1

For my parents,
Declan and Marian

To the dream
of a brighter future for the lowest among us
than a team of astrologers might divine for a king

Author's Note on Language

The original Irish text that inspired this story — contemporary to the Muskerry Gaeltacht of the 1840s — used characters and symbols no longer in general use today. Out of respect for those whose lives this book concerns, I have endeavoured to stay as faithful as possible to their Irish, when Irish is used, and to how they referred to themselves.

Though the story is primarily presented in English, the linguistic landscape in which we are placed was a dichotomy of Irish and English. A person's name may therefore be spelled more than one way, subject to the perspective being that of a native Irish or an English speaker.

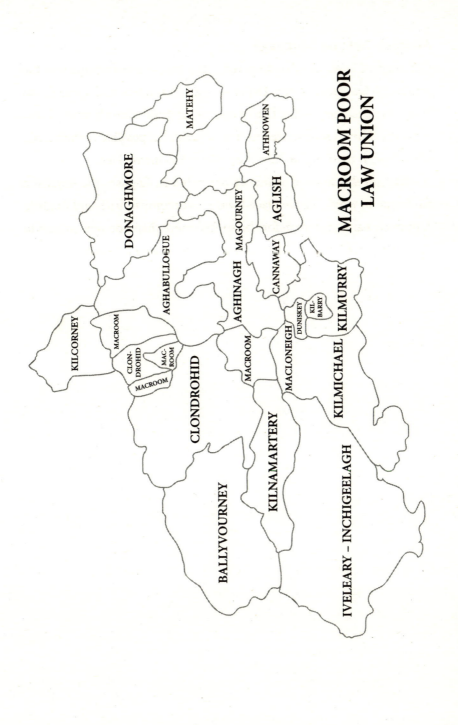

1847

EANÁIR

JANUARY

1

Between the Blows of the Wind

The cabin for its instrument, an insolent wind had been rattling and sucking at the door all the restless night. But when Cáit awoke it was amid descending silence and to the bite of frost in her nose and throat. The new year had brought the bitter cold, she realised.

Allowing her eyes to open, as though prised apart by the golden seam of light splitting the door from its frame, Cáit became suddenly aware that her husband had not yet stirred.

'Pádraig. Waken up, husband!' she whispered loudly and slapped the frigid shin across from her. When no response came, Cáit sat up in fright and shook Pádraig at the ribs until his body expanding quelled her fears. Pádraig groaned and drew a deep breath. But even with solace enough to close her eyes again, Cáit lingered a moment, sensing her task was incomplete.

'Are ye not going working today?'

'Mmmm…' her husband moaned, clearly out of his senses.

'Pádraig,' she yawned, rolling him back and forth.

'Ah!' he shouted, suddenly alert.

Laying back down, Cáit wriggled to get warm beneath the blanket and, hearing a slap, imagined Pádraig's calloused hands rising to meet his face. To the sound of more groaning, as she began to drift again Cáit foresaw him readying to climb through the portal of sunlight.

But slammed by the wind, the thwack of the wooden door ended the short dream and whatever warmth had been inside was instantly sucked out, replaced by an icy breath that filled the cabin and licked the walls.

Lifting the blanket, it banished every last drop of heat as, against her will, Cáit now listened to the thunderous splashing of Pádraig dispensing his waters against the dungheap outside, trembling as he did, the faint sound of teeth chattering in the cold.

Cáit felt the children squeeze themselves against her, wincing in their sleep too, when the sensation of a heavy coat landing on top told her Pádraig, come back in, had picked up the coat and thrown it over them. It was a comforting thought until Cáit realised she had forgotten something and, freeing herself from between the children, she was suddenly up, wrapping the small piece of griddle bread in a rag.

'Here you go,' she said, and reeled at the icy sting of his hand.

Seemingly unable to speak, Pádraig shivered too and, pulling his shoulders in tightly, managed but a grunt.

As crude as it was, Cáit understood the gesture as one of gratitude and watched him turn away, gripping the edge of the door as he pulled it out behind him.

Choking the shawl at her throat with one hand, Cáit rolled the rock back into place at the bottom of the door, turned the makeshift latch at the top and lay back down, finding her place between the little ones in relative darkness.

To escape the challenge of her day's worries for at least another while, Cáit tried once more to dream. But as so often had happened lately, to the sounds of the wind blowing violently against the cabin and the fast breathing of the little ones in her embrace, her thoughts went to poor Onóra in the workhouse, and with an absent prayer Cáit heard herself asking God to look after her sister.

Just as she was finally reaching the realm of comfort and peace that sleep alone afforded her, Cáit found herself suddenly alert, bothered by what sounded like some of the stones holding down the edge of the thatch come loose. As though swinging about in the wind, they clacked and clattered, making ill-tempered conversation. But the pattern changed as quickly and between the blows of the wind the sounds seemed to cluster with a gathering of all the clacks at once. As Cáit puzzled over how, though tied down with rope, a number of them might come together, the clacking died off and stopped. Her hearing strained, Cáit lifted her head in the darkness. The dull thud of something landing on the ground outside was followed by an intense creaking in the roof above, brought by some new pressure.

'Up, Síle!' Fearful of the roof collapsing, Cáit shot to her knees, gathering up Diarmuidín as she tried to get Síle going with the other arm.

'Mammy!' Síle called, as Diarmuidín began his crying too.

'Outside, quick!' Though she tried to control the panic she felt, Cáit knew her voice betrayed her, and the children startled at the apparent anger. But, at first merely concerned with getting them out, Cáit found herself filled with real ire at discovering that Pádraig, back and standing on the roof, was the actual cause of their fright.

'Pádraig Ua Buachalla, what in God's name? You have the children beside themselves, would you look?'

But maintaining his concentration, Pádraig answered without lifting his head at all: 'If I don't fix this now it'll get worse,' he said calmly. 'By the time I get home it will be dark.'

Behind her anger Cáit had to admit he had a point. But the shock of the elements and the effect on the children were enough to blind any clear thought. 'Well, you might have let us know before you started pulling the house down!'

With that Cáit ushered the children back inside and there soothed their crying as best she could, intending still to go back out. 'Whisht now,' she said, settling Diarmuidín. 'It's only your daddy. Good girl, Síle. You mind your *deartháirín* a minute.'

Outside once more, Cáit held the door with one hand and shielded her eyes from the sudden grey brightness with the other as she tried to understand what Pádraig was doing. Realising he well knew himself, she fought the urge to lecture him on keeping his place on the works and how much they were reliant upon it.

'I see what you're doing now,' she told him.

'You do?'

'I do. You go along now. I'll see to it.'

Turned to look down at her, Pádraig seemed to gauge Cait's ability to manage the task, but, following with a nod, he climbed over the back to descend the jagged ridge behind.

Though desperate to be inside now and stop the violent shivering, Cáit stood watch patiently. *He must really be worried about his place on the line*, she was thinking, *to give over the task of mending the roof to me*, when she heard Pádraig stumble down the last feet of the ridge. Limping out from behind the cabin, he winced and started down the hill.

'For God's sake, mind yourself,' she shouted after him, observing that he appeared sorer in his movements than usual. But the cold was probably to blame, stiffening his joints, she reasoned.

'Wrap yourself up, before you climb up there,' he called back, patting at his pocket as he went.

Making sure he hadn't lost the bread, Cait thought.

'I will,' she whispered, and bade him 'go along' with a wave, then took herself back inside.

―

By the time she'd settled the children again, showers of rain lashed the gable end of the cabin in waves so that the thoughts of going outside were even more daunting. And yet, Cáit knew she must do exactly that.

When next there's a break in the weather, she decided.

The wind had found a thread to pull at now and Cáit foresaw that, left to its mercy, the roof would unravel like yarn on a loom, leaving them completely exposed and in worse peril.

Elsewhere, her thoughts were of Pádraig, who was surely a long way from Macroom yet. Wherever he was, she hoped he'd found shelter; perhaps invited in by a kind stranger somewhere to wait out the squall by the glow of a fire.

'Mammamamammam,' came Diarmuidín's sudden cry as, sobbing, he pushed and pulled to get his head under the shawl and latch on.

'What's wrong with Diarmuidín, Mammy?' Síle woke up asking.

'Don't you worry, pet.' Without moving her arm, lest she disturb their unified warmth, Cáit bent her wrist to reach Síle's hair, stroking it at an awkward angle, until, agitated, Síle pulled her head from side to side.

'I'm hungry, Mammy,' she said, and began to cry too.

'Aw, pet.'

While Diarmuidín suckled aggressively, frustrated at getting nothing, Cáit escaped to the idea that they still had two days' worth of meal left of the last batch Pádraig brought home.

But despite knowing she needed only get up to cook a little stirabout from the sack in the corner, the same energy she had mustered that morning to see Pádraig off was now much diminished. Cáit kept her hand where it was, knotted up in Síle's curls, and, ignoring the sensations at her breast, tried instead to focus on the movement of the tears spilling from the hollow reservoirs of her eyes – slowly down one side of her face, then faster down the other.

It brought strange relief, to stop fighting for the first time … and give in to the fact that, just as it seemed, everything truly was falling apart.

Feeling a tautness in the area of her womb, Cáit breathed more deeply in the breath that came next, and longer out as it left. Was the hunger she felt her own, she wondered, or the sympathetic hunger of a mother for her suffering children? Cáit reflected that she did not know any more. But she no longer felt as hungry as she used to. Of that she was certain.

―――――

'Where are you going, Mammy?' Síle asked, when Cáit, having overcome the struggle of rising to feed them, wrapped herself in the big coat and braced herself for the mysterious task of fixing the roof.

'I'm just going looking at the roof, pet. You stay here and keep Diarmuidín warm, won't you? You be the mammy for a while.'

'I will.'

'Good girl. Keep away from that fire. I'll be down in a minute,' Cáit said, and, holding out the door, coached Síle through blocking it from the inside with the rock.

Above, in the wind, she struggled to gain her balance and maintain a grip on the awkward pitch of the roof. The long sleeves of Pádraig's overcoat did not help as, whipping her face with her own hair, the gusts mauled at her ears and eyes, making it difficult to see, much less untangle the twisted mess of ropes behaving just like her unruly hair.

Holding the loose wads down behind her ears, Cáit found her attention snagged by something in the distance and, abandoning the repairs, stood upright to discern a figure, limping in her direction.

Surely not. But yes. It was Pádraig.

'What happened?' she asked, meeting him at the foot of the hill.

"Tis too cold to walk to Macroom, and too cold to be working,' he replied.

With misery evident in his face, Pádraig limped forward, looking to the ground.

'What's wrong with your foot?' she asked, pulling his arm across her neck to support his weight.

'I think I cut it,' he said, and hopped, leaning on her.

Though hunched over and forced to stare at the lame foot, Cáit could not see where he was hurt; he had been smart enough to tie a strip of his shirt around it, she noticed. But as that was not the cleanest either, the makeshift bandage was filthy and, soaked with blood, it left traces in the grass each time he hobbled forward.

'Was it today or yesterday you cut it?' she asked, and remembered him limping off the ridge that morning.

'I don't know,' he said, shaking his head.

It must have been yesterday, Cáit reasoned. But he'd been gone a couple of hours. *How far did you walk in that bitter cold?* she wondered, with pity. For trying as long as he had, she admired him. But at being foolish enough to persist in such a state, she felt a small bit cross at him too. 'Well … we'll get you cleaned up and take a look at it,' she said.

'I'll be all right,' Pádraig laboured out, jumping his good foot in front.

'I know you will,' she added, 'and I tell you what else … as thin as you've got, to whenever we were married, there's a heavy set of bones in you yet.'

'Pffft,' he responded, seeming too frustrated for humour.

Trying to lift his spirits; in that moment, the wit Cáit administered had another purpose too. As they each contemplated the gravity of this latest frightening predicament, a distraction was needed.

For what were they to do, she thought, if Pádraig had to stay off that foot?

2

Cerberus at the Gates

'"Lucky"... What a name to give a sentient creature. I cannot account much for your good fortune, sallying up to a wretch like me for companionship.'

In the wall mirror, close enough to be shaving, Cornelius Creed examined himself slowly from brow to mouth then back for anything unusual, or familiar. Searching themselves, his eyes twitched between one another, though aware of the form in the background, nose along its paws, silent upon the floor.

'Maybe *you* have been lucky?' Creed said, turning back to the dog. 'Did someone save *you*? Or that funny eye of yours – were you lucky to keep it?'

Up again, the creature's head followed him, curious.

'Are you some kind of Cerberus?' Creed asked. But this, he decided, was a thought too frightening. 'Cicero, that's what I would have called you. Something like that. But you're no ordinary dog, are you?'

Ignoring the faint murmuring of voices nearby, Creed sat back into the armchair.

'I suppose "Lucky" has an easy ring to it. You don't care much either way, do you?'

At each question, Creed allowed time for response, though none came.

'Dogs sleep outside, you know?'

The eyes of the animal darted away as it dropped its head back to its paws.

The chocolate-coloured eye was the one closest to Creed. But he wondered if the other one, sharp and ice-blue, was blind, or just devoid of colour.

'At least we're dry now.' Creed softened his tone at last, pulling the blanket across his shoulders as the fire sparked. Gathering the garment around his neck, he remembered how, just one day before in the same chair, he had shivered violently; he a sopping wet mess, and the strange dog another, saturated before him, as he'd considered, with shock, how they'd ended up together. Creed had slept most of the day on and off after. The night too. But staring now again at the creature, he found himself still undecided as to whether it was a beast, or a saviour?

Who had saved who? The thought unravelled inside him.

Can he have been aware of what he was doing? Pushing me back from the edge of the abyss ... Where had he come from? Had he been sent there with a purpose?

As Creed sighed, the dog's eyes flicked back to see what was happening.

With a sure memory of his own ambition, Creed saw again the shoes flying through the air, one tied to the other, sailing, drifting in a dance, their long laced arms outstretched against a backdrop of fast blue dome until, plummeting, blurred across the dense confusion of bare wintered branches at the far bank, they collided with the surface of the wide drifting stream. Slack-jawed, drawn to them as though by some magnetic attachment, Creed had begun to wade in behind, when, like innumerous minuscule daggers, the sudden penetrating freeze and the crunching stones beneath had contrived to numb his feet almost instantly – messages of danger at once ignored and disregarded as cold raced the ascending waterline to reach his highest part first.

But at the point when the surface of the water was fitting a noose gently to his neck, Creed's bombarded senses had registered the sound of something large, plunging in behind him.

As, now in crisis, his body heaved to fill with as much air as his lungs would accept, Creed found himself unnerved by the violent dunking and splashing that approached, then raced past him in the form of a frantic black and white dog.

Perturbed that his plan was being cut short by the happenstance of an early-morning passerby, Creed turned to survey the path in either direction. Expecting to find the dog's owner upon the bank, he was surprised to discover that, apparently, the dog was operating alone.

Just then the thrashing stopped and to Creed's frustration, the dog, having ceased swimming, thrust its head under the water and resurfaced grasping one of the hurled shoes in its jaw to make for the bank. As it climbed out, the other shoe appeared, trailing from below by its tether. The pair dropped onto the grass; their unlikely captor shook himself off and proceeded to bark wildly at Creed.

Now emerging from the water, headed also for the bank and quite displeased to be doing so, Creed was further disheartened when the dog ceased its barking and pulled the shoes further out of reach.

Vexed and out of breath, with frigid streams of water running down the goose-pimpled skin of his neck and arms, he addressed the creature: 'Come now. I have no time for this.'

Creed surprised himself, giving sense to the animal. But despite his annoyance, he could not help but register a strange curiosity at the dog's behaviour, as well as the peculiarity of the differing colours of the dog's eyes.

Wincing at the pain reawakened in his feet, Creed attempted to retrieve the shoes once more. But this time the dog surprised him by not taking the shoes further away. Instead, it abandoned them, then, with a look, beckoned Creed to follow.

Having confirmed again that no one else was watching, Creed ignored the dog and, grasping the knot that bound the laces together, stood upright once more. Turning to face the river, he swung the shoes once, then twice around his head, until, feeling they had gathered sufficient momentum, he released and hurled them as far as he could downstream. Propelled, as though increased in their velocity by the incessant barking that resumed behind, the shoes sailed again for a time, spinning and twisting until, much further away, they fell to earth once more, landing in the deep, wide thicket of reeds that hemmed the nearside bank some fifteen yards out from the edge. The shoes made a distant *gulk* as they met with the water, when Creed suddenly realised the dog was racing along the bank to throw himself among the reeds and retrieve them anew.

'No!' he cried, maddened, running along the bank in pursuit. But by the time Creed reached the spot, the dog had already worked its way quite far out, half-wading, but half-walking, climbing through the brittle yellow stems that bent and snapped beneath its weight. Eventually, it reached the point where the shoes lay tangled in the mess, as Creed looked on, frozen, at its wrestling unsuccessfully to free them.

'Come in,' he shouted after it. 'Come in, you damned thing!'

Either admitting defeat, or understanding him, the creature gave in and appeared to make for home, its eyes looking helpless as they met with Creed's. But within three or four strokes of its one black and one white paw, the beast turned tail to attempt its task afresh.

'No! Get in! Get in! Get out!'

Correcting himself, Creed attempted to immerse one foot among the reeds and start in the same direction, but immediately realised the futility of such an idea. Replacing his foot upon the bank, he blustered aloud at the unexpected irony.

Though evidently tiring, with a resilience most alarming to its newfound acquaintance, the dog repeated the whole first attempt, but again to no avail. When a third bid proved fruitful, seemingly filled with even more panic than Creed, it made with its bounty for the bank only to find the sorry items snagged and entangled once more before it could make much progress. Anxious beyond belief as he looked on, Creed coaxed the thing time and again to 'abandon the damned shoes!' and 'just come in!' Just as Creed had ignored the signs of danger to his own life only moments before, so now did the animal ignore the danger to *its* own life, and continuous entreaties besides from the party who had unknowingly sent it into the drink.

When within two yards of the bank the laces were caught up a fourth time, Creed abandoned his own safety and stepped into the depth of the unknown murk beneath. But, tripping between the reeds, he found himself in peril just as suddenly and fell headlong face-first into the water. One reaching hand landed upon the dog, being the only solid thing he could grasp. Gasping in fright, he unwittingly choked on a mouthful of water amid a panic of bubbles and silvery darkness as, trying to right himself, he worried he might be drowning the dog too. But, with the sensation of his toes finding anchor among the velvet slime of bottom silt, Creed experienced a sensation of great relief at re-establishing his gravity. Coughing and gasping, resurfaced, he spat the water out in reflex, and tried to regain a steady footing within the precarious density of reeds, lest he trip again.

His hand still on the stranded dog, Creed now struggled to haul the creature across the hopeless mess of cracking straws as it released its charge and accepted his help. Its weight and girth did not surprise Creed, but the creature's whining insistence, when finally deposited on the bank, that the shoes still be retrieved was almost too much.

For why he knew not, Creed now took one more careful step almost to the depth of his chin. From there, at the edge of his balance, the tips of his fingers felt the nose of one half-sunken shoe. Buoyed up by reeds, it rocked and bobbed in the calm ebb and flow that concealed the dark realm beneath.

Panting, the dog let out a single bark as Creed managed to grip the forlorn jetsam, pulling it close enough to step higher up the slope, where from the security of a more stable foothold he fought the bending reeds until with a snap, the long, determined limbs released their prize for the last time. Wide-eyed, his rump to the grass alongside, Creed stared out across the black murky depth. Imagining himself lifeless, tangled among the same reeds, he tried to process how differently his confused vision of the end had played out.

His task remembered, Creed stood, shivering, and cast a look to the dripping wet dog. Bidding it stay with his eyes, he picked up the shoes and began to walk away, when, with a start, the dog arose reinvigorated to follow.

'No!' Creed said, full of intent, pointing to its eyes with an arm fully extended. At this, the dog cowered, but resumed its tracking as Creed attempted to move once more.

The pattern repeated until, standing in the shadow of the bridge, with hopes of ending the reviled chain of ownership by drowning the shoes and himself both, along with whatever misery it was possible their existences might wreak upon the earth were they allowed to remain functional above, Creed made the shape of one last unenergetic throw.

But at this, the dog had barked furiously into the cavernous echo chamber of the bridge until, utterly spent, Creed had finally lowered his burden and slumped down beside the nameless cretin that, at least for the moment, had changed the course of his morning profoundly.

'Where in God's name did you come from?' Creed had asked the dog as he began to shiver uncontrollably. But huddled beneath the blanket now, one day later, both of them dry by the fire in the room above the shop ... now, he knew all too well. It was James Welply's dog!

'Do you believe him, James?' Paulellen asked in the kitchen, far out of her husband's earshot. 'I mean, do you think he's being honest with us?'

'Hard to say,' James answered, leaning in the doorway with hat in hand. 'I think... I think he's quite confused himself.'

'He told me he went for a walk by the river, but forgot to dress!' Paulellen's anxiety rose with the pitch of her voice as she shook her head in disbelief. 'Thank God he had a night-shirt on at least.'

'He may be holding back to spare us,' James suggested, thumbing his lip with eyes cast to the floor.

'Did he give you the same story, James? When I went to make the tea.'

'Well, more or less,' James answered, conflicted, Paulellen felt: perhaps protecting his friend, or worried she might not be able for his opinion.

'It doesn't really make sense, does it?' she asked, desperate for reassurance.

'Not really,' James admitted, gazing into the distance. 'Hopefully no one else saw him?'

'I don't think so,' Paulellen answered, feeling herself close to tears. 'It was still very early when he came back. Oh, if you'd seen him, James – it was frightening. He looked far worse, if that is possible … drenched … a mad stare in his eyes.'

―――

'Ah! Lucky! You found Lucky!' James had exclaimed upon entering; the dog got up to greet him excitedly.

'Lucky?' Paulellen had asked, clearly as surprised as Creed had felt, he now recalled, awaiting the results of their confab about him.

A fab about Con, he thought, and tittered quietly, staring into the fire, where amber flames licked at a small mountain of reddened slack.

'This is *your* dog?' he had asked James, echoing the surprise upon all three faces; he sitting, the others standing, when Paull had returned that morning with James in tow.

'Was, yes!' James remarked. 'He went missing about two weeks back. Oh, we thought he must have been shot. And now Paulellen has just told me a bit about your unfortunate swim yesterday?'

'But I've never seen this dog before,' Creed protested, 'when did –?'

'Oh you must have, Con. How could you not have? Anyway, you've seen him now, and I'm very glad you have. How are you, Con … are you –'

'James, will you have some tea?' Paulellen interrupted. 'I'll go and make some tea.'

Is there anything James Welply does not have? thought Creed.

'Well, it seems he found you,' James smiled, apparently oblivious to Creed's frustration. 'Actually, we got a new puppy just before Christmas, the children were so broken-hearted,' Creed remembered him saying.

'Ah bless them,' Paulellen sympathised, kneeling to pour the tea from a tray bearing silverware and a pot.

'Didn't you just –' Creed asked, confused at how suddenly she seemed to have reappeared, when Paulellen and James looked to each other, seeming confused also.

'I did. But I was gone a while, Con,' Paulellen continued, and Creed wondered if she had come back so soon to keep an eye on him.

'I'm sorry to say we had you down for dead, Lucky.' James tossed the dog's ears. 'But I think you've found your new master.'

'What?' Creed feigned surprise, not fully sure how he felt, though there was certainly some element of relief.

'You weren't much fond of the gun anyway, were you?' James asked the dog affectionately. 'Gun shy,' he told his human audience. 'Probably why he ran off in the first place. It's not the first time he went missing, in fact. As you don't shoot, Con, it's perfect.'

―――

Alone at the window, Creed could see the store-shed below. Inside it, seemingly moments before, he had stood at the edge of his existence. But while, perhaps against his will, he was now a chasm's distance from the realm he had occupied then, most of him, as yet, felt like that; somewhere else, caught between worlds – a sense increased by the realisation, looking down, that he was still without shoes.

3

CRACKS

Untying the rag around her husband's foot, Cáit peeled back its layers to assess the healing. The cracks she had discovered in both feet on New Year's Day were still easily visible. Growing wider from the pad of his foot into the gap between two toes, the worst of them all was the source of the bleeding. Re-examining it now, two days later, Cáit remembered the moment she had removed the bloody strip of his shirt to reveal the gory mess beneath, and not one, but numerous other small wounds about its edges.

But the other foot had cracks in it too, Cáit had learned, and it did not take long to realise that through his habit of sleeping under the coat, on the outside of the fire, while she and the children took the blanket, with his body being too long and always closest the door, he had been exposing his bare feet to the harshest of the weather. The night before the appearance of the cuts had been the coldest yet all winter.

The only mercy was that the chill had numbed some of the sensation in his feet, sparing him some of the pain, Cáit reasoned. But, once thawed out, poor Pádraig had suffered at each attempt to clean the wounds since, as he did now.

'Ah …' He winced, and sieved the pain through clenched teeth as she held onto his leg, working by the light of the door.

'The worst of it all …' he hissed, talking to distract himself from the pain, Cáit imagined, 'if only I could have got there yesterday … down into the trench … then I'd be grand. I'll have missed the wages for another week now, if they settled out.' That this all was preventing him getting to the works and providing for his family was hurting him most, she understood. The pain was secondary. 'Maybe I can walk with a stick, or –'

'And ruin yourself?' Cáit cut across him. 'How would it be if you killed yourself getting there and they didn't settle out until next Saturday anyway? It might be the last wages you'd ever get. You'd be in a sorry state long before it.'

Cáit was surprised at her own reaction, but felt she had to discourage him.

'So what do we do?' he asked, at length, apparently seeing sense.

But across an empty silence, Cáit struggled to think of the answer. 'I'll find a way to get us over the next few days,' she replied. What if she had to go 'providing', like Máire Ruadh, she asked herself, and felt angry, still, at the prospect. When, a few years before, she'd left her homeplace to go with Pádraig, Cáit could never have imagined herself going begging to support her family, she thought, though she could hardly ask more of her husband. He was not to blame either.

She would go to Fr O'Brien in Clondrohid, she decided, and see if he could help them. Rumour had it he was only helping widows and orphans, that with so many seeking assistance he had to choose the worst off. But she might take Síle along too, to help him see how much they were in need.

4

Who Talks of Death

'Tis good to see you back.'

Against a backdrop of the morning's hammers and a stiff breeze that, blowing across their heads, bleated its promise of a scattering rain, Ned Swiney looked to the ditch adjacent and studied the condition of its weary occupant.

'You're in bad shape … though you must be better now than you were … that you couldn't get here a few days since … When the worst of the weather passed … and still neither sight nor sign of you … we thought you were done for … though granted, I hear 'tis still bad in the hills.'

Kffft!

Biting the muck, Ned's spade hit a stone, sending a shock up his arm along the handle while, to all appearances, Pádraig Ua Buachalla carried on unaware of his communication. But, despite the language obstacle, Ned knew there was understanding between them and carried on the one-sided conversation. 'There's men off their feet all about the place … gone to the union, a good whack of them … even men who, but one day before, looked relatively strong … carried off … the heart gone in them … not long for the last bit of digging they'll do in this world … God save the hearers.'

Keeerrrzhiou!

'Weaker men too, certainly … but strong men … who shouldn't be gone yet … I tell you … the man who begins talk of his failing health … who speaks of … or even begins to picture his own death … you may bet your hat … 'twill not be long afore 'tis him next who's in the ground … such are the times.'

Krzhuupth!

'A man must keep going … head down … ears back … plough on.'

Shchzzlaff!

Ned buried the spade, then rocked it back and forth to loosen the ground's grip on it. Willing himself to live his words, he bade the instrument chop away another wet slab of earth that, with a mixture of yellow-brown clay and grey detritus, held up the sides of his ditch.

'Scotch!' he announced, when Pádraig, raising his chin in a manner befitting curiosity, looked to the gang of new bodies idly gathered around the door of one hut. Somewhat cocksure, their purpose, as yet, remained a mystery to Ned.

'Whatever about them …' he thought aloud, 'does not bode well.'

Kiiiiirft!

'Roberts … gone!' Ned vied for Pádraig's attention, then, allowing the spade to rest against his chest, turned down his lips and dusted his hands one against the other, demonstratively. Turning to face Ned, his tall comrade, with a gesture, expressed a wish for him to elaborate.

The announcement seemed to have commanded Pádraig's full attention and Ned was happy to append his analysis: 'The chap who went in a few moments since … Roberts' *replacement* … *new overseer*,' he added, accentuating the point.

Pádraig's expression seemed to signify his understanding well enough.

'*Harnet*, I think his name is … one of Gordon's lackeys, might be … Did not take him long to show his colours in any case …'

Looking to his work again, from out of the wet, sucking ground, Ned plucked the long dull spade and reverted to his usual cadence of speech.

'"Do you pay O'Connell's rent?" says he, to the first fella looked for bread on time … "I have done, and will again, when I'm able," the poor divil replied, unsuspecting … "So you'd pay it if you had the money then?" Harnet asked …'

Keeerrrzhiou!

'"I would," the man replied … "Then go and ask *O'Connell* for bread," says Harnet, barking, "but take yourself out of here first," he told him … "that you'd presume to pay it with my money!" … sent the poor man packing … What a rotten so-and-so … to snare a poor fellow like that … He'll have that man's death against his soul, before long.'

Kishoouwhh!

———

At the short suck later that morning, sat on the ditch chewing the second corner off his bread, Ned looked to Ua Buachalla: a relatively young man, his feet so damaged by a life of want and inflamed predicament, who, on the meagrest of rations, at the risk of worsening his health at every step – or of losing his life – was dragging himself back and forth a measure of miles each day by the aid of a stick! All for a pain-filled pittance more often granted weeks of toil apart at a time.

It was a cruel time to be alive, Ned reflected, amazed.

That they were all of them now starving, ever so slowly, was ever more apparent and increasing with each passing day. In this season of life or death by virtue of the smallest mistake, each man of them was necessarily far more cautious now than he had been but weeks before: daily conserving, sparing and counting each morsel and crumb to keep his loved ones alive.

In view of it all, the seemingly tiny sacrifice Pádraig had made to him on Christmas Eve was seen by Ned in the enormity of its significance. The surprise on Pádraig Ua Buachalla's face as, silent, he now accepted the gesture in return told Ned that neither the gravity of his own deed some weeks before nor Ned's answer to it this day were lost on him, either.

5

The Oar Against the Swell

*F**air enough, Denis. I'll grant you shoes would be an advantage, at times like this.*

Weary and limping, Pádraig conceded to the quiet wisdom displayed by his forlorn companion of old. Reluctant to give up the one shoe he possessed, Denis had repaired it over and over, however useless it seemed to those around him.

How have you fared since, I wonder? Pádraig asked his absent friend, fondly. But, in the absence of an answer, or any word of Denis since he'd fallen injured off the works a month previous, Pádraig presumed the worst.

Tripping on a hidden rock and wincing as he recovered his balance, a tired Pádraig had to remind himself why he was driving his body on like this. They would die if he did not, came the answer, and at least this way he would know he had given his all.

One full week into January, not yet relinquishing its grip, the devastating cold was still driving frost up into the hills, exacerbated by the wind. This was his third day back on the works, Pádraig reflected, and the skin of his feet was still cracking and splitting, with more channels and trenches opening as he refused to stay off them. The makeshift dressings Cáit was applying refused to hold, but there was little Pádraig could do except hope the weather would ease before long and allow him to heal.

If only fleetingly, the imagined repartee with Denis brought Pádraig some relief as he tried to keep up the pace. But the pain affected not only his feet. The muscles of his legs and his back ached too: a consequence of tension built up while, struggling to walk, he sought to withhold the full weight of each step.

The small bag of meal that Cáit had got from Fr O'Brien was now exhausted; in order that they might have anything to put in their mouths before the wages were next settled – come Saturday, Pádraig hoped – the question of how he might get some bread on time from one of the new gangsmen was at the front of Pádraig's mind. How to get seed into the ground again for the season ahead came next, with the question of whether it was even wise to try after two failures in a row; then, how he might pay back the loan, if he got it, his mind circled back. And before that he should manage yet to buy something for the weeks ahead after losing so much time this last fortnight.

Pádraig tried to think of all these things as he limped on through the cold. But for now, it took most of his concentration to simply put one sore foot in front of the other until he could get himself strong again.

Most of all, it was probably the wind, Pádraig reckoned, the cause of the damage – dry as it was, sucking and tearing at him whether walking or asleep. At times it seemed to be seeking him out, and that he was now so unsteady, walking, did not make it any easier to resist.

Battling to cover ground on the first morning, when coping with the injury had been a new experience, Pádraig had marvelled at the wind's characteristics: how, unlike a river, whose path was obstructed by land, rocks, and mountains of earth, the wind was boundless. There was, in reality, an ocean of wind overhead, the length, depth and breadth of the sky, with little to impede its building momentum in search of whatever it sought.

So preoccupied was he with its hunting him, by now Pádraig could almost smell the surge before it arrived. This morning it had come with renewed ferocity in its tail and, as though lying in wait, vying to knock him over, it had pummelled him as soon as he'd stepped outside. Leaning on the stick, Pádraig had bent to stay upright then, splashed by the waters it threw back at him, cursing all the while.

And now, an hour later, though it had thrice abated only to renew its force, the elusive foe was before him again, behind and above, swirling and pushing; lashing his skin with its icy breath and ripping the air from out Pádraig's nose before his lungs could take the full benefit of its elixir.

Pressing down upon the stick, an oar against the giant swell, Pádraig resorted often to using both hands, and wondered if indeed it could just pick him up and hurl him aside if it wished to. But the wind was not so playful as that.

This wind, when it met resistance, howled in protest like a tormented spirit.

To Pádraig, it felt, this day, to be almost attached to the hunger tunnelling through his body and stirring the pain in his feet. Permeating and absorbing him one wave at a time, the blast threatened to gouge out the remaining contents of his bowels and his spark in the process for good measure.

A coffle of miserable, haunted souls, it screamed and groaned as though to vomit upon him with not one but many voices. Unseeable as they were, Pádraig could easily distinguish them by their differences. Stretching its neck out, one, dominant above its class, leaned into his face, bawling continuously, not with words, but a bottomless retching. Somewhere between the pitch of a man and a woman, fed by the depthless chasm of air above, it needed no new breath but growled continuously its tuneless wavering, threatening to distort his balance.

Squeezing out a whispered gasp, a second laboured like a corpse on its deathbed, eternally stuck at the end of its last breath; while below, some unharmonious dirge fought, scraping alongside like a glacier forcing its way through a corridor, bullied, losing out to the stronger forces. Lower still, a chaotic form could be heard railing in and out its broken, endless blabbering; not struggling to be heard, but prating like an *amadán*, tripping over its own shoes. There were others too, bound up in the wounded cacophony: one sucking; one screaming; the lost, and the searching; some less distinct than others, but all contributing to the lamentable *olagóning* deluge.

Combined, they made for what seemed to Pádraig a forlorn scraggle of sleepless beings, tied together at the midriffs, dragged and driven through the world by a relentless master: Death, who whipped them on; not on their way to hell, but from it. For life itself had been the greater part of their damned existence.

Already tired, inclined to woe and the entertainment of his fears, Pádraig worried that the voices beseeching him might be the souls of people he once knew. Frightened by the thought, he reeled as it was born within, and, as though to avoid an incoming blow, whipped back his head, instinctively. Flailing and thrashing their naked branches, the trees next joined the storm of sound unleashing its violence upon him, as Pádraig tried, but failed, to banish the thought, instead seeing the faces of old neighbours and relatives, even of his father – who, so far as he knew, was still living.

'Jesus above! What is happening to me?' Pádraig cried aloud to himself, when the wind raced to invade his open mouth. But stealing his words and molesting his thoughts to turn him against his own was the final indignity, and in that moment Pádraig's ire was roused to fury.

'Not yet!' he shouted at what, now, were fully fledged in his mind – ghosts on the wind, come to take him. 'I'm still strong yet! Feet be damned!'

6

Paróiste

'Next!'
Stepping into the hut, Pádraig passed another, leaving. When he stopped short of the desk, the hollow thud of his stick meeting the timber floor seemed to call the clerk – a young man, sat over an open ledger – to his senses.

In the dim light behind the clerk sat a second man, hunched over what, to Pádraig, looked a fortune in stacks of silver and bronze coins, while to Pádraig's right stood the least conspicuous of the cabin's inhabitants: someone of Pádraig's own class whose function, for now, remained a mystery.

'Name?' the clerk asked.

'Buckley, Patrick, Clondrohid.' With still no taste for them, the words fell uneasily off Pádraig's tongue.

'Clon …' the clerk said, and traced an imaginary line down one column, in the poor glow of the oil lamp. 'Hmmm … Clondrohid. Is that a townland or a parish?'

Momentarily frozen, Pádraig was struggling to voice his confusion, when the man, hitherto silent, on his right revealed himself to be a translator.

'Baile fearainn, ná paróiste?' he asked Pádraig. Townland or parish?

'Paróiste,' Pádraig replied promptly.

'Parish,' the translator relayed back to the clerk.

'Well, that might explain it,' the clerk said, flipping to a section near the back, where, crossing the columns of a short list, his pen hovered over various figures.

'Here it is … Patrick Buckley, Clondrohid … three days and one half-day … December twenty-eighth … to December thirty-first … deductions for light throughout.'

As Pádraig watched intently, the man at the back, suddenly busy, echoed the clerk's figures as he made note of them.

'Moving three cubic yards and four-tenths of earth …' the clerk dictated, 'with five and three-quarter hundredweight of stone.'

'What's he saying?' Pádraig begged of the translator.

'Three and a half days, from the twenty-eighth till the thirty-first,' the interpreter drawled back.

'And what of the weather?' Pádraig pushed him. 'From New Year's Day until Thursday last, I was prevented from getting here by the weather.'

'Says he couldn't get here due to weather, Mr Preston, from the first, until –'

'Weather? We've had no snow here,' the clerk responded, with a look of scepticism in Pádraig's direction.

'The snow,' Pádraig insisted, 'it did this to my feet,' he said, and gestured for the clerk to look down at them. Pádraig knew it hadn't snowed, but it might as well have, so bad had been the cold.

Having followed with his eyes, the clerk looked back to his book and began to talk at length.

'He says, out of three hundred and twenty-nine on that road,' the translator relayed to Pádraig, 'you're the only man listed as coming from Clondrohid. We are told payment, and indeed employment, is only to be given those who fall inside the bounds of Macroom parish. I have no instruction in this instance, Mr Buckley.'

'But my name is on the list. I am doing the work,' Pádraig pleaded as politely as his voice would allow, rattled as he was.

'Yes, I see that.' The clerk tapped his now upside-down pen upon the desk, seemingly still undecided. 'Furthermore, we are this day only paying out for the week ending Saturday, January second. You'll have to inquire again as to any days following that, if you are still here.

I would suggest you find a works nearer your place of residence, Mr Buckley.'

Father O'Brien submitted my name to the Relief Committee of Macroom and Clondrohid, with the result I got on these works, Pádraig longed to say in his defence. But he thought better of pushing his luck.

'The first and second, sir, with the weather,' he said instead, aware that he was protesting more than he'd ever done before. But he was a desperate man. He just hoped he could elicit some understanding on the clerk's part.

'I'm quite unsure as to what to do in this instance,' the translator conveyed. 'To be entitled to weather compensation, the Relief Commission states one must be prevented from working by snow or heavy precipitation, and, although you may have had snow in Clondrohid, there was none here. You must appreciate this complicates my position.'

In the silence that followed, Pádraig anxiously awaited the decision of the clerk, who, casting a glance to his injured feet once more, fixed his eyes upon the ledger and spoke blindly to his assistant.

'Two half-days: first and second.'

'Yes, sir.'

Meanwhile a bang upon the door was followed by some statement of impatience outside, as the clerk muttered something under his breath.

'I expect I may be admonished by the paymaster for my –' the translator began, but was waved off by the clerk from sharing any more of what was apparently irrelevant.

The sound of coins chinked in the background. 'One and sixpence.' The assistant came forward and placed the money before the clerk, who, having counted again, moved the tiny stack to the front and recorded the number in his own ledger.

Leaning back, Mr Preston flipped the wad of pages back to one marked with a blue ribbon and, nodding to the translator, looked again to Pádraig, who stared back with the money in his hand.

'Next,' called the interpreter, and, banging on the wall to someone outside, returned to a benign stance with his hands joined before him.

Poking the floor, Pádraig's stick began its hollow cough anew, as, with head down, he left the cabin and limped past the queue to begin the slow march into the dusky twilight of the hills beyond.

It was a poor satisfaction, he felt, on top of everything else, to be walking away with a new uncertainty over his place upon the works.

7

Fat Dogs and Paving Stones

Removing his cap, Ned stepped wearily through the door.

'Hello, Antoinette,' he said, greeting his wife's younger sister, who, with one of the children in her lap, was sat upon the apartment's only stool. Ned liked Antoinette and was happy to see her, but he had been looking forward to occupying that very spot, with hopes of eating something Mary might have prepared for him.

'Wait till you hear, Ned. Tell him, Antoinette,' Mary coaxed, but, typically, took to telling the story herself. 'Coming along Main Street this morning, she was –'

'Just out of the lane,' Antoinette took her cue.

'And who did she see only that Gordon fella, the engineer,' Mary continued.

'Oh?' Ned responded, his attention piqued, while, too tired to stand, he took to leaning against the door frame.

'Climbing onto his car, the very one,' Antoinette confirmed.

'Did you approach him?' More than curious, Ned was invested in the outcome, having suggested they might get Antoinette's husband Eugene onto the works by doing just that.

'I did,' she replied. 'Nice as barley I was, despite all the God-awful things we do hear about him. I said, "Excuse me, Mr Gordon, sir. So sorry to delay ye. I'm but newly married, and my poor husband can't get a place on the works –"'

'Anty?' the little one interrupted. 'Anty?'

'Whisht, child, let her talk,' Mary said.

Demented with the hunger, Ned watched the steam ascending from the ladle in his wife's hand. 'Let your aunt speak, and talk when she's finished,' Ned added. 'Go on, Antoinette.'

'I said, "Could you please give him a place on the works? I beg you," says I, with me hands like this, praying and imploring, "to save him from starvation," I said, says I.'

'And wait till you hear his response,' Mary said, stoking Ned's anticipation.

'With not a word up till now,' Antoinette said, 'he turns away, and, looking straight ahead, says, "Men can't starve while fat dogs and digestible paving stones are in the country."'

'Now …' Mary said, as though challenging her husband to make sense of the impossible.

'You're joking?' Ned let out, in disbelief.

'As true as God,' said Antoinette, and signed herself with the Cross.

'Credit that,' Mary said. 'And what did you say?' she asked her sister, so that Ned realised they must not have got further than that before he'd arrived.

'I was in shock, being honest. But still polite, withdrawing, I said, "I'm full sorry for having taken up your time."'

'And that was it?' Ned asked, disappointed, and wanting every detail as he foresaw himself imparting all to the men next morning.

'Oh, he said not another word, nor looked at me again. "Madam, could you please step back?" the young lad holding the door said. My mind was a blur after that. I suppose the driver give the horses the strap, and sure I was left to stand and watch it go along the street.'

Ned was lost for words. 'Men can't starve …?'

'While fat dogs and digestible paving stones are in the country,' Antoinette reminded him.

'*Digestible paving stones!*' he repeated in horror.

'Where would you get it?' Mary sighed.

'Nowhere,' answered Ned, 'you'd get it nowhere but in this God-forsaken country.'

'And here, do you think he noticed … did he look at you?' Mary gestured to Antoinette's condition.

'Anty, what's in your belly?' the child asked.

———

'All clear?' Ned asked again, feeling a mixture of trepidation and excitement; in his hands, a copy of *The Cork Examiner* that he and the men had put in for at the potentially life-keeping sum of sixpence.

'Clear, Ned,' the voices reassured.

'Are you sure 'tis in?' one asked.

'Front page,' Ned replied.

'Bejesus, give it to us so, before someone comes along!' came back, in earnest.

Amazed at seeing his own words in print, Ned cleared his throat and began.

> Sir, –
> Thank God, the times are so altered that a poor man is now suffered to speak openly and call public attention through such a pure and wholesome channel as your inestimable journal, to any hardships under which he may labour …

'This will cause some storm,' a body to Ned's right interrupted.

'Shhhhhh,' another beseeched, 'read on, Ned.'

> I have the greatest antipathy to bring the character of any individual before the public, nor should I do so if the injury were confined to myself; but when I see, with my own eyes, deeds, the most unjust, perpetuated upon so large a number of the class to which I belong, I

cannot refrain from the adoption of those means for their redress, sincerely believing these persons are so hard hearted that nothing short of a newspaper punishment can call them to a sense of their duty to God and man.

'Oh Lord, God bless ye, Ned!'

Over the corner of the page, realising how important this act was to the other men too, Ned saw Jeremiah Fitz kneeling, as though God, at last, was hearing his prayers.

You are aware, I should suppose, and I regret to add, so are the poor people here, that a Captain Gordon is the Engineer of the Board of Works in this district.

'I helped with that line!' young Lehane shouted, and thrust his fist in the air, causing Ned to hide the paper, for fear of attracting the stewards.

'Jesus, do you want to see him strung up? Will ye be *quiet*, men, and let the man read.' Con Riordan, the strongest among them, whom no man would argue with, took to keeping order as, blowing out his lips, Ned raised the page again.

So multifarious are the deeds of this military gentleman, that I would not trespass upon your invaluable paper, to recount his conduct in detail. I will plainly tell but one of his doings, then let proper pronouncement be made upon this unpopular official.

'Men can't starve while fat dogs and digestible paving stones are in the country,' so says Scotchman Gordon. Do not startle, 'tis fact!!!

'The pig!' Denis Manley of Cooldorrihy spat.

'Shhhh!' It was Pádraig did the hushing this time, Ned noticed. Anxious to get through it all, he continued.

'Men are *incompetent* and *disqualified* if they speak their religious or political feelings, and under any circumstances you shan't pay the O'Connell tribute,' says Mr. Harnet, one of the foreigners under Gordon here.

Sixteen Scotch and strange pensioners are here at present, getting two shillings *per diem,* stopped by Gordon out of the labourer's task work until these intruders are employed on the roads. God knows I am heartily sick of such conduct.

Mr Gibbon, financial inspector over Macroom, is most unquestionably the very officer to bring the entire satisfaction of all parties. I very much hope he is a reader of your esteemed journal.

With profound respect, I am sir, your obedient servant.

Ned BRIEN SWINEY, Sleaveen Road.

Ned finished to effusive hand-shaking and proud expression by those around him whose weakened spirits and bodies, like his, seemed to experience a momentary skip of strength and buoyancy. Now that he had alerted them to the cruelty and corruption of their official, he hoped Gordon's superiors would take him to task.

'You'll be the talk of all Cork, Ned! A labourer, writing to the paper,' Paddy Lehane said, cocking his head.

'He'll want your head on a platter!' Con Riordan warned, a look of fear in his eyes. 'You should not have put your name on it.'

But Gordon was likely too busy and lazy to read the papers himself, Ned imagined, and by all accounts the works were coming to an end anyway. What was the worst Gordon could do? he reasoned.

'Anything else in there, Ned?'

'Mr Limerick!'

Gordon spread his arms wide along the desk until his posture best befitted the scorn he felt.

'Yes, Captain Gordon,' his assistant replied, arriving promptly from the other room.

'What line is Mr Harnet on?'

'That's the road that was moved, sir; the one through Mr Conor's land. The one five one if I'm not mistaken.'

'One five one.' Frowning, Gordon inscribed the numbers across the article. 'Fetch me the list for that line.'

'Right away, sir,' Limerick replied, turning tail as Gordon completed the note with a weighted thump of his pencil.

'And bring the roster of pay clerks while you're at it,' he told Limerick's back.

'Pay clerks. Yes, sir.'

Through the window, Gordon stared off into the distance, flat and empty but for a tree or two, then turned with contempt to the text once more, the sound of footsteps returning.

'Paving stones indeed, Mr Swiney,' he said below his breath. 'You may soon have one yourself. A marking stone. If you don't fatten some dogs with your *own* bones first.'

8

THE LAYERS BETWEEN

Uncertain as ever as to why he was continuing so aimlessly in his tasks other than that he had received no instruction to do otherwise, Thomas French unlocked the safe to retrieve the large iron key to the stores.

Instead, within, French's hand fell upon what it immediately identified as an envelope. Having received a remittance by the same means some weeks prior on New Year's Day, his instant hope was that it might contain a payment. To his surprise, that envelope had contained quite a generous remuneration for his troubles. Removed to the light, however, the newer example revealed itself as a sealed packet addressed to *The Cork Examiner*.

'The *Examiner*,' French whispered, disappointed, yet too much distracted to indulge his feelings. For, inside the safe, he now spotted what appeared to be an accompanying note, fallen to the bottom.

Mr French. Kindly post on Mr Creed's behalf with the next dispatch.

Rising, French stared with deep concentration at the envelope, inscribed by Mrs Creed's hand.

Why would she ...?

The only logical explanation was that Mr Creed could not bring down the letter himself, meaning he was unwell. *Or worse!*

But, were that true, surely Mrs Creed would not keep something so monumental from him? French felt his eyes growing wider at the implications.

While he had heard obvious signs of life upstairs in recent weeks, French had not even seen Mr Creed since Christmas Eve. Clues that someone else had been active in the shop since, while French himself was absent from the premises, were abundant. Naturally, he'd presumed it was Mr Creed: the books disturbed, items moved, the lock upon the stores, all normal signs of life.

But the shop floor, sodden with footprints on New Year's morning, he now recollected – something of a great mystery still; the abundance of animal hair he presumed was from the unseen hound he had heard give off a solitary bark above: such things as these were unexplained.

It was all of it strange, French considered, as he eyeballed the ceiling.

Mrs Creed he *had* heard from, if indirectly: kindly, she sometimes left out soup for him to bring his mother; and, some weeks before, he had found a note upon the counter, requesting he daily bring the paper from now on – something Mr Creed had, hitherto, always fetched himself, French remembered, worryingly.

Mr French,
As part of your duties, will you please also bring the paper each day – use coins in the safe – and leave at the bottom of the stairs with the coal each morning.

But beyond abstract communications, there had been nothing, and French had the abiding sense that, purposefully, Mrs Creed was avoiding him.

He would have never sought to address her on matters of his employment in the past. These were not usual circumstances, however, and, perhaps sensing his desperation, she was staying clear accordingly, he supposed. Whatever the reason, it had only furthered the isolation he lately felt.

Heartsore, at what he was seeing in the streets coming and going from work; at the slow degeneration of his mother at home; and at necessarily spending the rest of his time here at the shop, alone, French had come to accept the ghostly emptiness of his existence.

One year since, even six months ago, he had been a busy employee, working discreetly between the stores and the back of the counter to the frequent sound of the bell above, heralding, not alone custom, but life; activity; and the music of human voices, however impoverished and poor were they who came and went under its calling. Providing dependable income for him and his mother to live upon, working for Mr Creed had come to represent the pinnacle of French's adult life: a distraction and an answer to his worries in an otherwise cruel existence that promised only hardship and the certainty of struggle otherwise.

Closed since mid-December to all but those redeeming pledges at Mr Creed's instruction, the shop French had been inhabiting these past six weeks had, by comparison, transformed to one of quiet loneliness, devoid of vitality. The bars protecting the counter and its occupants had become a prison; the bell that brought amusement and entertainment, an alarm, sounding only when he himself answered the incessant knocking of some desperate soul he had likely to turn away. What distractions from worry he had hitherto enjoyed had all been replaced by more uncertainty than he'd ever had cause to suffer, and endless time to dwell upon their loss.

Most grievous of all to French was the absence of his employers – for Mrs Creed was surely now as elemental as Mr Creed. However benign a force she had appeared before, by *her* absence too, French realised that he missed them *both*. But conjointly, Mr and Mrs Creed had become as elusive to him as the creatures that nightly disturbed his sleep, scratching beneath the floorboards of his mother's house.

If for a moment, this morning's envelope had held the promise of an emergence of sorts by Mr Creed, following a month-long absence. But how far from reality that seemed now, French realised. What if Mr Creed was not upstairs at all, and Mrs Creed alone was active in the house, with a dog to protect her in his absence? That would explain much!

Despite such doubts, Thomas French ensured there was no one looking over his shoulder before, passing under the counter, he brought the envelope to the window, wiped away some of the condensation, then held the packet to the light. Hoping to gain a clue to its secrets, he squinted hard at the layers of translucent script within. Impossible to decipher, they spoke of nothing but his own confusion.

He would just have to post it, and wait.

———

Hoping it might reveal the envelope's contents of two days earlier, with the paper under his arm an anxious French unlocked the shop door and silenced the bell before closing it behind him. Certain he was completely alone and the safe held no mysterious parcels or notes, he set about scouring the pages for any sign of Mr Creed's writing, or renewal of his 'To Let' advertisement – which so far had not reappeared since the fourth instant. Scanning the columns in vain, he jumped from one sub-heading to the next.

AUCTION OF DAMAGED INDIAN CORN

'FIRST COST SALE'
OF A SPLENDID ASSORTMENT OF PLATED GOODS

'EVERY MAN HIS OWN MILLER'
Hand grinders for Indian meal

'Every man his own miller!' French scoffed at the arrogance of the claim – there were literally thousands in any given direction with nothing to mill, let alone the cost of a grinder to mill it.

Elsewhere were articles on the 'closure of Skibbereen Workhouse'; 'THE CORK WORKHOUSE INQUIRY'; 'Coroner's inquest on the suicide of Mr Patrick Barden'; yet another article on 'the ether-assisted PAINLESS SURGICAL OPERATIONS' conducted before an audience at Guy's Hospital in London and hailed as a monumental advance in medicine.

Startled by a creak of the counter under his elbow and conscious that he should bring the paper to the bottom of the stairs soon, French redoubled his focus to sift through the remainder of the columns until his eyes fell upon an inconspicuous paragraph boxed among the last section of the final page. Apparently anonymous in source, it lay beneath a banner the editors often lent a piece:

STATE OF THE COUNTRY

The Pawnbrokers' shops in most towns of this county are closed against receiving any more property as pledges, at present.

This is the case in Skibbereen, Mallow, Fermoy, and here in Macroom too.

It is melancholy to behold once comfortable farmers, coming distances of ten and twelve miles to raise money upon trifling household necessities.

Shopkeepers through the county also have their trade at a standstill except bakers and coffin-makers.

Searching again, French confirmed it was the only thing in the paper that could possibly have come from his employer. Some of the writing was not of Mr Creed's usual tone, French adjudged. But he had posted the envelope himself.

'Here in Macroom too!' he repeated aloud. *Surely this is Mr Creed. Holy God!*

French did not know why he was so surprised. There was nothing in the piece that was news to him. Most of its contents he had known for weeks, in fact. But something was odd about it, he thought, when, alarmed by the sounds of life above, Tom French carefully closed the newspaper and, placing it at the bottom of the stairs, picked up the empty bucket to go to the carhouse.

9

Cleaning the Slate

Collecting the bucket of coal from the bottom step, with unbraided hair, Paulellen tiptoed down the stairs, lest she alert Thomas French to her presence. From above she'd heard him in the yard and, confirming through the window that he'd be busy for some time, took advantage of the opportunity to retrieve it. Lately, her waking routine was to gather up the pail and get a fire lit upstairs to draw her husband out of the damp bedroom where for almost a month he'd been languishing in a melancholic state, preferring to keep the curtains drawn.

Every Monday, Wednesday and Friday she had left the paper in the parlour, hoping it might motivate Cornelius to arise and come back to himself, but, until today, had found no sure sign that he was reading it.

This morning, she had awoken to discover him already up and situated in the front room, perhaps stirred from his hebetude by the calamitous storm that had passed during the night.

As Paulellen's foot felt the carpeted warmth of the lowest step, she felt greatly relieved that, by his own volition, her husband had, at last, raised his head to stand in the light. This day, he needed no enticing, but she would light the fire anyway before heading out on her errands, she decided.

With the bucket handle in her grasp, however, something of Paulellen's curiosity induced her to let it drop and continue down the last step. The state of her hair forgotten, toward the back door she followed the brittle sound of something being scraped, as though stone upon delicate stone, and outside found Thomas French sweeping up a pan full of broken slates.

'Oh no. Is that from our roof, Thomas?'

'Eh, eh, good morning Mrs Creed, ma'am. I'm – I'm afraid so.' Clearly surprised by her presence, the clerk stopped dead, loaded pan in one hand and a brush in the other. ''Twas the most violent storm ever I remember.'

'Indeed it was. Frightening to say the least, Thomas. I was praying half the night it wouldn't send the roof in on top of us. I dare say we'll hear some dreadful tales in the days to come.'

'No doubt, ma'am.'

Paulellen strained to assess the damage for herself, but was not tall enough to see it clearly. 'Is it bad?'

'Not as bad as some roofs I saw, ma'am. There were quite a few slates down on the square.'

'The thought of any poor family out in the wilds, with no cover.' Paulellen tutted dolefully and shook her head. 'Will you arrange a carpenter to fix it, Mr French?'

'Of course, ma'am.'

'Thank you, Thomas.'

'Uh, ma'am?' Turning to go inside, Paulellen detected an apprehension in the clerk's voice.

'Yes, Thomas?'

'If … if I may have a word, ma'am …'

'Of course.'

Putting the pan down, apparently keen to employ the privacy of a room indoors, the bulky clerk attempted to inhale his girth and sidled past. But Paulellen did not even want to confront her own thoughts on her husband's condition, let alone discuss it with someone else, if the impending question was of such a nature.

'Ma'am … the advertisement … appears to have ceased running … eh, ha– has Mr Creed had a change of heart with … with regard to the letting of the premises?'

Unprepared for the question, Paulellen wrestled with what she herself didn't know, while, despite the morning's coldness, she couldn't help but notice the beads of a hotter day's perspiration gathering and rolling from beneath the red hair of French's brow.

'The advertisement, yes – I'm not sure where Mr Creed stands on that right now, Thomas. We should consider it a matter in abeyance.'

As a multitude of thoughts gathered in Paulellen's mind at his observation, Mr French seemed to be searching her face, she felt.

'Mr Creed instructed me to stay on, ma'am, taking care of the stores, redeeming pledges, and such.' As unable for conference as ever, Paulellen observed, pulling a handkerchief from his back pocket as he spoke, French mopped his forehead, then returned the well-used rag to its compartment, stuffing it in. 'My mother and I are, are naturally so indebted to your and Mr Creed's kindnesses, ma'am, and … well, I wish to reaffirm my commitment … that I am willing to continue on a … as long as you both would like me to, ma'am.'

'Thank you, Thomas.' Paulellen smiled.

'But if I may … speak discreetly, ma'am …'

'Please do, Thomas.'

'Thank you, ma'am. Eh, Mr Creed being somewhat absent … eh … unavailable, ma'am … Could you speak to anything of his plans for me, eh, I … I … Would … would you think it … wise of me, to begin looking elsewhere, ma'am?'

'Thomas … who else could Mr Creed count on? He is relying upon *you*. Indeed, *we* both need you here.'

Looking into his sad blue eyes, Paulellen realised that, desperate to maintain the illusion of normality – something that had been helping her to hold everything together – she had not taken any time to consider poor Mr French, who, after all, had the weight of his own predicaments to consider. Still, she was yet conflicted: the instinct to protect her husband being paramount, she found herself resistant to saying more, lest anything of his condition might slip in the process.

If, later, she could manage to get any sense out of her husband, she would tell him of Mr French's concerns.

'Thank you, Thomas. You'll let me know the cost when the roof is mended?'

'Yes, of course, ma'am.'

A defeated-looking French bowed politely and, retreating backwards toward the counter, left Paulellen at the bottom of the stairs, where she picked up the bucket and struggled aloft under its weight.

It *was* unreasonable he be left to work on indefinitely with no communication on the matter of his wages, or the running of the shop, she reflected, breathing hard to climb the steps.

Before the present crisis, she had never needed to take stock of how much he shielded them from. There had been the recent spell, of course, extended though it was, when in December last they had gone out to Leades so Cornelius could take some time to recuperate. Even then, she now realised, Mr French, running the shop single-handedly, had not been anything she had considered.

But, in light of her husband's condition, and with the likelihood of any recovery being a somewhat drawn-out affair, Paulellen found herself suddenly forced to see the clerk's importance in a whole new light.

She had always supposed that *he* was dependent upon *them*, when, in fact, it was now the other way around.

She was not reliant upon Mr French for money, food, or for any other life-giving necessity. But, so long as Cornelius remained indisposed above, she now conceived, if Mr French were suddenly to abscond for any reason, she alone would inherit the overwhelming task of running the business and ministering to the countless paupers banging upon the shop door.

French, with his ruddy complexion. Gentle and inoffensive. A grown man who looked as though a boy lost among the world, still tied to the hem of his mother's shawl as he yet nursed her towards death and his own completed loneliness. Paulellen had always worried that through his habit of showing no obvious ambition to personal advancement, or indeed any apparent drive to win the companionship of the fairer sex, poor Thomas French's general simplicity and tendency to timidness almost guaranteed he would simply tread water for as long as he could, until one day the rolling current of life became too strong for him.

But, seeing the clerk in such a light as she never had previously, Paulellen now considered that perhaps she should be more mindful and appreciative of how delicately all three of their fates were hung together.

For now, though, she had better see to her husband and make sure he was warmed, she thought.

———

Nearing the end of the hallway upstairs, Paulellen found the parlour door ajar. Through it she overheard something she had lately forgotten: the sound of her husband's voice. Quietly lowering the bucket to the floor and steadying herself with a hand upon the architrave, Paulellen moved to peer through the narrow space dividing the door and its frame. Gaining no account of his position this way, she took to employing her ear to gather what was coming from the room and picture the scene instead.

As Paulellen tuned in, she realised her husband was talking to the dog. A consequence of his speech being underused lately, his voice sounded raspy and even a little weak: 'Ever since Adam climbed down from a tree and stood upon a thorn, man has been obsessed with protecting his feet. And so, he invented these curious appurtenances, though I expect in many forms and classes before reaching this design. But what is it that you found so invaluable about this particular pair, my friend … that you would risk life and limb, though you yourself cannot employ them? Myself, I do admit to finding them quite … enchanting.'

Trying her eye through the gap once more, to her surprise, Paulellen found she could now espy him partially, in profile. Standing by the fireplace, Cornelius had trained his attention upon something before him, upon the mantel. Though she could not see the item, Paulellen presumed it was the pair of shoes he'd brought back from the river on New Year's Day.

What significance he'd attached to a single pauper's footwear intrigued and worried her both. But the mixture of surprise and affection she had felt approaching the room had now turned to something of sadness and an anxiety to understand whether her husband was recovering at all, or indeed slipping further into a realm of his own making.

Staying absolutely still, Paulellen strained to hold her breath, turning away only to exhale, after which, her lungs refilled afresh, she peered through the gap once more.

But, no longer speaking, Cornelius had moved now.

Paulellen was contemplating what was going through his mind when from behind the door the dog gave a sudden bark and growled deeply, causing her to hide. With eyes tightly shut and her forehead against the back of her hand, Paulellen admonished herself, but felt sure her husband had not seen her.

When, at last, assured by some sense of his resuming his fascination with the objects before him, she eyed the sliver once more, Paulellen perceived him leaning toward the silvered mirror above the fireplace, studying himself in a manner most concerning. Pulling the skin of his face down from one eye, Cornelius spoke to his reflection.

'Is that you … or is it me?'

Finding his turmoil too disturbing to bear, Paulellen left the bucket and, as silently as she could, retreated towards the kitchen, the weight of a stone sinking in her heart.

There, with her face held in her own hands, Paulellen made up her mind that, however long she would have to keep him upstairs, no one would see her husband like this. More than ever now, she hoped the article in yesterday's paper would buy them some time, and stop people from wondering if he had lost his mind. Just so long as nobody realised it was *she* had written it.

The deception would seem to have worked on Thomas French, at least, and being so close to them on a daily basis, for Paulellen, his belief had proved a comforting litmus.

10

A Pawnbroker's Ticket

Out in the hallway, the deep sound of a knock preceded the voice of Mrs Stephenson, announcing in her narrow drawl, 'Someone is here,' a ritual lately all too usual.

'Yes, Madam?' Unsurprised by the diminished appearance of his visitor, Reverend John Torrens Kyle greeted a woman who, either for added effect or because she had no one else to care for them, had brought three of her children along with her. Whatever the reason, the effect was the same and there was no doubting their poverty.

'I'm here to beg you recommend my boy to the works, sir,' the woman answered, the hood of her shawl still engaged, one child at her leg, with another upon her hip, asleep. But it was the adolescent boy that she pushed to the front. 'I'll not lie to you, sir,' she said mournfully, 'my husband is on the works already. But we are nine in the family, and no matter how we manage it, his wages falls far short of putting food in our mouths, with the result five of the children are this present moment lying down with influenza.'

As he listened to the mother, Kyle observed the posture of the boy she proposed he add to the lists. It was hard to guess his age, his features being already altered by hunger, but the child did not look strong enough to withstand the work required of a labourer.

'Where is your abode, madam?' Kyle asked, already decided on accompanying her there. Taking his coat from off its hook, he summoned Mrs Stephenson, requesting of her, discreetly, to 'please bring a selection of victuals'.

As it turned out, the woman's husband was among those laid up at the cabin, Kyle discovered, his legs swollen, likely with dropsy, which did not bode well. No doctor, Kyle did not have the confidence to verify if it was fever or influenza afflicting the rest, but for their sakes, he hoped the latter. With some luck the provisions allotted them might help the husband's recovery. But in the meantime, Kyle felt he could not deny the mother's request and would recommend the boy in his father's place. The boy was much too weak to manage the physical demands of such a role, but it was the family's only chance, he believed, if the mother herself did not go.

Leaving the hovel, Kyle discovered a stranger had been awaiting him outside. With no introduction, the man thrust a piece of paper into his hand.

'I beg your mercy, sir. For the sake of my poor family, would you be so kind as to retrieve this from the pawnbroker's in Macroom?' he asked, with full sincerity. 'I've no money to do it myself, but could pay in kind, doing work as you see fit.'

Returning home upon the car, Kyle reflected that all around him, people were being forced to such bold and unusual undertakings.

It was, he imagined, only at reaching their lowest ebb, having exhausted every other refuge but the workhouse, that so many of the Catholic poor were lately given to approach him, or indeed come to the door of the rectory.

———

With concentrated sentiment and a hand poised in readiness, Kyle prepared to begin the scrawl. Even on this day, when under usual circumstances he would retire from his labours after Sunday morning service to write to relatives, or enjoy the observances of some ecclesiastical passage, he could not distance his mind from the events that, by the day, were growing to resemble those Biblical scenes of famine and plague in the long-ago times of heathen man: scenes Kyle had hitherto considered would never be repeated.

But besides the hope that, through writing, he might purge from his mind the anxieties of such terrible things – following the example of such fellows as Dr Dan Donovan and Rev. Charles Gibson, who, in visiting the hovels of the sick and dying with little or no regard for themselves, then bearing witness to the suffering in periodicals and journals, were amassing a dedicated readership – Kyle was fast learning that to make his experiences public was the best way to raise funds for the enterprise of ministering to the poor of his parish.

Clondrohid Rectory, Jan 31st

To the EDITOR of the CORK CONSTITUTION
'Famine is here, and the cry of hunger ceases not.'

Dear Sir – The annual distribution of the blankets has occurred. In parishes like this, wild, undrained, and destitute of gentry, the poor always suffer. But this year, their condition defies description.

Today a woman asked if women were employed on the roads; for her father, who had a labour ticket, was sick, and she had no brother, but five sisters.

To numbers, relief under the Board of Works will come too late. The frame, weakened by long fasting, will yield to the effects of the severe weather, if no dreadful malady will close in death the sufferings patiently endured.

'A Catholic Lady' in Cork read of the privations of our poor and sent me her mite through the Post-office. She will not have her name made known, perhaps feeling that good deeds, when vented, lose their fragrance.

An English Officer lately shooting here learned the craving wants of the people – he writes to his wife and relatives in England, and in a few days put their liberal offerings into my hands for a soup kitchen in aid of the sick and needy. Let us hope our Soup Fund will not derive all its support from strangers alone, but those connected with the parish too, through monthly contributions to our cause. How much suffering would our poor brethren have been saved, if soup kitchens were timely got up in every locality?

Two men lately came to know if I could 'give any account when the works would begin?', saying all they and their families had had for the two days previous was 'a little warm water with a grain of salt in it'. They'd left home fasting and would have nothing to eat upon their return, they assured me. One has six, the other seven to feed.

A woman came here to have her boy recommended to the works; her husband and five of her children were 'lying down' with sickness. I was in her cabin – her sad tale was true.

As I left the hovel, a man put a pawnbroker's ticket in my hand; he asked if I could have the mercy to redeem it on his behalf. Another came to tell me he'd 'change', if he could only get something for his children. I remarked he must think badly of our religion if he supposed we bought converts. He felt my rebuke, but repeated that he'd do anything to feed his children. The patience of the people is very remarkable.

The parish of Clondrohid is nine miles by seven; the pauper population: three thousand, five hundred souls. We are about to set up two boilers, and shall put into them the best materials the small fund at our disposal will allow.

– It is more blessed to give than to receive –

If in any of your readers, when surrounded with all the comforts and luxuries wealth can give, the thought rises, how fare the poor this bitter weather on the bleak hill or by the dreary swamp? Then for the wretched of Clondrohid, let them become, as it were, fellow workers with God; in feeding the hungry, and in supplying the sick with some of the necessities their sorry condition demands.

Contributions to the Clondrohid Soup Fund will be gratefully acknowledged by JOHN PEARSON, Esq., of Mountcross, Macroom.

My appeal on behalf of three thousand and five hundred famishing men, women, and children will, I feel assured, not go unanswered by some of your generous readers.

– Be good to the poor, as God gives thee store –

Yours very truly,
John Torrens Kyle.

FEABHRA

FEBRUARY

11

Swallows of Night

Lying on his side, Creed flitted between bouts of melancholia, restlessness, and thoughts constructed to convince himself that he was feeling better.

Terrified by the visions he perceived as 'blooms', he nightly battled sleep. Reminiscent of those stains a lighted lamp sometimes burned into the sight of his tired eyes, strange pools swirled in the darkness behind his eyelids. Yet, with no source of light to cause them in the small hours, Creed found the patterns unsettling. Seeping in like chemical droplets dissipating through the waters of his mind, one after the other they appeared out of nothing. Hopelessly, he reasoned that they were merely the functioning machinery of his fledgling dreams. But weary of the slopes of his mind, Creed startled and resisted when the blooms became vivid, taking the form of faces and objects and, all too often, what he'd come to fear most: the turbulent river. For weeks, this cycle of running and hiding had gone on, until, at some point nightly, like sirens on a dark nocturnal shore, one formless blur would transcend to something comforting and peaceful, tricking him to the realm of his dreams; or until, so tired, he simply lost consciousness.

Waking reality was often stranger than the dreams and the thought of venturing out – to walk the dog, at Paulellen's suggestion – had seemed distinctly unpalatable at first. But breaking the empty darkness of the room, the dog's reassuring presence by the bedside had been giving Creed the will to try and, of late, the secret test of late-night walks around the shop downstairs had helped him to accept that one day soon he would have to go outside.

Yet, it was the other creatures and their going that finally led Creed to feel that this episode was coming to an end.

Lying awake sometimes in the moments before dawn, he would hear the noises. As unaffecting as the first raindrops of a shower on the wind it would start. Then he would realise that, making themselves conspicuous in short bursts, it was the coming and going of bats swerving and swooping to land under the barge boards of the roof outside.

Taking off after a moment's rest, or chasing prey, their wingtips would clip the window panes or some other part of the structure. But how elusive they were. He had never even seen a dead one, let alone a living specimen, Creed realised. Drawings, perhaps, in some journal or periodical. And yet, if he was not imagining this too, here they were: secretive and magical, almost to be believed on faith alone.

This morning, having anticipated their arrival from the state of his half-waking, but still dreaming, Creed found himself alive to the sound again. Picturing the silvery fur of their charcoal bodies, he imagined them gliding at hurtling velocities, not with feathers, but the lustreless skin of paper-thin wings.

Wondering if, this time, with bleared vision, he might confirm what his ears told him, Creed arose and took himself to the window, the top blanket around his shoulders, trailing off the edge of the bed behind him.

Ready to behold their darting flights, he waited for his eyes to adjust. It was still too dim to make out much. But soon, against the burgeoning dawn, like swallows of the darkness, small objects blurred and plunged in silhouette, and with breath arrested, Creed gazed, enraptured.

They were beautiful and perfect: silent, invisible, and breathtakingly graceful. However reviled the bats were by the daylight world and its sensibilities – though unjustly so, Creed believed – how perfectly suited they were to the vacuous ether of this opposite realm.

Creed watched their acrobatic flights until his neck grew so strained he was compelled to lie down. But before long, seduced again by their increased activity – spurred on, he imagined, by the disappearing darkness – he arose a second time, to glimpse, and to store with his eyes, what was his vanishing privilege to witness: the spectacle of their mastery.

When, by the growing glow of light – too violent for their sensitive eyes – the bats began to arrive less frequently, soon could be heard the sounds of their retreat: somewhere above him, inching their way through the roof by a fissure or crevice he could not see; their outstretched wings folded now, turned to ungainly elbowed stilts.

Invisible and unseen for another long day, they left nothing but the empty morning.

But one more, it seemed: a black shadow out of the right, moving west towards the river. This time the light was bright enough for Creed's eyes to latch on and track the motion, when, with surprise, he realised this one was no bat at all, but a crow: the first of the morning, flying past in a straight line.

Everything he'd witnessed had occurred across a span of minutes, Creed supposed. But how quickly, he marvelled, that just like that, the night was over. *The first bird of the day, ready to fall in as the last of the night falls out. How finely attuned is nature, when unmolested by the habits of man. Not a moment gone to waste and everything abiding its purpose.*

Through many mornings across the month, he had listened in wonder, captivated by the gentle presence and quiet beauty of the creatures.

But, through watching, they had inspired him, Creed realised, to better brave, with less fear and resistance, this other state to which he had found himself confined. That such a creature existed, who could not only see, and hunt, but even fly in absolute darkness, making a virtue of overcoming the impossible: that was a revelation to Creed, who knew that this day, he must stay standing and attempt the world once more. He was not so foolish as to presume that *his* troubles, nor the tremendous woes of the masses around him, would be willing to disembark so conveniently as the night did for the dawn. But stirred by the magic and the poetry of what he'd seen, however tired he felt, it was time.

12

O Redeemer!

Coiling the scarf about her head, readying herself to leave the shop, Paulellen heard the bell knocked into life, and turned to find the clerk.

'Ah, Mr French, I was so sorry to hear,' she said, commiserating.

'Thank you, Mrs Creed.'

'When did she –?'

'Friday, ma'am.'

'Oh,' Paulellen sighed for him. 'Did she go easy, Thomas?'

'In her sleep, ma'am, mercifully.'

'Ah … that's a blessing … Will you not take some time?' she asked, concerned, as he closed the door.

'If 'tis all the same, ma'am, I'd prefer to keep my mind –'

'Of course. That's understandable,' Paulellen said, forcing a smile. 'If you change your mind, I'm sure Mr Creed will be very understanding.'

'Yes, ma'am,' French said, as, pulling out the door, Paulellen watched him going to the counter, his head low and sorrowful.

―――

Slowing, the horse's shoes pinged upon the cobbles as John Torrens Kyle prepared to climb down and straighten his back after the arduous journey from Clondrohid.

Three times he'd stopped since setting out that morning: once, necessarily, to relieve himself amid the cover of the trees before getting too close to town. But the stop he pondered now was the one he'd made for a struggling pauper, evidently on her way to the workhouse.

'*Tig na mBocht,*' she'd pleaded, her legs so swollen she could not have made it far otherwise; her mouth gaping open to so many missing teeth. When he'd got as close to the door there as he could take her, helping her down off his cart Kyle had observed with much pity that the woman's condition had deteriorated even since he'd picked her up, and with doubts she would ever leave the workhouse, he'd found it hard to shake her face from his mind since.

Here on the square, Macroom seemed as bustling and piteous as ever for its abundance of beggars and paupers. He was some correspondence lighter leaving the Post Office a few moments later, but with newly arrived letters to replace those he'd dropped off. These, he hoped, would carry more donations to restock the boilers of his poor kitchen at the Rectory.

The envelopes safely inside his coat, Kyle was crossing the street for CORNELIUS CREED PAWNBROKERS when a feeble voice he imagined to be that of another pauper seeking alms engaged him side-on.

'Reverend Kyle.'

'Mr Creed!' he replied, surprised at the sight of the broker who, with an animal at his side, seemed changed in appearance.

'Yes, the individual before you is a somewhat disordered version of the one you are accustomed to,' said Creed. 'I was unwell for a time, Reverend Kyle. But coming back to myself lately, I find my importances *re-*ordered. Walking with my friend here is among them,' he added cheerfully.

'I'm happy to hear it, Mr Creed.'

'Would you like to come inside?' the pawnbroker asked, holding out his keys, as though introducing them to the door. 'It seemed you were calling anyway?'

'Thank you, I was,' Kyle replied, and, stepping back to allow his host access, observed a 'CLOSED' sign hung in the glass. Painted by a careful hand, *it* seemed more in keeping with Mr Creed's usual comport, but it was hard to decide what to make of his present state, Kyle thought. More was sure to be imminently revealed.

Inside, the shop was eerily quiet. Save for the dying ring of the bell, the only sounds were of the broker's keys crunching as they settled upon the counter and the rapid panting of the dog, who had clearly been recently exerted.

'I must thank you for the kind reference, Mr Creed.'

'Reference? Forgive my state of mind, Mr Kyle.'

'In your writings, you referred to me once as – well, it's quite embarrassing to say it myself: "the poor man's friend".' Kyle heard himself smiling. 'It has been quoted often to me, since.'

'Ah! Indeed. As I have said, my memory is rather foggy. I don't recall the article, Mr Kyle. But I have often described you as such, and rightly so. With the exception of its beneficiaries, perhaps I, more than most, have been witness to your work on behalf of the poor when each year there is a sudden influx here of the blankets you distribute – becoming a kind of currency, as they do, among the needy of your parish.'

As he listened, Kyle studied the broker. Smaller, unshaven, with his clothing in want of some repair, Mr Creed more resembled the poor who frequented his shop than the man Kyle had often regarded at committee meetings. Though not someone he associated with extravagant dress, even for Mr Creed this was a somewhat conspicuous decline, and Kyle worried for the man's health, if he admired, and even applauded, his insouciance.

'Actually,' said Mr Creed, 'Saint Vincent de Paul have red-painted all blankets with the letters SVP this year, requesting pawnbrokers do not take receipt of them.'

'An interesting device.'

'Yes. But unfortunately for the wretched souls who frequent my shop – and those you serve among them, Mr Kyle – I am no longer in a position to accept any blankets at all. Though you may consider that a mixed blessing, I exp–'

'Not entirely, Mr Creed. While I wish they had no need for a pawnbroker at all, is it not better they can call on a good one?'

Ready to introduce his reason for calling, Rev. Kyle found himself startled at something that seemed to have taken place as the pawnbroker had finished his last thought. As though feeling morally responsible, or even ashamed, a great sadness had come over him and, his ears moving back at some realisation, he was frozen, staring, lost in his mind.

But just as the broker could attest to the minister's deeds, Kyle, in turn, had been witness to many of Mr Creed's and he admired the man. Sharing the table with him at Relief Committee meetings over many months, he had witnessed Mr Creed's battles at first hand and knew him to be one of a rare breed who, in all things, perhaps now more than ever, put his soul and his concerns for the poor before anything of business. Yet, clearly, he was wrestling with his conscience and perhaps this was the cause of his altered health, Kyle thought.

'Mr Creed, do not struggle with your morality. There are far worse amid the would-be prophets and those who profess themselves as such among our community. I have watched you in the lair of your enemies and admired the courage and integrity you have shown. Yours is a voice I find comfort in hearing and in reading.

'Despite the trade announced above your door and what it comes to represent, out in my community I have seen what good you effect by your actions, quiet and otherwise. Hold your head high, Mr Creed. You are a man of honesty, and one so valued amongst those in this realm who recognise goodness and honour when they see it.'

'Mr Kyle ... that is ... well ... I am at the mercy of my ineptitude to respond.'

'Think no more of it than a sharing of the truth, Mr Creed, from one who regards himself a student of intention.'

'Kind you are, sir.'

Worried at the signs Mr Creed might become as broken down emotionally as he was in appearance, Kyle moved to, at last, make known his reason for visiting.

'If I may, Mr Creed – I noticed the Closed sign in your window. But are you redeeming pledges, I wonder?'

'That is the one service still provided, Mr Kyle, yes.'

'Oh good! Calling to a cabin in the course of my work in recent days, a ticket was produced and handed me. A young man, the father of a family in Clondrohid, entrusted it to my –'

Fumbling to find the item on his person, Kyle observed the expression of the pawnbroker to transform greatly once more, from brimming emotion to one of earnestness.

'Clondrohid?' he said aloud, and, as if slipping from the present reality to another dreamlike state, his eyes glazed over. Whether landing in the future or somewhere in the past, Kyle felt the gaze pass through him. Mr Creed was of a sudden absent and vacant.

'Clondrohid, yes, Mr Creed: the man requested I redeem the item on his behalf, and, as he was clearly in need of it, I felt bound to oblige him.'

'Name,' he inquired anxiously, 'what was his name?'

'I put it in my, eh ... coming out ... I have it here somewhere, I'm sure of it.' Distracted by the intensity of Mr Creed's concentration, Kyle continued to search his garments blindly, fixated and somehow unable to break the stare that met with his.

'The item: do you recall it? Was it shoes?'

'Eh, a coat, I believe.'

Upon this announcement, like a pig's bladder cut with a knife, the atmosphere deflated and began instantly to resume its previous character, while Mr Creed's aspect turned to one of disappointment if not outright apathy.

'Ah! Here it is! A coat, yes. Carroll is the man's name – see here – of Dromanarrig.' Kyle held out the ticket.

'Would you like me to fetch it, Mr Creed?' spoke the clerk, a diligent employee, appearing from the back – having heard their conversation, it would seem.

Mr Creed held the ticket aloft and delivered it blindly, saying, 'Thank you, Mr French.'

Here, Kyle noticed that the dog had resumed its panting, only realising in hindsight it had stopped – perhaps as anxious as he was to see its master returned to a state of grace.

'Have you ever in your travels, Mr Kyle, come upon a Pádraig Ua Buachalla? Or Patrick Buckley, perhaps?'

'Hmmm, not that I recall. I expect that's quite a common name in my parish, Mr Creed, with Buckleys in most every townland. My door, if you will, is largely avoided by all but the most stricken poor. Though lately that has come to be a great many.'

'I understand, Mr Kyle.'

'We have, in recent weeks, just opened a soup kitchen, however –'

'Oh?'

'Yes, so I believe we'll be encountering more visitors as winter persists. Would you like me to … keep a look out?'

'Reverend Kyle, I would be most grateful. If you hear of, or cross paths with, anyone of that name, you might make me aware, or acquaint me with his whereabouts.'

'With pleasure, Mr Creed. Eh, this man – may I ask –'

'I have something I dearly wish to give him,' the pawnbroker said. 'I had him as dead, but I'm encouraged by the appearance of this ticket, and how you came upon it, that he may, in fact, be alive.'

'Very well, Mr Creed. I'll keep watch.'

'Thank you, Mr Kyle.'

'Here you are, sir.' The clerk returned with a heavy woollen coat. 'Patrick Carroll, Dromanarrig.'

'Oh, wonderful! How much to redeem it?' Kyle took out his purse.

'Shall I find the entry, Mr Creed?' Currently blocked by his employer, the clerk attempted to retrieve something from beneath the counter.

'That won't be necessary. No charge, Mr Kyle.'

'Thank you, Mr Creed. I'll not refuse your kindness. Necessity forbids. But rest assured, whatever's saved will go to hungry mouths.'

As Kyle stood by, the pawnbroker whispered something to his clerk, who, opening the safe, returned to load what sounded like coins into his hand.

'For your boilers, Reverend Kyle,' said Mr Creed, placing two crowns before him on the counter, 'may they continue to bring relief and solace to all who require it.'

'Mr Creed, you are indeed a gentle soul. Though I did not expect this, I cannot feign surprise.'

Gathering the money, Kyle fastened his coat, then held out the retrieved item between them. 'On behalf of Mr Carroll, gentlemen, I bid you good morning.' He bowed.

'Thank you for calling, Reverend Kyle.' Mr Creed returned the gesture. 'Come, Lucky. Let's go upstairs.'

Springing to its feet, the dog drifted silently beneath the counter as its master held the door open.

Outside a moment later, Kyle exchanged a silent greeting with the lady going in: Mrs Creed, he presumed.

Paulellen found the shop empty but could hear the faint voice of her husband upstairs. Abandoned upon the counter was the latest instalment of the *Cork Examiner*. Drawing her eyes, one article read:

TO PAWNBROKERS

A PERSON who was in the Pawnbroking Business for a long time Wants a Situation as CLERK. Testimonials as to character, &c., can be seen by applying to T.F., via Examiner Office. No objection to Town or Country.

'T. F. … Thomas French? Oh dear!' Paulellen whispered to herself.

13

A Sparrow's Meal

'I can't do it. I can't do it. I just can't… I thought I could go back, but it's too much …'

Thomas French felt his eyes widen with shock at what he was hearing. Five minutes before, he'd been going about his business, moving items back and forth, when a key had been frantically jostled in the front door lock. The fumbling had stopped, followed by a ping outside, as though the key dropped to the ground, at which point, certain Mrs Creed was upstairs, French realised it must be Mr Creed.

Ducking under the counter, eager to assist, French banged his head, then, wincing, felt the lump as he opened the door. Confirming his intuition, a panicked Cornelius Creed burst past under the frightened bell and made straight for the back, offering no more acknowledgement than a gasp of emotion.

'Is everything all right, Mr Creed?' French had called after his employer, and felt the cold air that followed in his wake. But in place of an answer had come only footsteps, hurriedly ascending. A sort of whimpering went with them, conspicuous even after the door at the top had slammed shut.

Now two steps from the bottom, French stood in the shaft of the stairwell, desperately sorry for the man who, but days before, had reappeared as though from thin air after five solid weeks of absence, a ghost of his former self.

'Oh no … what's the matter, Con?' It was the voice of Mrs Creed overhead. 'What at all has happened?' she begged; and by the smothered moan French heard, the impression he formed was that in the kitchen Mrs Creed had pulled her husband into her embrace.

'Shhhhhsshh …' followed a sibilant hushing sound. 'Tell me, tell me, what's the matter?' she said, imploringly.

For a long moment nothing was returned. But, when Mr Creed eventually spoke, it was a somewhat more controlled version that re-emerged.

'I went to the boardroom … for the Relief Committee.'

'Yes?'

As it seemed Mr Creed was finding the courage to share whatever had befallen him, attuning his hearing to the tiniest sound, French climbed higher up the stairwell, ever careful not to make the boards creak.

'I have not been well, Paull,' the answer came.

'I know. I know … but you're better now?'

'I thought I'd come through it, and I *am* better than I was, but –'

'But what?'

'Everything else is worse. Outside the shop this morning I was approached by a man I've often seen passing: an athletic, powerful labourer. His appearance was dreadful: faded form; attenuated body … Would I submit his name, he asked – with nine in the family, he could find no employment.'

French struggled to fix the identity of the labourer, but, hoping Mr Creed would turn to talk of the shop and his plans for it, listened on intently.

'Much like the man that *I* encountered, Nicholas White observed he met a poor soul coming across Sleaveen Hill this very day. The poor fellow cried bitterly. Fourteen days on the works he'd been, without receiving a penny; though ten shillings were owed him that would keep his family from starvation. Instead they were dying of hunger at that very moment, he said. It is shameful, Paull.

'If the poorhouse should be closed – as it probably will on Saturday next – what will be the consequences? Swathes of these unfortunate creatures will be found starved in the street. The House has gone utterly to ruin.'

Enough of the damned poorhouse, French thought in frustration, *what of the shop, and the man in your employ – left to run the premises single-handedly?*

Despite his own selfish concerns, French was frightened. The country was in deep crisis. That he knew. But to hear it fall from the mouth of Mr Creed, by whose word his own compass was always set, gave it a terrifying reality.

French had just lost his mother. His position of employment had hung in the balance for some time. The world around him was approaching a realm of plague and disease of medieval proportions. And now, that voice of reassurance – which somehow by its absence had been preserving hope – had reappeared, every part as damaged and as broken as French himself felt.

'Can it be true that among the lanes of the town, not a single morsel of food enters the mouths of the inhabitants from one day to the next with the exception of a drop of long porridge; that they exist without the slightest covering or protection against the elements? Where is their clothing? Where is their bedding? What circumstances have compelled them to part with both? How can people allow this to happen and exist and go about their business regardless?'

Either so upset by what she was hearing, or willing him to purge the poison from his mind, Mrs Creed appeared to be staying quiet. But most puzzling to French was that, as though reborn, Mr Creed was describing things like someone with no memory at all of the trade he had been plying for the last two years, or, indeed, why anyone had needed to avail of it. What realm was he returning from, French wondered with anguish; was it madness? He could find no other explanation.

'How have these people been surviving so long without employment?' Mr Creed asked, fast regaining his habitually righteous tone.

'But Cornelius,' Mrs Creed said, finally breaking her silence. 'You mentioned the boardroom. What of *it* had you so upset?'

'Oh,' Mr Creed sighed, defeatedly, 'I had almost forgotten how ill at ease I am in the company of such men.'

'What men? Who was there?'

'This fellow Captain Brooke, for one: Gordon's replacement. At least that's *one* thing improved; there is now only one Gordon in the Muskerries, though it remains to be seen how effectual, or *ineffectual* his replacement …'

Still concerned for his employer, Thomas French had little or no interest in these minutiae and clutched his face at Mrs Creed's having asked the question, helpless to prevent himself from losing concentration until something was said of interest.

'After a fortnight's delay some of the creatures employed upon the road were paid *one shilling* for *a whole week's labour!* Reverend Barry – Father Lee's curate – pointed out. That amounts to *two pence a day*. With horror and amazement, I ask you – is this not merely a dream? A coinage of the brain? How can any public officer possessing the ordinary attributes of a human being, and he having but one ray of compassion in his whole nature, suffer such a state of things to endure for even a single day?'

Tired from standing so long in one position, by now French had carefully lowered himself to sit upon the creaky stairs, but became unnerved when it sounded as though Mr Creed was up, pacing the room. As long as the diatribe continued, the door would not open, he reassured himself.

'And then Massy *Warren!*' Mr Creed continued, bringing French to think that they were getting to the heart of it now. 'Oh, to all this, Massy announced, "They have not earned nor deserved more!" Can you *fathom* that? As brazen as you care. "On Pound Lane it is notorious", said he, "the labourers carry their crowbars to the fire to warm them." These shivering creatures! "They do not half-fill their barrows, but roll them a short distance, then shift them from one man to another," he said, and by this humane defence he feels justified that those men have not earned more!

'"They did not work *hard!*" he had the nerve to – Gracious *heaven!* How would Massy H. *Warren*, were *he* reduced to the labour-mendicancy of the public road, "work hard" on *his* share of two pence a day? What could he possibly know of the conditions these men toil under? Make it your own case, Mr Warren. Then *you* will understand something approaching the enormity of the man's guilt who compels a human being to toil for such a recompense. I'd like to see *him* wield a crowbar, or trundle a wheelbarrow on a cupful of watered-down porridge! Such wages would not give a pound weight of food in the day to a whole family, with sometimes six, seven, even eight children to feed. That's less than a quarter of a penny worth of food each. Such an amount would scarcely sustain a sparrow!

''Tis a sentence of death upon the labourer – if Mr Barry's statement is to be believed – and even Massy Warren did not deny it: he, in fact, confirmed it – that a sparrow's meal has been the sole support of a human creature – and one labouring upon human roads at that.'

Mr Creed fell quiet, when, ready to jump, French gripped the rail, suspecting he would hear nothing more than the door opening. But Mr Creed was not entirely finished.

'And hear this! Mr Barry himself questioned the overseers and was told that, in many instances, the labourers received four pence a day *less* than the amount *allocated* to Captain Gordon! Is that not alarming? "I move that we don't hear any further discussion," Massy suddenly declared! What convenient hypocrisy!'

Through the top of the stairwell, akin to an extreme draught, a sucking sound along the threshold told French the dog had smelled him, even with the door closed.

———

At the sound of the bell below, Paulellen remembered Mr French had been downstairs and wondered, with some alarm, how much he might have heard.

14

Death of the Master

'Onóra! Wake up, girl!'

Onóra was roused violently from sleep by the sound of Matron's voice, accompanied by a sharp pain at her earlobe; apparently the woman was bent on extracting her from between the warm bodies among whom she fought to hide herself.

'Ow!'

Somewhere behind the candle Matron yanked her ear again. 'Up, girl. Come.'

Though disoriented, frightened at the prospect of displeasing the woman she feared so much, Onóra climbed to her feet, trying not to step on any of the women who blanketed the sleeping platforms from one end of the dorm to the other. At a pinching grip to the back of her arm she winced again, being marched along the middle aisle with the candle's light flickering before her.

Onóra dared not question where she was being taken, or why. But, eventually brought to a stop, she realised they were standing outside the Master's quarters, the door to which was slightly open; a yellow glow spilling from within, she noticed.

'Take this, girl. Go to the surgeon's room and fetch Doctor Crooke, who will be sleeping. Tell him the Master is going. Knock *loudly*, girl. Do you understand?'

'Yes, Miss.' Onóra could hardly believe what she was hearing.

'If he is not to be found there, he'll be in the fever hospital, beyond the infirmary. Do you know how to find it?'

'I do, ma'am.' Worried *she* might have to stay with the Master if she said no, Onóra had lied.

'Good. Go quickly.'

Why did Matron always choose *her*, Onóra lamented? Only that so many of the staff were ill with fever, she supposed. Frightened by the passing spectres of idols and statues that loomed out of the darkness along the way, Onóra felt her heart racing and hurried as she went, guarding the delicate glow of light in her charge as, one after the other, her quickening feet kissed the cold stone of the floor.

Through the blur of her thoughts Onóra tried not to think of what Matron would do if she failed to find the doctor in time, or got lost in the darkness somewhere, looking for the fever hospital.

What will happen if the Master dies? she asked herself. This place and its meals had kept her alive, however cruelly it did so. *Will we all be put out, to fend for ourselves? God in heaven.*

Reaching the surgeon's room, Onóra was relieved to find that within moments of knocking, life could be heard within and the door was soon answered by Dr Crooke, leaning on a cane.

'What is it, girl?'

'I'm sent by Matron to fetch you, sir. The Master is going.'

'Indeed.' Frowning sleepily, the doctor rubbed his hand the length of his face. 'Indeed. Indeed.' Flustering, he turned and retrieved his coat from the back of the door. 'Lend me your light, girl.'

'Yes, sir.'

'Carry this, please.' Giving Onóra his bag, the doctor took the candle instead and began to lead the way. At how steadily he seemed to manage the light, Onóra felt reassured walking behind the tall man – clearly stiffened and sore with age, as he tried to move at pace.

'Sir, what will happen if … if the Master –?'

'Manners, girl. Did you see him?'

'I did not, sir. Matron sent me directly.'

Back the way she had come, Onóra followed in the shadow of Dr Crooke till they reached the Master's quarters where, from within, she heard Matron greet the doctor, who did not return speech. 'Just in time,

I fear,' the woman added.

'My bag, girl – bring it here, please.'

Knowing her place, Onóra had stopped outside until she was summoned, but now entered, bringing the bag. Though she tried not to look, she could not help but perceive the Master, laid out upon what seemed an incredibly high bed; his face and neck thrust backward so that his head sank deeply into the pillow, his jaw unhinged to its widest. He was indeed, it seemed, in the final stages of death.

'Hurry, girl,' Matron implored from the far side of the bed, while, struck by the foulness of the air, Onóra struggled not to grab at her face as she approached.

In the vicinity of the bed, the dim light gave up two chairs and a locker laden with various basins of cloths and liquids. Taking the bag, the doctor unbuckled its top and reached inside to search for something. Not to be caught staring, Onóra tried to focus on the floor, but, feeling completely absorbed by what had filled her vision elsewhere, felt her eyes roll slowly up to steal a glimpse of the bare-headed Master and his tortured frame. A ghastly sound came and went through his opened mouth as, otherwise still, he seemed oblivious to his condition, his eyes closed as if he had already passed from the world. Seeing him like this, Onóra felt for the first time that O'Brien seemed just as human and vulnerable as she or any of the other inmates did.

Producing a vessel akin to a glass cup, the doctor applied it to the chest of the Master and, bringing his ear to the other end of the receptacle, listened, studying a watch at the pocket of his coat, alongside. At that moment the Master's breath seemed to catch and for a long time made no sound. But while Matron held her mouth in alarm, the doctor's expression showed no change. When, finally, the body exhaled and began its slow rasp once more, Dr Crooke straightened up and, regarding the watch-face, seemed to make up his mind.

'He is *in extremis* now. It will not be long. Can you hear me, Mr O'Brien?' he said aloud, bending close to the ear of the patient, when, to Onóra's horror, the Master's body jolted as if trying, but unable, to move. Somewhere inside there was life yet.

'Is there nothing to be done for him, Doctor?' asked Matron.

Her voice full of pity, Matron's eyes followed Dr Crooke, who, with a look of reluctance, shook his head but, seemingly for her benefit, began to feel the Master's head, hands, feet and shins, one at a time, with the back of his hand.

'Breathing is shallow … discharges have continued unabated … pulse is weakened … extremities livid and cold. Mr O'Brien's body has been reduced –'

Apparently noticing Matron's face, which, usually hard-hearted, showed more emotion now than Onóra had ever thought her capable of, the doctor cut short his appraisal, sighing heavily.

'Poor Mr O'Brien.' Matron bowed her head as Dr Crooke returned the cup to his bag. 'First the schoolmaster, and now …'

'You'll send for me if anything changes?'

'You're leaving, Doctor?'

'I am but one physician who requires sleep, Mrs Horgan.'

'Can you spare one of your nurses to stay with him?'

'The fever ward is beyond what can be managed already. And as Mr O'Brien refused to be treated there …'

'But Doctor, you said yourself, 'twill not be long.'

'It could be ten minutes or ten hours, Mrs Horgan. It's impossible to tell.'

All the while, between them on the bed, the Master's body continued its mortal sucking and blowing, either to beckon or to ward off death, Onóra imagined.

As the doctor left the room, she could sense well what was likely to happen next, confirming as much when Matron, likewise, prepared to leave.

'Knock on my door when the time comes. And don't go to sleep.'

'Yes, Miss.'

Twice across the hour that followed, believing the moment *had* come, Onóra woke Matron, only to find upon their return that the Master had resumed his struggle for life. The most offensive fluids continued to leak from his body throughout, as though, in advance of death, he had already begun to putrefy from the inside.

The third time Onóra felt cause for alarm, the Master's body jerked violently as, simultaneously, the flame of the candle behind his head faltered, threatening to go out for no obvious reason. Sucking in his longest breath yet, O'Brien seemed to swallow all of the room's air, choking on every ounce until, when he had wrestled for what seemed a short eternity, a long coarse sigh of death left his body sinking and deflating at every corner and, eventually, it lay completely still, devoid of life.

More fearful than she had expected to be in that moment, Onóra did not move for some time. Such a tyrant in life, the loathsome and cruel stain of the Master's character yet remained upon his body and, however beaten and empty the vessel seemed, Onóra could not help but imagine that, at any moment, he might yet rise up and, out from between the soiled sheets of his sickbed, lunge toward her, naked and skeletonised, having produced his dastardly whip from beneath.

But such a painful death as his was surely God's retribution for all the suffering he had enjoyed serving up across his lifetime, she conceived. Gazing upon his exhausted remnants, his jaw still thrust wide open, halfway through its last agonised bite, Onóra imagined it all was some sort of balancing of the scales. That this man had experienced just such a gruelling and torturous death as all those poor souls he had professed superiority over was a thought that brought unexpected comfort.

But Onóra's attention was suddenly drawn to something pasted upon the wall by the Master's head. It being the only such thing around the room, she instantly realised what it must be. How had she missed it? The sign so many inmates had whispered about; the one it was said O'Brien had pinned to the wall of his quarters, the ethos of the workhouse upon it.

Onóra could not read the letters in their black ink. But she knew what it said. Everyone knew what it said!

THE LOT OF THE ABLE-BODIED INMATE SHOULD BE LESS TOLERABLE THAN THAT OF THE LOWEST LABOURER.

THEY ARE TO BE WORSE FED, WORSE CLOTHED, AND WORSE LODGED THAN THE POOREST OUTSIDE.

What an evil thought. What a sickening idea to aspire to, she considered. And here; a real thing; in such a position that, upon waking, it was surely the first thing he had seen every day.

How vile! How cruel!

Images flew through Onóra's mind of the women she had seen sick and dying all around her: smothering under the fetid smell of their own filth and dirty clothes; cold and shivering; babbling the names of their children. Staring at the simple evil of the sign, in the presence of its instrument, Onóra felt the urge to spit upon it with all the anger and venom she could gather at the sickness of its meaning.

Bringing her face closer, she searched the hard, square lettering for any sense of humanity. The harmless piece of paper yielded yet nothing. But Onóra felt her mouth begin to fill. Tightening her lips, she drew a slow breath and imagined herself raining disgust upon it. But such a thing would be noticed, she realised. Instead, she turned to stare intimately at the horrible face of cruelty alongside her, even in death retaining its air of supposed nobility: eyes closed in ignorance; nose in the air; head held high in pious superiority. With an explosive, shivering convulsion of her entire being, Onóra unleashed every drop of the hatred bound up inside her, then watched the sputum that lashed and clung, rolling silently down his pathetic face.

For the hundreds of people at that very moment suffering in the wards around her, agonising in the dorms and the fever hospital; for the pitfuls of innocent, helpless children, old men and women already committed to the dark clay of the workhouse graveyard; for herself and what she had become; and for any of her family that might yet suffer the same fate.

It was not enough. Watching the slag that made its way slowly down his waxen skin, erasing and changing nothing, Onóra felt helpless and tasted the tears that – as though wept by all those poor souls – gathered and ran down her own face, washing and cleansing with purifying salt.

Remembering that Matron might come along and discover what she'd done, Onóra wondered if she ought to wipe it away. But in that moment she did not care. Instead she stared, and through the glass of her tears, even felt sorry and ashamed, pitying whatever was the caring element of the monster before her; for he must have cared for something …

———

When Onóra awoke she realised she'd been asleep for some time. For how long, she could not tell at first. It was still dark. The body had not moved. But the candle was now much smaller, she realised. Remembering the Matron's insistence that she not fall asleep, Onóra instinctively crossed the hallway and knocked lightly.

'He's gone?' the woman asked, tightening her belt in the open doorway.

'Will I fetch Dr Crooke, Miss?'

'Right away … Oh, God in heaven,' she gasped, peering into the Master's quarters as Onóra left hastily, 'bring the Chaplain, too!'

Returned with the doctor, Onóra watched as he tied a rag around the Master's head, attempting to bind the jaw closed, but to no avail despite the use of some force.

'Good heavens, how long since he passed? The body is cold, entirely.'

Onóra kept her head low as the chaplain began his preparations and Dr Crooke estimated death as having taken place at least two hours prior, looking to his timepiece once again.

'Mrs Horgan, please inform Mr Burdon at first convenience, the death of Mr O'Brien occurred in the small hours of the morning, Thursday, February fourth.'

'Yes, Doctor.'

'Send two able bodied paupers to confer his remains to the mortuary, in the morning. There is no point in moving him now.'

'Of course.'

'The jaw will have to remain distended, unless it is to be broken. *Rigor mortis* has long set in.'

Passing a look of disdain to Onóra, Matron barked, 'Be back here first thing, girl. And bring two more with you, to clean up this mess.'

'Yes, Miss.'

'They will need some lime of chloride from the infirmary,' Onóra heard Dr Crooke tell Matron as, bone-tired, she left to look for a place among the crowded boards of the women's dormitory.

15

Sickness in all Parts of the House

Refusing to acknowledge the taut ball at the pit of his stomach, Cornelius Creed entered the yard of the workhouse on Saturday morning, the sixth of February. It was the reawakened sense of civic duty that had motivated him to come, he told himself. That, and the seismical news of the Master's death. But, whatever courage he had earlier felt – bolstered in his decision to return by the kind words of Reverend Kyle that week – with each step that brought him closer to the building and the group of men at its heart Creed seemed to remember that courage less. Instead, old feelings of heaviness had returned, bringing him to anticipate questions and judgements he was certain to face at his lengthy absence.

Following the fog of breath that billowed from his mouth, traversing the largest crowd of paupers he'd encountered yet on the grounds, Creed's increasing sense of tension told him he was somewhere he ought not to be. Attending Tuesday's calamitous Relief Committee, he had somehow escaped the questions. But, barely recovered from the ordeal of their expectancy alone, now finding himself back in the same injurious place, Creed angrily questioned his own ability to make sound decisions. The renewed fear was nearly enough to send him back to the shadowy darknesses of the bedroom and of his mind. It was not the crowd outside that frightened him, but the crowd within. Still, despite the urge to turn tail for the comfort of the upstairs room and his effortless society with the dog, as if by practice, within moments Creed found he had negotiated the great human obstacle and was climbing the stairs to the boardroom.

The estranged sensation of being freshly shaven – at Paulellen's insistence – felt better to fit the room where a mostly unfamiliar complement of Guardians would soon double in number, Creed supposed. The first to catch his attention was a stranger, whose trade was rendered instantly apparent by the toolkit laid out before him and its similarity to the one rolled up under Creed's arm. This man was not a Guardian, but a reporter!

Hello, Creed thought to say, introducing himself. But an instinct to caution bade him remain anonymous and he walked to the end of one of the table's three great flanges to choose a seat. Conspicuous by their absence were the room's stalwart inhabitants, Creed noticed, but he felt relieved at having managed to remain uninterfered-with thus far.

The one Guardian he *was* looking forward to seeing was James Welply: the courageous friend and ally whose presence was sure to lighten the feelings of apprehension Creed was at that moment in the grip of.

'Mr Creed.'

'Mr Murphy, hello.' With some relief Creed turned to discover Cornelius Murphy, his ruddy-cheeked acquaintance, pulling out a chair.

'Very glad you've come back to us, Mr Creed. You have been missed – by some of us at least. Though I doubt you've missed us!'

'Well …' Creed registered the ambiguity of his own response, but felt powerless to change it.

'Much has occurred,' Murphy carried on in his flat country brogue, clearly intent on bringing him up to speed.

'So I understand,' Creed answered. 'Was it … foreseen?'

'O'Brien?' Murphy replied. 'I believe so.' Settling his chair, he looked around, then leaned in. 'As we speak, I'm told a number of the board are becoming acquainted with the condition of the House, first hand. And 'tis not strictly voluntary, mind, but on foot of a recommendation at Tuesday's Relief Committee.'

'By Father Lee?'

'Oh, you were *there* on Tuesday, is right,' Murphy said.

Distracted, Creed watched as, lapel in hand, an officious gentleman entered, so well presented that Creed could not decide which part of the man's grooming impressed him most: the centre-parted hair laid neatly over his skull; the stiff white collar brimming thick above his finely cut suit; or perhaps the moustache that unified the lot. With no one to greet him, the man surveyed the room's detail – as might an inspector, Creed imagined – before going eventually to the window.

'Anyway, the doctor and the clerk are along with them. They'll be on the way back now. One was violently sick: Ashe, according to the porter.'

'Oh!' Creed winced. 'Who else is with him?'

'So, Ashe, Philip Cross, Dan Lucy,' Murphy counted on his fingers.

'Warren?' Creed asked, hoping his nemesis was among those being schooled in the realities.

'Massy? Heavens no, man. I believe he as much as told them where they might *conceal* their tour of the House. Henry Howard was another, and –'

'Howard?' Creed remembered the name, but not as that of a Guardian.

'Oh, you'll have missed that, of course. There's been a changing of the guard, literally. The annual re-election took place in January. The result: Pat O'Riordan was voted out; John Pearson; Welply too.'

'James? No!' Creed complained.

'Afraid so. I don't think he was too unhappy himself, though, is the impression I got. Here they come – John O'Connell was the fifth!'

The party name-checked by Murphy filed in, bearing the collective expression of a gang clearly not the better for whatever they'd seen. If Ashe had been sick he hid it well, Creed observed. Dan Lucy, if anyone, looked greenest in the gills.

Assuming the presiding chair, Ashe shook the hand of the unfamiliar man and, by the gestures that went between them, appeared to invite him to the most active bar of the table. When the room was called to order, Creed was still reeling from the news of his friends' departures; a shock only exacerbated when with a silent gesture before the chairman spoke, Creed enquired of Murphy the identity of the young correspondent.

'*Southern Reporter*,' Con whispered. 'They were desperate in your absence. Maybe it's temporary.'

Whether from an accumulation of the whole morning's tensions and revelations, or the impact of this news alone exploding upon him, as though his mind had been rendered blank of all thought and emotion, at this Creed suddenly felt as withdrawn and as numb as those five Guardians looked who'd just fallen in.

'Gentlemen,' Ashe, standing, began. Sweeping the room, his gaze fell momentarily upon Creed and their eyes locked. But in the tacit exchange, Creed sensed Ashe's agreement that larger items were at stake than the relative triviality of one correspondent's absence, and the chairman broke off his gaze.

'I am sure you are all by now aware of the distressing news of Mr O'Brien's death. Within and without we are in treacherous straits. By what means we are to traverse the crisis remains elusive, but we must do what is necessary to not wholly succumb to that which threatens to overwhelm us.'

With a breath, the speaker's tone switched from one of gravity to practicality and Creed sensed the introduction's conclusion. 'In the short term, for the purpose of devising some means for the adequate government of the House – being currently in a dreadful state for the want of proper officers – Assistant Commissioner Burke has joined us here today.'

With an open hand, Ashe recognised the visiting gentleman, and sat.

'Mr Chairman, gentlemen.' With a bow to each, the Assistant Commissioner arose earnestly and acknowledged both Ashe and the board with an air of solemnity. 'Today you must determine whether or not to close the House. *That*, it would seem, is the ultimate predicament you face. But I strongly suggest you first address the appointment of temporary officers, until permanent replacements are fixed, being that you need to get the House under control either way.'

To Creed, who felt somewhat recovered, it appeared the hand of logic was at work, and around the room he sensed a general reassurance at Burke's words.

'Now, I understand you are advertising both for a master and a schoolmaster. Correct? Has this been undertaken? No. When will it be issued?'

'Monday, sir,' Burdon answered.

'Good, and you have agreement on the details?'

'The board resolves to advertise for a master at a salary of thirty pounds a year; a schoolmaster at fifteen per annum, Mr Burke.'

'Fifteen pounds?' Burke sounded surprised.

'I've suggested we get a schoolmaster who can teach something to the boys other than reading and writing,' Ashe proposed.

'Surely one of standard capabilities will suffice, given the present difficulties, Mr Ashe?'

Edward Ashe appeared taken aback and quietly submitted to the officer's logic.

'There has been no response to that advertisement on account of the inadequate salary,' Lee argued. 'You cannot get such a person as the chairman recommends for fifteen pounds a year.'

'Yes, let's return to that,' Burke said, checking his watch as though on a schedule. 'Literature suggests in the region of fifty pounds for a master; the same for a schoolmaster. Your offer is *far* below. I suggest you reconsider both salaries, lest you be left waiting.'

'The salaries proposed are in keeping with our financial status, Mr Burke. The House is on the brink of bankruptcy.' Creed recognised the dull voice of Philip Cross, who, awaiting an answer, remained upright.

'If you do not get someone to run the House adequately – and soon,' Burke replied, 'bankruptcy will be the least of your worries, sir. You should offer forty pounds at *least* for a master,' he told the chairman and the clerk. 'I should think twenty at minimum for a schoolmaster, which is not as pressing.'

'All Guardians in favour?' The chairman lifted his hammer.

'Hear, hear,' came the ubiquitous reply, and Ashe struck the block.

'If only this man were a permanent fixture,' Con Murphy whispered, as Creed himself reflected that Burke's presence was certainly having a rapid effect.

'For shame, it takes the death of a *staff member* for them to send someone out,' he bemoaned, picturing myriad bureaucrats at Dublin Castle.

'Now, what in the meantime?' Burke pressed the chair.

'In the meantime …' Seeming desperate to spare them embarrassment, Ashe looked to the room.

'There is a Mr Brennan,' Fr Lee offered, his tone reeking of opportunism, 'a capable young man.'

'How young?' Burke squinted.

'I believe seventeen.'

'Seventeen. Are there any alternatives?' Surveying the T-shaped table to no avail, bridging the chasm of silence that resounded, Burke spoke again: 'The death of the Master, who I'm sure was a *very proper man*, has placed your board in a position where energetic steps are necessary, gentlemen. I recommend Mr Brennan take charge of the House until you find a suitable appointment and that afterward he be continued as an assistant, so long as the House requires.'

Creed was astounded. A boy, to run a crippled institution that cradled within its hands the fates of more than one thousand human souls! Yet, other than the young reporter's pencil scribbling furiously at the far end, not a sound issued along the triune surface of the bench.

'With regard to the schoolmistress in fever, I am told there is a sister of the Matron, a very proper person. You should appoint her in place, *pro tem*, at a salary of five shillings per week?'

'All agreed?' Ashe proposed, having surrendered wholly to Burke's direction, it would seem. From around the table came another, almost mandatory, 'Hear, hear.'

'What *is* the state of the House, currently?' Still standing and seeming far more to be so now, the Assistant Commissioner pressed on relentlessly.

James Burdon arose sheepishly to answer and, though already small, bent low to refer his notes. 'There are in the region of eleven hundred persons in the House. The exact number is difficult to ascertain in consequence of the Master's death.' Clearly eager to finish, Burdon rubbed nervously at his neck and looked relieved to return the floor.

'Very well. I believe some of you undertook a tour this morning. Might anyone offer an appraisal?'

At length, in the absence of a Guardian volunteering, the doctor stood, and Creed braced himself for what he expected would be a no-nonsense evaluation.

'Dysentery is on the rise among the inmates. Besides the want of proper government, this I attribute in great degree to the number of able-bodied paupers, who, instead of being given work, are lying down in all parts of the house, or crowded around the fire in total idleness –'

'I have made application for eight or nine to scrape the streets of the town.' In a manner Creed perceived as deliberately rude, Fr Lee cut across the doctor in the middle of his dissertation. 'I can take four or five more to draw water for the soup depot,' he proposed. 'The Soup Relief Fund would be willing to pay for them.'

'Any man employed and paid for his labour would have to quit the house,' Burke stated firmly, putting paid to Lee's suggestion.

But what a contradiction in terms. This was the kind of ministration Creed was more accustomed to from an officer of the Commission.

'Doctor, will you continue your description of the House?'

'Certainly, Mr Burke,' Crooke replied, as Lee raised an eyebrow, seeming to imply favouritism, but offered no verbal argument.

'It has been asked of me in the past,' Crooke began anew, 'not to spare the board the reality of matters concerning the state of health presiding within. If the board will bear in mind the books of the house being imperfect, I beg to report on what has prevailed this past week.'

'Please,' Burke encouraged.

Steadying himself with one hand upon the table, his cane idle against the chair, Crooke held his record book high enough to sight over his bifocals. 'There are on this morning one hundred and fifty-two patients in the infirmary and idiot wards: the majority of those being small children suffering from bowel complaints. All others are either up and well, or convalescent.'

At the doctor's statement, Creed was suddenly alive to the gulf of difference between the numbers he'd heard when he'd last attended in November and the exploded picture of sickness the House had since become.

'Also as of this morning are one hundred and two cases in the fever hospital, including several infants admitted with their mothers. There were thirty-one deaths during the week, sixteen of which were children or infants who only breathed a few hours. Five were aged people. Children generally throughout the house are doing very badly. This I attribute principally to the bad quality of the milk. As I have frequently informed the board, the hardihood of the contractor has been increasing latterly. So far as I can tell, he now usually mixes one-third, sometimes one-half water.'

'Who is the milk contractor and why are such things allowed to go unchecked?'

'There is no one contractor, Mr Burke,' Burdon offered. 'We get Lucey's milk at five pence seven-eighths a gallon and Fuller's at sixpence. Lucey's was the milk complained of.'

'Well, and how is he paid?'

'He is not paid at all, Mr Burke,' Ashe underlined. 'It has been resolved to advertise for contracts.'

'Indeed. Is that the conclusion of your report, Doctor? Burke asked.

'I regret to state the Master died of fever on Thursday last. For some time past he'd been overwhelmed with work and was of bad constitution. My name, signed, Warren Crooke, M.D.'

As the doctor lowered his report, Mr Burke took the floor faster than Fr Lee, who seemed also ready to speak.

'It was not fever the Master died of, but debility. I suggest it be recorded as such.' Burke said deliberately, as though he wished to change the minds of all who'd heard the doctor.

'Hear, hear,' called two stinted voices, as though confused, in response.

By degrees, the young reporter ceased writing, then lifted his head out of his notes. Realising Mr Burke was now speaking directly to him, he looked nervously to the chairman, perhaps for support. Yet seeming to want no part of it, Creed deduced, Ashe stared straight ahead, fingertips caged before his face.

Apparently feeling no impediment to speaking *his* mind, however, Lee shot to his feet once more. 'I can hardly believe my ears,' he told the room. 'The Master was a strong, able-bodied man. A military man! In place of the dead schoolmaster he was teaching in the school on Saturday last. I know not your aim, Mr Burke. But whatever your ink says, in every instance, from the pulpit, and in the sight of heaven, I will relate it was *fever* he died of.'

And nor could Creed believe *his* ears. What was Burke's aim? *To somehow preserve the Master's dignity?* he wondered, looking to Con Murphy, who seemed equally perplexed. *Perhaps the Commissioners would have fever remain a* poor *man's disease!*

'And Doctor Crooke!' Lee continued, perhaps resuming the offence he'd been mounting. 'You seem almost content with the number of deaths?'

Surprised, Crooke leaned forward in his chair as though to account for not standing. 'In the Bantry workhouse, out of only seven hundred and fifty, forty died last week.'

'Poor comfort,' Lee replied.

Somehow unusually at odds with the doctor, Fr Lee's attacks seemed to speak to a recent disagreement Creed was blind to. 'If *I* may offer more than but a rudimentary summation …' Lee proposed, to which Burke raised his chin, willing, Creed surmised, to ignore the condescension on the promise of some curious truth.

With a telling slap Lee threw open his own tattered notebook. As it landed upon the table, he dug his knuckles into the green baize on either side, and, as though to draw from the object all the power he could muster, lowered his head to fill his lungs with a pregnant wind.

'On Tuesday last, I suggested the Guardians visit the House to see for themselves what terrors are unfolding there; that they might turn what horror they'd learn to effectual action. I found myself heartened this morning to discover such a journey was underway.

'And yet ... it appears there is a desire on the part of *some* to keep back the real state in which the house is placed.'

Here, as though winding up a spring, Lee rolled his head on its axis.

'As none of its latest visitors seem able, I feel it my duty to share some observations relative to the conditions within. As a priest of long standing, and one accustomed to visiting houses of the sick, in cholera and in fever, I must declare, I would go back tomorrow to the awful scenes I witnessed in years past, sooner than continue the duties this house requires of me, presently. I myself went over a great part of the establishment yesterday. I say a great part, for I found it almost impossible to go through the whole.

'In the girls' school room I saw eighty or a hundred sickly-looking little creatures, all huddled together, shivering with cold; while I myself found the atmosphere too warm and close to be comfortable for more than a minute! I had to go out for air, lest I be sick from the ... ahem!'

As the priest seemed close to re-enacting his feelings, Creed felt himself equally upset. But, through flared nostrils, Lee recomposed himself to continue his description. 'Every countenance betrays the symptoms of acute suffering. For the most part all are wretchedly clad, the majority clearly in the clothes they wore prior to admission. I'm not surprised disease should be the consequence of such a continued state of uncleanliness. It is a pitiful spectacle to behold so many young creatures in such wretchedness and misery.'

Turning a page, Fr Lee crimped the book to ensure it stayed flat.

'*That* was the school room. I proceeded from there to the nurses' apartment where in a still more disturbing scene I found a number of women around a fire, with infants in their arms literally *gasping* for a breath of fresh air. How their lungs could bear such a fetid atmosphere is, to me, a matter of much astonishment, though Doctor Crooke's report has shown that some, in fact, could *not!* But that the result of continuing to breathe such noxious vapours must be calamitous, no one who saw them could doubt for an instant.

'The women's day room and the infirmary present the same appearance as the girls' room: the same condition of the inmates; same sickly-looking, suffering countenances.'

When no challenge came to speak, Lee seemed only too willing to go on with increased authority. 'The probationary wards were in a worse condition than the rest. Cooped up in these small rooms and the hall are upwards of *one hundred* persons provisionally admitted during the week, but who *await* still a space within. *Their* clothing too comprises only the rags which have been their shelter from the winter's cold before they were obliged to seek refuge here; starvation is plainly stamped upon their faces, gentlemen, in marks too deep to be mistaken.'

From his position opposite the priest, Creed could easily see that Lee was working off simple one-word cues in his notebook, each written heavily in pencil and underlined. 'Probationary' and 'Gleeson' were all that filled the current page. The rest, it would seem, was fresh enough in his memory.

'To repeat the expressive phrase of Mr John O'Connell,' Lee gestured to the Guardian at his flank, '"They did not walk, they crept," to where their fate was to be decided – here – in this room.

'As I left temporarily, I perceived two men dragging a third – in the last stages of destitution – up those stairs. Enquiring of him but a half hour later I was shown into the male probationary ward where the unfortunate man lay dead, on a board! ... I learned from the porter the man's name was Gleeson, from Aghabullogue. He had been in the probationary ward for *three days*.'

Out of grief, and respect, Creed felt, Lee seemed determined to speak the man's name aloud, a sentiment he sympathised with.

'As lamentable as the facts are – and words can but convey a very inadequate idea – I am sure my statement will be borne out by any of those Guardians who visited the House, this day.'

Burke rose to interrupt. 'Thank you for your candid detail, Father Lee. If that concludes your sharing of the conditions within, we should move to potential solutions.'

So fast that the legs of his chair clacked violently upon the floor, Fr Lee sat, expressing either great relief at being stood down, or the most abrupt note of his song. But, as though remembering something cardinal, he stood hastily again before any speaker might replace him. 'The paupers should go through a process of cleansing upon entering the House. This has not lately been done. Then there is a great want of clothing. Unless something can be done, and that speedily, the consequences will be unimaginable. I was obliged to go about the town this week looking for straw, in order that the poor creatures might throw themselves upon it. I believe a great number of the recent deaths are to be attributed to cold.'

More gracefully than the first time, Fr Lee took his seat once more.

'Thank you. I too trust this state of affairs will be remedied as quickly as possible,' Burke said, turning to address the room. 'It is inhumanity to admit anyone else currently. How many are already in the probationary wards, waiting days to be processed?'

'There are one hundred and twelve on the provisional admission book. We are so overrun, on some days numbers of the inmates cannot be fed until two o'clock at night,' the clerk answered, with a remark so in contradiction with his position that the chairman regarded his neighbour with an objectionable expression.

'Does anyone wish to add anything else?'

At Burke's invitation, Creed had the impression of a surge of opinions bursting through a loosened gate, the source of each apparently sensing a last chance to be heard for some time, perhaps; or at least by anyone with the power to effect any change.

'They have been going lately in their hundreds,' Mr Leahy said. 'A girl who left the House last week dropped down dead on the road.'

'Paupers are complaining patients sick with fever are being sent to sleep with them,' said O'Connell.

Arising beside Creed, Con Murphy spoke for the first time: 'There are surely numerous other buildings available for negotiation?'

'I hope this is not said sincerely, sir?' Burke scolded. 'There was mention made of the House's liquidity?' He moved on, and wanted to close the floor as quickly as he had opened it, Creed perceived.

'The letter, Mr Burdon.' Though spoken directly to the clerk, Ashe's prompt was necessarily loud enough to hear.

'Yes, sir.' Burdon rifled his papers. 'I have here from the Provincial Bank of Cork a letter by which is stated: *it is our duty to inform the Guardians ... Unless money can be procured by the board they will have to close within a fortnight.*'

A tumult of noise followed the revelation.

'Will you close the doors today, Mr Burke?' Fr Lee demanded.

'That will be for the Guardians to say.'

Again, Burke had reverted to what Creed imagined his habitual bureaucratic default. But more surprising was Fr Lee's request. Though Creed perceived the priest had indicated a wish to see the House closed, surely he did not; for it would spell catastrophe to all within, as well as those within the town.

'I vote another physician is wanted. I would like to give notice of motion for the appointment of one,' Dr Crooke added.

'We are not discussing this matter at present,' came Burke's abrupt answer. 'Can the house accept more paupers or not?'

'What accommodation could this room offer?' Lee suggested, offering what seemed a preposterous scenario, as though to force a result.

Across another hour, as various statements flew in heated debate, Creed listened but found himself increasingly overwhelmed by waves of anxiety breaking over him; nervous at what he might say if someone referred to him directly; at what the future held for those suffering in this terrible place; for his and Paulellen's own health in proximity to it.

Offering nothing himself, and no longer required in the capacity of one recording, Creed questioned why he had come back at all and what he was still doing there. The only reason to remain was the fear of becoming conspicuous if he left.

'I wish to propose the following resolution.' Lucy forced his way amongst the voices, bringing the room to a relative calm. 'We will on this day fortnight move that the resolution of December last, relative to a second physician not being necessary to the House, be rescinded; that in consequence of the great sickness and its fatal consequences to the Master and the schoolmaster – and also the report by the Matron that sickness prevails in all parts of the house – a second physician be appointed.'

'I'll second.' Con Murphy stood again, making sense now of the whisperings and notes he'd been exchanging with Daniel Lucy.

Their motion then put to the board, with a *trunch* of Ashe's hammer, was passed by clear majority.

And here again was Father Lee: 'If the board passes a resolution to close the House, as chaplain, I will be placed in a very disagreeable position. At the same time, looking to the state of the House, I do not see anything else they can do.' Once more, Lee seemed to be talking in riddles, when suddenly his true aim was revealed: 'Mr Burke might state if the Guardians may give relief to the poor outside?'

'It would be against the law!'

'If the house is closed there will be a great many deaths!'

In hindsight, Creed could see now that all along, Lee had not wished to see the House closed at all. Rather his stratagem had been to ensure the House remained open, but – by suggesting that neither closing nor remaining open was sufficient alone – sought to propose the solution of administering outdoor relief, as the board had *illegally* done the previous October. While Lee's attempt had been admirable and clever, as an officer for the Castle, Burke was, unsurprisingly, completely against it.

'Gentlemen, we must move to admissions. There are many waiting,' Ashe said, and retook the reins for the first time since they'd begun. 'I personally was here until nine o'clock last Saturday, admitting applicants.'

Squeezing his eyes shut, Creed gripped the chair to hold back an involuntary exclamation of anguish, but failed as, suddenly, he felt himself overcome.

Blackness and turbulence; freezing ether; petals of a strange blossom; gases gushing, enveloping. Tractionless, suspended, perfectly fitted liquid realm: Leviathan – calmly, swallowing struggleless prey: insect, drank. Timeless void. Fight to surface. Ambushed, shocked, weightless, confused. Eyes bulge; convulsing. Lungs. Kicking. Running. Grasping gripping nowhere nothing. Breach. Panicked air sound rushing. Water glimpse. Night. Cold. *Stay up. Breathe! Grab! Nothing.* Buoyant. Too heavy 'Fathe–' Spit! 'Hel–' under black … *Don't swallow! Is this?* Convulse. *Up!* Breach. 'Hel–' Swallow … Paull … *choke, sound … voices …*

'… eed … Mr Creed!'

At the touch of a gentle hand, Creed, blinking, turned, finding at his sleeve a concerned Con Murphy. 'Are you unwell?'

'Uh … some air, perhaps.'

16

A Drift of Snow

Bent at the knees, clutching her shawl at the throat, Cáit leant forward to gather another lump of wood. The children groaned less for their hunger when they slept, she was learning, but they were sleeping too much.

For now she had work to do. Yet, reaching for the next fallen branch, a realisation came: she could hear the wind, but not feel it.

Through the hood of her shawl, she listened. Around her it was blowing; circling and whistling, hemming the ring of the hill; catching the dead briars that guarded the ridge and pushing flat the dead, bulky grass. But it did not touch her.

Flung from her hand, meeting the pile, the hollow limb voiced its empty *clunk*, when at the corner of her sight Cáit perceived something tiny, gently falling to earth.

Dreamlike, as though something merciful from heaven, a drift of snow was descending from over the mist-shrouded peak of Mullach an Oís. White and imperceptibly slow, it too seemed unaffected by the wind.

Caught in its beauty, Cáit revelled at the sensation of her body suddenly relaxing. With the expectation of something akin to the kiss of sunlight's warmth she closed her eyes to welcome the arrival of the tiny white spears. But a sting of cold recaptured her awareness instead, as, permeating her shawl, the first flakes made their icy contact with the skin of her back. Cáit drew a lungful of the frigid air and felt her body arch.

At the sudden realisation of what the arrival of the cold would mean to so many, the spell was broken. 'Onóra! No!' Cáit shrieked, and raced to fill her arms with as much as she could before she, or the woodpile, was covered over.

'Can anyone hear that bell?'

'What bell?'

'I hear a bell somewhere.'

To the sound of women arguing, Onóra awoke sweating, her bones uncomfortably met by a hard surface below, hands in place of a pillow, the feeling of straw stuck to her face. Unsure of where she was at first, her eyes followed the light high up the whitewashed walls, to the sills. Outside, she could see, it was snowing.

She had only been dreaming, Onóra realised; no longer a little girl, this was not her bed in Carrigadrohid, and the women she was squeezed between were not her sisters. It was Monday morning and this was the overcrowded female ward of the Union Workhouse where, on one side of the gangway, between two souls unfamiliar to her, she was lying upon the raised boards of the sleeping platforms.

Inches from her face was an ashen-haired woman, whose features, in sleep, drooped like melting wax towards the floor and, were it not for the open-mouthed snores coming and going like the wheezing of a bellows, Onóra reasoned she might have easily convinced herself the woman was dead. Blind to the identity of the other woman whose shoulder, or elbow, was pressed into her back, still with one foot in her dreams, Onóra longed to discover it was one of her sisters, Íomhaín, Síle, or Cáit.

Feeling invisible, encouraged by the sounds of others purling sorrowfully around her, Onóra reached out to Cáit, her little sister, who, though younger, she had always looked up to.

'I'm frightened, Cáití,' she whispered through her tears as a surge of heat coming over her brought Onóra to realise a night's sleep had not changed the condition she'd felt coming on the day before, despite her many prayers.

Opening her eyes, Onóra looked to the falling snow. It was peaceful, if only to her sight. But an image of Cáit and the children filled her mind: huddling under a snow-capped roof in the hills, for it was surely snowing up there too. Hoping they were warm and getting food somehow, Onóra tried not to contemplate her own condition.

Allowing her gaze to lower, she found her neighbour's mouth had closed. So wearied with age, the woman resembled an ancient tree, and Onóra imagined she was of the people from among the thicketed river forest, near Annahalla. *Bean Ghaoire*, Onóra thought, in place of a name: the woman of the wooden river. Perhaps she was Meascán Maraíocht, one of the ancient spirits who protected the forest, sent to watch over her, she fantasised.

But it was not only Bean Ghaoire, Onóra decided; every woman there looked to have been ravaged and dragged through a tangled mire of *sceach*; out of a graveyard even, some of them – herself included. Onóra imagined there was barely a trace of femininity or care left among them.

Besides Onóra and the few long-term inmates that wore the awful uniforms – the union stamp of vermillion-red lettering sewn across the back – she knew that beneath the blankets, every woman lived and slept in clothes that were falling asunder with the dirt and wear of year across year living in paupery; bodies and faces ingrained and encrusted with layer over layer of grease, ash and smoke, caked into every crevice of their smothered, withering skins.

The collective smell of the unwashed, neglected lot hovered thick from the floor to the rafters. It was an unholy, God-forsaken smell, Onóra thought; for the most part so all-pervasive it became necessarily forgotten by the senses until, disturbed by the tiniest movement, as Onóra was being forced to remember, it spiked with the foul effluvia of urine and excrement, vomit, fermented sweat, dried menses and, perhaps most offensive of all to her awakened senses, coughed-up phlegm and bad teeth.

Her eyes shut, Bean Ghaoire coughed again, directly into Onóra's face, so that she squeezed her own eyes shut too, to avoid the spatter. She tried in vain to tuck in her chin, but, prevented by the lack of room, used her sleeve to wipe her face instead, before propping her head up at the ear again, using her hands for a pillow.

'Can nobody else hear that bell?' the woman near the door called again, her voice slovenly, as though she was drunk.

'What are you on about?' her neighbour lamented. 'There is no bell. You're mad.'

'I hear it again. 'Twas in a different place afore. 'Tis closer.'

This was their second day left alone like this. Yesterday had been the first time they were ever even left to sleep late on the ward, and, lying here, Onóra had listened as, around her, the voices speculated that the House must be closed.

'The Wardmistress is dead,' someone announced to great reaction. 'Well, she must be. 'Tis a week since ever she was taken sick, and no sign since.'

'Why do you think the fires have not been lit?' another asked.

'The Master is dead, you know?' Onóra heard, and recalled how, almost a week before, she'd been warned by the Matron to *not breathe a word to anyone!*

Already aware far in advance of the rest of the women, Onóra had not felt so disturbed by the news: resigned, perhaps.

Suddenly, she supposed the Matron might be dead now too: a thought that arrived with mixed emotions, for along with a sense of poetic justice, Onóra realised that if the Matron was dead, she herself would likely be next, given that they were both present at the Master's dying.

'Why has nobody come for us?' a frightened voice asked, high and surprised.

'Maybe they are afeared of fever,' came an answer.

'O'Brien is *dead?*' the frightened woman asked again, seemingly lost in disbelief.

'Sure, the bell in the yard hasn't rung for two days,' she was reminded.

Before then, it had been unusual even to hear an inmate shout, Onóra pondered, let alone voices conversing. But that was yesterday. Now …

'She's twelve years old. Martin is seven.'

Through her back, Onóra registered a deep sigh from the body of her neighbour, as, on the yard side, a mother had begun to babble aloud about her children: 'He looks like his daddy, does Martin. My children will grow up proud and strong when they leave this place … except little Margaret is not well … she doesn't be talking any more.' The woman's voice shrank with pity. 'But the Liberator is coming for us. He'll take us out of here and give my Martin a job on his estate.'

Somewhere down the other end, Onóra heard a woman sobbing to herself. 'You'll come for me, won't you?' she blubbered, appealing to someone only she could see, in a kind of Irish Onóra was unused to.

Tired and weakened, Onóra was falling into sleep again when the sound of a bell in the corridors sharpened her senses and stirred the other women.

'Someone is coming. Oh, God, help us,' a voice prayed.

'I told you I could hear it,' the bell woman claimed.

Onóra sensed apprehension amongst the women, but relief too as the sound echoed, growing louder through the dank stone of the building.

'Up with ye, layabouts,' came the voice of the Matron, as the door was unlocked and opened. 'You can all thank God I've not abandoned you.'

Out of habit or fear, there followed a huge commotion as, like the soldiers of a strange, sick barracks, the women clambered up off the platforms, stirring up the terrible smells, groaning and wincing as their dilapidated bodies refused to co-operate.

'Oh, thank God for you, Miss Horgan,' the unbeliever's voice grovelled among them. But, too sick to move, Onóra lay back, nauseous and light-headed from attempting to sit up.

'Out to the dining hall if you want some food,' the Matron barked loudly as, under Onóra's head, the boards quaked with deafening vibrations from the weary stampede.

'Any woman not upright and walking will be taken to the fever hospital.'

As the room emptied, it became apparent to Onóra that at least two other bodies still prostrate on the platforms were not moving, while, behind her, the sound of heavy boots grew louder along the walkway.

'You: fetch the doctor,' Matron ordered – talking to someone who'd not managed to squeeze out the door yet, Onóra supposed. 'And you: tell the porter bring four able-bodied men to carry out these unfortunate wretches.'

'Yes, miss.'

'If any of you don't want to lie in the pit, you'll get moving now.'

Behind her head, the footsteps ceased, when to the creak of bending leather Onóra felt herself rocked at the hip and cried out in pain.

'Onóra!' the Matron shouted, surprise colouring the pitch of her voice. 'Up with ye, girl!'

'I am unwell, miss.'

By the time the overseers accepted that the snow was going to stick, it was late afternoon and almost home time anyway. Setting off, Pádraig knew he was in trouble. Within a half-mile, the numbness overtaking his already damaged feet told him the race against the weather was one he could not hope to win.

Before long it seemed the entire landscape was being hidden under a white blanket and Pádraig had the feeling it would only be worse ahead. It was coming from the hills, always from the hills, he thought, as Cáit and the children came to his mind. But with head down, facing into a wind that was quickly becoming a driving gale, Pádraig's immediate concern was to get himself in out of the storm. With the weather alone it was getting harder to see by the minute, but to compound matters, darkness would not be long behind.

Suddenly, as though his mind was playing tricks on him, Pádraig noticed every sign of humanity had vanished. Was it he alone caught out in the squall? In the absence of the living, his old friends had returned; those ghosts upon the wind, howling in his face, this time hailing their razor-sharp breaths upon him, stinging and lashing every part of skin that he couldn't hide. With chin down, hands buried in the pits of his arms, Pádraig braced himself and leaned his body into the fray. Finding nowhere to stop, increasingly alarmed at the stone-like sensation in his feet, he pushed on, opening his eyes for a squint after every few steps, scanning for any sign of cover. But every feature he perceived to be promising turned out to be a rock or the stump of a tree. Hoping to discern some strained voice beckoning from a friendly house, Pádraig listened hard through the howling winds. But none came. No Diarmuid Ua Laoghaire to pull him to his feet, and no one of his like to offer him refuge.

'Please, God, don't leave me out here to die!' Pádraig pleaded aloud, but heard his words lost to the void, sucked from his mouth and scattered in splinters, like a rock beneath a blow of his clinking hammer.

The aching in his feet appeared to be climbing up his legs and Pádraig moaned at the pain. Grunting with each step, feeling increasingly hopeless, he had the sense of being taken over from the ground up and from the face down. Matching the increasing intensity of the wind, his moaning grew until the two began to blend and tune, and Pádraig could no longer separate his own voice from the others, howling and dirging in awful harmony: the screeching one; the sucking one; the *amadán*, tortured and dumb below; and another – a new one – somewhere before him. Up ahead, it came out of the ground, closing in as he stumbled toward it. But when his foot touched the ground by what seemed its very source, it struck him across the shin and howled even louder.

Opening his eyes in fright, Pádraig discovered a shape in the snow. He had tripped upon a body, almost covered over by the drift; a man, he decided – the moan had come from a living being. Standing above the man, Pádraig was stunned. Where had he come from? Who did he belong to? Blinded at every turn, he walked in a circle, searching for somewhere to take him. No cowhouse; no cabins; no farm.

With the weather only worsening, Pádraig realised he had to find shelter, with or without the stranger.

It must have been a hundred steps back, beside the fallen limb, he remembered. There had stood a broad tree with what looked a small hole at its base. He'd been hoping for something better, but told himself it was at least a possibility. Turning hurriedly, Pádraig marched back the way he had come, relieved to have the wind behind him for a change. To his amazement, he found the fallen trunk after fifteen or sixteen steps. But the broad tree with the hole underneath was nowhere to be seen. Instead, in its place was a half-fallen giant: snow-laden and leaning against two sister trees, its entire rooted foot, plucked from the ground, had exposed a dark hole in the earth below.

With no time to waste, almost colliding with a rock in the snow, Pádraig jumped across the ditch and threw himself in, determined to see if it could take a man his size, then another alongside him.

With the light rapidly fading, Pádraig could sense better with his hands than he could see. Though ready to claw at the muck and roots, it became instantly apparent that not only was the space big enough, it had recently been used by some other unfortunate, either temporarily absent, or given up their scelp. Though Pádraig could hardly believe his luck, the hole was lined with grass and leaves, and even smelled of a fire. The next question that came to his mind, as, with gritted teeth, he slapped at his feet to banish the sting, was how he would get the stranger across the ditch that separated the road from the scelp – if he was even still alive by now. Either way, with the sudden fear that he might struggle to even locate the hole again himself, there was no time to lose.

Facing the onslaught of the frozen spray once more, this time Pádraig felt his way down, then back up the outside of the ditch: about a yard and a half wide and a yard in depth, he assessed. Climbing in would be a safer option, and the only way with his companion.

From the moment his foot met the road, so that he would not miss it coming back, Pádraig began to count the steps to where the man lay. *Seven, eight, nine.* He must be coming close. But no moaning this time? *Thirteen … fourteen … fifteen.* Unable to see, he slowed and listened. Nothing. *One more. Sixteen.* On hands and knees, fearing he had strayed and lost the track, Pádraig swept the ground around him, blindly patting the snow. Was he gone? Could he have just got up and walked away, vanished? Was it all a dream? The pain inside his frozen ears told him it was not. The wet leaking through his trouser shins said no. Then a moan to his right. Pádraig reached out as far as his arm would stretch, but, finding no prize, followed the sound on his knees.

'There you are,' he whispered. Landing a hand upon the mound of snowed-over cloth and bones, Pádraig felt himself overcome with emotion at the relief of finding he was not alone.

Locating the man's arm, he pulled him, half frozen, up to sitting, so that he could get his own shoulder under; then, counting in his mind, bounced upon his heels to ready himself and, with everything he had, reaching three, lifted and tried to get his load to stand. It was pointless. There was not the strength of a single step in the man and with his back to the stranger, Pádraig now pulled the arms across his shoulders and began to drag the man back the way he'd come, his legs dangling through the snow behind.

Four paces later, blind to what lay ahead, Pádraig estimated he should take two steps to the right, having wandered off track finding the man; one now, the other when he'd counted sixteen, he decided – lest he stray too close to the ditch and upend them both in the process.

Ten … eleven, along the corrected path. *Twelve … thirteen …* Were his steps the same length with the man on his back? He'd have to take his chances. *Fifteen …* and the extra step to the right. Carefully, he found the edge of the ditch and let his man down.

Still holding the arms, Pádraig began to slide himself down the ditch until, his foot reaching the bottom, he pulled, leaning forward. But when the man's legs slid over the edge, with double the load now coming at speed towards him, Pádraig felt himself slammed against the inner bank, the stranger's weight on top of him, so that each let out an involuntary moan on impact.

'I don't know how you'll do it, but you're going to help me get up this ditch now,' Pádraig shouted, with one side of his face against the snow and not entirely sure if he was talking to himself or the man oblivious at his back. Yet as though his prayers were answered again, spreading his arms as he readied to lift, he found a break in the ditch on his left side; it was barely a notch, cut in by the flow of a stream, perhaps, but enough to gain a foothold and prise them up and over the gully to where, with some relief, he felt the fallen limb beneath his hand once more. Heaving, Pádraig dragged the man along it until, gripping one of the tree's skyward-pointing roots, he turned and lowered his cargo, collapsing into the hole behind him, then following face-first with little more in reserve than the man he'd been carrying. All that was left was to manoeuvre the fellow deeper in and fit himself alongside, after which Pádraig felt he had accomplished survival, at least, and could allow himself to settle for now.

There was just enough room for them both, Pádraig decided; one of them was probably sitting on the remains of the fire, hidden under the grass bedding somewhere.

'What is your name, I wonder?' Pádraig asked, realising by his voice that he was shivering badly. 'Do you hear me?' he repeated, and shook the man's arm, but to no avail. Nothing but the coarse rasping of the man's breath came back, just loud enough to be heard over the howling and whistling that, to Pádraig, sounded incensed and intensified in its anger outside: at having lost its grip on them both, perhaps.

'If you were listening, I'd tell you my name is Pádraig Ua Buachalla, of Doire Liath,' Pádraig said, blowing into his hands. 'You'd tell me yours, and where it is you're from.' Wondering at the sense in talking to a man who couldn't hear him, Pádraig found himself pulling his neighbour closer, as if, in spite of himself, his body knew best how to find heat.

'I don't know if I'm sent here to warm you – or if you were sent to warm me. But we're both better off, no matter which, and I'm glad of it. We'll stay here until morning, sure. Maybe you'll tell me then.'

But quietly, his eyes awake in darkness, Pádraig did not much fancy his friend's chances of seeing the dawn's light.

How long had he been there in the snow? It couldn't have been long, Pádraig imagined, since the snow had only come in hard that evening. But how long would it take, lying in the snow, before you'd freeze to death? A half-hour? An hour at most, surely.

Had he been coming from the works too? On a different line? Why would any man be walking the roads in this weather, otherwise? But, with his mind fuzzy and tired, Pádraig supposed it was perhaps just his own circumstances that brought him to draw such a conclusion. The man could be anybody, caught out in the weather for a thousand different reasons.

'Who'll be worrying about you, I wonder? Have you a Cáit, a Síle, and a Diarmuidín? It won't be long now until Cáit is wondering where I've got to. It'll be a long night for mine at home.' Drawing a slow breath of the cold, biting air, Pádraig blew out his worry and gave it away to the wind. 'We're in a bad way, my friend.'

Shivering against the stranger beside him, Pádraig rubbed his hands together and fitfully dug his toes into the matted grass, to cure the bitter numbness that still had a grip on them.

Come the morning, he'd have to brave the elements with something around his feet, he decided. With his feet the way they were, and miles left on his journey …

As the wind picked up again, in Pádraig's mind, the falling snow turned to leaves.

At first light, cold and stiff, Pádraig awoke to find himself huddled in a dark hollow. Quickly remembering the events of the night before, he shifted to check on his companion. But before he'd even turned his head, the resistance he met in the shoulder pressed up against his told him the poor man had already passed, expired sometime during the night.

For a moment, out of fright and shock, Pádraig started, with the intention of getting himself as far away from the corpse as he could. But, realising the absurdity of his fear, he sat back against the wall of the hole to gather his thoughts. Whatever harm could have come to him by way of this sorry fellow had long passed.

Outside, the wind was low and mournful, barely blowing, while the light, blue and dim beyond the wide open hole, had yet to penetrate the interior.

Turning to glimpse the stranger, Pádraig found he could see no more of the man now than he could the night before, with him half-buried in the drift and Pádraig blinded by the driving white blast.

'Oh, you poor divil,' he told his neighbour, and, losing all fear, reached across to touch the man's face. There, above the line of a beard Pádraig imagined brownish-red, the back of his hand felt the waxen cold cheekbone of a tall but thin soul. The skin was tough and well lived in, he guessed, and, from that one touch – all he could bear before withdrawing his hand – Pádraig saw a man, not very young certainly, but not very old.

Coupled with what he had unthinkingly gleaned of the man the night before, putting the picture all together now, Pádraig was convinced he might nearly be sitting alongside a version of himself, so similar were they in stature and in make-up. With a chill he found his mind momentarily stuck upon an image of the reverse outcome: with the other man waking to discover and feel *his* cold cheek instead.

The vision was enough to remind Pádraig that he had people to get home to, and with a long way to go yet, the lull in the weather might be his only chance to get going again.

There was nothing more he could do for this unfortunate soul. Perhaps he had, unwittingly, already given the man as good a burial as he was going to get, under the circumstances.

It felt a strange sadness to remove himself from the dead man's company, knowing he would never hear more about him. And nor would anyone else, for that matter, Pádraig realised. But there was little he could do to change that. Time would not permit it and, departing, he thanked the man for his warmth, and for having had someone to weather out the storm with, in place of who knew what other eventuality.

Had he not stumbled upon this mysterious twin, fallen in the snow, Pádraig now realised he might have wandered on far past the hole and fallen himself, before long. Perhaps he owed the stranger his life.

'May God in heaven recognise the kindness of your face, my friend, and know you by your good in this realm.'

Crawling out with some difficulty, Pádraig arose to straighten himself out and, attempting to get to his feet, found the road as eerily deserted as it had been the night previous. By the time he crossed the ditch again, making a few steps along the road, he was painfully reacquainted with the same aching numbness in his feet and realised he'd forgotten to dress them before starting out.

Stopping to decide *how* he might rectify his mistake, Pádraig's eyes fell upon a conspicuous lump in the snow. With a nudge of his foot, he discovered a black shoe, but looking around saw no other.

Instantly understanding the gravity of the revelation, shaking off the first to hide it under his vest, Pádraig made straight back for the hole, but searching down the other Pádraig's shins found only his bare, cold feet.

Crawling out once more, he retraced his steps, along the fallen limb then down the bank of the ditch to where the flow of the stream had made a notch in the wall. And there it was. Caught in the cleft on the way up, it must have fallen off.

'Merciful God,' Pádraig exclaimed, staring at the thing before he picked it up.

For all his cursing about shoes in the past, this was a gift to soften his cough. He could not believe his luck. But before setting off any further, he turned back for the scelp once more to attempt the man's coat.

He would not leave him naked, out of respect to them both. But he was sure the man would call him a desperate fool were he to leave a body in a scelp, wearing a coat that left *him* warmer, dead, than Pádraig, living; shivering up the road in the cold.

No: a vest would do him, and the trouser he had on. He would leave the stranger with those – and with his dignity. But back inside the scelp, Pádraig soon realised it was too late. From the man's head to his heels, he was as stiff as the fallen limb outside, and no amount of pushing and pulling was going to change that. Save for ripping or cutting it asunder, there was ne'er a hope of getting the coat from off his stone-hardened frame. The only thing Pádraig could do now was to search the poor sinner's pockets. But alas! they were as dark and as empty as his own were: as dark as the hole in the earth had been before they had taken shelter there the night before.

'But you've given enough, my friend,' Pádraig said, trying the shoes on his broken feet. 'Rest easy now.'

For the last time, Pádraig hobbled down the side of the ditch, wincing at the restrictive sensation that bunched his toes together, making the road beneath him as flat as the floor of a church at every step. But for now, at least, it was a feeling preferable to the encrusted snow against his damaged skin.

A few hours later, when he finally reached home, the pain in Pádraig's legs was severe. Before his hand reached it, the door of the cabin opened to reveal the face of a weeping Cáit.

'Thank God you're alive. I was worried sick. Come inside and get you warm,' she said, then caught her breath in her hand as her eyes perceived the way he'd come.

Looking back, Pádraig discovered the same red marks he'd seen when she'd helped him up the hill a month or so before. Only now the tracks were in the snow. The stranger's shoes had protected him from the deadly cold, and saved him inflicting new injuries upon his feet. But the price was that they had reawakened the old wounds just the same.

The wet sensation he'd been ignoring for some time turned out to be his blood.

'Oh, God … what are we going to do?' Cait asked through her fingers, her eyes staring, scared, into his.

'Come on,' Pádraig told her, 'help me get these things off.'

To the sound of crows prattling their want overhead, Cornelius Creed watched as steam arose from the pungent yellow liquid boring a hole in the snow.

The dog lowered its leg and, distracted by something up ahead – a bird perhaps – stiffened its ears, then bolted away in pursuit. Deep in thought, Creed followed slowly.

It was Thursday morning and, as of an hour ago, the snow seemed to have stopped for a second time since its unwelcome arrival on Monday. But what remained would not be gone any time soon, what with the cold and the threat of more, he estimated, consulting with the sky.

Accompanied by the periodic tap of a cane he had taken from the shop on the way out, Creed walked at a gentle pace along the bank, where the hissing roll of the passing waters signified the unending tendency of nature to be proceeding, whatever the circumstances. The river appeared narrower, Creed mused: tapered between strips of grey ice that, creeping out, encroached upon its black depths, stealing the reeds slowly as they went.

Yesterday morning had made for a pleasant change when, after what felt like so many days cooped up within, the snow had first stopped and after the briefest of walks with the dog – a daily routine Creed had come to lean upon since re-emerging – the break in the weather had afforded a first chance to respond to the call of an old acquaintance. Arrived on Sunday last, the request had come by way of a letter from Fr James O'Driscoll, who, in his characteristic beautiful script, but without much explanation, wrote:

Dear Mr Creed,

On behalf of the starving poor of my district, I earnestly beg that you will call to me at your earliest convenience. You will find me at St Enda's in Johnstown. I am your very Obdt Servant

James O'Driscoll,
P.P. Kilmichael

Believing that since the time O'Driscoll's letter had been first dispatched, the frightful weather could only have exacerbated what hardships the people in question were suffering, Creed had met the unexpected plea with matching urgency, he remembered.

But, still processing the traumatic scenes he had witnessed there as, dusting off the planks of a waterside bench, he prepared to sit a while, Creed reflected that had he known what misery and abject destitution he would behold at the other end, he might well have regretted even opening the letter.

Yet, as darkly as the entire experience lay upon his memory, Creed knew well he could never knowingly have ignored, or refused, the appeal laid at his doorstep.

Alighting from his car in Johnstown, Creed had been met with the greying O'Driscoll, returning upon his own car from a mercy call, he'd said, having set out to deliver emergency provisions to a family he'd found in a stricken state that morning.

'Alack. By the time I got back to them, 'twas too late, and all but one of the poor family were destroyed by the fever,' he told Creed wistfully, 'but such is no longer an unusual circumstance in our district, I fear.'

'I regret to hear that, Father.' Creed had attempted to offer consolation. 'The times we inhabit are hard to reconcile.'

'Anyway, I cannot thank you enough for coming, Mr Creed. Come inside and sit by the grate, till I explain why I sent for you,' Father O'Driscoll said and, releasing Creed's hand, turned to lead the trudge inside.

'I hope your journey was not too arduous?' he inquired. 'I didn't expect you quite so soon, given the severity of the weather.'

Examining his own steps as they crunched the well-trodden snow of the path, Creed answered, 'Oh, some winter scenery can make for a pleasant rest upon the eye, the treacherous element aside.'

'Indeed it can – if you're warm,' O'Driscoll answered.

As they thawed themselves by the fire, Fr O'Driscoll proceeded to tell Creed how much heart he had taken from his writings; that in his opinion, being one of the few consistent voices advocating for the poor of the barony, Creed had cultivated a certain respect amongst the readership of the *Examiner*. With the neglected condition of his own famishing poor in mind, O'Driscoll wished to take him on a tour of Kilmichael, he said, that he might see what privations they were enduring, and falling prey to in their droves.

'I myself am taken up night and day, tending the sick and dying here, Mr Creed. When not on the way to the abode of some emaciated family – to issue last rites, and the like – then 'tis to or from the dreaded graveyard I am going. Of course, I make no presumptions upon your time and how it is taken up,' O'Driscoll had said, with black rings around his eyes such as Creed had never before known him to have.

The flickering fire offered a sombre portrait of the man who, like many other people Creed was familiar with, had aged somewhat rapidly, it seemed, in a short space of time and the observance led Creed to wonder whether O'Driscoll saw the same effects on his expression. 'I'm sure you have sorrow to occupy you in the town, Mr Creed, without an appeal such as mine to assist a far-flung district, largely unfamiliar to your steps. But 'tis because I know you – not only through your writing, but through our longstanding friendship at the Repeal Association. You are a man who cares, is why I have reached out to you. And with your already established connection to that esteemed journal, well … perhaps, through its pages, you could bring some attention to the plight of a people such as ours: fallen between the towns and blind to the world beyond.'

Creed had sat listening to the priest's eloquent introduction, unable to find any good reason to interrupt. Apart from his morning walks with the dog, by way of occupation at that moment, there was precious little he could think of to excuse himself from the task that, morally, O'Driscoll's gentle platitudes were coming to bestow on him. Despite even the distant feeling that, at the risk of his health, his agreement might expose him to a tissue of human suffering he could not yet even imagine, the need for some new sense of purpose had compelled Creed to remain quiet.

'Mr Creed, I'm ashamed to say I have imposed a trickery upon you. I can offer you nothing in return. But that at the cost of your time, the deed I entreat of your good will is one that will sit well upon your conscience and perhaps your soul. If, behold, you find granting my request beyond the scope of your time or inclination for any reason, rest assured I hold you under no obligation and will trouble you no further.'

With an earnest expression, O'Driscoll then fell silent, seemingly to allow his guest a chance to digest his proposal or decline gracefully.

'If, on the other hand, you find it desirable to put yourself in harness, I will take you on a tour of some of the habitations lying under the span of my cloak, as it were, whenever you wish it, or even immediately. Either way, I suggest we fill you with a bowl of soup and waste no more of your time.'

Finding himself nodding, Creed awaited some valorous impulse to feel himself worthy of the man O'Driscoll thought him to be. When none came, with some reluctance, he spoke honestly: 'Father O'Driscoll, I half expected that, having called me here, you might petition me to release some of the belongings of your poor entrusted to my care. Beyond the complex administration of such an idea, I might have been amenable to examine it in principle. Yet at eleven miles distant, I suspect there is likely very little, and that was not your aim. I will admit to finding myself somewhat surprised at your faith in me. I thank you for your kind words. My health, for some time, has not been … as I would wish it …'

'I see.' It was O'Driscoll's turn to nod as Creed tried to solidify his thoughts behind the uncoordinated answer he was delivering.

'But it is improving.'

'That I'm glad to hear, Mr Creed,' O'Driscoll replied – looking hopeful, but as uncertain of where the conversation was going as Creed felt.

'Huh,' Creed let out. 'I think what I mean to say to you, sir, is that I can find no valid reason to deny your disarming appeal, and –'

'Yes?'

'As I am already here …'

'Yes?' Sitting up further in his chair, the priest again interrupted, seemingly desperate to tease from Creed's mouth the answer he was seeking, though quicker than it would leave.

'We should proceed, Mr O'Driscoll, that I might see as much as I can, then oct my car for Macroom before too long, with the uncertainty of the roads.'

'Of course, of course,' O'Driscoll had said, when, rising, he had seemed almost surprised at Creed's acceptance. 'Mr Creed, you cannot know how pleased I am at your answer. You have my eternal gratitude,' he had said, gripping Creed's hand firmly between his own, shaking it vigorously.

'Your car or mine, Mr O'Driscoll?' Creed had asked.

'Oh, mine. I insist!'

It was not so much that by answering O'Driscoll's distress, he had bitten off more than he could swallow, Creed thought now, staring at the river. Neither was it that the things he'd witnessed at Kilmichael had overwhelmed his sensibilities and shocked him to the core, though he suspected that, in part at least, they had done just that. The overriding sense was that there were just so many things clouding the waters of his mind, and all of them vying for his attention. Much like the countless tendrils of the willow on the opposite bank, each one drooping low, hoping to spy its own reflection bestilled upon the surface of the stream. But, too volant to give them any of its time, the river tumbled past.

When, what seemed like an age ago, he had been in the habit of submitting his work regularly, Creed had always found it best to write while his thoughts were fresh. But despite the urgency of the case he was to represent now, yet, he did not feel hurried to begin. The letter he would write was a chance to do something new. He would take his time to do it well, he was decided, even entertaining an idea that he might travel the barony further and report on more of its forgotten inhabitants.

Then I might find Pádraig Ua Buachalla, the thought came quickly. For ever since Rev. Kyle had brought in that ticket from Clondrohid and Creed had seen a spark of light in the darkness of his own mind, he had not been able to loose the idea from his head that the pauper with whom all his moral wrongs had come to rest might, in fact, be still alive.

'Where in the world is Thomas French these days?' Creed asked his wife upon his return. 'I thought he might be busy in the stores, but he was not even there, when twice I looked. He seems to be here only as much as he is not, this last week.'

But Paulellen was preoccupied with something in the paper, he noticed. 'Merciful heaven,' she remarked, before she answered without lifting her head, 'Eh, Tom French? I don't rightly know, Con.' She looked up, present at last. 'Oh, I did get the smell of poitín downstairs on Monday, though, which might account for something.'

'Poitín? Sweet Thomas French?' This was too hard to believe, Creed thought.

'Since his mother died, he hasn't been himself, the poor man. I think he's very lonely and melancholy, Con. And he hasn't much to do.'

'Oh dear,' Creed answered. But he would give it some thought later, he decided. 'What is that you're reading?' he asked Paulellen, curious as to what had engrossed her so much.

'Massy Warren's letter.'

'Oh?'

'To the *Examiner*, of all papers. You must have heard of it?' she said, turning in her chair, searching his reaction, Creed felt.

'I did. I read it yesterday before leaving for Kilmichael.'

'You never spoke of it?' she remarked, sounding surprised. 'Well, I suppose 'tis a good thing you're not overly fussed. But a letter from Massy Warren, to your own *Cork Examiner*? I thought it would have caught more of your attention, is all – given the history.'

'Before the day is out, I will be writing to the *Examiner* too,' Creed said, embracing Paulellen, who seemed happy to stay there, 'but *not* in response to *that*,' he added clearly.

———

'Lord God, heavenly father, I beg of you, hear my prayers this day. So many of your poor have asked of me to pray for them. They've not the strength to help themselves. We are doing all we can here. But we are stretched, Father. We are stretched.'

On Friday morning at his house in Slevean East, knelt upon his simple wooden prayer desk, Father Thomas Lee had begun his morning devotion below the crucifix upon the wall. As spent and exhausted as he had ever felt, he blinked hard to fight off the sensation of having grit or sand in his eyes, periodically breaking his prayerful grasp to rub them clear.

'I know in your infinite wisdom, 'tis nature as you created her, Lord; keeping balance among the elements.'

As, spilling across his lips in quiet restraint, the words came, as thoughts more than prayers, struggling to shake the grip of sleep, Lee centred his attention on the feeling of his knuckles, digging into the cold skin of his brow.

Over and over he saw them: the famished, huddled creatures he was daily, hourly ministering to, in seemingly endless rounds to every corner of the town; the dying occupants of squalid rows of drab little houses lining the lanes; clinging to each other for warmth, under pathetic, hole-filled roofs.

In his ears rang the cries and the moans, and – most disturbing of all – the silences of barely living creatures shivering and fading to nothing in darkness: the one and only thing protecting them from the horror of what their bodies had become.

Inside his tunic, Lee found the wooden cross around his neck and held it in his fist, reliving the scenes he'd encountered the evening before: at Jeremiah Cronin's in Walton's Lane; the cabins of Hanora O'Sullivan and James Wallace too; Mary Kearney and John Murphy, neighbours to each other in Batten's Lane, each on the brink of death and unlikely, he'd imagined, to see morning; at Holland's Lane: the O'Connells, Corcorans, Ellards, Horgans and Lehanes.

All through the town, in habitations of the simplest mud walls, the sick, the dead and the living were now lying together in their own filth, too weary and helpless to slop out their cabins; entire families of fathers, mothers, children and grandparents sharing tiny one-roomed spaces serving as kitchen, bedroom, living area and privy all at once. While, from the papers, he knew this was happening everywhere, Lee could scarce imagine how any locality could surpass the wretchedness he was witnessing.

Exhausted and helpless, Thomas Lee, the priest, hoped God would hear his thoughts. Lost in the snow now too, perhaps, Thomas Lee, the mortal man, sought desperately what certainty the cloth had provided him in bygone days – a feeling very distant at this moment in his life.

One house at a time. One hour at a time, he told himself anew and, pressing the wooden cross to his lips, before replacing it to hang beneath his tunic, Fr Lee arose to take his bucket to the privy, the sagging board of the *prie-dieu* groaning under his knee.

At eight o'clock he would meet Fr Barry and Fr Foley at the reading room in Lucey's Lane to decide who would go where this day.

From a sleeping curl by the stove, discovering its master preparing for the outdoors, the dog yawned and stretched its front legs with excitement.

'Out for your morning walk, you two, is it?' Paulellen said, observing the ritual that had lately grown.

Indirectly, her husband answered through the creature. 'We must take our exercise while we can, mustn't we, my four-legged friend?'

'Oh, do you think we'll get more snow?' Paulellen asked, worried at the thought.

'It's certainly cold enough,' he answered, pulling on his gloves. 'We won't be long.'

As though pulled by some invisible cord that ran between them, Cornelius followed through the open door to the sounds of the dog bounding awkwardly down the stairs.

Moments later, hearing the bell below, Paulellen went quietly to the window, and watched. Spotting them before the pane fogged up, they were crossing the Square toward Castle Street; unlikely to turn back now, she was sure. Still, with an air of trepidation she headed for the stairs.

Producing his article on Kilmichael, she presumed, all that morning and much of the evening before, Cornelius had closeted himself into his study: that secluded realm he had not otherwise inhabited of late. If anywhere, it was there she might learn something of his true state of mind. For, while she was anxious at going behind his back, her fear of his going before the public unchecked was greater, and Paulellen was desperate to see what he had written, before it was too late.

There was little danger of her being discovered by Thomas French, who was almost never at the shop lately, but Paulellen left the door ajar, that she might hear, just in case.

The first thing to catch her notice was that the desk was unusually disordered, with writing implements left out; drawers open; papers piled up. But it brought great relief to discover that, on this occasion, he had not exercised his sometime habit of leaving letters sealed in their packets and stewing upon the desk. Instead, in position were a series of pages in her husband's characteristic, still meticulous hand.

Preparing herself for their insights, Paulellen sat carefully before them.

To The Editor Of The Cork Examiner

she read, intrigued at the singularity of seeing one of his articles in raw form. And he had titled the piece. Already Paulellen had learned something new: that those headings she'd always thought designated by the editor came from Con himself.

SNOW GRIPS THE DOOMED CABINS OF CARRIGBOY

Setting foot upon the soil of another district one confirms that what is local is universal; that what unfolds in one place is happening everywhere, differing only by degree. Everything we feared might come to pass is now happened, and we are delivered to the point of unenviable catastrophe. The consequences, no longer preventable, are what we behold, instead.

Kilmichael, Macroom, Friday

The degree of destitution existing at present in this ill-fated district far exceeds any idea previously entertained. Indeed, it would be difficult to conceive of a misery exceeding that now prevalent. Every field and road teems with gaunt witnesses to the presence of starvation.

In the company of Fr O'Driscoll, I visited several wretched road-side hovels. In the first, from an almost dilapidated stable, we heard low groans issuing forth. Through heaps of the most disgusting filth we got to the door and there met a young man, upon whose features starvation and disease had already written their stake. His mother was sick of dysentery and he was out of employment. But by the kindness of a neighbour they had been allowed to lie in that stable, where two or three horses were already present. The floor within, we found, was covered with heaps of manure and straw and – learn this, readers! – atop one of these lay the wretched woman, scarcely clad at all, and to all appearances in the last stage of disease. I suspect that, so long as I live, I will never loosen that tragic image from my mind.

A visit to several other cabins nearby was sufficient to confirm that in many cases an equal degree of destitution and misery existed there.

We next proceeded to the district of Clasbrethane, where, a short time since, the Curravayain road was in progress, affording considerable employment to its labourers. But in a bout of vindictive negligence – some might call it wilful murder – Captain Gordon stopped those works. Over two hundred peasants were at once thrown out of employment thus – left helpless to perish with their families in the hills. I have never seen a district to present such a wild and dreary appearance as this one at the hour I ventured in. Composed of rugged, stony hills with deep morasses between – and those entirely covered with snow – the whole scene presented a picture of the most stern and sombre character. A few miserable mud-built hovels, embedded in heaps of snow, were scattered over the sides of the hills. Over fifty cottages, I was informed, have been left tenantless in this district, their occupants preferring to risk starvation upon the roads over perishing inside their miserable cabins, unknown and uncared for. But for the small stirring of the wind there, it was so quiet and still. This I found most affecting.

A traveller will find no indication of the industry formerly seen on every side here. No fields dug or ploughed. No labourers working, or cottages rising. All uncultivated and desolate, nothing meets the eye but untilled fields, tenantless hovels crumbling to ruin, and haggard skeletons, the very shadows of what once were strong and cheerful peasants.

Naturally, the extreme severity of the weather has only added to the suffering in terrific degree, and, needless to say, it is quite impossible for those holding places upon the works to earn anything at all for their families when the snow lies still on the ground as though it had just fallen. When to these calamities the most dangerous and destructive diseases are added, the extent of suffering is, I am very sorry to say, much easier imagined than described.

It is scarcely possible to adequately convey the state to which these people have been reduced. The townland I speak of is the property of Mr. Hickson, an absentee landlord.

Two pages in, Paulellen stopped to consider that, for a moment, she had almost forgotten the author, so entranced and absorbed had she become by the plight of the subjects within. But compared to his usual tone, the writing did not sound like Cornelius. Perhaps it was that had influenced her feeling, she reflected. This was more to the point, somehow, and calmer than the Con she knew.

Finally, he might be recovered, Paulellen supposed, with a sigh. And just maybe he was even a little stronger for it all; his priorities changed for the better, to something more in line with his civic pride, and worthy of the good soul she knew he had.

Most encouraging of all, where Paulellen was concerned, was that, true to his word, Con had not taken the bait to engage with Massy Warren in a public exchange across the *Examiner* columns.

But, while feeling a little guilty for having doubted her husband now, Paulellen could not help but wonder if his reluctance was – in any measure – guided by fear. After all, his longstanding rivalry with Warren had almost certainly played a significant part in his recent debilitation.

Either way, Cornelius had steered a course away from more disaster – the best outcome she could have hoped to discover, Paulellen thought as she prepared to read on.

Let Massy Warren do as he pleases, she told him in her mind, *he has not half the moral fibre of my husband.*

In Kilmichael itself, the portion of those destitute amounts to between six and eight thousand, or two-thirds the entire parish. Hitherto a dependable source of local employment, even the farmers are reduced to almost utter destitution.

Both workhouses in reach of the vicinity are crowded to excess. Dunmanway, with more than eight hundred paupers currently, has more than doubled its allocated capacity, while Macroom, built for six, is so rampant with contagion that its doors were closed to any further admission one week since, bursting at the seams then with upwards of fifteen hundred.

Thus, it will be seen, the poor of this locality are thrown entirely upon the support of the Relief Committee, whose work, of course, is vital. Nonetheless, it must be stated that – composed of a mere eight gentlemen in this district – however valiant their efforts, little more can be achieved than to check in slight degree the brutal progress of such widespread starvation and death.

Though the greater part of the parish is the possession of more absentee landlords whose assistance should be rendered their tenants in such times, not one of these gentlemen has subscribed a single farthing and contributions collected since the beginning of last August here scarcely amounted to two hundred pounds.

Soup is sold at the very low rate of a penny per gallon, with twelve hundred quarts daily supplied. Until last week, the Committee distributed a quantity of the soup gratuitously, to such inhabitants as were unable to procure it at any price, but for some reason this arrangement has since been prohibited to great controversy by the Chairman, Benjamin Sweete.

The extreme prevalence of fever and dysentery here is most alarming. I am assured there are at present three hundred cases of fever in the parish, and that at the lowest calculation. The Clergy are so continually taken up visiting the sick and dying that ''tis but rarely' they are afforded an hour's rest, 'til they are inevitably called to confer last rites over some or another victim.

Almost entirely full before the crisis, Kilmichael Graveyard has become more a dumping ground of death than a Cemetery, every day receiving new tenants still. The bodies are rarely interred in daylight, however – the reason of this: that precious few can afford the luxury of a coffin. Instead, those victims of hunger and sickness are nightly conveyed in stealth inside and hurriedly flung into haphazardly dug holes, uncoffined and uncovered save for the rags that yet hang around the emaciated corpses' limbs. Heaven only knows how many lie elsewhere, abandoned or unattended.

C. Creed.

Paulellen whimpered to herself, greatly moved, but also relieved to have reached the end with her husband's grace intact. Filled with pride at such renewed strength and dignity, she straightened the papers and laid them back the way she had found them.

Lest she leave some careless clue to her presence, with hands suspended above the desk, Paulellen took a moment to survey the whole bureau. However unusual it was to behold such disarray, she felt satisfied it was as disorderly as when she'd first entered.

The chair creaked as, deciding it best to quit the room in good time, Paulellen leant forward to rise. But for the first time, beneath some books to the right, she now spied the corner of another sheet of writing. The date, it was, had snagged her attention. For it too appeared to have been written that morning. Perhaps an earlier draft, she imagined, as with one hand resting upon the books she questioned her first instinct.

But her husband's drafts usually went to the basket by his feet. Why would he keep this one, and hidden at that?

As, carefully, she moved the books aside, exposing two more freshly written pages, Paulellen's instinct told her something was terribly wrong this time. Yet she knew she must read them, and sighted their exact position before lifting them from the desk. Like the wilting wings of a dying bird, they lay lifeless across her hands, so that, before reading a word, Paulellen sensed that their wounds, in turn, were her own wounded hopes, and, surrendering the pages to the desk once more, she took a breath.

To The Editor Of The Cork Examiner

Macroom, Feb 12th, 1847

As, for the second time that morning, but this time upon mute lips, she read the date, unable to help herself, Paulellen succumbed to the lure of something that called her eyes to scan four or five lines ahead and, there, discovered the words her mind wished were only a dream:

M. H. Warren

'Oh, Connie, no …' Stricken with grief, Paulellen covered her eyes for what seemed a long time before she accepted that she must face whatever lay among the lines below – at the very least to know before anyone else would.

Sir,–

While ready to acknowledge those qualities which have given you, deservedly, so influential a position as a journalist, I had no idea – until your paper of the tenth instant, promising in your next number a letter from M. H. Warren – that you had so strong a mixture of waggery in your composition. Nothing has occurred in this locality since the days of O'Connell's monster trials to cause such excitement as this announcement. All were anxious to know by what process of reasoning notorious facts could be controverted, with not a few indulging in the hope that Macroom would have the glory of being the birthplace of the eighth wonder of the world – Baron Munchausen being the seventh and last. The only thing that could excuse you was the hearty laugh this precious morceau caused when it did appear.

Closing her eyes, Paulellen brought her palms to her eyes once more in hopes of staving off the despair she was feeling. This version of her husband, when compared to the one she was proud of, sounded a raving lunatic. However farcical and mocking he was attempting to be, she for one was not laughing. On the contrary, Paulellen's face had never felt quite so long or devoid of mirth.

To do Mr Warren justice, he admits that the once active and powerful labourer is no longer able to work as had been his wont to do. Neither does he deny the statement made by Father Barry that, on the Pound Lane road, the unfortunate labourer had been cut down to two pence a day – a shilling a week to support himself and his wretched family. But he attempts to palliate the injustice by stating that this cruel experiment was only tried for one week. How well may Capt. Gordon exclaim, 'Save me from my friends.'

Surely Mr Warren cannot be ignorant of the fact that in many instances the payment to the poor labourers, so wretchedly small and irregular, is quite inadequate to sustain life in either themselves or their famishing families; or that the system has forced many into a poorhouse already far past capacity, and from the poorhouse to their cold graves.

What a commentary on imperial legislation!

Thousands of our unfortunate peasantry dying by the ditch-side in the forty-seventh year of our Union with the richest country in the world, the 'envy of surrounding nations', while our gentry are to be seen like supplicants,

Kneeling before their masters' doors
Hawking their wrongs; as beggars do their sores.

I have just heard – and upon enquiry found it to be fact – that able-bodied men working on the Carriganne road were paid the extraordinary sum of three pence halfpenny each day, or one and nine pence, for the week ending Feb sixth Inst. Mr O'Sullivan, pay clerk.

Have we a Government? Have we rulers? Have we a Board of Works? Have we Gentlemen in the country? Have we anyone who will step forward to protect the starved and dying labourers?

Oh! God help the poor!

I have the honour to be, Mr Editor,
your obedient servant,
A LOOKER-ON

'Dear God,' Paulellen whispered. That he had gone back on his word was something perplexing and frustrating enough. But the idea that he was not, after all, as well within himself as he was purporting to be was wholly devastating. In that moment Paulellen felt hopelessly unsure of what to do with her excessive emotion. Her only consolation was that he had signed the letter under a pseudonym. At least he was not proclaiming this madness to the world openly!

Pressed against her face once more, the skin of Paulellen's down-turned hands felt moisture when a slow trickle loosened from the well of her eyes to spill upon her knuckles.

What reaction will this *maunderous babble elicit from the community at large, let alone Warren himself,* she wondered … *Oh God, could Cornelius be identified in any way through the article?* Just then the tiny flat sound of something dropping tapped upon the desk below her head. Opening the shutters of her hands, Paulellen realised with fright that a droplet of her tears had struck the page. Spreading wider, it would imminently loosen the words, whose edges began to blur as though they themselves were now weeping too, with her.

'No! … Oh, no!'

Sniffling to avoid further damage and drawing her tear-streaked face away in panic, Paulellen grabbed for the kerchief beneath her sleeve and pressed it down hard onto the script. Lest she smudge the ink and make it worse, she dared not move it at first. But, suddenly remembering the Kilmichael letter beneath, she picked it up instead and began fanning it frantically to dry its moisture.

Horrified at the slip-up and fearful of her husband's inevitable return, she spotted the candle upon the bureau shelf. Bracing herself, Paulellen positioned the page taut above the flame so that a glow appeared through the translucent porthole of moisture. Slowly she lowered the page closer to the light, but kept it a safe distance above the tip of the flame.

It was as the paper began to assume its colour again that she noticed the tiny wisp of oily smoke, creeping around the edge of the page. Withdrawing it so fast, it cracked like a whip, and again Paulellen's breath seized at the thought of having ripped it. But it had not torn and, checking its underside lest she'd clumsily soiled it with soot and smoke,

Paulellen discovered all was well. When the page moved of its own accord in her hand and rippled a crack once more, Paulellen felt a draught from beyond.

'Paull, dear?' called the voice of her husband.

'Yes?'

One, two, three, the books were stacked above each other and before she knew it, Paulellen was in the kitchen, heating the teapot upon the stove.

'Now, you two will mind your Daddy, won't ye?'

With sadness in her eyes, Síle nodded slowly, seemingly unsure of what she was agreeing to, Pádraig sensed.

'Don't cry, my little love,' Cáit told Diarmuidín, and thumbed at his tearful cheeks.

'You have the meal bread?' Pádraig asked.

'I have,' Cáit answered, checking herself once more.

'Don't eat it until you're fit to fall down, do you hear? The trip home is harder,' he added, 'and you're sure today is Saturday? You couldn't have miscounted while I was down?'

Cáit answered with a nod as they shared a knowing look. 'I'd better go while I can,' she said, with her hand upon the door.

'If it starts up again, come straight back,' he said, and stared at the objects that, like a strange extension of her shawl, covered her feet to keep them from touching the earth floor. Two scuffed, hard-edged hooves; he imagined her struggling in the things, just as he had: tripping, too long as they were; one identical to the other, equally uncomfortable no matter which foot they were on.

As she opened the door, Pádraig stared out in terror at what looked and sounded like the frozen wastelands at the ends of the earth. It was no longer snowing, but the wind was high.

'Do you hear me? Come back if it starts up again,' he insisted, to the sound of Síle getting upset.

'Stop now,' Cáit said, 'of course I'll come back.'

'Jesus above!' he said, 'and don't get swindled leaving the huts.'

When she was gone, Pádraig hugged the children and made them rest easy in the blanket where he warmed them and they warmed him. Listening to their whimpers, he felt his eyes stuck fast, drawn into the fire's light. What if she didn't make it back at all?

There was more potential for disaster now than ever there had been.

While the children slept, Pádraig sat up, and, propping himself against the wall, rolled back the coat that was covering his legs. The rags were off now and, anxious to gauge the progress of his healing, he knew it was good to let the air at the wounds.

Wincing, he recoiled at the first sight of his feet. His skin, blotched all over with pink and blue cold, was otherwise a mess of scabs, some parts soft and some hard. The sores at the edges wore yellow crusts, with inflamed pink rings where the new skin was growing. It was where they were soft that the problems were. They were in a bad way and he knew it. *Some day, before ever long, these terrible times will have passed us yet,* Pádraig told himself, and considered the untiring use his feet had given him before the weather had wrecked them completely. A hundred days and more they had carried him in and out of Macroom, wounded and healing, but never refusing, as, wearily, he had walked and stumbled on through the pain. At more than six miles in and the same back out, Pádraig estimated he had walked at least twelve hundred miles in the four months since he'd started going for outdoor relief in October; all of it on barely a morsel a day and what scant reserves his body had stored up over the course of a poor lifetime.

It was a miracle they had lasted so long, Pádraig reckoned, with a sentimental gratitude for what he had subjected them to; two wounded limbs, as battered and sore as a butcher's block.

'Well the cold and the snow has finished that all now,' he thought sorrowfully, 'but please God, Cáit will be all right,' he whispered, and closed his eyes, wondering how far she might have travelled by now.

'Daddy?'

Startled at realising Síle had been awake, Pádraig covered his feet as fast but as gently as he could, taking a painful breath.

'Are you going to die, Daddy, like Labhrás Ua Duinnín?' she asked, with tears in her eyes.

In extreme discomfort and already hungry not half an hour after she'd eaten the griddle bread, Cáit reflected that the journey so far had been harder than anything she'd imagined. The snow being ever present still, her limbs and kidneys ached from the cold and she was having to stop frequently when, with numbed fingertips, she would adjust the rags stuffed into the shoes, sometimes reducing or adding to the lumps in the toes. Too little of the material and it seemed her feet moved around, agitating the sorest parts. Too much and the restriction was equally as painful. The blood around her toenails confirmed why.

But Cáit consoled herself that, as cumbersome as the shoes were, she would never have got this far without them. Proof of that came all too easily when, taking them off to relieve her ruptured blisters, the feeling of days-old snow cutting at her skin combined with the cold to a walking agony. Putting them back on, it took almost half a mile before the cold ache subsided and Cáit decided to not take them off again.

Men's shoes, stuffed with rags. Bent forward, the hood of her shawl pulled tightly around her face, Cáit swapped her hands often: one to clasp the neck of her raiment, the other to thaw beneath her arm. Leaning into the wind, she tried to ignore the multitude of sensations her body sent in alarm: raw at the heels, along the sides of her feet and between her toes. Clumsy and tight and benumbed inside, it was as though hard wood was pressed against her feet from every side.

Overall, Cáit could not remember having ever felt like this, and was convinced that – the shoes aside – her health had fallen far lower than she'd realised. She had been aware, certainly, of her deteriorated appearance, the loss of herself, the greying hair, fallen-out teeth, even her inability to feed Diarmuidín – but to find herself leaning on a tree, so out of breath at having to walk a few miles, was an unwelcome surprise to add her many worries.

Walking any distance had never been a struggle before. But with the exception of going to see Fr O'Brien recently, for the most of two years, she had ventured no further than the stream, for water, Cáit realised.

Only now did she fully appreciate what Pádraig must have endured before he'd eventually been put off his feet – though he never complained, or spoke of it, she reflected: the same frightening deterioration, and the same agony that she now felt; just over a longer period.

Remembering how worried he was at her leaving that morning, Cáit now understood why. But there had been another reason she'd been so adamant about going to Macroom in his place. And although she had had no other choice but to come – since he could not, for the wages – Cáit had withheld the real motivation from her husband. Part of her regretted not telling him. But at the risk of his not understanding and only worrying more, it had been better to keep it to herself, she had felt. For this might be her only chance to find her sister, or learn something of her fate, she had determined. And even though that meant having to visit the fever-ridden workhouse, nothing would stop her from trying.

But first, the wages.

———

'Doctor,' said Fr Lee, meeting Valentine McSwiney at the corner of Massytown Road.

'Father Lee, I'm glad I found you.'

'Oh?'

''Twas rumoured at the Relief Committee last evening a woman had died of starvation in Massytown.'

'Yes, I'd heard that,' Lee replied.

'So that it might be published in the event of confirmation, 'twas resolved I should call to the house and ascertain the facts. With a priest in tow if possible – it was suggested – to confer prayers over the woman.'

'Right. I was too waylaid to attend the committee, but planned to reach the house in my own travels. Shall we walk there together?'

'That would be convenient, Father.'

'This morning I sent Father Barry and Father Foley south and east of the town,' Lee elaborated, to the sound of their footsteps ambling over the trodden snow. 'I elected to cross the bridge and cover west and north, with the aim to work my way towards the Union and close out the day there. It has taken me all morning to get clear of Pound Lane and Barrack Lane alone. I was just finishing up there when you found me, Doctor McSwiney. How are things at the dispensary, dare I ask?'

'Oh, as you might expect, Father. But I supposed if I didn't come now, I might not get away at all. Tomorrow or yesterday would be no different.'

Drawing a long breath that seemed to bear the weight of a hundred more, the young doctor wore a tension that Lee himself knew all too well. It spoke of a strain built up in the carrying out of such grave duties as were theirs to discharge, Lee thought.

'Truth be known, Father, I needed to get some air in my lungs and relished the thoughts of a break from the barrage there,' McSwiney continued, impressing Lee.

'It's well you heed the instinct to ease your burden when it gets too cumbersome, young man; through prayer, or whatever wholesome means you find at your disposal. To ignore that inner voice is to do so at your peril,' Lee warned. 'I saw good men go to ruin, who failed to observe it.'

'Wise words, Father. I'll endeavour to take care, thank you.'

Counselling the doctor, Lee realised his advice carried wisdom he had needed to unearth for his own sake as well.

'Anyway, I found you easily enough,' McSwiney added. 'That boy who brought me to you was not the first to ask if I was looking for the priest.'

'Is that so?' Lee replied with sad rhetoric. 'This world is a strange playground, for him and his brethren, doctor – growing amidst the most horrendous time in the history of their people.'

'Well put, Father,' McSwiney replied, as, shuffling on, Lee reflected that the houses in Massytown were in better condition than those of the town-dwelling poor; something owing to William White Hedges' insistence upon letting property only to tenants interested in improving and slating their domiciles.

'And God help us, we've another Presentments upon us,' Lee said, noticing that the snow had begun to give up the cobbles beneath again.

'It's been announced?' McSwiney inquired.

'Next month,' Lee told the doctor. 'It only appeared in yesterday's number. Let's just hope it bears more fruit than the last one. It can't be any more of a fiasco, certainly.'

'The house of Dick Walsh, young man. Do you know it?' McSwiney asked a figure in an open doorway when, from a position of cradling his head upon his knees, the young man looked up and pointed to a spot further along the opposite side.

'Thank you, sir,' McSwiney replied.

As the boy's head returned to the same forlorn position, Lee estimated his age as being no more than twenty-one. A fully grown man, yet still a boy, it was indelibly written across his face: the sorrow his soul withheld seeming to manifest in the rosing of his cheeks. Were he to be standing he would be quite tall, Lee observed. But his limbs, in the folded position they held, put the priest in mind of the delicate bones of a bird's wing, stripped and robbed of its flesh.

Though his pride and grace forbade it, there was a call for help in the young man's eyes. He had answered their question, but by his expression offered only silent despair at not being saved by the men who had suddenly appeared.

Walking on, a tinge of guilt fell upon Fr Lee's heart. He wished he had time to stop. But his duties at the Walshes' and the Workhouse beckoned. 'Did you notice which house he pointed to?' he asked, sighting the lines along the street for a revelation. 'Dr McSwiney?' he asked, turning, when the doctor did not answer, to find a man as though somewhere else, tears welling in his eyes.

'That boy,' McSwiney remarked, looking straight ahead, 'he might as well have been … it was my nephew … I mean, everything … the same eyes … same gentle quietness.'

'Do you need to stop, Doctor McSwiney?'

'No, no,' he insisted, wiping his tears. 'There, I think.'

Behind a wooden cart left broken in the street was the house he had pointed to: a small cottage with its roof in disrepair. Under a crooked lintel, they found the door ajar.

'Good day, ma'am. We're sorry to intrude,' said Lee, finding a woman in semi-darkness within, two grown children at her side, crouching near a fireless hearth. 'Is not there a woman dead in this house, ma'am?' he asked, to precious little forthcoming.

'There is,' was as much as the woman volunteered, in a sombre, almost peaceful lull.

'Where, ma'am?' the doctor seconded.

'There,' said she, pointing to a bedstead, partially hidden by an old settle.

Blessing himself, Lee approached, with the doctor close. Over the furniture, through the dimness, Lee could spy the outline of a body, but with the shape of another alongside.

'Are there two dead here?' he turned to the woman.

'There are not,' came the sepulchral rasp of a male voice, small and weak, apparently one of those laid out. 'I am not dead yet, but soon will be,' the voice added, struggling.

'God in heaven,' Lee said, aghast, and felt the surprise of McSwiney alongside. Lying beside his dead wife since the night before, this must be Dick Walsh, he realised.

'I'll fetch a candle,' said McSwiney, and left hurriedly, as Lee prepared himself to issue last rites to the man.

'My poor wife,' Walsh moaned as, producing his beads, Lee placed them in the man's cold hands to comfort him.

'Thank you, Father.'

'Have you any sins to confess?'

'A great many, I suspect,' the voice said, weeping.

'Anything particular that worries your soul, Mr Walsh?'

Expecting none but the general sin of the poor, Lee meanwhile considered that administering extreme unction would take an appreciable time to perform. Unsure as to how close death was at that moment, it would be best to confer a single unction upon the forehead, he decided. The soul of the woman was beyond unction, but it was of urgent import to see to that of him still living, capable of salvation while he was.

'I wish I could have helped my family more,' came the eventual confession of the man, upon strains of gentle sorrow.

With blessed oil upon his thumb gouged out from the tin beneath his soutane, Fr Lee now marked the shape of the cross into the man's brow. 'And the prayer of faith shall save the sick man. And if he be in sins, they shall be remitted to him,' he recited aloud. 'In this is fulfilled what St James the Apostle says: if anyone be sick let him call the priests of the church and them lay hands on him, anointing him with oil in the name of the Lord.'

Gratified that, right then, he was forming the all-important conduit between the dying man and his God, Lee felt instantly restored of his earlier doubts. Not only was he bringing Dick Walsh comfort as he prepared to leave his mortal coil, but saving his soul at the moment of most critical importance, when its fate would be fixed for all eternity: either cleansed of mortal sin and saved by the sacraments, or in danger of the long torment of infernal punishment were the rites not conferred in time.

When – having completed the singular unction – he was content the man's soul was no longer in such danger, Lee decided he could now fulfil the entire sacrament and began to issue the oil in cruciform markings upon the other organs of external senses: eyes, ears, nostrils, lips, hands and feet, as, all the while, the man continued to gasp.

'Through this holy unction and His most tender mercy may the Lord pardon thee whatever sins or faults thou hast committed by sight, by hearing, smell, taste, touch, and by walking.'

Behind him, by the growing halo of light illuminating the yellow-brown tones of burnt umber upon the walls, Lee knew McSwiney had returned. Moving and thinning as it administered the rites he perceived his own shadow, stretched like a gaunt devil against the light.

Preparing to conclude the ritual, leaving his hand upon the shivering skull of the dying man, Fr Lee could now see that Walsh was wasted and almost entirely devoid of fat. 'Holy father, physician of souls and bodies: as the healer of every disease and our deliverer from death, heal also Thy servant from the bodily infirmity that holds him. By the intercessions of Saints Barra, St Coleman, Saint Fachtna and all the saints, make him live through the grace of Christ. *In nomine Patris; et Filii; et Spiritus Sancti; amen.*'

'God bless you, Father,' the dying man said as Lee covered him over, and edged his way around the bed to reach the body of the woman; making room for the doctor to examine the man before he'd begin his judgements on the cause of the woman's death and its being starvation or not. At this point in times past, the daughter or the mother of the house would have led a keening lament, Lee ruminated, while, instead, their quietness brought him to regard how low the people had come.

'Apologies, Father,' McSwiney interrupted, 'there is a request for your presence in the house adjacent. The man of the house there is very close to death: a weaver, by the name of Murphy.'

'I see, I see … right,' Lee said, and blew out the tension he felt overtaking his body. In the woman's case, a cursory prayer would have to suffice in favour of yet another soul preparing to depart. 'Thank you, Doctor.'

Marking the cross upon the cold forehead of Mrs Walsh, Lee imagined her corpse could not have weighed more than a bushel of wheat straw. Closed in death, her eyes seemed the only feature exempt from stress and desolation.

'I recommend to Thee the souls of those who were most devout to the passion of Our Lord; to the Blessed Sacrament and to the Blessed Virgin Mary, the souls who are most abandoned; those who suffer most; and those who are nearest to the entrance into paradise. *In nomine Patris, et Filii; et Spiritus Sancti; amen.*' Lee signed himself with the cross.

Repositioning the tin of oil beneath his garments, he hastened to leave. 'When I've completed my duties adjacent, I'll continue on for the Workhouse, Doctor McSwiney. It being two days since I last visited, I suspect my work will be measured up for me there.'

'Of course, Father,' McSwiney answered, resting his bag upon the settle.

———

Within sight of the huts and the gangs of souls swarming around them, Cáit felt great relief that she'd found the line, at last.

As she approached, most all of the men lining up exhibited as grey and dreary a condition as Pádraig, at his tiredest, did, coming home from the works. But these poor men looked too cold to work and, as the snow yet remained, Cáit presumed they must only be here for the same reason she was.

If slowly, the labourers appeared all to be coming and going from the second hut. A wooden structure, it looked new and sturdy, but somehow not permanent.

This has to be the wages, Cáit thought, and confirmed as much when the next man came out, counting some coins, his head sorrowfully bowed.

'I'm here for my husband's wages,' Cáit told the man guarding the door.

'You'll have to join the queue, like everyone else,' he said, blindly, before looking her up and down, the face of disdain.

Showing a decency far exceeding his, however, the men at the front made her a space despite him, the most elderly among them removing his hat for a woman's presence.

'Suit yourselves,' the guard said, and went back to poking at the dirt under his nails.

'God bless ye,' Cáit told the labourers as, next in line, her turn soon came.

Though it was not as much as Pádraig had hoped for, ten minutes later, Cáit felt relieved to be leaving the hut with near five shillings – or even anything at all, given his recent experiences with the pay clerks. This she put down to her having the advantage of at least some English, where Pádraig had none at all.

'How do we know you are who you say you are?' the clerk had asked, seemingly to tease out any deception in her attempt.

'Because I am an honest person, and I have walked six miles on the strength of my name,' had come her answer, proud that she still had her self-respect. 'Here is my husband's ticket,' she had added, producing the tattered yellow slip from out the side of her shawl.

'Will your husband be coming back?' the young man had inquired near to the completion of the transaction when, by his tone, it was as though his delivering the coins was dependent upon her answer.

'He'll have to eat first,' she had responded, standing firm, but secretly shaking and praying they would not make her journey be in vain. But it had seemed the right response and Cáit was glad that something had cut through the pattern of the men seeing so many forlorn creatures that their pity was often asleep to them.

Limping more acutely with the pain now as she went, Cáit was unable to stop the tears of relief as she left the site of the works.

But despite her worsening condition – it having become so apparent that she could not hope to make the journey again any time soon – the idea was only solidified in Cáit's mind that she had to get to the workhouse.

In the absence of any more news of her sister in the long four months since Pádraig had seen Onóra there, Cáit knew this was her only chance to find out if she was alive or dead. It was a colossal risk, given that she would be exposing herself to, then potentially carrying home to her family, such disease and pestilence as was rumoured to be present at the Union right then. But she had to know.

───

'Water … please … water!'

Through the blur of her vision, with arms outstretched, Onóra could see the outline of a female figure approaching with a jug. With every ounce of her entire being she hoped the liquid inside the vessel was being brought to cure her insatiable thirst.

But the shape drifted past with the whifting shuffle of clothes in movement.

'Nurse Sullivan, some water here, please!'

The voice was on the other side and, burning and tired, Onóra's arms fell once more.

With eyes closed, she found herself by the Láinne, licking its way across the rapids on the way to Harding's Mill. Lying forward there, she lowered her arms, reaching for the cool, clear water. But seeming as far away as the sky above her, it might as well have been a sea of clouds.

Water, nurse, please, came a distant cry, changing shape and colour, when the mill wheel jammed and stuttered, trying to go. Again, again, again, again; a cutting, choking noise.

Not choking; she was coughing, Onóra realised, sending pain to the muscles of her back, her thighs, legs and arms. Burning her throat and hurting her head until her eyes ached.

'Water!' a man shouted. Sounding terrified, he cried fitfully amid the coughing and rasping that ebbed and flowed throughout the ward, and Onóra remembered she was upstairs in the fever hospital. The platforms here were broken into sections, one apiece, and between these she was lying on a pitch of straw.

Two paupers from the men's ward had carried her aloft. 'Women and smaller men upstairs,' had been the doctor's direction. Delivered to her current position then, Onóra had wondered why the beds were low and high. But she had soon understood. Intended for doctor's access, the gaps between had been utilised as extra beds and, lower than her neighbours were, Onóra had frequently to endure the fluids that ran down the sides of the higher boards, like rain off a gutter, soaking her space. This had happened often when the little old man who died yesterday lost his waters.

'Someone douse that fire, please,' a voice pleaded. The same poor woman had been complaining all week, repeatedly told they would all freeze to death if there was no fire.

'Water,' Onóra gasped, hoping it would be her call answered this time. But her body drew a huge breath so that she could not speak. Caught on her wind, the phlegm sucked down her choke, bringing her to cough violently again into the black darkness behind her eyes.

'Nurse. A pan here, please,' the doctor's voice called as, in the shadow of the figure, Onóra felt herself rolled onto her side. Retching into the pan from the depths of her stomach, her entire body convulsed to send yet more of the thick, dark fluid up. Blue and grey, but streaked with blood when it came, the bitter substance clung to her mouth and to her insides, bursting out but not wanting to leave.

Old Dr Crooke and the young woman she'd come to know as Nurse Dwyer were speaking, but with words she could not hear. Frightened, Onóra sensed that whatever they were saying was not good.

'Water … water!' The word was everywhere but where she needed it to be.

'Doctor Crooke,' a voice called, from a different room.

'Stay with her, Miss Dwyer. When this bout ceases, administer water. But not too much. If the discharges do not slow, I may issue a decoction of logwood to stay their frequency.'

'Yes, Doctor.'

To Onóra, lying back as a rag wiped at her mouth, the beams overhead resembled the hard peak of a church roof. It was so painful to keep her eyes open. *The strange woman's rag*, she thought.

'Drink, just a little,' a soft voice said, but removed the cup from her lips too quickly. Grabbing at the hands, Onóra tried to pull it back and managed one more suck when some of it spilled upon her skin, bringing instant relief. But already her tongue felt as dry as leather and, sifting over her broken lips, she searched out every last droplet.

At the pain of another bout of coughing Onóra clamped her eyes shut, then, behind them, saw the Master once more, gasping for air on his deathbed. Staring at his gaunt face, she tried to spit. But, dry and cracked, her mouth had nothing. Awaking inside herself, Onóra wondered if maybe the Master had cursed her for her deed. Perhaps her mouth being so dry was punishment for her terrible deed!

'Water … please!'

The incessant moan echoed up and down the ward. But the nurse was gone. Footsteps came and went in the stairwell, travelling the boards on this side and the other. The swooshing of the water wheel; lapping in a bucket; stirred with a stick by an army of washerwomen; she dreamed.

'Good day, Father Lee.'

'The House is assuming the appearance of a battlefield hospital, Doctor Crooke.'

'There is no comparison, Father Lee. This is far worse, believe me,' the doctor answered.

Coming and going from her self, Onóra listened to the heated exchange, broken by shouts for 'water,' and 'something to eat, God save us!'

'You have patients sharing accommodations now?' the priest asked.

'Father Lee, the House is so overcrowded it is near impossible to separate the sick from the healthy and space has rendered it necessary to place two, even three, to a bed in some instances. I've managed to restrict the practice to other wards, for now. But you must recall the House was never envisaged to deal with large numbers of sick at all.'

'When will the House reopen, Doctor?'

'That is beyond my control, Father Lee.'

'I say, you – as physician – are the *only* person to control it, Doctor Crooke.'

'If you can somehow limit the sickness, we can reopen, Father. But neither your god nor mine seems able to accomplish that, sir. In the meantime, I must make do with what I have at my disposal.'

'How many have passed since last I came?'

'More than I care to recollect, Father Lee. Mortality is high, not only due to the appalling conditions, but because nearly every person lately admitted is a patient.'

'So how long? A week?'

'Under the current circumstances, two at least. That is, if the situation does not worsen.'

'Two weeks? With scores outside at any given moment, and hundreds in the probationary wards. And the dead?' the priest asked quietly.

'Committed almost immediately, they pass to the burial ground adjacent.'

'God have mercy on me. That they should go to their deaths with their souls yet burdened, uncomforted by the solace of repentance, or a kind word of prayer. Will you please direct me toward those closest to passing, Doctor?'

'There are two men, swollen up with severe dropsy downstairs; a woman across the hallway very weakened in her breathing – and at least one here. You might begin with that.'

'Thank you, Doctor. I'll see to the men below.'

'Someone stay with me,' a lonely voice whimpered when the doctor and the priest had gone, echoing Onóra's feelings of solitude, as she noticed the shivering and the feeling of cold had returned.

'Don't leave us here alone … please,' the same woman repeated; a young mother, Onóra imagined, though she had no idea what the woman actually looked like.

'Doctor! Nurse!' a man sputtered, grief-stricken. Over and over he called, until, when no one came, he vomited, unaided by anyone.

It was when the staff were away and the calls died down that Onóra felt lowest.

Not far from her, a woman opposite was breathing rapidly. Onóra could not see her from there, but she knew it was her. When Dr Crooke came again, it was to count the speed of that woman's blood as, simultaneously, there came the scutter of Onóra's bowels, squelching in spite of her. Unleashed of their own accord, they relieved some of the sharpening pain in her gut, but sent hot liquid down her legs and up her back, like fire, so that her inside linen was wringing with filth. The passage of her privy felt raw, and she cried. It was better when she was unaware, Onóra thought in misery.

With her gaze fixed upon the roof of the white sky through the broken squares of the casement behind her, for the third or fourth time this day Onóra felt the heat of the liquid growing and spreading throughout her otherwise hardened clothes. 'Pulse at one hundred and thirty,' the Doctor pronounced quietly, perhaps to the nurse.

'Water,' Onóra attempted to say, as feeble and quiet as an old woman at first, then louder with the craving. It was hard to speak, because her throat was so dry.

At that moment the nurse arrived, accompanied by another set of steps.

'The new cook, Doctor, Mr Mahony,' Nurse Dwyer announced.

'Mr Mahony, thank you for coming. As you can see, I have my hands full here and am unable to leave.'

'Of course, sir.'

'Mr Mahony, it is of utmost importance we discuss what you intend to serve as diet to the inmates at this time, that the wrong food be not administered to the detriment of those suffering.'

'I understand, sir.'

At the sound of this, Onóra's stomach might have ejected more, but that there was nothing to send forth.

'You might share – Nurse! A pan, please!' The doctor interrupted himself, apparently at another patient's vomiting.

'Coming, Doctor.'

'What is it you plan to serve, Mr Mahony?' Dr Crooke said, sounding as though he were doing something physical, lifting or turning a patient.

'Certainly, Doctor. For some months since, I have been cook to the Lismore Union Workhouse, administering the soup from Count Rumford's essay there, sir. The same has been adopted to economical effect by Fermoy Union, I'm told.'

'I am unfamiliar with Mr Rumford's recipe, Mr Mahony. Could you elaborate on its substance?'

'I have the rudiments in my notebook here, sir. Would you like me to –'

'Please, Mr Mahony.'

'Yes, sir … In Count Rumford's *Essay on Food*, Soup Number One may consist of barley, peas, salt and water, with cuttings of wheaten bread, or biscuit, in the proportion of one pound of peas and one pound of barley to one gallon of water. Each quart is about two pounds four ounces in weight and costs three farthings. The barley, ground whole, should be given with all the bran. Of course, meat would improve the soup but then the price would be greatly increased. A quantity of peas and barley, in soup, will support a much greater number than if cooked separately. Do you wish to hear all of this, Doctor?'

'Please, Mr Mahony.'

'Yes, sir. The peas, whole, should be soaked –'

'Is it trying to kill us you are? We are dying of hunger, for God's sake.' Seemingly frozen, the young cook stopped reading, when, from the end furthest from the stairwell, a patient protested in torment, the sounds of phlegm impeding his objection.

'Thank you, Mr Mahony, that will suffice,' the doctor said, sheepishly, seeming to recognise the cruelty pointed out to him. 'The reason I inquire is that we're finding soups, and aliment in fluid form, grossly injurious to the gastric condition of those labouring under fevers and dysentery.'

'I understand, sir. If it is agreeable, I will proceed with the use of bread and milk until directed otherwise?'

'Thank you, Mr Mahony.'

'Will that be all, Doctor?'

From her viewpoint, shivering, Onóra watched the young man leaving the ward, a book beneath his arm, away to school like one of those better-off boys.

'Nurse Dwyer?' the doctor called.

'Water!' someone shouted.

'Yes, Doctor?' the nurse answered, arriving.

'When he is next free of obligations, you might tell Father Lee this woman should be next in line for his attentions.'

'Yes, Doctor.'

'And please bring water for those in –' he called after the nurse. 'Blast. I need more staff.'

'Water!' the cry continued.

―――

When Onóra next came to, the priest, across, was babbling his prayers. For some long minutes he talked in Latin over the woman until, at last, it seemed she had died before him.

'Oh, Lord, how many more this day?' Fr Lee whimpered, pitifully, as though alone, and Onóra heard a sound she imagined him dropping to his knees.

'Water … please!' a man begged.

'The Lord's mercy!'

They could not even stop their coughing or crying for the woman's death, Onóra lamented. *Will it be like this when I go?* she pondered, weeping to herself, lying in her own excrement.

To the sound of someone returning, Onóra perceived the priest shuffling to his feet once more.

'How is it outside, Father?' This time Dr Crooke addressed the priest with a sympathetic tone, as though understanding what had preceded his return.

''Tis the same all over Macroom, Doctor. And worsening at an alarming rate. Not one hour before I met you here I was in Massytown, where, after a day of this, I found a living man lying by the side of his dead wife – a corpse since the night before. Half an hour after I acted over him, that mercy denied him in this world was, I hope, vouchsafed him in the next,' the priest elaborated, solemnly. 'When he died, I was tending to another man in the same street – his neighbour, in fact – destroyed by the labour mendicancy of the Public Works. Denis Murphy. A weaver. Dead from hunger before I could finish blessing myself, the poor man. Two men, directly adjacent, expiring within minutes of each other. The population of the town will be decimated if this keeps up. I asked the neighbours how they allowed such an occurrence. The answer I got – if you can imagine it – was "'Twill be our turn next." The tops of leeks, alone, had sustained that man and his family, four in number, for some days before. God help them, that they have one less mouth to feed now.'

'Father Lee, there is one other here.'

'Oh …'

'She's been coming and going from delirium for some days.'

'This poor girleen?' she heard the priest ask, through her dulled senses.

Onóra worried, as footsteps approached – at the mess she was in, soiled and filthy. Was it her they were coming to? she questioned, squeezing her eyes tightly. A touch at her leg brought shock and confirmed it was her they were discussing.

'No! I don't want to die,' Onóra cried, aloud, without deciding to.

'Shhhsh, now.'

'No … No!' She struggled.

'Easy, now. What is your name?'

'No, I'm too young to die!'

Leaning in, the shape of the priest loomed large above, and Onóra hid her face to escape.

'Onóra Waters,' Dr Crooke said, in a gentle voice.

'Water! Water, please!' someone shouted, strained and hoarse.

'Onóra Waters.' The priest repeated her name and, kneeling, moved closer along her berth to find her hands and pull them down from her face.

But something strange: hearing her name, all other sounds in the room seemed to die away, and Onóra found herself surrendered to the sensation of someone taking her hands, clasping between them a string of beads.

Behind her head, as though falling up from the world, the snow looked heavenly, and Onóra felt ready to leave the rest behind.

'Have you any sins to confess, Onóra?' she heard the gravelly voice say, soft, slowing everything down. And although she was shivering, she felt warm and still beneath the touch.

No, she told herself.

'I do not,' she answered.

'Very well, child. Lord have mercy.'

Dr Crooke whispered something to the priest, before his steps creaked upon the floor, leaving.

Allowing her eyes to close again, Onóra felt the crude but careful rub of the priest's strong thumb, spreading his oil across the skin of her forehead, one way and then another. It smelled of something sharp, wild mint, but of something holy and sacred too, making her chest rise of its own accord.

From her brow, the priest moved to mark the same pattern upon her lips, eyes, and ears, incanting strings of words across the air like the circles and knots of those beads gathered between and spilling over the sides of her hands. And as the oil reached her hands and feet, each with a new round of incantations, Onóra's body floated amongst the snowy plumes that filled her eyes. Gone were the jut of the water wheel and the crack of the master's whip.

'Onóra,' she heard from far away.

'Onóra …' It sounded closer, a voice she knew intimately, the face in the water too becoming clear as she stared into the settling ripples.

———

''Tis closed, ma'am. You've divil's hope of getting in,' the old man told Cáit, as she turned up the avenue leading to the Union. Now walking with the aid of a stick, she sighted the eerie group of structures ahead, behind a huge surrounding wall.

Instinctively Cáit felt different to those who, wandering about, lay down on either side, and gathered near the foremost building. They had decided to come here, she reasoned. She was only passing. But otherwise, as she neared the door, it was not hard to realise that she herself was as poor and as frail as most anyone else around her.

'There's no use in knockin', girl,' said a woman, sat on the ground, an old sick man leaning against her, dying, Cáit understood. 'A week since, it's been closed – and if they'll answer at all to any paupers.'

So far as Cáit could tell, the woman wasn't lying. There was a sense that the people scattered around and resting nearby had only lingered because they had not the strength to try their luck anywhere else – but no one was near the door itself.

'Have you come far, dear?' the woman asked. 'If you're left out, you can take the night's shelter by the bridge.'

As exhausted as Cáit was, she had no intention of staying, and something told her to keep her distance, even from those who looked least likely to be carrying the sickness.

'Who are those?' Cáit asked, seeing two men carrying something as though they'd come out through the boundary wall. A moment later they disappeared through the gap of a smaller wall to a field adjoining the grounds.

'The dead, darling. That's the Union burial ground. I wouldn't go in there!' the woman called after her. But with so little time, she could not hold herself.

Ignoring the pain, Cáit rounded the corner of the high wall in pursuit of the same men, who, returning empty-handed, disappeared through a gate somewhere near the far end of the complex. With darkness soon approaching, desperate to find out anything of Onóra, Cáit followed the giant wall for what felt like a hundred yards, to where, coming from behind a tin-covered black gate, she heard the voices of two men.

'Yes, ma'am. Yes, Matron,' they said, subserviently responding to the ill-tempered voice of a woman barking instructions: 'There's another upstairs when you're done with that. And one in the infirmary.'

Cáit startled as the gate opened and the men came through, two paupers struggling with what she now saw was the same long box they had carried in only minutes before – a coffin, she realised in fright.

Turning as they passed her, the man facing seemed stunned and unprepared to be met by anyone outside.

'Please ... could you tell me –' she called after as his eyes kept her gaze.

'I'm sorry, ma'am,' he attempted, before something behind Cáit unnerved him.

'Who are you?! What are you doing up here?' a loud voice boomed, making Cáit jump. Its owner, a sour-faced woman, now blocked the gate with her large presence. The Matron they had been speaking with, Cáit surmised. 'The workhouse is closed t'all admissions. And this is not the entrance for paupers. Clear off out.'

'I am not seeking admission, ma'am.' Cáit blurted her request, afraid, but not put off so easily. 'Please, I'm after word of my sister. She's within.'

'You'll have to inquire with the Guardians around the front,' the woman said, and moved to close the gate.

'But it's closed, ma'am. Please, Onóra Waters, ma'am. Onóra Waters, of Carrigadrohid. I've come an awful long way.'

The woman was taken aback, Cáit felt – hopeful that it was at some recognisance of Onóra's name, if not at her determination and impudence. At the same time, another young woman, appearing inside, looked up to her superior as though in expectation of a response.

'There's no one here of that name. Along with ye now!'

The huge gate screamed as, stopping abruptly but inches from her face, the force of its wind brought Cáit's shawl to flutter about her ears.

'Please, ma'am. I'm to take her home with me,' Cáit cried over the high wall, to the sound of boots marching away behind.

'Have mercy … please!' To an uncaring silence, with her shoulder to the gate, Cáit continued to beg, her voice weaker each time, so overcome with emotion. But, realising it was pointless to expect pity from such a cruel woman, she turned at length and began to walk, weeping at the torment of having come so far only to learn that she might never know more of her sister.

As she limped along, the *pulk* of the stick fell, lonely, between the sounds of Cáit's footsteps, twisting upon the strange surface of tiny broken stones. To her right, the path was hemmed by snow-laden grass. But while the path itself had thawed, the point at which the high wall met the earth to her left remained hidden by a bank of unmelted snow, as though kept frozen by proximity to all that lay inside, impenetrable to kindness and feeling.

But with the next fall of the stick, Cáit heard a click: a quiet but mechanical sound, like a latch. Turning, she was met once more with the face of the younger woman, this time appearing around the gate's edge. Having cautiously gauged it was safe to do so, she came after Cáit with light steps.

'I'm so sorry, ma'am. The Matron is a hard, cross woman. But if 'twas my sister, I'd want to know. You say you're after Onóra Waters?'

'Onóra, yes. What of her?' Cáit covered her ears and contorted her face, frightened at what she was going to hear.

'I'm so sorry, ma'am.'

'No. No. What is it? What?'

'She passed this morning, ma'am.'

'Passed? What do you mean? No! What happened? Oh no! Please …' Feeling herself falling apart from the inside, Cáit grabbed at the girl's arm to stay standing.

'Fever, ma'am. I'm so very sorry. But she went easy, and was seen to by the priest.'

'No! It can't be …' Cáit shrieked to catch her breath, but, devastated, held her mouth.

'Please, ma'am, I must go back. I'm not supposed to be out here.'

'Just this morning? Oh no …'

'I'm sorry, ma'am. I must go now.'

'Thank you. Bless you.' Cáit let go and listened as the gate lock clicked once more.

Though she knew she must go, for what seemed an age, Cáit stayed leaning between the stick and the wall, weeping, until she slid down its cold stone face to be bundled in a slump at the snowy bank of its foot.

With flashes of their childhood, thoughts and memories of Onóra's beautiful face mixed with a horror-filled imagination that but guessed at her suffering in those final moments – and all she must have endured in the months leading up to it. Cáit could not remember their last meeting, but thought it was probably when Diarmuidín was baptised at Inchinlinane. She regretted terribly now that they'd not seen each other since the move to Doire Liath. It had been all she and Pádraig could do to just survive since late Forty-Five. But what long periods of deprivation must have led her to such a lonely, sad end, Cáit wondered, filled with sorrow.

When, booming once more inside, Cáit heard the mean-spirited voice of the matron, she found herself filled with rage. Pulling herself to her feet with the aid of the stick, the nails of her other hand clawing at the wall to climb it, before she knew her own intention, she had battled and struck the tin surface of the gate's face so that, as though inhabited by her voice, it roared in anger and tore the air, echoing violently.

When this time the matron's face appeared, it was with an altogether changed expression. At discovering Cáit wielding the stick high above her head, ready to strike the door again, this time it was she that wore the fright. 'Agh!' Wide-eyed, the woman recoiled, cowering at what she must have perceived an incoming blow.

'You heartless, uncaring wretch of a woman,' Cáit bellowed, the liquid of her tears wet and cold upon her cheeks and her chin, 'all you see is paupers, and corpses! Can you not see people … with feelings, and memories, with love for their children and their loved ones? With hopes and fears?' Feeling herself baring the whites of her eyes, unsteady and shaking, Cáit lowered the stick to lean upon it. 'You treat us as if we are already *dead* … as if we were *born* dead … Well, we are *not* dead … We are alive! And if you cannot see that, then perhaps it is *you* who is dead inside … Go on, close your door … close it on your own soul!'

To the sound of the gate locking for the last time, Cáit turned away, shocked by Onóra's death and by her own anguish in the face of it.

For the guts of a mile she limped aimlessly toward home; up the Sop Road to the sound of the river, then out towards the hills, until the last few of her kind dwindled to solitude and she was crunching the snow in relative silence once more, the rhythm of her limp badly uneven. Out among the elements with nothing but her grief and the intensifying bite of hunger, the road led Cáit closer with every step to utter weariness and exhaustion.

Although she had not promised outright, when she'd left that morning, Cáit had had every intention of trying to fulfil Pádraig's request of her. Her plan had been to look for the scelp on the way back, and, if it did not take too much out of her, to try and remove the clothes from the poor soul he had dragged out of the snow that night. The value of their warmth was not lost on her and she knew how attached Pádraig had become to the idea.

But by now, it had become an altogether unrealistic and potentially fatal task. With half her journey still to go, her pace much slowed, and darkness but an hour or so away, it would be task enough to make it home safely at all, let alone before the night's cold set in.

Limping on, her pace weakened to such a slow drip that, as dusk came on, she felt as though she was making no progress at all.

The whine of the wind seemed to rise up in torment when, with a dart of agony, Cáit wondered if that had been Onóra's body the men were carrying past her outside. But, deciding she could not afford to dwell on such things now, Cáit was forced to contemplate the very real danger she was in. If she did not get home soon, she would likely not survive the night. Instead of bringing home Pádraig's wages and more of the dead man's clothes, it now looked as though the wages would go to the benefit of whoever found her – in just the same way as the shoes had come to her husband.

Undertaking the trip had been foolhardy and far too much of a risk, she now realised. Helpless at home, her family would starve, unable to do anything for themselves, or for her. Distraught and faint, feeling she was saying goodbye to her life, Cáit followed step after weakened step, praying that by some miracle, in her absence, her family would be spared, to somehow survive and see through this terrible time.

'Help me, Onóra,' she called to her sister, and lifted her face to the sky, only to discover by the first flakes – gently kissing her brow and settling among the lashes of her eye – that a drift of snow had begun to fall.

Still she traipsed forward and, just as she had on the way in, bade her feet follow the tracks of hooves and wheels that had beaten down the snow to the frozen mud beneath.

Cáit did not see the slush-filled rut that splashed and caught her feet so that she stumbled and, losing balance, found herself meeting the cold road with a hard landing at her shoulder.

'Pádraig,' she moaned, and with her eye at ground level sighted the channel of the wheel track stretching out before her. Through the ice-cold snow against her head, Cáit imagined she could hear them … the horses pulling … wheels veering under the creaking car, cutting their way through the snow, traces jingling in harness … hooves and wheels … louder and nearer as she closed her eyes. Tired … the sharp coldness inside her breath … moisture soaking her through on one side, and new snow falling upon the other.

'Whoa! Whoa!' came the voice of a man as the hooves stopped and the creaking, moaning sound of metal seemed to settle almost above her. 'Easy now.'

The hot air of the horse's breath sprayed across her face, snorting, physically excited, out of its gallop.

'Oh dear.' The footsteps came down. 'Are you alive? Hello? ma'am? Can you hear me?'

Cáit moaned, hoping to enlist the stranger's help in finding Onóra. 'My sister,' she tried to say.

'Dear God, you're alive. Can you get – of course you can't, you're lying on the … road.' The man's voice laboured as he sat her up. 'Now, can you hear me, madam?' Two hands gripped her at the shoulders.

'I can …'

'Here, drink this.'

A liquid brought to her lips, though cold, poured fire upon her mouth and throat. Instantly spluttering, so strong and bitter was its taste, Cáit shivered, awakened at the core. She had swallowed most, but was aware of the horrible sound she made, trying to regain her air.

'Yes, it has that effect, certainly. But it may revive you.'

Some class of spirits, Cáit thought. Its effects had brought her to her senses somewhat, though she struggled still to understand what had happened.

'Come on,' the voice said, 'let's get you up. The Glebe in Clondrohid, I go that far. Were you headed that way?'

'Clondrohid! Yes!' Cáit answered loudly, displaying her relief, then groaned at the pain in her ribs as, feeling herself lifted onto the car, she opened her eyes and, trying to focus, saw the form of a man, in fine dress. His clothes were dark. But it was the white preaching tabs, falling down from his neck, that, even through her soft vision, registered in Cáit's mind as being part of a Protestant minister's attire. The Glebe, he had said. *Of course.*

'Reverend Kyle, Madam. Can you tell me your name?' His voice had a northern edge, and sounded educated.

'Ua Buachalla,' she managed to get out, 'Cáit Ua Buachalla.'

'Ua Buachalla? Good. Good. Here, I'll put this over you and we'll get going.'

From under the seat, the man retrieved a coat and hung it about her shoulders, then, taking the reins, eased the horse back into a gentle pace, though the car bumped and threw them at first, traversing the rut she had fallen into.

'Are you able for food?' he asked, a ring of caution in his tone.

'I am. Please. Bless you.'

'A little bread …' The end of a loaf was produced from the bag he wore across his person, and as Cáit began to eat, he took a small chunk more and offered it too.

'Thank you,' she said, and, taking it from him, attempted to maintain an element of dignity while chewing, putting the second piece inside her shawl.

Returning to her senses, Cáit contemplated just how close she had come to her own death: were it not for the torch attached to the vehicle, its driver could not navigate at this hour and would never have found her.

Swaying this way and that, blinking, hypnotised by the music of ringing hooves, the last thing Cáit registered as she felt herself slipping to dreams was the silhouetted majesty of a giant tree. Fallen back away from the road, its wide, ancient trunk glistened with ice among the shadows; its roots, broken from the ground, pointing to the sky.

MÁRTA

MARCH

17

A Worse Hunger

At the first sound of Cáit approaching the door, Pádraig pulled himself up frantically to open it. Closing it as quickly behind her and dropping to his knees, he poured water into the skillet heating over the fire.

On either side the desperation of the waiting children was palpable as Cáit untied the bag and poured the yellow flour into the sizzling liquid. Instantly, the powder formed lumps and islands, as though to resist the water. But, mixing the lot, Pádraig doused and broke them against the sides until, with the consistency of mud, the resulting paste began to resemble the dense flat cake that would be the griddle bread. Sweet intoxicating smells filled the cabin as, transfixed, all stared ravenous over the substance.

Impatient at the sight of bubbles appearing through the surface, Cáit shovelled and flipped the batter over so that it seared and spat violently, sending wafts of steam up Pádraig's nose, intensifying the agony of his hunger.

Seconds later his hands were in the pot, jostling to grab as big a piece as he could stuff into his mouth of what tasted like fire and smoke, unable to swallow fast enough as the drive engulfed his senses. Around, and within, were the sounds of mouths tossing their prize amid piping heat; hands fumbling amongst each other and ripping the bread away; everybody inhaling each morsel faster than the last. Somewhere inside himself Pádraig had the sense of a wild animal devouring a live creature, pinned down and torn apart lest it break free from his clutches and bolt, leaving him famished, and desperate to survive.

Swift and blackened, the hands came and went until the last crumbs that clung to the sides were being scraped out by Cáit's spoon. Attacked by the children as they left, Pádraig gulped the last chunk from his hand, sending it down with barely a bite.

The frenzy over, it took great restraint on Pádraig's part to not suggest they cook more. But by the amount already gone out of the small sack, he knew they had eaten too much. In their haste they had not measured the flour and would be eating smaller amounts in days ahead to conserve what was left. When that was gone, they would fast again until more could be got and the cycle would begin anew.

At the sight of Diarmuidín and Síle still hungry and searching the floor like scavengers, Pádraig felt a ferocious guilt. They had all eaten something, he had told himself while shoving the last bite into his mouth, but only in proportion to their size. The most disturbing realisation was that, on some level, part of him had been ready to guard his share, compelled to fill his own belly first, he had noticed. Watching on as they searched their hands now, Pádraig was startled and horrified. That – overwhelmed by greed – he would put his own needs first, before those of his children! There and then, he vowed never to be ruled by hunger again where it came to feeding his family. But a shame that would haunt him for many days yet had already taken root, Pádraig sensed. Looking to Cáit, he saw great sadness on her and, by her stare, imagined she could see inside of him.

It was a devastating thought, he reflected, that – even with food in his gut – there was a hunger worse than hunger still. Foreign to his soul, it was consuming him from the inside.

18

The Chime of Eleven

On a weary Monday morning, feeling unwell and not himself, James Burdon sat at his desk adjacent the boardroom of Macroom Union Workhouse.

It had been a task to venture out this day, given his condition. But following the Guardians' meeting of Saturday last, it was his paramount task to put to tender the numerous positions left vacant by members of staff lately deceased.

But one month to the day since, he had advertised the positions of master and of schoolmaster, and thankfully both those places had been settled. Outstanding yet were the appointments of two competent wardmasters, one wardmistress, and a licensed apothecary. There was also the matter of issuing a repeat notice for a nursetender to the infirmary: unanswered thus far, despite being re-advertised already, one week ago, on March first.

The position of second physician to the workhouse was one no longer requiring attention. Though officially that had gone unanswered too, the advertisement had been a mere formality, it being concluded from the outset that Valentine McSwiney would be the only candidate considered come the election on February twenty-seventh.

Coughing politely, Burdon produced a rag from his pocket and mopped his nose and mouth before stuffing it back into its velvety purse.

The repeat notice to begin with, Burdon decided – for which the hard work was already done. He merely needed copy his notice of the week before and correct the date.

Opening last Monday's *Constitution*, for reference, Burdon brought his pen to the new page and blew out his cheeks to unblock the inflated feeling of his sinuses. Focusing on where, and where not, to use capital letters, he transcribed exactly:

<u>MACROOM UNION</u>

ELECTION OF A NURSETENDER.
THE GUARDIANS of this UNION will, at their
MEETING to be held on SATURDAY the 13th
MARCH Instant, elect a competent NURSETENDER
at a Salary of Ten Pounds a-year and rations.
         By Order of the Board,
            JAMES BURDON,
                Clerk of the Union,
Macroom, 8th March, 1847.

The last dot put to the first notice, Burdon released a wistful sigh.

A glance to the clock confirmed the next dispatch was two and half hours away. He *could* proceed straight to the next notice, he considered, or, instead, do something that felt distinctly uncharacteristic: abandon his all-consuming duties momentarily and follow the overwhelming urge he had to talk to another human being.

James could never bring home to his wife most of what he witnessed at work. But neither was there anyone here he could relate to as an equal. Forming an isolated bridge between the Guardians – who held little or no respect for him – and the many hundred paupers he wished to stay as far from as possible, the position of Clerk to the Union had, to James Burdon, become a distinctly lonely one. An island amongst an unending stream of human traffic, the occupation that, but a few short years ago, had promised great security was now an extremely dangerous one.

For many months it had been in James' mind to answer a letter from his cousin, John Walsh, and, staring out the window now, his utter loneliness led him to suddenly feel he could delay it not a minute longer. There would never be a convenient time to divert from his endless tasks. But James had awoken with a frightening sense that, did he not soon stop to consider his troubled feelings, fate might overrun him. Picking up his pen, Burdon hurriedly drew another sheet of paper and began:

My dear Cousin,

I beg you will forgive of me my tarrying reply. As you know, the position I hold here places great demand upon my time and requires that I be present during many hours each day. The journey from Currahaly to Macroom alone – one hour each way six days of the week – only adds to the accumulated time so that I am scarcely at home with Mary and the children at all. I fear I have become a stranger there.

Burdon paused to cough again, when his pen touching the desk coincided with a loud knock.

'Yes,' he called out, hiding the page upon his lap. Mr Powell, the porter, he supposed. But Edmond Walsh instead appeared, showing only his head and neck around the top half of the door.

'Mr Walsh, good morning, sir,' Burdon offered, with the nursetender notice positioned to feign its finishing touches.

'And to you, Mr Burdon. I am out of coal again and don't see the porter. Could you have him bring some to my quarters?'

'Of course, sir. Will that be all?'

'Thank you,' Walsh said, retreating.

'Very well, sir.'

Even with the Master gone, Burdon waited some moments before raising the letter again from below. On February seventeenth, 'Edmond Walsh of Carriganimma' had been elected to the mastership by a majority of fourteen to seven at the Guardians' choosing. But here, a fortnight later, Burdon still quietly maintained they had picked the wrong man.

'If hereditary integrity and personal worth be recommendations, a better selection we could not have made,' Edward Ashe had announced jovially, congratulating his friend.

James Burdon himself was not so sure. If Walsh was all Ashe said he was, what need would he have to take the position of Master of the Workhouse during this, the lowest, most explosive and pestilence-ridden ebb in its short history? Pending Walsh's ability to re-establish order, Burdon had decided to reserve judgement and nothing had changed his mind yet.

The one candidate Burdon *had* thought worthy was not even the recipient of the seven opposing votes counted against Walsh. Thomas T. Herley, it was, had Burdon's eye. Unknown to the board, but clearly an industrious individual, *he* had questioned *them* on various matters, including salary. Insisting their offer was much too low, he withdrew before voting even began.

I know you wished me to recommend you for a position here,

he continued,

but take my word on the matter: a Union Workhouse is no place you'd wish to find yourself, especially at this juncture. Macroom WH accommodates – rather *holds* – fourteen hundred paupers currently. As by no possible mode of compression could a greater number of human beings be crammed together, the Guardians have been compelled to rent a large store in the town, to shelter many others awaiting admission. So habituated are all here to seeing wretched beings lying down to die in every part of it, but the last resource of the destitute is now closed in consequence of the severely overcrowded state of the House.

A dreadful fever rages within. Even the Master succumbed, the schoolmaster too, among others. The Matron, schoolmistress, and the nurse are at present in its clutches. Needless to say, the inmates themselves are falling into the grave by the score. And yet, there is great pressure to reopen. How can the House reopen, I ask, when not only the inmates are dying, but the staff like so many flies, too?

Death is now shorn of a great many of its terrors and I wonder that I myself am becoming far too accustomed to it.

Filled with melancholy, Burdon closed his eyes.

The bother to his chest and to his senses: he wanted to put that down to the strange clouds of dust blowing in from the east all week on cold, harsh winds. But the muscular pain and the gastric symptoms – he could not put those down to dust.

Unsure if he should divulge so much of his feelings, to his cousin or even himself, James Burdon stared frozen at the empty part of the page until, set in motion by a telling click, the chime of eleven struck. He had yet to draw the other notice up. But if he finished the letter quickly, he could send the lot at once, he decided.

Broken from the trance, the weight of his obligations felt once more, Burdon would have to finish the letter and get on and finish his work.

I very much fear that before a month expires there will be great difficulty getting sufficient food for either the workhouse or the town. The price of carriage has more than doubled in six weeks due to the carriers' horses dying in great numbers and almost all of our provisions travel from Cork.

As we are not to have government railways in Ireland, I think some of the well-fed cavalry horses at Ballincollig – a distance of fifteen Irish miles – should be employed by Government to deliver meal for the Relief Committees. By this a considerable saving of their expenditure would be effected.

It would be far better that those idle horses should assist in the transport of food for our starving people, than be seen prancing in all the pride of mimic warfare within the walls of Ballincollig.

Speaking of which – given its proximity to Iniscarra, I propose you look for a position at the gunpowder mills.

My sister Helena speaks of you often.

I remain, your Obdt Servant,
James.

19

THE OTHER PLACE

'You, sir. Are you not the husband of Cáit, the woman I found in the snow?' Reverend Kyle asked Pádraig, as he reached the top of the queue.

'I am,' Pádraig replied, understanding the question translated for him.

'Your *name*, sir?' Reverend Kyle asked, in quick succession.

Patrick Buckley, Pádraig almost volunteered, his instinct sparked at hearing the English word he had met with so many mornings on the works.

'Is mise *Máirtín Ua Buachalla*,' he answered instead, thankful for his presence of mind, holding fast to the preconceived plan. 'I am Máirtín Ua Buachalla,' he added, just the way Cáit had coached him.

Regarding him with pity, Pádraig felt, the inquisitive rector looked him up and down, and, considering his feet, issued some quiet instruction to the man dishing up the soup. Doing as he was instructed, it seemed, the same man delivered a generous helping to Pádraig, who thanked them with a nod and turned away.

He was tired and it was cold still, but, walking out towards the mountains, Pádraig felt light. Perhaps with the strains of exhaustion, he imagined. At three miles distant, Reverend Kyle's Glebe was still more than half-way to Macroom.

A month had passed since the February snow; it had taken him until mid-March to recover from the damage. But, leaning upon the crutch he had fashioned, Pádraig had managed to reach Clondrohid at last, where the soup committee at the Protestant church had decreed that while offered to all others at a halfpenny a quart, soup would be given gratuitously to widows and the sick. Clearly unfit to work, Pádraig had qualified and gratefully availed of the benefit until he walked the strength back into his legs.

But feeding the family required more than a single soup ration. So with the last of the wages Cáit had collected, it was with a stone of flour upon his shoulder this day he was returning home.

For now they had meal, Pádraig accepted. But they desperately needed a new plan.

There was another new burden that weighed on him, however. With the Protestant Glebe house being at the far end of Clondrohid, heading for home he had to pass the Catholic church, and Pádraig kept his head low approaching it. Among the queue there, of mostly widows, were the sets of eyes that set their glares upon him like stones hurled from a sling. As far as they were concerned, the meal he was carrying could only have been got from one location, and that was *the other place*. He might have carried it all the way from Macroom, he reasoned. But somehow they seemed to know, and nor could he hide it from himself.

Pádraig tried not to care what they thought. Each family had to do what was necessary for survival and he was doing what was best for his. Their decision to go to the Glebe instead of St Abina's had not come easy and he had taken a lot of convincing after Cáit got back from Macroom. But in the end, everything had pointed to this being the only way.

As Pádraig saw it, their situation was complicated by his falling off the works in Macroom. There was no way he could go back to Fr O'Brien asking to be put on the lists again for Carriganimma or anywhere else – not when he'd left the place he was already given, and hundreds behind him still waiting for any turn at all. Maybe the priest would have understood. But at the risk of being refused – ending any chance of his resubmission to the lists – Pádraig had reasoned his only option was to go to Rev. Kyle, who was also on the Relief Committee and, consequently, had the power to add him too. He would just have to submit himself by a different name there, to conceal the fact he'd been on the lists before, he'd decided.

But there had been another reason to give his name as false.

'The Reverend, as soon as he heard my name, asked me if my husband was Pádraig, or Patrick,' Cáit had recalled to him, back from the snow. 'The pawnbroker, Creed, requested he look out for a man of that name,' she said Kyle had told her. 'Pádraig Ua Buachalla, or Patrick Buckley,' she'd repeated.

Mercifully, even delirious, Cáit had been present enough in her mind to feign weariness or incomprehension at the question.

Contemplating what the pawnbroker could possibly want with him, Padraig had considered that, pawning the shoes, he'd been given ten months to redeem his pledge. If not redeemed by then, his debt would be cancelled and considered a sale. He'd keep the money and the broker the shoes. But those ten months had long since passed and that the man would come looking for him now made no sense at all. Either way, parting with any of the wages that were all that stood between his family and the dirt had not felt like any trouble to be invited and, lest he had it wrong, Pádraig was not going to take any chances.

He'd not be able to pawn the dead man's shoes at the same shop now, was the only thing. He'd heard of many a huckster cropping up across the barony lately, though. Maybe he'd go to one of those. There was another pawnbroker in Macroom, too, he remembered.

However he would do it, it was the question of the dead man's shoes and pawning them that Pádraig's thoughts had moved to now as, struggling up the hill, he could sense the door to home.

But more important, he considered, was how, wisely, they would spend the money?

This time last year they would have put it all to seed. No question. But there were grave doubts about the wisdom of such a decision this season.

Pádraig had yet to sound out Taidghí Críodáin and his brother on their plans. But no matter what came of that discussion, if it *was* to be seed they'd decide upon, he would need to bed it in soon or wait all the way to October for it to flower with the late crop. To get the seed at all, though, he would first have to pawn the dead man's shoes, Pádraig thought, his tired mind going in circles.

The sense of lightness long gone off him, leaning on the crutch with his hand to the door, Pádraig was far from sure he could manage a trip to find a huckster yet, let alone a broker beyond in Macroom.

But with a stone of meal to let down inside, for now hunger was everything.

———

'It'll be time to pawn the shoes soon,' Pádraig told Cáit, when the madness of his hunger had been bought off for another while.

'Will it be?' she returned, seemingly asking for more of his plan.

'Question is, do we put to seed what we get for the shoes, or obey sense and spend it on meal – so that at least we're sure to get something for it?' he suggested, watching her carefully.

Her silence left to hang in the air, Pádraig sensed a heaviness on her: the grief that she'd been wearing for poor Onóra, he imagined. 'Sounds like you've your mind made up,' she said, looking away.

'If we put seed in, we might get nothing again, come the autumn. But if we don't have food in the meantime, there might be nothing left of *us* by the time we find out,' he said, attempting worriedly to discourage her from dwelling in sadness, through something that required her attention anyway.

Combing her fingers through Diarmuidín's hair, Cáit stayed quiet another while – mulling over their dilemma, Pádraig hoped.

'Husband, sometimes you have to take two risks to get only half of what you wish for,' she said, leaving Pádraig at a loss for her meaning.

'Look at what came of my mistake, walking to Macroom.' Turning, Cáit looked him squarely in the face. 'I know, I learned my sister is dead, and I almost died in the snow. But something good came of it too. If I hadn't gone, there'd have been no wages, and without them we'd surely be dead by now. But I met that Reverend Kyle, is more, and, when all other options seemed finished to us, that has made the difference since. We could never have survived on five shillings this long, but the soup held us out till you could walk. There's surely a lesson in all of that?'

'Oh, we're paying enough in other ways,' Pádraig argued, the judging stares still fresh in mind. But his point was aimless. Everything she said was true. And still, he was confused somehow. It was as though she was making two points at once, or was lost somewhere between.

'Reverend Kyle is a good man, Pádraig. No one is asking us to give up our God. That night I got back, and you cried on me, and I cried on you, and we held onto each other crying. Weren't you glad to have me home then?'

'Of course I was!'

'Well, wouldn't you never want to feel that kind of sadness ... if I didn't make it back and I was lost to you altogether? If you lost me, or one of the children, God forbid. Maybe all of us, gone at once. Look at them!' she urged him, with pain in her voice.

Staring at her, and at the sleeping children, Pádraig understood perfectly what she meant in that sense. 'But what about seed?'

'What I'm saying is, I think we have to do both,' Cáit said. 'You are right. Blight or no blight, if we put it all to seed, there might be nothing left of us to meet it, come the autumn. But if we don't put seed in, we'll have nothing left anyway by the time the harvest comes around, and with nothing in the ground what'll we do then, come winter, next spring, and next summer? The answer has to be we bet on both.'

Pádraig lowered his head and, staring into the fire, understood at last. They had to risk everything in two different ways.

Clerk

To the clink of an empty bottle rolling across the floor, French startled himself awake and, still drunk, went straight to the WANTS A SITUATION column of the *Examiner* he'd picked up stumbling home from the Bridge Tavern the night before.

Sighting hard with one eye closed, he spotted the word MACROOM.

MACROOM UNION

THE GUARDIANS of this UNION will, on SATURDAY, the 27th day of MARCH, Instant, appoint a

CLERK OF UNION

in room of Mr. BURDON, deceased, at a Salary of £50 per annum.

Sealed proposals mentioning the names of Two Solvent sureties to be forwarded to me before the hour of Meeting, 12 o'Clock, Noon, when the personal attendance of the Candidates will be necessary.

By order of the Board,

THOMAS T. HERLEY,

Clerk of Union, *pro tempore.*

March 15th, 1847.

'God's blood!' French exclaimed, standing to meet the shock when, keeling to one side, he knocked another bottle down, reaching out to stop himself. Inside his skull the lancing pain made him close his eyes hard. 'Devil curse you,' he spat, hoarse and low, in reply.

Smashing instantly, the second bottle had not been empty, French now realised, its acrid contents wafting up from the floor: the urine from earlier that morning, when he'd been too inebriated to go to the bucket, he remembered. Disgusted, not only by the smell of the fast-spreading fluid, but by himself too, fermented with liquor and sweat, French ran coughing for the corner and retched his bile into the bucket – where he should have gone in the first instance, his mind taunted.

Cooling his back against the cold wall, Thomas French groaned miserably, sorry for himself, but for Mr Burdon too. Picking the *Examiner* up again, he took himself to squat upon the low bed where his knees brought it almost to his chest. 'Oh, a shame to hear of it, Mr Burdon,' French mourned, reading the article once more, 'from one clerk to another. I hope you didn't suffer.'

Despite his anguish, however, French couldn't help but allow his eyes to settle upon the line that mentioned salary. 'Fifty pounds,' he read, now more alert. A dangerous job it most certainly was. But such an amount was nearly enough to blind a man to that!

French's own advertisement – *seeking* a situation as clerk – could not have been more poorly timed, he now knew, landing one month since, just when pawnbrokers the county over had begun to shut. Devastatingly, it had brought nothing but silence. But at this, it might have been answered yet; his mother looking down on him, to help him from his fallen slump, French imagined, with a tearful smile.

He had been all but forgotten by the Creeds, French felt. They hadn't even bothered to find out why he'd been coming and going as he pleased lately. *I might as well be dead,* he had grown often to think aloud, drunk and alone in the darkness of his house, listening to the rats.

But were he to become *Clerk of the Union* – a job he was almost certain he could manage – French would have no need to trouble himself with the Creeds, or their wretched shop and stores, any longer. Undoubtedly, they'd been good to him – before the crisis had sent Mr Creed over the edge of his nerves. French felt so angry that they had abandoned him at such a time. They had needed to look out for themselves, perhaps. But he needed to do likewise now, and fifty pounds was over twice what Mr Creed paid. With that, he would move himself into much better accommodations, perhaps even make himself attractive to a woman of equal standing. He might meet a member of the staff at Macroom Union! Someone to settle down with when all of this passed over.

All he had to do was clean himself up, French thought. A glance confirmed the appointment date as March twenty-seventh. Just over a week away. Standing again, more sure-footed at last, French searched the remaining soldiers upon the table and found one still half full. A sniff confirmed it was reasonably safe. 'To your honour, Mr Burdon.'

Tipping it back, French felt the warm, stale brew race to the back of his throat. Vile, it made him shiver. The other bottles jingled as he replaced it alongside them, uttering a noise of disgust.

But for the first time in weeks, there was a sense of possibility, French thought, staring at the darkened walls. Too sick now, he would sleep a while longer and clean himself up later.

Máirtín

'The lists! How did I never think to check the lists?' Creed had shouted to himself, struck by his almost obscene dereliction. In all the weeks since Rev. Kyle had come to him, clutching a ticket from a pauper in Clondrohid, Creed had never thought to consider that, not only might Pádraig Ua Buachalla be alive, he might even be somewhere near! The lists! The Macroom and Clondrohid Relief Committee even sat together – a singularity across the barony of West Muskerry and its sixteen parishes – and being on that committee himself, Creed had access to those relief lists!

It seemed ridiculous now, but what was even more astonishing was that when he did check the lists Creed found that, right under his nose, one 'Patrick Buckley' – of Clondrohid – had been on the Macroom works all along! Until mid-February, five weeks since, that was, when the same man suddenly vanished, having not returned to the works after collecting his last wages.

Though he continually dismissed it, Creed had the recurrent sense that pursuing these thoughts was potentially dangerous: that they led a path back to that strange realm where suffering in the dark for a whole month had sometimes felt like the briefest of moments, while at other times an eon. He could just abandon the whole idea, he supposed, and get on with recovering. But it felt to Creed that *not* getting the shoes back to Ua Buachalla, now that he was possibly still alive, might lead somewhere even worse.

He was not just chasing a ghost to some pointless, maddened end, Creed told himself. Ever since that terrible moment of reckoning in the stores, Pádraig Ua Buachalla had come to represent all his moral wrongs and, now – since he had checked the lists – a potential path to correcting them.

Over and over in his mind Creed foresaw himself handing the shoes back to that young father, and, in doing so, imagined a giant burden lifted from his soul. The hows and wheres were yet to be unveiled. But the promise of attaining something higher resided beyond his instincts, Creed felt.

Of course, any logical mind would question if the Buckley on the list and the Ua Buachalla from the shop were one and the same person, he reminded himself, halfway through his journey out. But they had to be, Creed was almost certain. The pieces all just fit too well!

Once over the anguish he'd felt at realising he had barely missed finding the Patrick Buckley on the works, thinking practically, Creed had next considered what information he *did* have to go on. A man simply dropping off the public works was never a good sign, he had come to learn. Invariably, it meant the man was either dead, nearly dead, or gone to the dreaded Union Workhouse. But finding no trace at either the recently closed Union or at Dr McSwiney's dispensary had only fuelled Creed's hopes afresh.

Fr O'Brien, the Catholic parish priest of Clondrohid, was the man most likely to have put Ua Buachalla on the lists. But, seeming guarded – perhaps unsurprisingly so – the priest had treated the questions of a pawnbroker with suspicion and that proved a dead end too.

Between trips to Clondrohid and local inquiries throughout March, Creed knew he had spent far more time trying to raise the elusive pauper than he ought. But the one last thing he wanted to try, before he might be out of ideas, or before Paulellen would begin to ask questions, was to talk again with Reverend Kyle, Clondrohid's Protestant rector.

Of all the avenues he'd planned to search, this was the least likely to bear fruit, Creed believed. Not only for the fact that a house of the opposing faith was the one source of charity most Catholics avoided, but also because Creed had already asked Kyle to look for Pádraig Ua Buachalla. But that was near two months ago and Kyle had reported nothing since.

Yet, climbing off his car at Clondrohid, the sight of so many paupers lining up excited Creed's hopes afresh. He had forgotten all about Kyle's soup kitchen and, landing as it was underway, Creed realised his timing could not have been better. In anticipation of meeting the rector, he did feel a *little* foolish, however. For what might Kyle think of his expending so much energy chasing this one elusive figure, he thought?

He would announce himself under another guise, Creed decided, and unpacked his writing equipments from the car. That would do it.

Intent on examining as many individuals as he could among their ranks, he had purposely halted *outside* the gate, that he might walk the queue at his leisure: inevitably, he would be greeted by Kyle and, from that point on, at the mercy of someone else's guidance. Whatever insight the rector might share would come regardless. But given this might be his last throw of the dice, Creed was determined to be thorough.

With the horse tethered, passing into the churchyard, Creed estimated the line comprised a hundred souls or thereabouts; each weary member downcast so that their true heights were obscured when viewed from behind. Most of their heads were covered, Creed noticed, hidden beneath the hoods of the ever-present black shawls to shield them from the rain, which – falling in light but incessant sheets – was of the kind particular to March.

With the realisation that the group was made of mostly women – with little or no representation of taller men among it – Creed's heart faltered once more. Yet still he looked to each face, hoping for some revelation.

Faint voices carried from out of the far distance, he observed, while amongst those nearest, who would wait longest, there was only silence. But no sooner had he named the void than, perhaps awoken by his striding, from the loosened hands of the forlorn soul Creed was passing, there dropped a wooden bowl that made its hollow plea upon the ground beside him. Though its language differed, the sounds it made were words still, from a voice to fit its owner's hunger. Stooping to collect her bowl, Creed caught but a glimpse of the woman, who hid her face from his. Though instinct bade him lend his aid, for the sake of the woman's pride, he walked on.

The line did not lead to, but bypassed, the small glebe church nearer the road, Creed had noticed, with the kitchen erected outside the larger residential edifice, much further in. This was likely in consideration of the poor's aversion to accepting soup from the Established Church, and the resulting stigma it brought them, Creed theorised.

In Donoughmore, a couple of parishes over, it was reputed 'strangers' were going to the poor, distributing tracts and papers, saying, 'No wonder the potato has perished in your country, you have no Bible!' Another story Creed had heard was of the Bibles handed out by one Mr Cotter to the poor of that same district – 'Books' the people took home and used on the fire to boil up the meal they'd been given as bribes!

Yet, while rumours of such things were not in short supply, so far as Creed could tell, Rev. Kyle was not the kind to seek conversions in return for his charity. Kyle was kinder and smarter too, Creed believed. He would most certainly have pondered the repercussions of such details as the kitchen's location.

Though an array of chimneys were visible from the road, the bulk of the inordinately large house that only now appeared was made invisible to passers on the road by the encirclement of grand trees that must have made for elegant grounds many acres deep, Creed estimated. But in the immediate moment, he was only concerned with the group of people leading toward it.

They were a collection of grave and dejected faces that revealed an aspect of masked humanity to Creed's senses. Moving faster than they were, he had the impression of a chain of souls disappearing one by one into a void somewhere behind him, until, finally nearing the front, he accepted that no one resembling Ua Buachalla was among them.

'Mr Creed, to what do we owe this unannounced pleasure?' came Kyle's greeting, tall and noble coming out of the house. Kyle's features had always put Creed in mind of the youthful Robert Emmet. 'Have you come to see our kitchen?'

'Reverend Kyle! It took longer than I thought, but I got to accepting your invitation, eventually,' Creed returned, restraining his joviality out of respect for the condition of those around him.

'Many underestimate the encumbrance of the slight climb toward the hills, Mr Creed. Where is your car? You surely didn't come by coach?'

'No, no, I set down just beyond the gate, there, lest my wheels flick mud upon those availing of your kindness, Reverend Kyle.' Turning, Creed took the opportunity to view the last few faces that, interrupted, he had not yet chanced to see.

'That'll be one penny, ma'am,' the server told the girl at the front who, having produced her money, departed in haste with her soup.

'So you've come to us in your professional capacity, Mr Creed?'

While Creed had become fixated upon the queue's foremost members – three women and a middle-aged man – Kyle appeared to have spotted his writing satchel, and, remarking, sought to recover his attention.

'I'd like to submit a report on your operation, Reverend Kyle.'

'Oh, this is very good news.'

'With your permission, of course, sir?'

'The more public notice we can call to our enterprise the better, Mr Creed. Let me show you the running of it?'

Though now greatly preoccupied with the subject of the customer they potentially shared, following the rector's prompts, Creed began a summary description of the soup kitchen. After all, he *had* brought his notebook, and Kyle's initiative was more than worthy of an article. Taking note of the three boilers, Creed recorded the primary benefactors along with a list of those exemplars of the community deserving of praise for their charitable donations: that their selfless charity should be 'made known, as incentive to others', at the rector's suggestion. Creed's own feelings at the level of degradation on display, too, were made mention of in his notes.

Various other nuanced details documented of his own accord were, admittedly, unlikely to be relevant to his article. But Creed indulged himself nonetheless, taking note of the spoked fanlight that spanned the wide doorway with its carved timber pilasters on either side.

'Reverend Kyle, as I'm here, I don't suppose you ever heard more of the young man I mentioned to you back in my shop?'

'Oh, forgive me, Mr Creed. I did ask my staff here when I returned that day, but nothing turned up that I recollect. Then, I've been so preoccupied with our kitchen …'

'I understand, of course,' Creed said, embarrassed at having asked.

'Mrs Stephenson, did you ever come upon a – what was the name, Mr Creed?'

'Pádraig Ua Buachalla, or indeed, "Patrick Buckley", as it might be rendered.'

'I know no one of that name, I'm afraid, sir,' the elderly woman replied, addressing Kyle alone. 'I expect there are many Buckleys here though. And Patrick, of course, is very common.' Though not meaning to sound unfriendly, Creed gauged, the woman's tone was dismissive and dour.

'Come to think of it,' Kyle's expression changed to one of scrutiny, 'I recall now we had one possible candidate: a Buckley or Ua Buachalla, with no English, you say?'

'That's right!' Creed encouraged him.

'This man … he had definitely no access to shoes, though – walked with the use of a makeshift crutch; feet in a terrible state of recovery – from having worked so long with none, I expect.'

'That would be in line with the man I seek, Reverend Kyle.' Creed fought to conceal his excitement. The rector had apparently confused one detail, thinking he was to seek out a person *with* shoes, not one who had pawned his. But that was a minor detail of no consequence, Creed decided.

'This fellow went by the name of Máirtín, though,' Kyle said, and shook his head, evidently remembering, 'I don't suppose that's any –'

'Máirtín?' Creed replied, more than surprised by how at variance *this* detail was; shocked, in fact.

'Yes, I happened upon a woman during the bad snow, back in February, almost dead upon the road: his wife.'

'Oh ...' Creed lifted his head, feigning interest. But he had already lost the air of what the reverend was saying. 'Máirtín' was a far cry from 'Pádraig,' and Creed felt himself quite annoyed. If Kyle had just said there'd been no one of that description, Creed would have left, grateful, if disappointed. But to have made such a glaring blunder, and to have gotten his hopes up into the bargain: Creed found that exasperating. 'Oh, well,' he told Kyle, keen to depart, 'I'd better be heading back, I suppose.'

'So sorry, Mr Creed. If we hear of anyone else we'll let you know. You'll keep an eye out, won't you, Mrs Stephenson?'

'Of course, Reverend.'

Creed was not hopeful as he descended the steps.

'How soon should we hope to see the, eh –?' Kyle probed.

'I'll aim to have it written by Friday. But it will only print subject to the editor's approval, you understand, Mr Kyle?'

'Naturally, Mr Creed – though your writing is, as ever, most compelling. I'm sure they'd dare not pass on it.'

'Oh, one other thing, Mr Kyle.' Creed turned, thinking to inquire of *his* lists, in case there should be anything in the pipe they would not have seen in Macroom yet. But in the light of all that had just occurred, before Kyle even responded Creed had changed his mind and decided it was pointless. He himself could access any new lists, from Macroom, in a matter of weeks. Kyle had got enough wrong of one request already.

AIBREÁN

APRIL

22

DESIDERATUM

Lest he be prevailed upon by the pitiful souls loitering beyond, Creed stayed just inside the doorway of Mary Hogg's on the South Square and, in the light of the window, opened his sixpenny copy of the *Examiner* to begin a sweep of its columns.

It was with a vested interest that he'd stopped to look. One week prior, through a handwritten note, curiously titled *Desideratum*, John Francis Maguire – proprietor of the *Examiner* – had entreated Creed with such fancies as *we have sorely missed your contributions; several readers have communicated likewise*; and, rather directly, *I would personally appreciate if you'd consider attending and submitting a report upon the proceedings of the Adjourned Presentments Sessions to be held at Macroom, on April 2nd.*

Held the previous Wednesday at the Courthouse, the opening Sessions had ended in controversy, by all accounts, *but with no one there to record the minutiae!* Maguire had lamented.

As Creed had it, far from fulfilling its intended purpose, the meeting had quickly descended to a public hearing on Captain Gordon and his many wrongs within the region – mostly precipitated by his appearing with the incorrect paperwork that day. It was said there was scarcely a gentleman in attendance who had not had a shot at the military man – but to little or no effect, as, evidently, Gordon had laughed at the entire proceeding. When that meeting had adjourned, the unenviable officer left the courthouse followed by some wretched hundreds whose execrations remained loud and continuous behind him until he'd reached his lodgings in the town: a scene that painted an indelible picture upon Creed's mind.

At understanding Maguire's request, Creed's reaction had been one of apprehension.

In another season – he had replied – *I'd have been wholly charmed by such pleasing blandishments, Mr Maguire. But as lengthy reports on many meetings have in past times amounted to a great strain upon my health, I have lately decided that, henceforth, I will best serve both myself and our poor by limiting my contributions to personal observances.*

If it pleases, however – Creed had suggested – *on this occasion, I shall attend, and forward a general impression of the proceeding.*

In the meantime, I enclose such a personal commentary as mentioned for your readers' contemplation. As ever, a faithful devotee of your fine journal.

Necessarily, Creed had responded boldly. But to his delight, the piece appeared. And here it was, halfway down the closing page. A quick perusal, he decided, before he would continue on, en route to those very adjourned presentments.

AWFUL DESTITUTION IN MACROOM

TO THE EDITOR OF THE CORK EXAMINER
March 28, 1847.

Dear sir,–

So many doleful communications have appeared in your inestimable journal for some months past, descriptive of district and village scenes of poverty and human wretchedness, that I fear I shall not succeed in attracting public attention to, nor riveting it upon, the appalling horrors to which humanity is reduced in this ill-fated town.

This morning, a man who could not get into any house last night was *found dead* in Sleaveen road, Ned Brien Swiney, a labourer. Stretched on the public street, *three more* were prepared by Fr. Lee, P.P., this very day, *where they afterwards died.*

Groups upon groups of beings, *looking* like human creatures, are incessantly besetting every avenue, individual and door in the town, evidently bearing in their dreadfully emaciated persons contagion of all kinds: beings who regularly disturb the nocturnal quiet and repose of the much-harassed inhabitants of the town by their nightly screams from wisps of straw cast promiscuously down by the market house, and other wall sides. For that is where these miserable and exhausted wretches lay their shrivelled bones, regardless the torrents of rain, or the inclemency of the night. Borne on men's shoulders daily to the graveyard are seen eight and sometimes more white coffins inside of which sometimes two and even three are *stuck together*. As to the country *trade* in that way, 'tis fearful.

Our inestimable curate, Father James Barry, is in a most desperate fever. Our truly excellent parish priest, together with his indefatigable and exemplary other coadjutor, Father Dan Foley, are in such a state of mental and bodily debility that it is much to be feared, unless they receive some auxiliaries in the discharge of their spiritual functions, they too will fall victims to either the desperate malady, or their own over-zeal and efforts to attend to all the dead and dying.

Fever is now catching all in this neighbourhood indiscriminately; many country gentlemen have fallen victim. Many more are sick and likely to share the same fate.

I remain dear Sir, faithfully yours,

C. CREED

As he prepared to leave the shop, the gratification Creed felt at finding his writing intact proved short lived; for directly afterward, Maguire had conjoined it to another that brought his heart lower still.

The following touching extract from a letter to this office by Father Lee, himself, the heart-broken pastor of Macroom, more than corroborates the painfully sad letter of Mr Creed :–

We are truly in a shocking way. The people are dying in the public streets. We are as if living in the City of the Plague; so surrounded are we by fever.

My indefatigable Curate is in its clutches, with little hope of recovery. I feel ill myself, and have made exertion to write this to you.

Believe me, ever sincerely yours,
THOMAS LEE

How much suffering must we endure? Creed asked himself, as, forlorn, he stepped out, folding the paper. From the castle gates at his left to the market house opposite and across the square, the vista of misery on display told him no gift of prophecy was required to answer. Nor was one needed to imagine the future awaiting those other countless thousands the country over, or the man now before him, soliciting alms.

'God be good and the price of a half a loaf you'll spare for a hungry family,' the pauper beseeched. Pulled by a kind of ruthless gravity that would not allow him to look away, Creed stared into the man's eyes as he spoke. He appeared to be blind yet had walked directly forward, cap outstretched, dragging his feet behind a miserable stick.

'Thank you, kind soul,' he said as Creed dropped a solitary coin into the makeshift purse. 'Beware the kiss that falls upon your ear, sir. For when it comes it will already be too late.'

Turning as he finished his edict, the man gently bowed and retreated, leaving Creed stuck-mouthed and awed; silent on the one hand at the apparent profundity of the man's words and preoccupied on the other with getting to the courthouse. When, moments later, the soul had vanished around a corner into the lanes, Creed wondered if he had ever been there at all.

23

A Looker-On

Approaching the courthouse on the far side of the river, it became apparent to Creed that this visit would prove an even more sombre experience than those heavily attended landmark events still clear in his memory from the year before. Nowhere in sight were the crowds of worried labourers blocking the doorway in their droves; absent the hundreds who, down from the hills, had come to let be known their gravest concerns. But the needs of the poor were now far too immediate for the luxury of speculation, Creed supposed, their silence conjuring ghostly remembrances of the din that had tortured the air outside and lacerated the roof within.

After all their suffering and hardships their worst fears had manifested in catastrophe, he reflected. In the hour of their greatest need they'd hoped the landed classes would come to their aid, or at the very least secure employment enough to save them from slipping off the last rung on the ladder of disaster. But how many voices had been permanently quietened by the inaction of those he now surveyed upon entering, Creed wondered, bitterly. And how many more, barely hanging on, would be lost and gone too another year hence? Climbing the stairs to the empty gallery, a vision awoke as remembrance in his mind: the haunting panoramas of vacant, abandoned dwellings scattered across the snow-laden landscape of Carrigboy. If he had not been witness to that himself, he might not have had a sense of the answer at all.

So far as he could tell, the Bench were about to proceed to business when, in the absence of none other than Gordon himself, it was deemed necessary to postpone until he be present. As though through the eyes of the absent labourers, Creed found that, observed from above, by the tops of their heads alone, the court's participants looked suitably ridiculous.

To Creed's bemusement, the chairman announced, 'We are not so much assembled to grant presentments, gentleman, as to vote a sufficiency of money for the completion of those roads, already passed, that are presently stopped for want of funds, by which thousands have been disemployed and thereby subjected to the tortures of starvation.'

However worthy of appreciation he found this account, determined to stick to a general impression, Creed had elected to not bring his notebook and, across the hour that followed, he simply watched as, under the great Venetian window, the Bench jostled and argued like so many scorned children, wasting more time and getting more of nothing done with every minute that passed. As Gordon had seemed of no great significance to the Sessions of October last, it was hard to see what was different now. Yet, over and over, the room passed, debating whether to sanction the offender for trifling with them; treating them most discourteously; and for delaying them from their business when they'd come great distances.

'He delayed us by an hour the last day,' Robert Warren piped up, 'and when at last he found it convenient to attend, he barely scribbled a few lines. But here another hour has passed.'

At half past twelve, on the agreement of the Bench a police constable was dispatched to relate the wishes of those assembled to Gordon. Soon returned, the constable relayed the message that Gordon would appear 'a few minutes hence'. When another half an hour had passed, the outrage was doubled and a vote of censure, proposed by Massy Warren, was only abated by a calm few desirous of keeping the meeting on track to achieve some meaningful result. Warren was usually Gordon's *defender*, thought Creed, at the contradiction.

Next, with a voice as inept as it was youthful sounding, Captain Brooke arose to state that when he left their quarters a short time since, Gordon had been dressing, and was all the night previous occupied without going to bed. Brooke did not specify by what means his associate had been occupied. But by the man's reputation, Creed believed many present would fancy it hard drinking. It was the first time Creed had put eyes on Brooke, replacement to *Inspector* Gordon, 59th, who'd lately been moved to Clare. *That* Gordon – Creed imagined, with a lick of irony – would not be missed half as much as this one was.

When more significant time elapsed, and, amid the growing chaos and disorder, Creed for a moment almost wished he'd brought some paper along to make sense of it all, the constable – dispatched a second time – returned with something and passed it along.

'I have just received a note from Captain Gordon, which I beg to hand the chairman,' Brooke announced, engendering immediate silence. In a voice Creed thought befitting of his wig, the chairman then read aloud, 'Macroom, April Second. Eighteen Forty-Seven. My Dear Brooke – Will you be so good as to tell Captain Wallis I shall decline attending – unless the Bench guarantees I be not insulted, as I was at the last sitting. Sincerely yours, Charles Edward Parke Gordon.'

At this, Creed observed, the result could not have been more the opposite of Gordon's demand.

'It is his duty to attend and he should do so unconditionally!' roared the chairman, whose role it was to keep the order, Creed reflected. But the flames had reached the top of the tree and the atmosphere of anger increased until, hammering the plate, Captain Wallis seemed to have come to his senses, restoring the room to order enough for individual speech.

A pall of weariness descended over Creed as, once again, Massy took the floor and began a drawn-out, lambasting indictment.

'That letter only convinces me that Gordon has deliberately insulted the Bench. I will therefore proceed with and read my resolution: that insomuch as Captain Gordon, Seventy-Fifth Regiment – the Engineer in charge of the Barony of West Muskerry – has not thought proper to attend said Session at a quarter past one o'clock, despite being sent for two or three times whilst most of the magistrates and cesspayers were in attendance along with several Relief Committee members – we conceive such conduct as trifling with us and calculated to retard the public business of said sessions – we therefore pass a vote of censure on Captain Gordon, and request of the Commissioners of Public Works to remove the officer from this Barony, as well for his conduct on the present occasion as for his inefficiency at all times. I will now move that resolution, whether seconded or not!'

Throughout the applause that followed, Creed sorely shook his head. If Macroom had been the scapegrace of the country on the occasion of last year's Presentments, this year, when the poor were most in need of their active function, those at its helm were so pathetically embroiled in their own bickering that approaching the second whole hour, they had not raised a single grant even to the point of consideration. If only Fr Lee was on his feet, he would bring this body to focus.

Though not imbued with the persuasive charm of Thomas Lee, the Rev. Mr Daly, of Kilmurray, at last brought *some* reason to the proceedings, Creed felt, when he pleaded that were he merely to consult his own feelings, he might not take such a different view from Warren's, but that 'seeing the consequences, and the number of poor who would be injured by adopting such a course, it would surely be wiser that Captain Gordon be given the guarantee, that the day's business might be proceeded with'.

'Twas but a loose 'Hear, hear' arose in support, Creed lamented.

The Rev. Henry Sadlier stood solemnly to say he cared not 'for the rank or station of any man' when he had a conscientious duty to discharge and, on the last day, consequently felt he could not keep silent whilst persons were dying of starvation around him. 'If I used any uncourteous expression on that occasion, however, I am ready to apologise,' he said, to the seeming disgust of Massy Warren.

Daly, pressing his point, added that on the day in question he had heard the phrases 'infamous' and 'disgraceful' applied to the conduct of Gordon, and believed that 'certainly a gentleman of his rank and position might feel insulted at such terms. I therefore do not think it unusual that he would seek a guarantee.'

The gentle Daly was seemingly nurturing a growing chorus of support, Creed observed.

'Did Captain Gordon tell you to repeat those phrases?' Massy interrupted fervently, seeming the sole voice against progress now.

'Certainly not,' Daly replied.

'Then why repeat them?' Massy pressed absurdly.

'My sole motive in interfering is the public good, Mr Warren. We have evils enough to contend with, without the introduction of personal collisions.' The statement by the gentle priest had won out the day where Creed was concerned and produced the largest approbation yet.

Ultimately the chairman stated that while he could not approve the way the Bench had been treated, he was prepared to give Captain Gordon every support and protection. The support was not for Gordon himself, who was deserving of all their contempt and more, Creed felt, but for the only course conducive to good that the remaining session could pursue.

'Captain Brooke,' Wallis moved, 'please communicate a reply to Mr Gordon and request him to attend.'

Watching smugly from above, Creed heard a generous 'Hear, hear,' though Massy, with arms folded, was clearly not among those who upheld it. 'I must say we have been most grossly treated by the gentleman,' Massy said with a sulk, among the settling atmosphere that awaited.

When, to an expectant hush, Gordon shortly afterwards arrived, Massy arose and addressed the chairman: 'Sir, as I shall never be found to say anything to a gentleman's back that I would not to his face I will now proceed to move my resolution –'

But Captain Wallis forestalled him with a hand. 'Now let us proceed. We have agreed to take the business first.'

'Well, I accede,' replied Massy, sitting once more, all his idle puff petering out, Creed took great delight in beholding. To save face, it would seem, Massy had been all too happy to withdraw his attack when, rather conveniently, the chairman had yanked his rope.

As Mr Johnson, Secretary to the Grand Jury, stood to speak, Creed tried to, but could not, stifle the cough that escaped his mouth in the ensuing silence, and, for the first time that day, feeling the eyes of many below peering up at him, remembered himself and shrank momentarily.

Though it was far too late to achieve much of what might have been, Creed mourned, he was relieved when Johnson proceeded with the list of extensions for works presented. By Gordon's representative signature, sums amounting to fifteen thousand nine hundred and five pounds were passed, along with seven hundred and fifty pounds more, passed at those sessions held the Wednesday previous.

How far fifteen thousand pounds could be made to stretch were it spent directly on Macroom's poor, Creed imagined with cold frustration. But typically, the government would never allow such things. Rather they would support initiatives that filtered money down to the poor, but first through the coffers and estates of their friends. The clergy aside, this was essentially a committee of the rich, squabbling to get their hands on government money. For all their bluster, it seemed they needed Gordon more than he needed them, and that explained why, ultimately, they had acceded to his intolerable behaviour, Creed understood at last.

The reason the poor labourers were so noticeably absent was not just because they were unable to come, he now supposed, but because it had been emphatically proven to them, these people would not be their saviours. Creed himself had known that for some time since, but now the poor could see it too, it seemed. How many lives might have been saved through examining new projects, Creed reflected, as, rising from his chair, he sought to escape.

Much to his annoyance, half-way down he encountered an inspired Massy Warren climbing the stairs to meet him, conveniently out of earshot, it seemed.

'I notice you have withdrawn from our usual forums, pawnbroker. I suppose you think you are above us now?' Massy said, blocking his path. 'I saw you, you know?' With this remark, Massy's face changed from a recognisable expression to something Creed had never seen.

'What the devil are you talking about, Massy?'

'Splashing about that day, with the dog …'

Feeling as though a raging wind had lashed him to a post, Creed battled to maintain his composure. Behind a façade, he scrambled to understand how Massy, of all people, could be privy to his innermost struggle. And what were the implications of Massy's holding such knowledge, given the manner of his confrontation here?

Doing some strange thing with his tongue, Massy gave Creed the impression of one relishing his agony. But sparing Creed the torture of conjuring an equitable response, no doubt in favour of delivering some pre-prepared blow he had been savouring, Massy himself finished, 'I'm so sorry I couldn't lend a hand, pawnbroker. I was merely "a looker-on", you see?'

24

That This Year Would Be Different

Cáit awoke to the sensation of being shaken by the arms, with Pádraig telling her, 'Cáit, you're at home. Wake up. Wake up.'

'I went there again, to the workhouse, for Onóra,' she told him, catching her breath with a stifled scream. Just like last time, and every time yet, the dream had begun with Cáit walking in the snow, too sore and too weary to reach her sister in time. And the dream had ended the same way on each occasion: 'I keep seeing her … buried alive,' Cáit cried, 'gasping for air, 'neath the lid of the coffin.'

'Ah now,' Pádraig told her, pulling her close and holding her there until she'd crossed through the tears.

Some nights she saw Onóra lying dead on the floor of the poorhouse, surrounded by other people, sick, with sores over their arms and legs. Only sometimes, she sensed, had Onóra been the recipient of any kindness there, perhaps from the young nurse who'd met Cáit at the gate that day. To discover she had only been dreaming should have brought relief. But instead, at the thought of what unimaginable suffering Onóra had endured, she'd spend the rest of the day haunted and plagued by lingering sadness. However she had pictured it before, seeing it for herself – albeit from the outside alone – Cáit had a new bitter hatred of the place they called *Tíg na mBocht* – the house of the poor.

'Tell me we'll never go into that place, husband,' she begged Pádraig, as he tried to rock her and himself, both, back to sleep. 'Tell me you'd never let me die in there, no matter how bad it got,' she pleaded, feeling new tears rolling down her cheeks in the darkness.

'I promise … I promise,' he answered, and shushed the baby reassuringly, until there was quiet again.

'Not if we're dying and laden with fever,' Cáit whispered herself after a while, half knowing Pádraig had drifted again. *She* could not get back to sleep so easily. But nor did she want to.

Wide-eyed in the darkness, Cáit decided she would never allow them to claim her too. Onóra would have wanted her to take that lesson from all this, if nothing else. Cáit could do that much for her sister.

Up early that morning, Cáit went to the stream to wash Diarmuidín's clothes and there found Kitty Uí Laeire, the one neighbour she usually took care to avoid. But today Cáit was glad of the distraction.

'Ah Cáit, how is Pádraig? Is he still off his feet?'

'He's rising, Kitty. With God's help he'll be fit to go working again before long.'

'Oh, that's good news in these terrible times,' the neighbour replied, lapping clothes in the water.

'Is Micilín still hoping for work?' Cáit asked, before the woman could press her first.

'Oh God, he is, Cáit, have you heard of anything?'

'Reverend Kyle at the Protestant Glebe is looking for a pauper to dig the graves, I hear.'

'Oh …' Kitty responded, then said no more. Head down, looking to her work, she lapped on, unusually quietened. Cáit had considered it knowledge worth sharing, but by Kitty's expression supposed the idea would never even reach Micilín's ears, whether for the stigma attached to the morbid occupation or the association with the Protestant Glebe itself.

Gathering *cipíní* in the woods on the way back, she pondered on how sad it was that she could no longer make the same suggestion to Máire

Ruadh, now that her poor Labhrás was gone. Maybe if Kitty could see it that way, she might better appreciate the gesture, Cáit felt.

Pádraig would probably have tried for it himself, if he wasn't holding out for a place on the works at Carriganimma, a mile or so east of them, Cáit thought. 'I'd only need walk through the forest to get to it,' he'd said. But two months now he'd been home and they'd been talking about Carriganimma so long, she worried it might be fancy alone: something they were telling each other just to keep their hopes alive. To make matters worse, there'd been rumours lately that the works were ending everywhere.

Cáit got back just in time to watch as, in a dreamlike repetition of the year before, but with much less strength, Pádraig took out a small cloth bag and was preparing to put in the seed he'd got with the proceeds of the dead man's shoes. Seemingly hesitant, he walked the length of their ground a number of times, staring and measuring something with his eye.

'What's troubling you?' she asked.

'I'm trying to remember which end got the worst of it last time, and had it to do with the wind up here, or the better drainage over there, where the slope is deeper,' he answered.

Cáit felt a fondness that was mixed with pity for how he always took care to weigh everything up and get the most of whatever they had, however hopeless. If the blight came again then the gamble they'd taken would amount to nothing at all. What if she was wrong and she'd pushed him too hard to risk it? Along with the shoes, he had sold the blanket Siobhán Ua Laoghaire gave them the year before too. 'There'd be hardly enough to go planting at all, otherwise,' she remembered him saying, angry coming back from the huckster at how little he'd got this time around.

But eventually, his mind made up on the two or three rows at the westernmost end, Pádraig walked up and down, planting holes in the drills with the long stick. Kneeling, he then dropped in the hopeful little slots. And afterward, when, with his finger, he had packed them all in, covering each with earth enough to nourish it and protect it, he called out the children and Cáit watched again as on either side of him, small and scraggy, they joined their little hands to say prayers over each tiny seed. At the last one, while the others waited patiently by, Síle squeezed her hands tightly to her chin and seemed to make an offering all of her own before Pádraig led them in blessing themselves. It was the most hopeful day they'd had all year, Cáit thought, and from inside the doorway she prayed too.

'Well,' Pádraig said, dusting himself down, back inside, 'it's in the hands of the gods now. Come October we'll know if they landed for us. There'll be plenty of signs before then, with the earlies and such.'

'Please God, that they'll come again,' Cáit said, wishing for all their sakes that this year would be different.

25

A Thread Untucked

'Sit with me, dear,' Creed said. Just back from his walk, taking Paulellen's hands in his own, he sat facing her, one chair to another.

'Con, is everything –?'

'Everything is fine. But there are some things I need to tell you,' he announced, looking hard into the green-blue flecks of her eyes.

'Oh, where to begin?' he said, searching himself before looking to her again. 'That day I came back from the river, soaking. Do you remember it? New Year's D–'

'With the dog?' she asked.

'That's right. With the dog.'

'Of course I do.'

'Good. Well, what did I tell you that day? I have little memory of it.'

'You told me you'd slipped and … that the dog saved you, somehow.'

'I see … Perhaps I did not share fully what transpired.' He blinked. 'Maybe I was shocked with the cold, or –'

At the confusion of trying to acquaint Paulellen with the scene, while somehow sparing her the fright in the process, Creed shut his eyes tightly. For all the walking he'd done that morning, deciding how and what to say, he felt more confused now than ever. But if Massy Warren was to uncover the truth first, it would be far, far worse; he was certain of that, and if one tiny thread was left untucked, it might all fall asunder with a gentle tug.

'I was very confused when I went to the river that day …'

'I'm frightened at what you're going to tell me, Cornelius,' Paulellen said nervously.

'I know this is sudden. Should I stop?' he asked.

'No. No. I'd rather hear,' she replied assuredly, and, redoubling his courage, Creed nodded as they each took a breath.

'That morning I went out with the intention of drowning a pair of –'

At the word, he realised, Paulellen gasped, her eyes filling with latent tears, ready to spill.

'A pair of shoes, I stress! A pair of shoes,' he continued. 'I wanted to do away with them, you see. Not myself. At least I don't think I meant to, I … I was very confused. Should I go on? Are you sure?' he said, at the sight of her weeping, clutching his fingers more tightly as she did.

'Please,' she urged him.

'If I stop, I won't be able to get it out,' his voice quaked. 'I'd gotten it into my head, somehow, that the shoes were … cursed. I know how it sounds. It was an innocent kind of a madness, you see.'

Partly laughing, Creed felt himself slowly coming undone until, with a burning in his nose, he was just crying.

'I saw they'd lain on the shelf of the stores for some time and … I remembered the pauper, a young father, who brought them in. I could still see his face … his young family. And I realised – by the date on the tag – he must be long dead.' With eyes open, Creed tried to see through the water, brimming at the edge of his eyelids. 'Then I thought of all the people I'd turned away, just like him, before I closed the shop. You see, I instructed French to stop taking pledges when we went to Leades. He was only to redeem pledges, which of course no pauper could afford at that time, or since. Am I making any sense?'

'Some,' she answered, mirroring his emotions, along with his attempts to compose himself.

Relieved that his wife was still before him, apparently calm and understanding, Creed sniffled and made a sound of laughter, bewildered by the complex stream of emotions. 'None of it makes much sense, I know. I cannot seem to put it coherently. But at the time, in the state I occupied then –' he said, quietly remembering the bird in the tree, and how he had laughed at his own reflection in the window of the stores.

'I suppose I blamed myself for their suffering. I still do ...' he said, breaking down, the gates unlocking on something he had kept shored up for a long time. 'Sometimes I think ...' Creed froze, lost.

'Con, you cannot burden yourself with – it's not for you to solve an entire crisis single-handedly.' Paulellen had got stuck too, but seemed to have found her words first on this occasion.

'I know that's true, Paull. But I still feel responsible for my part in ... turning them away, I –'

'The river,' she beckoned him back. 'You were going to the –'

'Right, yes,' he said, rising at the shoulders to fill himself with air. 'I went to the river, believing, if I could do away with the shoes, I could end their curse – because they had outlived numerous owners, you understand – I could alter one thing, and somehow begin ... reparations – for my contribution to all of their woes.'

'That's enough for now. Don't upset yourself further.' Paulellen seemed to understand and Creed felt her hand coming to rest upon his lowered head, easing him. 'One thing I don't understand, though, is where Lucky came into the picture?'

'This beast?' Creed said, tossing the ears of the dog, who at some stage had worked its head in under his hand, he realised, and was now staring up at him with its two different-coloured eyes. 'Believe it or not, he wouldn't let me discard the shoes. From out of nowhere, he appeared. Each time I'd fling them, no matter how far, he bally well fetched them out again, and before I knew it, 'twas me retrieving him. I didn't know who was saving who, in the end.'

'I knew there were things you'd kept from me,' Paulellen said, and shook her head. 'Sure I heard you, in January, talking to yourself about the shoes. You took a long road getting back this time, but I knew you'd find your way. You always do. You probably needed that,' she added after a moment of reflection.

Patting the dog's head, Creed found himself unsure as to where the truth ended and where the fog of his memory had intervened, replacing the parts he had tried most to forget. For now it was all he could muster.

With it all out, both he and Paulellen were acting as though they'd been relieved of a burden, he noticed. And perhaps they were. But Creed sensed a shared feeling, too, that they had narrowly escaped something quite unimaginable; something that he, at least, could not bring himself to contemplate.

'You *still* smell like that river,' he said, holding the dog by the snout, and bent low to rub its nose against his.

'You've come past it now, though, haven't you?' Paulellen asked, searching.

'I have,' he answered eventually, feeling peaceful and somehow renewed.

'So what needs to happen, then?' she persisted. 'Why did you choose to tell me now?'

'In truth ... I am restless,' Creed answered, then waited, quiet, for a deeper answer from within. When it came, he faced his wife again: 'I *am* better in myself. But somehow I know I will not advance until I have balanced my error.'

At length, resolute, Paulellen replied, 'Then you must do what you must.'

26

THE RED MARK OF DISMISSAL

'I thought I heard you packing,' Paulellen said, appearing as, out in the carhouse, Creed was struggling to marry the horse with the trap.

'Was I so loud? … Argh … Thomas French usually does this part for me,' he said, distracted. 'I must find him and talk with him.'

'Well, we know where he's spending the most of his time,' she answered.

'And where is that?' Creed asked.

'The Bridge Tavern,' Paulellen said, matter-of-factly, 'dabbling in all sorts of sin, I was told.'

'And only half believe what you see,' Creed said flatly, still wrestling the harness, but feeling pity for the wayward clerk.

'You're right, I know,' Paulellen said, repentant and soft. 'So you *are* going then?'

'I decided to take your advice,' Creed replied, turning to find her holding a basket of clothes. 'Oh, they're the –'

'For the poor, yes. I'm taking them to the rectory now. You're sure you won't need these?'

Creed blew out his lips and shook his head with a gesture that might have come from the horse. 'I have clothes enough in the stores alone to last a lifetime,' he replied.

'Right so. I'm glad you're going, anyway,' Paulellen said, ''twill do you no bad to get away from all this and reflect on what you must do to proceed.'

'Yes, I think you're right,' Creed admitted, greatly appreciative of his wife's support. 'I just need to send off that article. Then we'll be ready, won't we, Dreoilín?' He patted the horse, secretly hoping Paulellen might offer.

'Is it ready to post?' she asked, taking the bait. 'I'll be going by the Post Office on my way out, sure.'

'Oh, perfect. Would you mind, dear? It's sealed and ready on my writing desk.'

'Of course not.' She nodded, grinning.

'Thank you, dear,' he said, and kissed her forehead. 'Be mindful of keeping your distance, won't you, from anyone likely carrying contagion?'

'Oh, God,' Paulellen said, turning away.

'We'll be back on the morrow,' Creed told her absently. 'There … that's it,' he spoke to the horse, finally getting the collar and hames to sit where he wanted them.

'How long has passed, old girl,' Creed whispered, starting up a one-sided conversation with the horse as they broke away from the roads of Macroom. 'How long since that farmers' race, when you wiped all their eyes, hah? *An Dreoilín* … the treacherous wren,' he smiled, remembering, as the mare started into a trot.

Feeling more like himself again with each passing day, Creed was increasingly aware of those elemental forces that were inseparably ravelling whether he liked it or not: it was such a crucial juncture in the crisis; for the poor; and for his own soul, and considering his part in it all, racing the clock, he felt compelled to think fast. Away from the town he would focus his mind on devising a plan, clear and unburdened for now by the piece he had written. The Strongest Description On Earth, he had titled it.

MACROOM, APRIL 21ST, 1847.

Dear Sir–

A miserable fatuity dogs the steps of the English Government. Each succeeding hour proves its dishonesty and incompetency better than the last. It decides without wisdom, and acts without forethought or calculation. Throughout the country, twenty out of every hundred labourers – *every fifth man, straight down the list, receiving the red mark of dismissal* – are bid go home and turn their thoughts to the cultivation of plots and potato gardens. After dooming these sixty or seventy thousand men and their families to a cruel death – *by an economical crotchet* – it suddenly bethinks at the eleventh hour, that there ought to be a harvest in the autumn of this year! Even if the people could be marched with the promptness and precision of soldiers on parade from road work to agriculture, they could not, in their condition, hope to retrieve this promise. They assume the land will be generally tilled. Though how can it be so, when the dismissal of workers only began on March 20th? Yet ministers shuffle them off the highways.

No sooner decided than commenced, the first subtraction of the half-starved has already been sent to wholly starved. But in three days hence, on April 24th, a further ten on the hundred will be sent to their doom, and, by a momentous May 1st, the apparatus of the public works is to be suspended and dismantled entirely!

With these hurried measures, ministers have bound up a provision. By the Soup Kitchens Act, they have provided for outdoor relief, to meet the awful results of dismissal: starvation. *The only problem:* the first part of the statute has come without the other. There is *no food – nor preparation made* – to keep the people alive in the meantime!

The strongest description on earth could not convey to you or the public an idea of the human wretchedness which prevails at present in this town. Nor is the appalling degradation of nature confined to the miserable hovels. Our market-house walls are literally lined with living creatures clearly indicating not alone symptoms of the most revolting stages of starvation, but all the other horrors incidental to man.

The poor house closed – works suspended – no outdoor relief – private charity exhausted – business abandoned – resident gentry absent – no resources. *What will become of the people?* The Omnipotent Being can only see.

Every avenue leading to this plague-stricken town has now a fever hospital, each having for its protecting roof the blue vault of heaven. Persons of all ages are dropping dead in every street and lane, many of them interred with much difficulty after rats have feasted upon their unfortunate frames.

The incessant and heart-rending moanings, the infectious and tattered rags in which they fester, only half enveloped. Oh, much as I admire the letter, and concur in the sentiments of Doctor Maglinn's scathing and much-aggrieved condemnation of the Colonisation Scheme, yet still is it not better to transport and expatriate thousands upon thousands of loyal Irish subjects than witness their prostration and premature deaths in the land of their nativity, victims of an unfeeling and alien Legislature?

Dear sir, faithfully yours,
C. CREED.

27

A Horse Named Giles

Stepping through the doorway, the first thing to catch Creed's attention was not the horse, but the much-deteriorated appearance of Maguire, the stable-hand, who stood with a brush around his knuckles and was accompanied by a young boy, equally dishevelled. Grooming the horse, Maguire looked to have suffered much since Creed had seen him last and was aged significantly.

'Mr Creed, I wasn't expecting you.'

'Hello, Mr Maguire. This must be your boy?' Creed asked. But so ragged and pitiful was the boy's condition that, at the back of his thoughts, he thought to say *urchin*, and pondered how the horse seemed luxuriously healthy compared with the two human beings. It was *they* who needed looking after most.

'My son's boy, Mr Creed. The whole family were struck. He's all that's left, and lives with me now. Has a fondness for the horses. I hope you don't mind.'

'Worry not, Mr Maguire. He's quite welcome where I'm concerned,' Creed said, removing his gloves, taken aback by the sorry tale.

'Thank you, sir.' Maguire bowed, graciously.

'What's your name, young man?'

'Pray, he doesn't speak much, the poor gossun. But he has a way of getting on regardless.'

'I see,' Creed said, and smiled kindly at the boy, whose eyes returned a sullen gaze, full of fear or distrust, he perceived.

'His father believed he had the gift.'

'The gift?' Creed enquired.

'With the horses.'

'Oh, the –' Creed was still unsure.

'When he grows up he'll give old James Sullivan a run for his money, isn't that right, lad? You've heard tell of Sullivan, Mr Creed?'

'I can't say I have, Mr Maguire.'

'Easy now, boy,' Maguire told the horse, and patted its shoulder before combing another circle through the bristle of its vivid brown coat. It seemed nervous at Creed's approach, and he knew he must be patient having been absent so long.

'James Sullivan, of Inishannon. The famed charmer of horse flesh, Mr Creed. With one word, 'tis said he could make a horse lie down on its back, the four hooves up in the air, so that a glass filled with drink could be balanced on each hoof. Now that's some trick?'

'Mmm …' a sound of reluctance escaped Creed's mouth. 'Sounds a trick indeed.' Reluctant to deprive the old man of his notions, Creed continued to feign ignorance. But, his memory stoked, he had indeed heard of Sullivan, he now realised: an awkward and ignorant rustic, known widely as 'the horse charmer' for his famed habit of breaking horses by certain mysterious means. It was the credulity of the rural people had bestowed the epithet upon him, from a collective opinion that he communicated his instructions to the animal by means of a quiet word in its ear.

How Sullivan's trade had been acquired, or what it consisted of, had been the subject of debate for many years at drinking establishments and firesides from Cork to London and back again. The singularity of his method only furthered the superstitious beliefs, it seemed, and the curiosity consisted in the short time requisite for Sullivan to accomplish his task: something performed in private and apparently without coercion. Every description of equine brute – horse or mule, whether broken or unhandled, whatever their peculiar habits or ill-health they were said to have all submitted to the magic influence of his art and in the short space of a few minutes became gentle and tractable by his workings.

Sullivan's consistent reputation and record were impressive and novel enough to have garnered Creed's interest too. With an interest in horses, he had not been immune to the intrigue of it all. But, a man of science, he did not subscribe to the generally accepted theory on offer. Of all people, Creed recalled, it had been William Shanahan, the old hawker – a charmer himself of the highest order – who, quite intuitively, had once proposed an alternative narrative that Creed found surprisingly intelligent and scrupulous. Dismissing the supernatural outright, during one heightened spell of gossip, Shannie suggested that what was generally perceived as a *sotto voce* in the horse's ear was, in fact, Sullivan getting close enough to nip the horse's ear between his teeth! This, Shannie proclaimed, was 'the common habit of every mare ever needed put manners on a foal' and therefore an action that each horse surrendered to, instinctively.

But, theory or fact, whatever the nuance of Sullivan's mastery, Creed supposed the truth would remain, now, forever unknown. 'This Sullivan is deceased now, is he not, Mr Maguire?'

'Arrah, he's departed this world, his lips sealed and his secrets gone with him. May he be basking gently in Elysian fields somewhere in the realm of his reward.'

'You've not been back since last year, sir?' Maguire asked, changing the subject.

'Ill-health prevented my getting here sooner.'

'A sorry tale, and I'm sad to hear it, Mr Creed.'

'Thank you, Mr Maguire. But my problems pale when compared to most.'

'The country is every measure of woe, Mr Creed. 'Tis a melancholy state no matter which way one looks, and appears to be only disimproving.'

Listening, the illusion occurred to Creed that the man's face, grave by its pouting, seemed even more seasoned now than when he had entered. Stooped, and rolled down at the shoulders, it was as though Maguire was aging by the moment. Weary in face and low at every corner, each limb of his body appeared to know how to assume the saddest posture, so that the overall effect accentuated the sympathy he felt for his fellow sufferers.

'Anyway, Mr Maguire, I did not come here to bring you more sadness.'

'Indeed, Mr Creed, let you be reminded of some natural beauty and the solace of liberated nature, here. He is a beautiful beast, aren't you, lad?' said Maguire. Dipping the bucket, he *swarched* the bristles across the glistening pelt of the stallion, to its apparent pleasure. 'It's a shame you wouldn't race him agin, Mr Creed. He'd fair flatten them all, I'd say.'

'I dare say he might, Mr Maguire. But is goodness not to hold power and use it only for kindness?'

'If you say so, sir.'

'Though some would see it the virtue of a horse, I do not care to see him under the whip.' Speaking softly, Creed furrowed his brow.

'Well … *Capall le ceanntacht* – a horse should be treated with gentleness – some say.'

Creed appreciated the idea, even if he felt Mr Maguire would have it otherwise in terms of racing the creature.

'Will you put him up for stud, Mr Creed? That would be of no harm to him: good for him, in fact.'

'I'll certainly consider it.' Patting his pockets as though to search for his key, Creed aimed to let Maguire feel he was not escaping, so much as he was pressed. 'Very well, Mr Maguire, I should unpack my things and get settled. Would you stable the horse and car when I'm done, Mr Maguire?'

'Of course, sir. Will I send someone to fetch the provisions?'

'No. No. Thank you, Mr Maguire. No one is to part with an ounce of what is scarce on my account. I have everything I need on the car.'

'Very well. Thank you for your kindness.' With that, the faithful man removed his cap and bowed his head with eyes closed; a ritual that presupposed forthcoming generosity, Creed was reminded: in patting his pockets he had inadvertently planted the seed himself. But the gesture seemed more desperate and more hopeful in this instance than ever before, and, producing some coins from his undercoat, he suddenly wished he could find more to part with.

That old feeling could still be traced, warning that being overly generous risked an unending line of requests. But that instinct was fading fast in Creed, replaced by a feeling of shame at stopping there when he had so much more, if not on his person at that moment.

'Oh, Mr Creed,' Maguire blurted out – at the unexpected amount, it seemed.

'You're welcome, Mr Maguire. That you've taken such care of the horse's condition is easy to see. I'll settle a bill for his keep before departing.'

'That would be fine, Mr Creed.'

———

At the sound of the bitter winds blowing outside, Creed found himself unable to sleep that night. He had come here to weigh insurmountable problems and to reconcile them with his own life and means: the poor, the crisis, Ua Buachalla, the shop. How to not only survive such a manifold complexity of problems, but take a meaningful step forward in the service of each. Hours awake in search of an answer; to his great frustration, he was finding nothing.

Let you be reminded of natural beauty. He heard the words of Maguire again, when, by the white and amber glow of the lamp that swung from his hand, Creed left the house and made his way to the stable.

Inside, he turned the wooden block over so that, landing in the makeshift receiver, it *clock*ed. In darkness, the rustle of hay signalled movement within the stall, where, invisible to him yet, Creed sensed the horse was disturbed at his entrance.

''Tis only I, beautiful boy,' he said, hoping to reassure the creature who earlier had seemed to consider him an unfamiliar. 'I should not interrupt your rest, I know. You're not used to visits at this hour.'

The sound of hooves, scraping then clacking, told Creed the beast had risen to its feet, as, opening the door slowly, he let the light in, cautious not to startle the huge animal. Any sound it usually made was one of contentment or excitement. But by the tale of movement alone, Creed gleaned only restlessness and, though compelled, knew he must be careful.

One part empowering, the other becalming, the urge to stand next to and observe the latent grace and power of the creature was something magnetic.

'Now, now.' Placing his hand upon the giant flank, he felt the muscles twitch with nervousness. Settling by degrees, swaying slightly, the horse made a gentle nickering as Creed's hand rested slowly but firmly upon the same spot.

Greatly relieved at the sound, which at last told Creed the horse remembered him, he revelled in lifting the lamp higher, and, out of the darkness, watched the colour of its rich chestnut hide appear, glistening in the light with lustre and vitality. Creed felt almost transformed at the sight of the dark veins, running like briars across the mounds of dense flesh. Lifting the lamp higher still, he caught a sparkle of light reflecting back at him from the beautiful black orb of the eye, its great neck turning to perceive him and connect with him. Putting his ear to the huge hip, Creed listened and tried to imagine the size of the magnificent heart pumping at the centre of the animal as its blood ebbed and pulsated thick and loud in his ear.

Powerful and sleek, Giles was everything Creed was not: masculine, strong, beautiful and intoxicating. In the presence of the horse, he could *almost* forget everything else. It was addictive and compelling. *What joy, what rapture, what tranquility,* he told himself.

It had been too long since last he'd felt so at peace and Creed wondered why he had not come sooner, when a flash of remembrance broke the fixation. The mute boy, whose whole family had been wiped out, an orphan, living with his grandfather.

In that moment Creed realised a part of him had secretly thought he could find refuge here, escaping the terror and chaos surrounding him and within him. But seeing now, and summoning the poor stable-hand — a human being who was merely looking after the horse so that he himself might enjoy this almost sinful allowance of pleasure by comparison – Creed was racked with guilt. What was happening was inescapable. Though stealing a moment of peace like this had ultimately helped him to see, escaping his troubles could not fix them, or him, or anything else. He had to face them, and face them fully, he realised. And by the morning Creed knew what it was he must do.

———

'How did it go?' Paulellen asked, as, without choice, Creed answered the dog's greeting first.

'I saw it,' he said, excitedly, 'I saw it in my mind.'

'What did you see?'

As they sat, Creed told her all about Maguire and the boy, eventually explaining, 'I've decided to let the animal to stud at Leades, and allow Mr Maguire the proceeds. The gift of industry.' He threw up his hands.

'That's very kind!' she said, seeming surprised too, exciting him more.

'I'm going to place an advertisement straight away.'

'Right!' she affirmed.

'But that's not all … I'm going to reopen the shop.'

———

STALLION

The well-known Horse GILES will stand this Season at LEADES, within Three Miles of this Town. He was the Property of ROBERT HARNED, Esq., and is now in the possession of Mr CREED, who will make the Charges exceedingly Moderate. To praise this *Beautiful Animal* would be perfectly superfluous as his name sufficiently illustrates his pedigree.

Macroom, Apr 22nd, 1847.

28

Gomack

Fair day was Creed's least favourite time to venture onto the square: full of stalls, with salesmen shouting and bartering over spit-filled, hand-clinched deals; hucksters exposing their wares on doorstep and shutter; fish jolters, with sprats and kindred fishes; cobblers and cheap Johns; the brogue-makers with their kishes.

'Here's your pottle a penny!' He heard Joan Begley's voice ring clear, as, navigating the islanded blotches of cow dung and sheep droppings that, over the course of the day, would be trodden and interwoven with wisps of straw into a dark green wax by the coming and going, Creed stopped and gave way to a drift of close-herded sheep that blocked the path. Moving again, he distractedly watched as, in a nearby doorway, a young man from the country was about to be relieved of what scanty bit of silver he'd brought to town. A 'trick o' the loop man' it was, evidently exercising all the subtlety of speech and gesture he possessed to catch his mark. The boy's expression resembled that of a hungry trout, who, though it sensed the danger, could not resist the fascination of the angler's fly, playing on the surface. But before Creed could see how it ended for the poor, soft gomack, his attention was commanded by the roar of a beast but feet ahead. Turning in time to clock the white of the bull's eye, Creed had the sense it might stampede at any moment and crossed in haste to avoid its path. Not the least extraordinary business was the frequent auctions of cattle distrained for rent, conducted by desperate men who no teaching could enlighten, and no amount of human suffering could appease.

Despite the abundance and clamour, by the hopeful stare of one girl that engaged his passing glance, Creed's awareness was painfully reacquainted with the great many, seen and unseen, to whom the market's riches were but a mouthwatering mirage. As though ghosts of a realm separated by nothing but an invisible veil, they appeared everywhere but were just beyond reach.

To see so much food and not be able to touch it, he imagined torturously. *If I was starving, I would be here too, hoping for some turn of kindness, a change of fortune, an easy drop.* To steal – which was the recourse of many – was to risk the squalor of a gaol cell and perhaps transportation, he contemplated fearfully. All the more reason to pursue his ambition, Creed decided, determined to effect the greater good.

Twice a year, and to a lesser extent every second Tuesday, on market day, he avoided this commotion. But retrieving Thomas French from the state to which he had fallen had become something of a matter of urgency to Creed.

Through the confusion he proceeded, until, from the open door of the infamous taproom, the long, melancholy quaver of a drunken voice carried a traditional song above the babble: 'There is a green island in lone Gougaune Barra, where Allua of songs rushes forth as an arrow.'

To the heavy reek of human sweat mingled with soured beer, Creed searched the faces, from those maddened with whiskey to the fools who clung to each other, holding hands with the slobbering affection that drink engendered.

How any one of them could justify the utter waste in times of such inexorable want, while, he imagined, their wives and daughters waited forlorn and distraught in some hovels beyond baffled Creed so endlessly that, unable to endure much more of the maudlin spectacle, he found himself relieved to discover French, by his ginger crop, sleeping upon a stool.

'Mr French,' he called, shaking the far bigger man by his lapels, 'Thomas!'

'Myself ...' his man responded, slovenly, with closed eyes.

"'Tis time to gather your bootstraps and pull yourself up.'

'Oh … Mr Creed …' Rolling his head up, momentarily alert, French, at last, had come to, but dropped off as quickly, as though a weight had sunk his chin.

'Come now, Thomas. We have much to discuss.' Creed shook him awake once more.

Outside, Creed listened as, into an abandoned corner, French rid himself of his stomach's contents, then, moving again, guided him stumbling through one street after the next to the disturbingly wretched accommodations that not long before had been a home to him and his mother. There, Creed listened while, either to punish his changeable master, or merely divest himself of his burden, with inebriated honesty, the clerk mumbled fitfully about an advertisement he'd posted to the papers, 'To Pawnbrokers, for a Situation'.

'I did not wish to abandon my position, sir. I just – at any rate it went unanswered,' he slurred, lying back onto his bed at Creed's insistence.

'That's not for today, Mr French,' Creed told him, removing his boots. 'For now, rest.'

'And you might as well know,' French added, confessing more of his apparent betrayal, 'I put myself forward at the Union … for the pozjin … James Burdon's posstion. God rest him.'

'God rest him, indeed,' Creed commiserated.

'Laughed at me, they did,' French whimpered, clearly heartsore, 'said I should … apply as a storekeep.' Only then, after a hiccup he politely asked to have excused, did French nod off.

Covering him with a blanket, Creed spent the next hours attempting to put some order and manners on his apartment.

When the patient awoke, from a pot bubbling over the fire, Creed brought a portion of soup so close that, however pale and unappetising, French daren't refuse it, but took the bowl himself and supped on a spoonful, if only for show, Creed supposed. Perhaps that was enough, to begin.

When, for embarrassment, the face before him seemed to wish to hide itself, sat by the glow of the hearth, Creed took the bit between his teeth and got to his meaning: 'I have decided to reopen, Mr French.'

His usual inhibited self once more, French did not answer.

'I know you have been though a hard time,' Creed continued. 'I regret I could not offer more of myself when you lost your mother lately. But I have had my own poor health and my own affairs to wrestle with.

'Now, we've noticed you have not been much at the shop. Perhaps you no longer wish to be there. I will understand either way. Much has changed. But if you wish to remain in my employ, you will need to present tomorrow at the usual *early* hour and quit this habit of driving yourself toward an early grave. Is that understood?'

'Yes, sir,' French replied, as Creed, rising from the chair, made for the door, turning only to speak from the outside step. 'Upon the sideboard you'll find a half-crown. It is to purchase a fresh clean shirt and shave off those whiskers, before Mrs Creed sees you.'

'Yes, sir,' French replied, sounding sorry for himself, or disarmed, 'but, Mr Creed?' he called through the last inch of the closing door.

'Yes?'

'They're all closed, sir ... brokers everywhere ... In this climate, it's –'

'I'm well aware, Mr French, thank you for your concern. You leave that end to me.'

With that, Creed shut the door fully, leaving French to his decision. If it was too late and the clerk was lost to insobriety, excessive kindness would not save him. Ultimately, the outcome was out of Creed's hands, but he was betting on the strategy that he'd given the clerk incentive enough to regain some self-respect, while not being so hard as to deter him outright. For Creed's plan to work he needed his clerk. But first, Mr French needed saving from himself.

29

Cornelius Creed Pawnbrokers

Suffering withdrawal sickness, Thomas French had found his already troubled sleep greatly disturbed by the wailing and keening he'd heard in the night. Much deprived of rest, he approached the square as though inhabiting a strange domain. To avoid retching forth, or even dying as he went – for he felt like his heart might presently collapse – he tried not to look at those same sad creatures that lately had populated the town. While he himself had latterly descended to a lower tier of existence than ever he'd been accustomed, it was, at least, not as low as these poor souls, he consoled himself.

The morning after Fair Day, French felt as low inside as the town looked: as sick and as foul as a gutter privy. But, at odds with much of what he was passing, he was clean shaven and dressed in a fresh white shirt. The feeling of his incongruous appearance only added to the sense of being pulled back in time. For, in spite of everything that had occurred in recent months – the whole crumbling disintegration – here he was at his employer's behest, opening the door to CORNELIUS CREED PAWNBROKERS as if it had all been a dream. OPEN AT 9, read a freshly painted sign in the window.

What did Mr Creed have in mind, French wondered with grave anxiety. Was his employer lost without a compass, and was he to be taken to the bottom with him in the resulting shipwreck?

The sound of the bell only further enhanced his bemusement, as, stepping in beneath it, French found Mr Creed waiting, in position, as though it was business as usual.

'Mr French!'

'Good morning, si–'

'Perfectly on time, and not a moment to spare. I have everything ready,' said Mr Creed, coming out from behind the counter that – clearly having undergone some unusual alterations – gave off the perfume of freshly milled timber.

Meeting French, Mr Creed took his coat and proceeded to reverse the sign in the glass. Just then, various clocks in the back chimed to confirm the hour. Mr Creed must have decided to wind them all in preparation for reopening, French realised. He himself had not been maintaining them, and when last he was here, most of them had stopped.

'Open!' announced Mr Creed, seemingly determined to progress.

'But sir, are we ready, sir?'

With a jangle, the door opened, before French could even finish asking.

'Well, that did not take long. Our first customer this year.' Mr Creed turned with an almost gleeful smile. 'Don't worry, Mr French, all is in hand. Just follow my prompts.'

'Yes, sir.' Though feeling as though he had just stepped onto a moving merry-go-round, French replied dutifully. For now, he had little choice but to do as bid, and, at Mr Creed's invitation, crossed inside, just as the customer approached the counter.

'Good morning, sir. What can we do for you?' Mr Creed asked the pauper, politely.

'Are you taking pledges, sir?' the old man asked, with barely the power in his voice to carry the question. French wondered how he had strength to stand, so thin were the poor man's legs.

'We are taking pledges, sir. What do you have?' Mr Creed responded, to French's astonishment.

'I have a bowl, sir,' the man said, producing from under his coat a piece of crockery with more cracks than the plaster of a fallen ruin,

French estimated. But nevertheless, Mr Creed began to process the item, logging it into the book without qualm.

'Mr French, would two shillings be a fitting advance on such an item, would you say?'

'Two shillings?' French asked, unsure if he'd heard right and feeling his eyes were growing as large as those of the pauper, who, on the far side of the counter, was staying quite silent. 'I'd say a sixpence would –'

'Agreed. Two shillings it is,' Mr Creed said, overruling French, who, had he been permitted to finish, was intent on saying that a sixpence would buy two such items, if they were new.

'One year or two, sir?'

'Huh?' the man answered, confused.

'Let's say two years, at one per cent accrued interest. Will that do, sir?'

'Uh ... yes,' the old man replied, seemingly stunned.

'Very well,' Mr Creed said, and readied his pen. 'Mr French, would you fetch the deposit from the safe, please?'

'Of course, sir,' French said, and, manoeuvring behind, found the safe open, readily stacked with coin.

'Now ... Mr –?'

'Cronin, sir. John Cronin, of Chapel Lane.'

Writing, Mr Creed repeated, 'John Cronin, of ... '

Back from the safe, French placed the coins upon the counter at Mr Creed's disposal.

'Now, Mr Cronin. Two shillings.'

French watched as, with spindle-like fingers, the man took the money from the counter to his pocket, his eyes awash with disbelief.

'Eh, the bowl, sir?' French reminded them both.

'Oh ...' the man said, seeming genuinely to have forgotten, 'of course, sirs.'

But as the pauper moved to lift up the bowl, Mr Creed interrupted: 'Oh, yes, that's a problem.'

'Sir?' asked a puzzled French, while, appearing as though he might flee at any moment were it not for his condition, the old man's eyes darted between the two.

'We have no room for a bowl here. Our stores are, unfortunately, quite full. Am I right, Mr French? I'm afraid you'll have to hold onto it yourself, Mr Cronin – in safe keeping – and come back when you have money to redeem it.'

At this, neither French nor the pauper had a single word to offer. But as Thomas French himself began to, it seemed Mr Cronin, too, understood what was happening.

It made no logical sense whatsoever. But irrespective of why it was happening, French enjoyed the feeling more than anything he had known for some time. Not alone at feeling appreciated in Mr Creed's, or in anyone's, eyes for the first time since the death of his mother, but to feel a part of something as intrinsically good as what was unfolding before him.

No sooner had the first customer left than another, Nancy Scanlon, of Donoughmore, arrived and was treated to the same fare, only, when the poor woman moved to divest herself of the blanket she had pledged, Mr Creed, having already paid her the advance, found fault this time with the item itself.

'Oh, that's a pity,' he frowned, discovering the painted lettering upon its end. 'V.D.P.' he read aloud, feigning disappointment. 'Do you remember the article, Thomas, requesting of all pawnbrokers that they not take any St Vincent de Paul blankets, this year?'

'I ... do, sir?'

'I'm afraid you'll have to hold on to it, ma'am.'

'I don't understand, sir,' she said, looking fretful.

'Oh, you can still take the deposit,' Mr Creed told her quickly, 'but you must hang on to the blanket yourself. For I cannot keep it here, on the premises. Is that agreeable, ma'am?'

French found himself almost overcome as the girl thanked them both and left.

Later that day, when, having processed numerous other cases similarly, they had a moment's rest, French asked a question of his employer. 'Do you believe they will make good on their pledges, sir; that they'll come back?'

'The honest poor, Mr French? Some will, at least. Some day.'

BEALTAINE
MAY

30

SALUS POPULI SUPREMA LEX

Like the cry of a vixen, calling her cubs to warn them of danger, the sound seemed to carry a great distance, echoing across the slated roofs and down the cobbled streets, a watery imprint of the elements in its tail. Awake in the blue darkness, Cornelius Creed sat still, picturing the trembling human forms at the source of the sickening noise. How much louder it must be there, under the arches of the bridge, he imagined, a haunted chamber of suffering.

'If William White Hedges *was* here, he'd probably abscond again, just as quickly,' Paulellen said, somewhere beside, leading Creed to wonder how long she'd been lying awake, silently listening, as he was. And she was right. Macroom Castle was perhaps the closest residence to the river, and to the sound.

'You're awake?' he asked, instinctively.

'Who could sleep through that?' she replied. 'The whole town must be alive to it. God help them,' she whispered, at length, with pity in her voice. 'Have you seen them?' she asked, when, after a while, there was a lull in the constant sound.

'I have,' Creed replied, but added no more. *I saw them again today, out walking,* he thought to add, but somehow could not bring himself to speak aloud of what he had seen. Instead, as the awful wailing resumed, he lay back down and there wrestled aimlessly, with as little success as his wife, it seemed, to find any comfort in the privilege of his pillow.

Carrying his writing equipment through the kitchen that morning, Creed picked up the last cut of toast from his breakfast plate, and, while licking the butter that rolled down his thumb, lowered a crust to the waiting dog. Swallowing it whole, it stared back intently, hoping for more.

'Not manning the counter this morning?' Paulellen asked, at the sound of life below.

'No. I'm determined to maintain my routine of getting out once a day and keeping up with my other pursuits,' he told her. 'Thomas French has it all in hand, besides.'

'Now, there's a new man,' she said, surprised. 'Well done to you, Cornelius Creed. You made a virtue of helping him out of that slump.'

'Well, it's good for us both. I can rely on him and … there is no disadvantage, in truth … How are you feeling today? Better?'

Paull, leaning hard on the table, looked tired. Rubbing her eyes in place of an answer, she took her face in her hands. 'I just can't seem to get a wink of sleep,' she said, at last. 'Those poor women and their children.'

Creed soughed heavily too. 'I know,' he said, after a time.

'Go,' Paulellen urged him gently, seeming to sense his need.

Followed by the dog, Creed found himself in the upstairs front room, where, away from the bustle of the shop, he hoped to focus on what was happening outside.

With a passing glimpse, he took in the mirror, wherein, some months before, rambling abstractedly about the shoes, he had examined his reflection, searching for something or someone else; another Creed, it had seemed. But both those Creeds were gone now, he realised, left behind to that murky window of the recent past. Here alone today was the Creed he knew of old: the one with purpose, who knew what to do.

Settling into the groan of the chair, he took up his pen, and, lifting his chin to the warmth of light radiating through the glass, Creed closed his eyes to recollect his last thoughts of the night before. Tossing and turning to the heartbreaking sounds that were coming from the river, he had meandered and drifted, considering what he would write in the morning.

Ah, yes, he remembered: the lingering controversy of Bishop Edward McGinn's public letter. Damning, to say the least, of the government proposal to relocate one and a half millions of the Irish peasantry to the wastelands of Canada, the Catholic bishop's vitriolic critique had fomented even more division across the already fractured array of patriotism. By his own feelings on the matter, Creed had felt inspired to open with a quatrain from Oliver Goldsmith's 'The Deserted Village' – famously written by the poet upon his witnessing the destruction of a peasant settlement to clear the way for a wealthy man's garden.

> Princes and Lords may flourish, or may fade;
> A breath can make them, as a breath has made;
> But a bold peasantry, their country's pride,
> When once destroyed, can never be supplied.

TO THE EDITOR OF THE CORK EXAMINER

May 1st, 1847.

Dear Sir–

The more soup, *Soyer,* and artificial means of averting the root cause of our appalling national prostration, the greater the mass of pauperism throughout the whole land.

The spot from which I write presents a spectacle as disturbed and convincing of British misrule as it is revolting in its aspect. Macroom at this moment is surely the most poverty-stricken town in the south of Ireland – at a depth of human suffering beyond even Skibbereen and Schull. Deaths are so numerous and sudden that the mind is wholly depressed of its wonted inclination to horror.

Removed from the market-house walls and the body of the town lately, thirty-six of the most miserable-looking creatures were obliged to find shelter elsewhere, and, some days ago, settled on the strand of the bridge. There, at risk to themselves and the rest of the community, they have lain since, exhibiting their dead, with and without coffin or shroud – for the purpose of securing some means of sustenance for the surviving group, one can only presume. Wretched coverings and tattered garments are long since *all but pawned* in order to procure a morsel for their little ones, while the parents themselves are left, not alone hungry, but bare and naked to the inclemency of the weather. The bridge being the town's only access from the Kerry side, the sight has produced much alarm among those travelling through by coach and otherwise.

Days ago at this new infection spot three men died, each leaving a family and wife, whose lamentations since, over the remains of their husbands – at the dead hour of night, when the swollen river seems to become the auxiliary of approaching death – would rend the heart of the most inhuman being in existence. For days, each of those widows, in turn, has *keened* the partner of her life in the most affecting manner. On yesterday, as I witnessed it, one of them evoked the curse of heaven upon Lord John Russell, not just for the death of her husband directly, but for the only source of subsistence to herself and her children. Of all people, she perhaps most must be keenly aware that, by his recent decree, *with the swipe of a pen*, the complement of labourers *nationally* employed upon the public works was *thrice decimated*, with the result that, in the parish of Macroom alone, hundreds of families were thrown off the works.

Traditionally the first day of the harvest, today has sounded the death knell on that source of relief to hundreds of thousands, who, when counted with their dependents, must number in the region of two million souls. We shall be harvesting *bodies alone*, before long.

In disbelief at what he was writing, Creed stopped a moment. One horror-filled statistic after another already spoke of incalculable suffering: and that in just his own locality.

Who was he writing to? Creed asked himself. How many could he expect would read his accounts when every column of most every newspaper was dedicated likewise? Was it to shame those who would not, or inspire those who could yet, into doing much more of what they ought? Was it himself he was trying to shock into some deeper feeling, or more extreme action? For posterity, perhaps? Did the answers even matter?

If even it was merely to find a release for his own feelings, there was one thing he did know: his instinct to bombard the paper had to be obeyed. For did he not have eyes to see? The gift of words? And from the pen in his grasp with an open channel to the *Examiner,* every tool at his disposal to utilise both? Should he not be damned if he did not put them to work given his singular perspective on this corner of the world? And for this reason, if no other, was it not his duty and obligation to form part of the fabric that would record, and hold to account, this gargantuan disaster?

Looking over the square, Creed's gaze fell once more to the vacated spot by the Market House. Upon the bare ground, but a lonely scattering of straw spoke to its former inhabitants, reminding him of his task.

> Through the humane efforts of *some* of the local Guardians, sixteen of the lingering creatures moved from the square were conveyed to the Workhouse last evening. Thank God it has reopened! The other twenty were left to perish beneath the arches of the bridge, attacked by wind and water from all directions. The unfortunate and care-worn mothers may be seen collecting watercress and some such food by the banks of the river. This the children devour, in fact, having little or nothing else to sustain life.
>
> Coffins are daily placed at the church gate, for interment. But in the plenitude of his liberality and commiseration for the poor, the Rev. Mr Swanzy has peremptorily refused any further accommodation in *his* grave-yard, thereby obliging the bearers to either lay down in the open street, or take back, the putrid and infectious remains of their loved ones. This question must be settled at once, and not have humanity outraged further by such wholly appalling and unnecessary exhibitions. Five young children were heaped in the butt

of a cart yesterday, all dying of want, but they would not be received at the Workhouse; the Master having been threatened by the Guardians on the Saturday previous for admitting four persons in the last stages of destitution, at the special request of Fr Lee.

Last Tuesday was the first day of giving out relief tickets for the Soup House. It was painful in the extreme to behold the congregation of moving rags but half covering the creatures whose frames gave incontestable evidence of every privation. No description can equal the sad spectacle.

By the wisdom of its *well-intended* law, the vast number thrown off the public roads, including those still stretched by the riverside here, must, with their families, *live on air* for fourteen days more before they can get their card. What a *mockery!*

In the adjoining parishes of Kilnamartery and Ballyvourney, persons taking corpses on their backs in pannions or *kishanes* to the grave, without any covering, is now so common a practice that no such extravagant idea as coffins or funerals prevails, with few exceptions.

It appears that all things conspire for the augmentation of the sufferings of the poor of this afflicted land, and that the conduct of the British Minister, and the doings of an unfeeling and migratory crew of officials, tend only to disprove the recognised and often inculcated doctrine *Salus populi suprema lex* – the health of the people is the highest law.

Yours faithfully,
C. CREED.

Relatively relieved at finishing, Creed downed the pen and blew out his lips, to the sound of which the dog started to its paws, apparently ready: a walk would be a fitting reward for its patience. But at its next reaction, Creed wondered which of them was sadder, for it grieved him to refuse.

'Not today, my friend,' he told the faithful creature, who whined but once and returned to its unhappy spot. 'I'm afraid we'll have to find somewhere else to walk, a while. I'll let you have a run around the garden ...'

31

Best by Hands are Anthems Sung

'Very fine work, ladies … Catherine, we must remember always to soap our hands before handling the cotton … Ellen, same … Mary, posture. That's it. Don't slouch.'

'Yes, Mrs Pearson,' the girl replied, as the instructress strolled between the rows.

Concentrating hard, pushing it through, Cáit studied the course of the needle. Too often she'd pricked her fingertips, struggling with the awkwardness of the thimble.

'Did you ever see one of these houses before?' her neighbour whispered, when Mrs Pearson looked away. But Cáit kept her head down. 'It's all so tidy and straight,' added Ann, looking aloft to scrutinise her surroundings.

Following with her eyes, Cáit silently agreed. For over a week, she'd been coming here, to the Big House, over Mount Cross. A foreboding place it was certainly, and away from the children, besides. But for the life-keeping allowance it afforded, Cáit was more than glad.

'Remember, girls, Reverend Kyle will be coming with a visitor today. We must show them not only our diligent work but the finest of our virtues too, which I know you all can manage. There is to be no staring. We will keep our heads and our eyes in our work – and there's to be no idle chatter, Ann Carroll.'

'Yes, ma'am,' Ann responded.

Cáit liked Ann, but sometimes worried the girl's talking put both their places at risk.

'Mrs Pearson.' The voice of Rev. Kyle brought Cáit to lift her head, but she bowed it as quickly, remembering their instructions, 'I'd like to introduce Mr Blennerhassett, rector of a most generous congregation in Dorset County. He's been touring the counties of Cork and Kerry these past weeks, with a commendable interest in the welfare of our poor.'

'A fine day to meet you, Mrs Pearson,' the gentleman said.

'Mr Blennerhassett, good *morning* and welcome to our humble school. We greatly appreciate you taking an interest in our community.'

'The lady of the house is being very modest, sir,' Mr Kyle told the guest. 'Mrs Pearson almost singlehandedly runs our *humble* school. We are newly opened – at the beneficence of Abraham Beale and the Society of Friends, in Patrick's Quay, I must point out. At present, we are supporting up to one hundred and nine families.'

'Most impressive,' the strangely named man responded.

'Thank you, Reverend Kyle,' Mrs Pearson replied. 'Reverend Blennerhassett, would you care to see what we make here?'

'I would like that very much,' the man replied, and Cáit found herself won over by his manner, though his accent was quite unusual. In age, Cáit guessed the rectors and Mrs Pearson were, all three of them, around the middle of thirty: much older than she and Pádraig were, but so much more healthy and youthful.

'We instruct around thirty women daily, on six days, all from the surrounding townlands,' Mrs Pearson said, leading the group in walking the room, as they looked in over the women's shoulders. 'After a breakfast of milk and bread, we set them to work, knitting, plain sewing and clothes mending.'

'Marvellous,' Rev. Blennerhassett replied. 'Mostly wool?'

'We do *some* woollen work, but mostly produce cotton stockings, like these.'

'Ah.'

'The long ones sell for one-and-threepence a pair; or short ones – like these – from threepence, small, to seven pence for the largest.'

'I must say, they appear to be of excellent quality, to my untrained eye,' the foreign man said.

'From personal experience, I say one pair of these will last *three times* longer than a pair made by machine, and they are every bit as comfortable,' Rev. Kyle cut in, with what sounded like his most pleased voice.

'Oh, I believe it,' the gentleman answered, clearly convinced.

'But the greatest of all about our scheme', Rev. Kyle added, apparently getting to the purpose of the visit, 'is that the sale of these articles has thus prevented the necessity of our women, many of them widowed, with orphan children, from having to work on the public roads.'

'I can think of no more noble aim,' the guest replied, solemnly, 'and with your permissions, I would like to represent your fine work to my own parishioners, in Sherborne.'

'That would be just tremendous!' Mrs Pearson exclaimed.

'Very well, then I should like to take some samples with me. I will purchase them, of course,' he added hurriedly, 'perhaps ten or fifteen pairs of each?'

Wearing an expression of contentment, Rev. Kyle looked quite proud, and to Cáit, it seemed all had gone well.

Looking up at the sound of Mrs Pearson's preparing of samples for the visitor, Cáit discovered that Rev. Kyle had broken away, and, talking to the women amongst the desks, was moving in her direction.

'Hello, Reverend Kyle.' Ann spoke first, when he eventually neared.

'Mrs Carroll, how are you?' he returned kindly.

'Surviving a day at a time, sir. But if it wasn't for you and Mrs Pearson … My Paddy and me are ever so grateful for what I get here at the school.'

'That's lovely to hear, Mrs Carroll. And you, Cáit, how are *you* faring?' he asked, with concern.

'I am well, Mr Kyle,' Cáit said, feeling far less prepared to answer than Ann had seemed. As kind as any man, Rev. Kyle had long since gained her trust. But, always uneasy and conscious of her raggedness in the presence of people of 'society', Cáit found herself anxious around even him.

'And your husband, Máirtín, isn't it? How is he, Cáit?'

'He's much better, and getting stronger, sir, thank you,' she said, more unnerved at the lie she was having to continue. 'Your generosity and the place at the school have meant a great deal to us.'

'It's the least we can hope to do.' Rev. Kyle smiled, graciously. 'May it continue to serve you well.'

Finding it hard to smile, with eyes to the floor Cáit bowed out of politeness.

'Such exemplary specimens of human kindness,' Mrs Pearson said of the men when Rev. Kyle had walked their guest out to his car, and, as though in their honour, she began to sing aloud,

Be a workman, O my brother,
Trust not worship just to tongue
Pray with strenuous exertion,
Best by hands are anthems sung.

Through the open window near to her, Cáit, at discovering the two men were striking up a conversation, strained her ears to hear it over Mrs Pearson's warbling. But the further the teacher drifted toward the front of the room, the more discernible the voices grew. Rev. Kyle, Cáit made out first, was inquiring of his guest's 'impressions'.

Commending their praiseworthy efforts, the foreign gentleman confessed to being 'alarmed at how much the general condition has deteriorated, compared to my visit of November last'.

'Sadly, your observations are well-founded,' said Rev. Kyle. 'Starvation, dysentery, and fever are making sad havoc in this dominion. Out of one hundred men employed until recently upon the road from Carriganimma to Clondrohid, *twenty-eight* died of starvation.'

'Oh, dear,' the visitor replied, with great sadness in his voice. Cáit herself was shocked at the revelation and, for the first time, reconsidered their poor luck in not being able to get Pádraig onto those works.

'In an ordinary season, interments generally amount to no more than twelve per week,' Rev. Kyle elaborated, 'but in the last three alone – the most favourable for some time – there have been in excess of forty burials per week.'

'Good gracious! Near four times the usual number?' the foreign reverend commiserated.

'The Public Works, criminally mismanaged, have sent many early to their graves,' Kyle said. 'They die so slowly that none call it murder.'

Having forgotten herself, Cáit startled at something falling to the floor beside her, and turned to find Ann Carroll, the face of shock, having dropped a large scissors.

'Is all well down there?' Mrs Pearson called. But on this occasion Ann seemed unusually prone to silence.

'Yes, ma'am,' Cáit responded, instead.

When, outside, the rectors resumed their talk, it was clear they were now aware of their proximity to the window.

'Well, Mr Blennerhassett, I know you have business in Macroom. I'll not detain you further. You're still stopping at the Glebe House tonight?'

'If that's no trouble, I'd be most grateful, Rev. Kyle.'

'No trouble at all. I'll tell Mrs Stephenson you'll be dining with us.'

Heading home that afternoon, nearing Clondrohid, Cáit came upon a crowd at whose centre she glimpsed two children, one laid against the ditch, the other kneeling alongside.

'A sister and brother, poor craturs,' a woman volunteered.

Though her view was blocked by the crowd, insofar as Cáit could gather they were both still alive, but in a wretched state and very distressed. With no sign of the parents or any such guardians, she wondered what tragedy had befallen them to be abandoned in such a sad condition.

'What is the matter here?' a strangely familiar voice interfered, and at the sound of a cart, Cáit turned to discover the English reverend who'd visited the school that morning; returning from Macroom, she supposed.

'The boy is dying,' a well-dressed gentleman answered.

'Someone help my poor brother, please,' the little girl cried, just as Cáit caught another glimpse of the children. Breathing hard, he was staring to the sky while his sister looked on pitifully.

To Cáit's great relief, Rev. Kyle's guest, having studied the scene, handed something to the same gentleman, saying, 'Please see the poor fellow is attended to.'

———

But on her way back to the school, next morning, Cáit discovered the boy was dead. For two days more, each time she passed, however much she hoped it were not so, still he was there, his little sister watching over him yet.

'Good God in heaven, would no one stop to bury the poor child?' Pádraig asked, angrily.

'I suppose there are so many,' Cáit said, at a loss for an answer, her thoughts taken up with consulting her conscience. 'I gave the girl some griddle cake, twice. But what more could I do?'

'God help that poor little child. Did she *say* anything, or *ask* for anything?' Pádraig persisted.

'She just cried for someone to bury her brother,' Cáit said. 'Who knows, maybe someone –'

'If you'd told me, I would have ...' Pádraig began, covering his eyes as though the image was too much.

'And what if they'd the fever?' she asked.

'Fever or no fever, they deserved to be buried, and not left to lie by the side of the road,' he cried, 'for the crows to –'

Cáit was used to seeing bodies by now. She'd passed two other men only that day, and with more around them not long behind.

Holding on tight to Síle and Diarmuidín, Cáit cried over them, unable to loosen the scene from her mind: that little girl refusing to leave her brother. In her heart it was as though those two little children represented herself and Onóra.

32

To the Last, to Hope

'Some have even been so ungrateful as to raise their voices and their arms against him who still exhibit marks of the chains which *he* has stricken off!' Father Lee proclaimed, his voice ringing through the lonely chapel, where, sitting alone, Creed listened on.

'But let no man antedate O'Connell's doom. Who dares anticipate the stroke of fate? Or outrun the speed of death? With the benedictions of the supreme pontiff, the monarch of the Irish heart, and of Irish *law*, restored to health and vigour, will return and, please heaven, live to achieve the favourite object of his heart: the regeneration of his native land.'

Shocked by sudden rumours of O'Connell's death, Creed found himself at a sparsely attended Sunday mass, in hopes of attaining some higher confirmation. But the closing words of Father Lee, having avoided the subject until that moment, brought no clarity.

'Go to your homes,' Lee croaked, clearly jaded, but recently recovered from fever. 'The rumours may not be true, yet. Hold fast for better news, and pray.'

It had been in the wind that this day would come, thought Creed, slow-footed, walking from the church. Whispers and reports of O'Connell's ill health had emanated steadily since Forty-Three. But by virtue, alone, of the pilgrimage he'd been undertaking over recent weeks – however the people would wish it were not the case – the great man himself seemed clearly to sense that his hour was fast approaching.

Still, with some hope, proceeding for home, Creed told himself, *a rumour is a rumour until facts can confirm or prove otherwise.* Tomorrow would bring more.

On Monday, at the shop and in the street, there was no other topic on anyone's lips, from the beggar at the castle gate to the coachmen passing through.

The *Examiner*'s piece only served to exacerbate the tension, as if it brought the lamp-oil closer to the flame. Having first locked the door, that he and French might absorb its wisdom free of interruption, a worried Creed read the foremost headline.

REPORTED DEATH OF O'CONNELL

MONDAY EVENING MAY 24, 1847.

The London journals of Saturday, which reached this city yesterday morning, brought intelligence rumouring the death of our illustrious Regenerator. The following is the announcement of the *Chronicle* :–

'The following letter, from our Parisian Correspondent, has just reached us:–

'The *Moniteur Parisien* of this night (Thursday) contains the following:–

'On ecrit de Nice que O'Connell est mort en arrivant a Gênes.'

'Meaning,' Creed explained, '"A letter from Nice gives the death of Mr O'Connell on his arrival at Genoa."'

Beside him, over praying hands, French seemed to equal Creed's apprehension. But he knew they must read on.

Although this important statement bears no date, we must observe it was communicated through the organ of the French Government, who received it probably by telegraphic dispatch, as it is worded in the form usually adopted when giving such communications to the public.'

Creed had the sense of following a trail backward across the continent. By the time this news had reached Ireland, he realised, it was substantially aged, and – by the already established pattern of one periodical quoting another – essentially hearsay. 'We'll have no confirmation this day,' he told French with some confidence.

But, exploring the language thoroughly, he spotted something that carried the promise of hope, yet.

'Wait … hear this,' he said aloud.

> This certainly implies Mr O'Connell died on his arrival at Genoa; but as the letters in London are dated a fortnight subsequent to his reaching the former place, we do not feel disposed to attach credit to the announcement in the *Moniteur Parisien*. Admittedly, the last accounts of Mr O'Connell's condition were such as to afford very slight hopes of permanent amendment, but on the strength of a vague statement, undated, and without any guarantee of its authenticity, we must await further and more explicit accounts. We cling, to the last, to hope.'

'Exactly!' Creed rapped the page with the back of his hand. 'This has been my thinking also.'

But still, the outlook was dismal, he knew, and, disinclined to the endless columns that would only amount to repetition, he left the paper to French. 'I've read enough. I must take a walk.'

―――

Tuesday's *Reporter* brought nothing more of Monday's speculation but a hint that the last letters received by the O'Connell family were of the kind to fully prepare them for a melancholy announcement.

Spontaneously, that evening, Creed brought himself to the People's Hall in Temperance Lane. Seeking consolation amongst fellow devotees there, at the outpouring of grief and affection, he found himself moved;

especially when his neighbour, the apothecary, Matthias Ryan, spoke of one of the Repeal Association's foremost members.

'The hall door of O'Connell's house on Merrion Square is said to be beset by inquirers. But even in Dublin no one can find anything out. Poor Tom Steele is said to be heartbroken, hovering about, scarce believing the stupendous blow has been struck.'

Steele had been a faithful friend, and the 'Head Pacificator', who'd followed O'Connell with such fidelity and devotion as to be almost heroic in its abjectness. Creed became watery-eyed at the thought of Steele's loss alone. But the gloom was general, and a mournful depression was observable in the expression of every man, woman and child he had encountered that day as each awaited the certainty, or otherwise, of their tribune's passing.

'Regardless of religion or class,' Creed told Paulellen, removing his coat when he returned home, 'the announcement will nowhere be read without some sense of awe being felt.'

———

Wednesday's edition of the *Examiner* was very ominously late. All day, through the window, Creed watched for the mail car, sending out French at every sign. But it was closing time when, at the sight of its torches crossing the square, Creed rushed out to meet it himself. Though realising, in his haste, one could not purchase a copy straight from the car, he found many others convening upon the spot, including the errand boy sent out from Mary Hogg's to fetch their batch of copies.

'Here's a sixpence,' he told the boy. 'You'll permit me a copy here, and deliver this to your employer?'

'Yes, sir,' the boy said, untying the cord around the stack.

'I'll do likewise.' Taking his example, others began to place orders while Creed started back for the shop, frustrated at gaining nothing from the print in darkness.

'Cornelius,' someone shouted behind, and Creed turned on the step, not only to discover Samuel Welply running to meet him, but to find a small entourage amassing in his own wake.

'You have it?' Sam inquired, looking to the paper, breathless from catching up and holding his knees. Without the means to purchase copies of their own and most of them likely 'without the letters', Creed supposed that those others gathering around were, like Sam, hoping to learn the truth and, perhaps, find solidarity in the moment too.

'Come in, come in,' Creed said, and, waving them past, held the door until eight or nine bodies had crossed the threshold, among them the widow Reardon of the shambles; John Kelleher of the square; Thomas Granger of the Protestant schoolhouse; and, at the last minute, Patrick O'Riordan, another old and dear acquaintance. The two exchanged a knowing glance as Creed closed the door. The sight of Paulellen appearing from upstairs coincided with the shriek of a woman on the square and a sudden murmur of voices beyond. Much alarmed, all within looked to Creed, who, moving, dropped the paper upon the counter.

'Sam, would *you* –?' Creed asked, when his friend acceded by action, collecting up the broadsheet and bringing it to the light. But the time it took for Sam to speak seemed, to Creed, the residence of an eon until, at last, he read aloud, 'O'Connell is dead!'

As though a statue, to the cascade of crying and moaning that began around him, Creed did not move, or blink. Paulellen, coming near to clasp his arm, brought sensation, and instinctively he returned the gesture, but he felt blank and stoic, in disbelief. As others took refuge against solid surfaces, to Creed it seemed everything was in conflict with everything; time with movement; stillness with sound; emptiness with a sense of collision.

'"This is the sad proclamation it is our painful duty to make,"' Sam continued, apparently in control of his emotions. '"O'Connell, the veteran leader of Ireland, and advocate of universal freedom, is no more.

'"He breathed his last, at Genoa, on the fifteenth of this month, in the seventy-second year of his age, at thirty-seven minutes past nine; the hand of the priest of God extended above him. There was no struggle, nor visible change upon his features. The spirit that moved the world took its flight so peacefully that all were in doubt if it actually had departed. He died as an infant sinks upon its mother's breast to sleep, and by the soft and beautiful transition of the prayers: we had suddenly before us, but the noble body of O'Connell, as if listening, hushed in attention to the summoning of a glorious immortality."'

As Paulellen and old Mrs Reardon began the rosary, akin to water trickling in a brook, the monotone purling string of prayer blended with Sam's reading to form a continuous soothing murmur. What would become of Ireland without him? Creed tried to contemplate, while Sam's delivery of the official report came and went from his hearing and awareness.

'"Full of years, full of honours, and full of woes, the illustrious *Liberator* … endowed with great intellectual powers and exalted attributes … a stricken land and its enslaved race …"'

'"It was his anxious hope,"' came the voice of Dorcas at some point, having seemingly arrived and taken over from Sam, '"that he might be allowed to reach Rome and kneel at the feet of the Pontiff. But that hope was …"' she sniffled, '"… frustrated by fate in the city of Genoa, and, far far away from the home of his affections, *The Liberator* expired."'

Across the minutes that next ensued, with Paull's head upon his shoulder, Creed noticed that the task of reading had become a shared ritual, moving presently to Thomas French. The door was now open, and, as though aimless and unaware of their movements, some left the group and some joined anew.

'"It will be hard to reconcile ourselves to the fact",' read French, '"that *he* – whose voice, a few years since, was heard above the murmur of countless listening thousands, on the hill-side and on the plain – is now hushed in death; that the eloquent energies which aroused and inspired the spirits of millions are but shadows of the past. The sad, crushing fact … is … that he is dead … never t–" Mr Creed, sir?'

At French sounding overcome, Creed was brought to his senses at last, and, feeling almost fatherly somehow, found himself taking up the mantle, directed to a section at the end of the page.

But, clearing his throat, he froze for a moment. Before him, enrapt, lit by the glow of the lamp, were the forlorn faces of neighbours and friends. Helpless and sincere, the widow Riordan stood foremost among them, her tear-brimmed eyes glistening, locked upon his, as though a frightened animal awaiting the final blow.

Then, finding the breath, Creed's voice seemed to carry the words in spite of him. "'In O'Connell's absence, our public is split, our councils distracted, our energies weakened – when the country demands that we should be united firmly. The great population of this fine and noble island should not be permitted to sink irretrievably into political, social and moral debasement, to which we are fast hastening under crude and vicious legislation; a grinding system of landed proprietary; an execrable and avowed desire to be rid of the people; and a scourging plague which rages fiercely, mowing down the poor in battalions …'"

Throughout the short reading, Creed felt a venom rising within, sharpening in his gullet with every word of discontent. But akin to a bird taking flight at the edge of a cliff, unfolding its wings to the effortless lift of air, with an acceptance of words that fell from his lips, his anger was suddenly transformed to a feeling of utter shock.

"'The history of Ireland and O'Connell are identified. For he was, through half a century, the impersonation of his struggling country. But alas! with the land he loved, he is stricken too. Ireland's sufferings were his sufferings. Ireland's joys were his joys. O'Connell and Ireland were one. Death has made a widow of her, Irishmen!

"'We can only pray his loss to us may not be eternal; that the Almighty will yet spare his spirit to guide us through our present difficulties.'"

Where Creed was concerned, the *Examiner* might just as well have announced to the Irish poor that God himself had died in Genoa, leaving them rudderless, and leaderless, to their crushing fates. For, to them,

O'Connell virtually *was* God. And wrapped about him like a shroud, the great sum of their hopes – countless lifetimes' worth of hopes – would go to the grave with him, their Great Emancipator.

MEITHEAMH

JUNE

33

KILCORNEY

For the sake of those still finding refuge below the bridge, whose peace, he feared, tended to be frustrated by the natural curiosity of the dog, Creed, at mid-morning, had strolled west along the Sop Road, to a different stretch of the river.

The fine June weather led him to stray, until, forgotten to himself among the fields, his awareness returned at the sight of large numbers of labourers, who – taking their break, he presumed – were marching, dreamlike, toward the house of James and Mary Welply.

'Hello, Mr Creed,' called a man, who, were it not for the whistle around his neck, seemed to belong to the others, but did not appear to be going with them.

'Do I know you, sir?' Creed returned.

'Thomas Barry, sir. I've been a customer, betimes, is all.'

'I see. Hello, Mr Barry. A fine day. Tell me: I was under the impression all works were ended? And why are your labourers descending upon the Welply residence?'

'Oh, 'tis a private enterprise for the railway coming, sir, though the conditions would be every bit the equal of the works were it not for the generosity the Welplys extend, at their own expense. I have orders from Mr and Mrs Welply to send to them as many labourers under my charge as required, for a breakfast. A fine thing, sir.'

'Indeed,' Creed replied, feeling much surprised. 'I confess, I was unaware of this meritorious charity. How long has this generosity been their practice, Mr Barry?'

'From my own observation, I can state at least a hundred men get food here every day, sir, and better than they themselves can afford, with the largeness of their families. I've been all winter an overseer here. And as many have been spared, thus, by their kindness.'

'Fascinating,' Creed answered. Just two fields over, the labourers were by now queuing outside the house and Creed decided he should avail of the opportunity to visit. This likely explained why he had seen so little of James in recent months, he realised.

'I thought it was just me had dispensed with the ragman roll of local politics,' he told his friend, walking to view the garden with him a short while later. 'I now see that, perhaps, we have reached the same conclusions, James. I too have withdrawn from the meetings.'

'If by "the same conclusions" you mean realising there are more ways to approach a catastrophe than just talking about it endlessly and doing nothing, then we are very much agreed, Cornelius. But we have always been of the same reasoning, have we not?' James smiled, stoking Creed's affection.

'Well, all I can say is, the utter gall of that "*Viator*", publicly castigating you –'

'Oh, pay that no mind,' James said, seemingly untroubled.

'Who could find fault with one who does so much for the poor?' Creed vented. 'And what business is it of anyone's if you *should* keep three or four dogs, finding the amusement and exercise they afford you necessary for your health?' Creed remarked. 'Whoever the devil it is, he was surely unaware of your extraordinary efforts here.'

'Such concerns are far from me, Con,' James said, slowing as they neared the plot. 'What do you think?'

'Oh, *look* at *these*,' Creed marvelled, at the stalks of the newly flourishing potato garden. 'This is *very* promising!'

'Isn't it?' James agreed. 'I'm hearing similar reports, all round.'

'Yes, me, too. I was shown equally luxuriant specimens at Timmy Murphy's. Robert Warren wrote to me, too, raving. I'll say this much: bloodsucking corn speculators like Edward Ashe won't be so pleased!'

'I expect you're right,' James concurred.

———

'LET ERIN REMEMBER DAYS OF OLD.' Wending his way toward home, Creed was smiling, if nostalgic, at the memory James had evoked before they'd parted, of the banner that led Macroom's complement of five hundred Repealers through the streets of Cork when, in Forty-Five, the Liberator had drawn a monstrous sea of over a million supporters into the city. That was as close as Creed and his Repeal friends had ever come to hosting O'Connell. At the prospect of entertaining him just a couple of years prior, they had erected the 'People's Hall' in Macroom; and the people's hall it was, in every respect. Though unremarkable from the outside, at its heart it was composed entirely of stones gathered from across the sixteen parishes of West Muskerry – carried mostly on men's backs to the site, in O'Connell's honour. Equipped with a library and a reading room possessing a breadth of the best works and authors, it was an edifice as fit for their king as they could manage. But receiving him, to crown it, was to be a dream unfulfilled. The state prosecutions had seen to that, setting O'Connell's poor health into a spiralling downward cycle.

BOOM! At the blast of a gun somewhere close to his position, Creed was startled from his dreaming and suddenly alive to the baying of hounds.

'Lucky!' he shouted, instinctively running toward the whimpering he understood to be the dog, bolting away frightened by the noise, or shot! In panic, blinded to the animal's whereabouts by scrub and gorse, Creed encountered a family hurrying to hide themselves within a scelp they were clearly inhabiting, the sound of horses and dogs thundering towards them.

Just in time, they got in, and Creed, finding the dog cowering upon the ground, shielded it with his arms, as the hunt – a barking quarrel of blood-lusting mayhem – barrelled past, murderous and chaotic, with horses at the rear.

But while the majority carried on, the last horse skidded to a halt.

'Well, if it isn't the pawnbroker!' a voice mocked at his back, amid the sound of hooves dancing on the spot.

'You!' Creed shouted, recognising the face. 'Of all people, a so-called *Justice* of *Peace*, allowing a calamitous butchery run riot at a time like this! There are poor people trying to *shelter* in this field.'

'Yes, I found two of them hiding in my loft the other night!' Massy returned, exultant. 'Next thing they'll be *dying* in there. I chanced this might scare them all out. But running into you was an unexpected boon.' He grinned, struggling to control the great horse, restless beneath him.

'You ought to keep those hounds under control, Warren. They are a public menace,' Creed shouted, to a horn blowing in the distance.

'I have one hundred dogs that need exercise, Mr Creed. Besides, it's my land you're standing on, and I'll do as I see fit upon it, with the inclusion of having you for trespass if you don't vacate. Consider that your official notice to quit.'

'How in *good conscience* can you keep and fatten *one hundred dogs*, Mr Warren, with human beings starving in plain sight all about you?'

'And *your* dog does not eat, I suppose?' Massy retorted, circling the horse, until, at the sound of another blast, he kicked his heels and set the beast to catch up with the pack, calling as he went, 'A fine set of standards you keep, pawnbroker.'

'One dog is not comparable to a hundred!' Creed shouted after him, seething.

'I should have known I was near his land,' Creed told Paulellen, admonishing himself, pacing the kitchen. 'Codrum House is right *next* to Gurteenroe. He and James are practically neighbours.'

'Do you think he'll pursue the trespass?' she asked, thumbing the paper.

'It would not surprise me in the least,' he huffed, 'but *I* was almost *bowled out of my standing* … by *him* … and his damned beagle pack!'

'Here,' Paulellen said, turning the paper around for him, 'it would appear, the spirit of the hour.'

Reluctantly, Creed sat, directed to an article headed 'KILCORNEY' – the name of a parish some twelve miles north, at the edge of the barony.

'I must go out, love,' Paulellen said, and kissed his forehead as he began:

> In the graveyard at Kilcorney, the consequence of mortal pressure has produced scenes of a nature so disgusting as to almost exceed belief. From the alarming extent of mortality in this district, the number of interments had lately obliged friends of the deceased to place their coffins within a very short distance of the surface, so that almost the entire of the yard was occupied by graves of but days' or weeks' formation, on which the red earth still indicated that the deceased had not long lain under it. Several hungry dogs, driven from the cabins where they had established themselves, being attracted to the churchyard, with very little exertion succeeded in rooting up the ground and tearing open the frail shells covering the bodies. The next step in this dreadful detail is too shocking to allude to. But in a few days, the coverings that once wrapped the bodies were seen driven in ribbons by the wind about the churchyard. A melancholy spectacle, the ground was literally covered with portions of coffins newly dug out; bones, skulls and other relics of humanity ruthlessly ejected, some long before their flesh had turned to clay. This fearful desecration attracted more numbers of starving animals to the scene of havoc,

and though many were shot by a respectable farmer of the neighbourhood, he could not scare them all away from the shocking banquet. An old horse was next poisoned, with a quantity also distributed over the carcass. This was then placed in the churchyard and, of course, voraciously devoured by the dogs.

The Rev Tuomy, of Droumtariffe, said on Saturday last, he met someone returning from Millstreet with a paper of poison for the purpose of endeavouring to destroy those that remained yet.

I believe it is the case throughout the country that the graveyards are too small for the accommodation of the dead; the consequence, that the inhabitants are all too easy prey to the newly learned conventions of these abandoned creatures who everywhere must be shot on sight to deter such grievous occurrences.

Greatly disturbed by the article, Creed sat still to contemplate a moral dilemma he had not foreseen.

At the sound of violent banging, on Saturday morning, Paulellen dressed and rushed downstairs. Ignoring the clamour of the shop, she followed the noise in the other direction, to the yard, and there found her husband hammering nails into the gated wooden fence. Shocked at the sight of his wielding tools of manual labour, she exclaimed, 'Cornelius Creed, *what* are you *doing?*' But by the time he stopped and turned, Paulellen had already discerned the answer. 'Could you not hire a carpenter to do that?'

'At the risk of an escape,' he replied, testing the structure, and looking to the dog, 'I'm strengthening the perimeter.'

Lolling its tongue, the dog lay at his side, watching, with all the innocence of a lamb, Paulellen observed.

34

As Many as the Stars

In the fading twilight of the longer evening, Pádraig lay back after smooring the fire over with ashes. Maybe with the light of the fire gone the children would sleep, he thought.

'Daddy?' Síle said, in the darkness. 'Tell us again about Daniel O'Connell, Daddy. Did he die?'

'He did, darling,' Pádraig said, realising she was wide awake.

'And were all the people very sad?'

'Oh, very sad.'

'What happened when he died?'

'All the birds stopped singing,' Pádraig said, tired, but happy to indulge her little fascination.

'And what else, Daddy?'

'A great mist rolled down the cliffs and told all the trees at his home-place in Derrynane. The giant big oak there shed all its leaves with grief, and 'twas said a black cloud of starlings cluttered the evening sky above the fields.'

'Why were the people sad?' Síle asked as Pádraig yawned.

'Oh, because he was their leader … the uncrowned king of Ireland.'

'How could be a king if he had no crown?'

'Well, you see, he was such a special king he needed no crown at all. Forty years he had battled England, undoing one law after another they concocted to keep our people down. He was a great scholar, you see. They say he could baffle any man with words. That with his great wit and intellect he beat the English even in their own courts, with their own language. Robert Peel himself, the chieftain of that land, said O'Connell was his greatest foe, and a genius.

'Oh, people travelled the length and breadth of Ireland just to hear him speak. Everywhere they went to meet him. Thousands, at first, waving boughs of green. Then tens, and maybe hundreds of thousands.'

'Is that a lot, Daddy?'

'Well … You know when you look up in the sky and see all the stars, Síle?'

'Yes?'

'Even more than that,' Pádraig said, and, looking at the sky himself through the hole in the roof, heard the wonder in the way her breath retracted.

'Did he like green?'

'Green was his favourite colour of all. And the people knew that. So they whitewashed their cottages and dressed them in more and more green, wherever he was passing. Daniel O'Connell, the *Liberator*, they called him.'

'What's a Libater, Daddy?' asked Diarmuidín, who'd been listening too, it seemed. Snuggling up to Pádraig, his little body fit perfectly the shape of Pádraig's own curled-up frame.

'It means when you let something free, Diarmuidín,' Pádraig explained, his chin in the boy's hair, 'like when you let go a little bird, to fly wherever it wants to. Daniel O'Connell wanted to free our people.'

'Are we free, Daddy?' Síle asked.

In the darkness, Pádraig froze, wondering what to say.

'Of course we are!'

Later on, Pádraig wondered why he had not answered Síle truthfully.

He could have told them that, because of O'Connell, people like them were free to go to school now; allowed to go to mass if they wanted, and to marry whoever they wanted. He could have told them that the Liberator had done so much for Ireland's freedom, but that the bold English were very strong, and that for forty years O'Connell had been like a boy talking to a cat with a bird in its mouth. That the English had just held on until he got too old, so that he hadn't fully achieved Ireland's freedom in the end. *Then*, he would have said, 'One day we *will* be, though …'

And maybe it was that, Pádraig realised: that he just couldn't bring himself to tell them he did not foresee it coming in their lifetime. Not now, with O'Connell gone. Even if, somehow, they lived to be old. And if that were true, he thought with a heavy heart, then maybe it was better to just let them live, believing that they were free.

At the sound of Cáit sneezing, Pádraig was pulled from his thoughts. She always got sneezing with the gorse in summer.

'Are you awake?' she asked, and Pádraig heard the exhaustion in her voice. He knew that feeling well, and even longed for it, still. But Cáit was doing all the walking now.

'I am,' he answered, realising he'd thought she was going to say something. Maybe she was too tired, like he used to be.

Throughout the months it had taken his feet to heal, Pádraig's time with the children had been rare and dear, he contemplated. But with the feeling of some strength returning had come a desperate longing – a feeling that said it should be *him* out there, providing for his family. And, by her tiredness, he sensed Cáit needed it, too, of him.

'I never thought I'd miss the works.' Pádraig broke the silence. 'With terror, I used to hear the clinking of the hammers … pelting the rocks, in my dreaming. Now I'd give anything to hear it again,' he said, closing his eyes, 'just to feel useful.' But the works were over! He kept remembering. And even if they were not, Rev. Kyle had advised Cáit against it.

Thank God you got that place at the Quaker school, he thought, presuming Cáit was probably asleep by now.

'Ann Carroll is dead,' she said abruptly, through the stillness.

'Dead?' Pádraig asked, stunned. 'Fever?'

'Three are all that's left, of a family of ten, Reverend Kyle said … in under a month.'

'Oh!' Pádraig drew a heavy breath. 'You never said she was sick?'

'Nobody knew. She just stopped coming,' Cáit said, and sneezed again, causing Diarmuidín to stir in his sleep.

'Poor woman,' Pádraig whispered, and looked back to the stars. How many more of the twinkling lights that were O'Connell's great poor would fall to shadow by the time this awful devastation ever ended?

35

THE CONTRAPTION

'"The beginnings of the disease may be so mild and gradual as to be subjectively indistinguishable from, say, a cold or a moderate case of influenza!" it says. "Ventilation is useless without first purifying the public streets. For what advantage is a stream of air, when, on the exhalations of privies, drains, sewers, and slaughter-houses, it carries the seeds of death through every open window, into hearth and home?"'

Agitated and tired, Paulellen sat listening as a worked-up Cornelius paced the parlour, searching one newspaper tract after another for a panacea she knew would not come.

'"Spirit-drinkers,"' he continued, as though preaching a sermon, '"enfeebling their bodies by dissipation, are rendered fourfold prone to attack, for disease always targets the dissolute and the abject poor, especially those inhabiting crowded, dirty, ill-ventilated situations."'

'But Sam and Dorcas would be the last to fit that description!'

'Oh, I know that,' he replied, blinking repeatedly, 'but I said it. I said it. As soon as I heard they were even thinking of attending that wake, I told Samuel it was foolhardy to go.'

'It was his *brother*, Cornelius – and a priest at that.'

'James did not attend!' he argued. 'John was *his* brother too. The man expired of fever, for heaven's sake. And a priest, yes, but however virtuous his own apartments, he was a priest in daily contact with people living in just such squalor as described here. Through every epidemic across the green face of Ireland in over three decades – be it regarding influenza, typhus, dysentery, or cholera – the advanced opinion of every medical practitioner has been that people *must avoid* the tradition of the wake during outbreaks. *"Do not attend wakes!"'*

'Are you finished?' Paulellen asked, which seemed to halt his ranting. 'They are family, Cornelius. If it was the other way around they would look out for us.'

'I am not saying you should not go over, Paulellen. But we must exercise rational caution. At this moment, on the Square alone – that you imminently intend crossing – there are twenty-two manifestations of the disease, and, reaching the other side, you will enter an abode where not one, two, or even three, but four are stricken. You said, yourself, for all intents and purposes it is a fever hospital!'

'In case you need reminding, Con, it's not just Sam and his three children labouring in fever. Our own godchild, Charlotte, is among them – a child we stood for since birth, in the sight of *God,* and who is as close as we will ever come to having a child of our own on this earth. We have a responsibility to her alone, if not them all for their constant decency to us.' Feeling tears in her eyes, Paulellen stopped. 'For God's sake, Con. And while we're at it: right below us, in off the *street,* you have a shop full of paupers, with any number of them up to their eave chutes in fatal contagion at any given moment.'

'Well…' he said, apparently stumped as to how he might return argument.

'How can you find it reasonable, I'd like to know, to allow every stranger in the barony bring disease in, while you have such trouble with us caring for our own?' Paulellen asked, genuinely concerned at the state of the mind behind such a contradiction.

'Now we are getting off the matter,' he began.

'No, I'd like to know,' she insisted.

'Please, I am taking every precaution to ensure fever will never cross the counter of –'

'How?' Paulellen heard a coarse rasp entering her voice. 'How do you suppose *you* can do what no one else on earth can do?'

'There's no need to be resentful,' Cornelius said, sounding hurt, looking out the window.

'Resentful?' she repeated, incensed.

'We are getting lost here –' he attempted again, meeker still.

'Right.' She stomped, rising scornfully. 'I'll be back to make the dinner. There's some mutton on the slate in the meat larder if you're hungry in the meantime.'

With the stroke of closing hour fast approaching, Creed descended to help Mr French with what, even through the floor, sounded like a busy shop. It had also become his custom of late to check the day's ledger for any sign of the elusive owner of those shoes still hanging by their laces inside the door of the padlocked stores. French was under strict instruction not to allow them leave the shop under any circumstances without his say-so.

Though unaware of the measures he'd implemented, Paulellen had a point regarding his hypocritical approach to the danger, and it was therefore with a heightened sense of exigency that he descended the stairs. For months, he had been chasing a ghost – but perhaps too carefully, or even too playfully, he now realised. If ever he was to find Pádraig Ua Buachalla, it would be by virtue of a chance that, doubtless, had been rapidly diminishing with each passing moment. He would have to step up his efforts somehow. Even with someone as central to Clondrohid's relief efforts as Rev. Kyle looking on his behalf, he had failed to turn anything up. And yet, a residual niggling – telling him not *every* stone had been overturned – had lately inspired Creed to contrive a way to *lure* Pádraig Ua Buachalla to *him* instead. And the resulting method he had devised had the added advantage of being one that would help his customers in the process.

'Hello, Mr French,' he said, approaching the counter from the back, while, through the bars that separated the shop into two distinct rooms, he perused the line of six or seven customers.

'Mr Creed,' his clerk replied, seemingly content at his work.

'Busy day?'

'Not a slow one, sir,' a casual French replied, downing the pen on the latest entry. 'Just a moment, I'll fetch that for you presently,' French told his customer.

Taking the clerk's place before the ledger, Creed worked backwards from the last pen mark, sweeping carefully through the Names column, but to no avail despite nearly two pages of entries. Satisfied he had not missed anything, Creed addressed the next customer in the line.

'Now, good afternoon, ma'am. Your name, please?'

'Mrs Kelleher,' the woman answered timidly.

'Parish?' he said, having already begun writing.

'Clondrohid, sir.'

'Clondrohid?' Creed felt his hand falter, momentarily, as he wrote. 'Clon … dro …' he continued.

Stealing a glance as he wrote, Creed confirmed the woman's condition was as tired as the colourless rags that hung, not only from her own frame, but also from the tiny figure of the child clinging to her hand.

'Don't worry, this won't take long,' he assured her, scribbling to process the woman's advance as fast as he could.

'Tell me, Mrs Kelleher, have you ever pledged anything here that went uncollected?'

At this the woman seemed suddenly nervous, stammering at an answer that would not come.

'There's nothing to fear,' he reassured her. 'We merely have a lack of space in our stores and are endeavouring to return as many items as possible to their owners.'

Creed saw clearly when the man behind Mrs Kelleher nudged her elbow, as though to prompt her. 'A blanket. December, twelve months since,' she blurted out.

'Very good,' Creed said, recording the detail on a paper scrap. *Kelleher, Clondrohid, Blanket, Dec 45.*

'Now, Mr Daley, your coat, sir,' French said, returning, and pushed something into the metal drawer of the contraption which squeaked and clanged, delivering the garment to the other side of the chute. To Creed, the noise of the springs made for a pleasant sound upon the ear. He was extremely proud of his designs, which, so long as fever remained a threat, ensured no contact between those behind and those in front of the barrier.

'Thank you, sir, thank you,' Mr Daley said, bowing as he retreated.

Checking the clocks, Creed confirmed it was already ten past six, and, continuing with his own customer, he dropped the coins into the money chute. 'Here is your deposit, ma'am,' he said, to the sliding chink of metal landing in the narrow trough outside. 'Mr French, could you retrieve this while you're in the stores? Thank you,' he added, passing his note to the outgoing clerk.

'Just a few moments more, ma'am.'

'Thank you, sir. God bless you.'

'Mrs Kelleher, I've been struggling to raise a cousin of mine in Clondrohid for some time, a very poor man. I fear the condition he and his family might have fallen to. Do you know any Buckleys, or Ua Buachalla, out there?'

'There are several around us,' offered the man behind, now clearly associating with Mrs Kelleher.

'There are?' Creed asked, excitedly.

'Well, there's John Buckley, Daniel Buckley. Ua Buachalla, though … Oh! there was an Aindrias, in Cillaclug. 'Tis a time since I saw them parts, though. Could be dead and buried for all I know.'

A short while later, with the last of the customers seen to, Creed decided it was safe to cross the deserted shop and lock the front door, lately reserved for customer use only.

'On the morrow,' he shouted to Mr French, departing through the back, 'please ensure the gate is *firmly* closed?'

'Yes, sir,' he heard faintly, stood listening, his hand on the key.

'How is Charlotte today?' Dr McSwiney asked, entering the room where Paulellen was keeping vigil over her niece.

'Still delirious, Doctor. But sleeping for now,' Paulellen answered, mopping the girl's brow with a wet rag. 'It's very good of you to call. The dispensary must be overwhelmed?'

'Beyond description,' he answered. 'But without patronage from such people as yourselves and the Welplys, the poor would have no dispensary at all. Therefore, given opportunity, we must return that kindness,' said the slight young doctor, who, to Paulellen, seemed unusually collected for his years.

'Thank you, Doctor. How are the others?' she asked.

'The young ones are faring best. John and Marie seem to be coming around. It's Sam I fear for most. Men are worse affected; and men of middle age ...' The mask of doubt, McSwiney shook his head as an exhausted Dorcas arrived from the other room, her face an ashen hue.

'How is she, Doctor?'

'Charlotte is young and strong,' he answered. 'She has a good chance. You are doing everything right, Mrs Welply – open in daytime, closed in the night with the windows; all in separate rooms as you have them; every item of clothing washed; floors cleaned.'

Dorcas nodded along.

'And you know the symptoms to watch for in yourself?'

'I think so.'

'Rising temperature, insomnia, headaches, and, of course, feverishness. Any sign of the stomach distending, or patches on the skin.' The Doctor's head lowered as though to emphasise his earnestness. 'This is for you and your husband too, Mrs Creed. Symptoms can take two weeks to fully develop.'

'I'll be checking on her, Doctor. Don't worry,' Paulellen offered.

'Good … and it's good you have help,' he told Dorcas, 'but you must get some sleep, Mrs Welply. Run-down constitutions make easy hosts.'

Looking to her sister, who appeared to be somewhere else, Paulellen tried to imagine how Dorcas felt: her family in such deadly peril and practically helpless to save them.

Just then, there was a knock at the door. 'I'll get it,' Paulellen said, reacting quickly.

'Right, I must get back,' she heard the doctor say, as, by her hand, the front door opened to reveal her husband upon the step.

'Hello, Mr Creed,' McSwiney said, squeezing past.

'What can I do to help?' asked Cornelius.

36

Last Leaf

Huddled beneath the coat, shivering in fever, Pádraig felt like his head was immersed in a lime furnace, while his body seemed unable to find warmth at all. Filling his ears, his breath heaved as, outside, the raging wind continued to pummel like a force battling the darkness; the timber of the door moaning and crying incessantly, tormented by the onslaught.

Any little mistake now, an echo of his thoughts told Cáit over and over, *anything at all might mean the difference between falling and standing, or living and dying. The tiniest thing in the world, and you're gone. We cannot afford a single mistake now,* he had told her, or at least he thought he had. When, he could not remember.

By now, though, the question was not so much where they had made a mistake, as what they could have done to avoid it, when disease was so rampant. All year they'd been on the alert, aware the sickness was out there, until, suddenly, it had been everywhere: in the cabins; stalking; jumping from person to person and family to family. He and Cáit had discussed keeping their distance from anyone with contagion. But sometimes people looked fine one day and sick the next. In the end, surviving had meant inevitably crossing paths with disease on a regular basis and Pádraig supposed they might have caught it anywhere: in the soup queues; from one of the neighbours; or at the meal depot. Cáit might have encountered it at the sewing school.

How they had managed to outrun it and last this long on almost nothing amazed him. Maybe they were meant to survive. He had to believe they were. In some backward way, perhaps all the time Pádraig had spent off his feet had afforded him strength enough to better fight disease than he could have were he as crippled and broken down as he'd been in January and February.

Lying there shivering, Pádraig felt like the last leaf on the tree; a leaf that had hung on all winter long, resisting, holding fast, clinging to the branch, a brittle twig. The fearsome wind, with all the suck it had, had dried, torn, and ripped the other leaves asunder. Blasted and trembling he'd watched them all go until he alone had remained. And when the winter with all its ice and snow still did not detach him, it had continued, blowing relentlessly like a winter's gale, all through spring and into summer, so that here, now, there was barely anything of him left at all, and even the tree itself had withered to a hollow shell. How long more did he have to hang on before it would lie down and give him some rest, Pádraig questioned. But on and on it blew. And on and on he suffered, until, shivering, waking, Pádraig wondered how many days they'd been there, curled up, dreaming, trembling, clinging, all four of them, ravaged under the coats by the beast inside them. Was it day or was it night? And how many days more would it torture them before it either finished them off or loosened its awful grip?

The blight had ruined the crop, and now fever had diseased their bodies.

But what next? Pádraig asked, as he had asked himself already that day or the day before, lying there in the darkness. *What next?* he asked again now, holding his children, listening to Cáit struggling, stroking her hair with his shaking hand. What else could he do to get his family past this impossible obstacle? And if he succeeded in that, what then?

October was still four months away. Four months until they'd know if the seed he had planted had escaped the blight. Even if the crop was good, he'd put in so little, there would barely be enough to sustain them for a few weeks, let alone another winter. *Another winter? Like the last?* Unable to bear the thought, Pádraig buried it, somewhere deep, dark, into the night-black, bog-drenched soil of his mind.

Moisture! Moisture! his mouth begged as Pádraig hugged himself under the coat. Their mouths had been so dry with the fever taking hold, he'd placed a pebble in each of the children's mouths to suck on – a trick his father had taught him one hot summer when he was young.

'It keeps the moisture going,' he told the children, just as his father had told him. But the stone in Pádraig's mouth was by now so dry it had stuck in place, rubbing against his teeth. Still, he refused to spit it out, every once in a while forcing it to move, until it drew whatever water his body could muster yet out of his gums.

After so long listening to the blast, Pádraig could no longer tell if the wind was real or imagined. But when the door burst in, he gasped, his breath stolen, as, somewhere inside, he dreamt the cabin had rolled off the hill.

Fix the latch, Pádraig, please! Cáit's frequent plea across the weeks rang through his memory, as under the blanket the wind came menacing, simultaneously tossing through the contents of the cabin. Too sick to utter words, with chattering teeth, Cáit, across, gasped aloud, and, imagining her torn apart by the wind, Pádraig felt compelled to get to it now.

Stripped of his own covering, he struggled desperately to move himself, heavy and disoriented, burning up at the movement. One hard-won inch at a time he began to drag himself across the floor. He choked, and swallowed the invading wind, as, out from under the coat, against their will, his eyes at last told him they *were* still in darkness; that it was night. But whether morning's night or evening's night he could not sense. Tearing the floor with his fingernails, dragging his flesh-poor skeleton across it, Pádraig struggled to cover the hardest three feet of earth he had ever crossed, just to get to the door. Screaming and silent at the same time, his shrunken bones felt every lump of the world beneath him. Dirt and straw blowing all around, Pádraig imagined himself every poor vein of that perished leaf, flapping fast against the raging storm, when, sending him delirious, a bright light burst into his eyes, leading him, deterring him, burning and taunting, a strange creature, flailing its many arms before him, sultry and terrifying, dancing, transfixing him as he rolled to its calm, mesmerising allure. When it was gone Pádraig realised he had blacked out, but for how long, he could not tell. A second, or an hour? But his hand was still gripping the edge of the door, and, with all his remaining might, as though it were the last thing he had ever to accomplish on earth, Pádraig strained and pushed, then, leaning and pressing with everything he had, held it against the wall until, the wind at bay outside, with the other arm pulled out of the dirt, he spent his last to move the rock back into place behind it. The wind rushed once more, rattling the door, then retreated, but blazed, sickened, in circles around the cabin.

Is that the worst of it? Pádraig asked himself, laying back to anchor his head at Cáit's feet. 'Are we over the worst of it yet?' he whispered aloud, directing his question past the sound of the wind combing the roof to God, overhead. Whether by *it* he meant the storm, the sickness, or the unending test of their endurance, Pádraig could not make up his mind. But behind his closed eyes, he hoped they had passed the worst of all three. Because, in that moment, he had not an ounce of strength left to fight any of them an inch more. Drifting, and saturated with disbelief that anyone might push open the door he had fought so hard to close, Pádraig thought he could hear the footsteps of someone approaching outside.

37

Rearmost Milk

Approaching the cabin, giddy as a child, Creed again questioned his cohort: 'Are you sure this is the right one?'

'This is the cabin of Pádraig Ua Buachalla,' the man said, holding the lamp aloft for them to see by.

'I don't see any signs of life,' Creed replied at the darkness of the miserable hut: a windowless pile of stone and earth, patted haphazardly with mud and straw. But feeling himself some kind of Dan Donovan, Creed put his fist to the door, and, giving two knocks, pulled the coat up about his ears.

'Is there anyone within?' he called as Mr Hallissey, his guide, drew back, Creed sensed – the light growing thinner upon the door before him.

'I wouldn't get too close, Mr Creed,' the man said, fearfully, 'there's plenty of fever around these parts, by God.'

But having come this far, Creed was not deterred, rapping thrice this time.

'Pádraig Ua Buachalla,' he shouted, feeling the words almost sucked off his lips by the surging wind. Losing hope, if only slightly, he turned his ear to the door and peered over his glasses in the direction of the car they'd left down by the roadside. So impassable was the way, they had necessarily come the last few hundred yards by 'Shanks's mare,' as Mr Hallissey had termed it: going on foot. Whoever Shanks had once been, his horse was apparently so poor that, more often than not, it had been faster to walk alongside it than ride on its back.

'Damn,' Creed muttered, remembering he'd left the shoes back there on the car.

'Perhaps we should come back another time, sir?' Mr Hallissey suggested, a comment to which Creed returned a *tread-on-the-tail-of-my-coat*-type stare, then turned once more to press the door.

'Oh, I wouldn't,' his companion replied, stumbling with the light as, to the sound of the crying hinge, the door swung inwards, disgorging a hot, pestiferous smell from out the bosom of the cabin.

Concentrating, Creed reached an arm back through the darkness and, listening for any sound, waited impatiently for his eyes to discern the void.

'Bring the lamp, Mr Hallissey ... or at least lay it down if you're too much a sheep to hold it yourself.' By his cowardice, Hallissey, a resident of Clondrohid who recently, at the shop, had responded at once to Creed's asking the whereabouts of Pádraig Ua Buachalla, was fast beginning to frustrate his newfound employer.

'As you wish, Mr Creed.'

The lamp laid down somewhere between them, Creed sensed, he turned, vexed, to collect it. But moving it that much closer had seemingly spilled enough of its glow to illuminate something of the scene within, and, to see for himself what had brought his companion to bear such a face of fright, Creed turned immediately back, abandoning his quest to retrieve it.

There, inside a hovel pregnant with pestilence and poverty, it became clear, was an emaciated family of seven or eight, all dead, the father closest the door with the youngest child apparently embracing him.

'God have mercy ...' Mr Hallissey said, at a distance, and began to babble some rapid prayer, his voice a-quake with emotion and pity.

Unable to register the cadence, Creed blocked it out, preoccupied and horrified, not only at the cruelty of *nature*, but of *time*, to have brought him so close, yet on the wrong side of such an immovable hour. For it seemed to him they had died but very recently.

'... rest their blessed souls,' Hallissey ended his offering, while, fallen to his knees, Creed found himself struggling to grasp how, on the very cusp of the salvation he had been determined to offer the man and his family, this could have happened.

Though overcome with sadness, if only to confirm this was the same soul he had met in the shop with Mr Shanahan that day, Creed inched closer to examine the dead father. But the cut of hunger and death, it was clear, had so changed the man's face from whatever it had once been that with the darkness of the hour, with the wind throwing his hair about, obstructing exactitude, Creed could only guess that it must be the same Pádraig Ua Buachalla: tall and gaunt, if much deteriorated.

Then, as though he had imagined it, Creed suddenly thought he had perceived some wisp of sound emanating from the man. Had it been the wind, playing tricks? Possibly. Yet something else. An imperceptible motion. From what quarter of the body, he had not discerned. But again, there. This time he saw it at the man's lips. *Calling for water, perhaps!*

'Mr Hallissey. Bring the light!'

'I'm sorry, Mr Creed –'

'Bring the damned light, man – please!' Creed whispered, terse, with no room for refusal, and, this time, Hallissey advanced the lamp to within reach.

Armed with the appurtenance, its handle rattling as he leaned upon it, Creed moved one knee over the threshold, bringing his head as close as he could, in desperate hopes to catch whatever sound might yet come.

Nothing.

Had he missed it, he wondered with dread?

Drawing back to examine the man's face again, Creed spoke. 'Pádraig Ua Buachalla, I have searched for you. Whatever your need, it is mine also … If you can speak, just … My name is Cornelius Creed.' Fearing the situation was, indeed, past hope, Creed scanned the shadows within for any other trace of life. But as the wind stirred anew in the trees above, he heard it again, a rush of air from the man's throat. Not a cough. An attempt to speak, he was sure.

'Water, Mr Hallissey. Water!' he shouted, realising the man's mouth was too parched to speak. 'Hurry, for God's sake!' Creed urged as the guide rose from his knees at some distance behind.

When another sound came, remembering Hallissey now had no light, Creed decided he could wait no longer and brought his ear as close as he could to the man's mouth. But what sound came forth was so faint that to better his balance, he leaned in further, and feeling his ear press the man's lips, as though he had implored the rearmost milk of a goat's teat, an utterance came at last.

But the word, something in the man's natural tongue, was a solitary stranger, followed only by a long breath that, leaving, met with, and was absorbed by, the drawing, hungry gust that circled outside, spiralling upward to the void of cloud and restless night above. Then Creed knew it was over.

Upon his return, apparently seeing the proximity Creed had reached, Mr Hallissey dropped the can of water and stood well clear. 'Mr Creed, what have you–?'

At the dull sound of the vessel releasing its contents upon the earth, Creed felt himself pulled back from whatever horizon he had crossed, only to recollect the advice of the old blind man on the square.

'Beware the kiss that falls upon your ear,' Creed mouthed his warning, 'for when it comes, it will already be too late.'

Stepping away from the door and the lamp, Creed turned back once more to behold the scene, painfully enthralled at what lay before him. Resembling a work by some sculptor of antiquity was a scene that might have been carved from the broken heart of tragedy, a man holding a child in his arms; its mother and five more about them, each ravaged, reduced to stone. *Eight souls more ... dead, at the feet of the Empire and its murderous Act of Union,* Creed declared within, feeling the image would be etched in his memory, and scored upon the face of that edifice for all eternity.

Rising from his knees, he too fell back, sat down by his own importance, Creed felt, tricked by his arrogance. That he had legitimately tried to save Ua Buachalla and his family, sparing God knew how many others the ignominy of such a death in the process, did not matter. All his attempts to put things right had now come to naught: grappling with his sanity and the curse; reopening the shop; the search for the man that he might return the shoes and thus rid himself of his guilt at the countless unseen injuries he had caused those souls turned away from his establishment. Unredeemed in the eyes of his maker, it all ended here.

'You cannot escape your fate,' he mumbled to himself, staring, from the cold seat of his rump, at the horror within.

'I'm sorry, Mr Creed?' Hallissey sounded taken aback.

'A prophecy ... from the ancient Greeks ... you cannot escape your fate,' he repeated.

'A strange thing to say at such a time,' Hallissey said, perhaps misunderstanding, Creed realised – as though he'd meant it coldly, reflecting upon the fate of those within.

''Tis not them I refer to ... oh, never mind.' Creed shook his head, defeated, and prepared, as he arose, to accept whatever judgement was given him, whether merited or otherwise.

Fully upright, Creed reached for his purse.

'Please keep the money, Mr Creed.'

'Keep–? I don't undertsand.' Creed returned.

'With the greatest respect, in the eyes of God I could not accept it now, sir.'

'Nonsense. You have done them a mercy yet, Mr Hallissey.'

'Sir?'

'One pound,' said Creed, extending the money to his hire. 'Please see to it these people get a decent burial.' Still hesitant, Hallissey stayed away, eyeing Creed's hand with some reluctance, until, by his mistake, Creed remembered he was likely now corrupted by the disease.

'I shall lay it down here. Wash it with lime.'

With that, Creed walked away somewhat dazed through the dark, in the direction of his carriage.

IÚIL

JULY

38

Wonders Never Cease

'How are you feeling?' Dorcas asked Samuel, returning from across the square.

'Mmm,' he returned, opening his eyes for but a moment, as though mustering the strength.

'You're through the worst of it now,' Dorcas said, pushing the hair back from his brow. 'Rest and recuperation will do the rest, doctor says.'

'How long?' Sam asked, as weak as a kitten.

'It's been over a month since you got bad the first time. The children recovered some weeks past. But you had a relapse, which Val McSwiney says is happening with great prevalence.'

'Last I remember,' Sam said, clearing his throat, 'Cornelius had taken ill –'

Nodding along, Dorcas confirmed her husband's recollection. 'Cornelius got it too, unfortunately.'

'How is he faring?'

'Oh … he is suffering greatly, Sam,' she answered, looking aloft for inspiration. 'This last week, Paulellen and I have been coming and going like I don't know what, keeping vigil for each other. Doctor McSwiney is trying something new he came upon through the medical journals, pioneered by a physician in London.'

Seemingly too tired for expression, Sam lay still and listened, with eyes closed.

'It involves draping wet sheets over the body to bring down the fever,' Dorcas continued, 'but wrapped in blankets, too, to bring on a sweating. I don't quite understand it.'

'He's a few years younger, Cornelius … Surely he –' Sam seemed unable to finish, but Dorcas knew what he meant, and, lowering her head, thought of how much she would like to sleep. To her surprise she felt Sam's hand take hers and, looking up again, found him attempting a smile. 'I'm sure Val is doing all he can do,' he said, gently squeezing her fingers.

'I do hope he pulls through, Sam. For Paulellen's sake, if nothing else. She'd be lost … Anyway,' Dorcas added, attempting to brighten herself, 'we're so relieved to have you on the mend.'

Rubbing his fingers, Dorcas breathed a great sigh containing hope, gratitude, and weariness, but anxiety too. So far, she and all of her immediate family had either survived or avoided the clutches of the desperate malady. It was just Cornelius who needed to recover now.

'Any good news?' Samuel asked, putting her on the spot; perhaps to encourage more of the change in her thinking, Dorcas imagined.

'Good news …' she responded, struggling to come up with anything of significance, 'mmm … Paulellen has … oh … maybe not.'

'Please,' Sam insisted, 'tell me.'

'Well,' she relented. 'Paulellen has been paying some of the poor young boys around the square to give the dog its exercise, in Con's absence, what with the yard being so small …'

'Yes?'

'When I was just coming back across, I saw one of them returning with Lucky, when a carriage pulled up. So a gentleman climbs down to meet the two, and … it took me a moment, but I soon recognised the cut of Massy Warren.'

'Oh …' Sam said, as his demeanour now matched the apprehension Dorcas had felt.

'Yes, he spoke to the boy, and next seemed to examine the dog, and I thought, oh, what is going on here? But then, didn't he slip the boy a coin, and, after exchanging a few words, patted him on the head, before departing. He seemed kindly, do you know?'

'Indeed,' Sam replied, surprised.

'Now …' said Dorcas, rising up, happy to have delivered on such a task.

Closing his eyes, Sam looked ready to sleep again. 'Massy Warren?' he murmured. 'Will wonders never cease?'

39

Hydropathy

Bone tired, in a moment's grace Paulellen sat among the stillness of the kitchen, reflecting on how, in the span of a few short weeks, she had gone from a place of relative security to one contemplating a future, widowed, with a decimated family.

As she worried that by not heeding her husband's caution, she had perhaps brought this fate upon him, the sound of someone ascending the steps did not change her tendency to stare into space.

A light knock came to the upstairs door which, appearing to answer itself, revealed her sister.

'Any change?' Dorcas asked, going straight to the hearth with something she had cooked.

Paulellen shook her head. 'Father Lee prepared him last night,' she said, abstractedly. 'You should be at home with Sam,' she added, coming out of herself temporarily. 'He needs you, Dorcas.'

'I won't stay long,' Dorcas replied. 'Marie is with him. I just wanted to check in, make sure you're eating.'

'Thanks, sister,' Paulellen replied, blankly. 'How is he now?'

'A little better, thank God,' Dorcas replied, looking relieved. 'We just need Cornelius to get well now.'

'Oh, what if he –?' Paulellen let out, beginning to weep.

'Now, you mustn't think like that,' Dorcas said softly, coming to embrace her, just as another knock came. This one proved to be Dr McSwiney, who, for the first time, appeared to be wearing the strain of his position.

'Ladies. How passed the night?' he asked Paulellen.

'Much the same,' she said, drying her eyes.

'*I'll* head out,' Dorcas announced, sneaking gently away, 'be back later.'

'Eh, how is the patient?' the doctor asked Dorcas on her way out.

'Coming around, Doctor, thank you. Just Cornelius now.'

'Good. Good. Shall we begin, Mrs Creed?' he suggested, and, when Dorcas had gone, Paulellen arose to lead him to the bedroom where she had sheets, water and clean blankets at the ready.

'How long can this treatment be continued, Doctor?' she asked, conscious of the feeble body she had washed in advance of his coming.

'As long as necessary, one supposes,' McSwiney answered, seeming to express his own doubts at the lack of success thus far. 'The authoritative physician did not find it necessary to apply the treatment on more than five consecutive days, to any individual.'

'And how long have we –?'

'So far, seven,' he answered with a sigh. 'Mrs Creed, I can discontinue if you wish it. I suggest we hold out another day or two, however. What do we have to lose at this stage, is my reckoning?'

With forlorn resignation, Paulellen acquiesced. 'Very well,' she answered.

'Thank you, Mrs Creed. Oh, one more thing,' McSwiney said, looking to his watch, 'I would very much like to demonstrate the method to Doctor Crooke. Would you mind if he called by? Insofar as it might be of benefit to the suffering humanity of the workhouse, he might venture an opinion on something I have overlooked.'

Paulellen signalled another consent with a wave of her hand and went to answer the latest knock, leaving Dr McSwiney to record something in his journal.

'Mrs Creed.'

'Hello, Doctor,' Paulellen greeted the older gentleman, who, with black hat and a topcoat tied at the neck, looked and sounded as a quintessential doctor should, to her mind: polite but direct; a man whose disposition was slightly gloomy, if marked with intelligence and authority. He grew to look even taller leaving the top step.

'I'll show you in,' Paulellen said, leading the way, floating with exhaustion. Entering the bedroom, she turned to watch the face of the visiting doctor for any reaction to her husband's condition. But, to her surprise, Dr Crooke made no expression at all, either of hope or damnation. Instead, both doctors seemed prepared to set straight to work, with Dr McSwiney leading his attentive elder through the process.

Paulellen, on the other hand, found it too difficult to look upon the object that lay between the sheets of the bed to her right, struggling for life. For within that distorted shell, at present, was barely a discernible fragment of the Cornelius she knew.

It would be strange enough to see him with his hair cut short, she thought, and without his ever-present spectacles. But swollen and purple across large areas of his body, disfigured in shape through his agonies, and most of the time not conscious of who he was, it was as if the attack to his mind he'd suffered last winter had joined forces with a new disease that threatened to take him away entirely and had no intention of giving him back. Most of all, with such suffering and pain as she had witnessed him to endure throughout the last week, Paulellen now wondered if it might be best for her husband to give up and let go. But, by his quietness today, perhaps he already had.

'The method I have followed has been this,' Dr McSwiney began. 'On the flock bed are placed three, four, or five blankets. Superimposed over these is the central apparatus: a wet sheet, wrung out of cold water.'

Paulellen looked on from the chair, while Dr McSwiney, twisting the doused linen sheet over the bucket, proceeded with Dr Crooke's help to lay it across the second makeshift mattress, stuffed with old flock wool for soakage. 'If *you* take one end, Doctor Crooke,' he continued. 'Thank you. Now, upon this the patient is laid, stripped, with legs outstretched and arms to the side. Mrs Creed, would you –?'

Remembering Dr Crooke's walking stick, Paulellen realised she was not to get a break after all this day. Instead, she arose to assist the younger doctor, who, pulling back the sheet, caused Cornelius to squirm and groan at whatever deluge of pains were activated across his bruised skin. Paulellen disliked this part distinctly, and, taking hold of her husband's ankles, awaited the doctor's count to lift.

'How are you today, Mr Creed? Are you ready to be moved?' Dr McSwiney asked the unresponsive Cornelius, then signalled to Paulellen, who lifted with all her strength as her husband howled in pain. Whether at their gripping his tortured skin, or the contortion of his bloated abdomen, she could not tell. But despite his apparent placidity it was now clear he was still suffering greatly.

'Thank you, Mrs Creed,' Dr McSwiney said, as the visitor swapped positions naturally with her.

'Now, the wet sheet is wrapped over the patient, from below, and drawn tightly around, up to the neck, like so, inclosing the feet at your end … that's it.'

Paulellen felt relieved at the sounds Cornelius made at the apparent sensation of the wet sheet enfolding his skin.

'Next, we close one blanket over the top,' Dr McSwiney said, 'then another, and so on, until the whole body is tightly packed, and in this state the patient lies, for anything from a quarter of an hour to one or two hours. As soon as a gentle perspiration commences, a wine-glassful of water is encouraged, as frequently as will be accepted.

'Now, although Dr Gill prescribes it for up to two hours, in the case of Mr Creed I have *not* found it advisable to implement the wet sheet for more than one, as doing so for longer periods caused the pulse to be accelerated, instead of lowered, which, of course, is the desired effect. But *after* the allocated time, or when the desired effect has been achieved, the wet sheet is removed, and the patient – returned to the bed – is well wrapped in three blankets and allowed to perspire for three hours; the blankets then being carefully removed, one at a time, to allow perspiration to subside gradually, leaving the patient between the bedsheets.'

'Notwithstanding the severity of Mr Creed's condition, I believe this is, without doubt, the most effective mode of quickly reducing the temperature of the body. If only temporarily in this case, I found an equilibrium is soon established between the cold of the water and the heat of the body, and, effectively, the patient becomes bathed in a natural vapour bath, as may be felt by placing one's hand under the bedclothes after a short time.'

'What food is administered, Mr McSwiney?' Dr Crooke inquired, addressing him for the first time.

'During the whole course, milk and water, or weak broths, are permitted *ad libitum*.'

'Hmm. Have you had any trouble with bowel congestion?' Dr Crooke asked. 'In my experience, a confined state of the bowels is frequently the effect of a wet sheet, for which I have found it necessary to resort to small doses of castor oil.'

'Interesting,' Dr McSwiney returned. 'I have mostly witnessed the opposite.'

'And where the fever runs high, and violent delirium is a factor?' Doctor Crooke pressed. 'Dare I ask, how does one administer the treatment then?'

'I suggest the sheet may be safely applied for short periods of two minutes several times in the day. While, thankfully, I did not encounter anything of a *violent* nature with Mr Creed's delirium, on one occasion I necessarily found the method a more effectual mode of reducing cerebral excitement than any other I was acquainted with.'

'And finally, Doctor McSwiney, I might ask how you found the application's effects upon an aggravated respiratory system?' Dr Crooke inquired.

'Yes, I must confess, I myself had great doubts as to the safety of the treatment, where the mucous membrane and the gastro-alimentary passages were complicated. But if anything I feel the decided benefit of the treatment was, perhaps, most marked in this area. The cough became looser, the rales moister, and expectoration was established.

'But many uncomfortable sensations, I believe, are relieved by the use of the treatment: muscular pains in the back, thighs and legs; the sense of aching and weariness; even the thirst becomes lessened and the dry tongue sympathises with its influence. I have observed the low moaning to subside, and, where the patient has struggled to sleep, it has brought him to doze, especially since the hair was cut short.

'So there we have it,' Dr McSwiney said, seeming to have concluded his demonstration. 'Despite the lack of a sustained result in the present, unusually difficult case, I'm confident the method has at least been checking the progress of the disease somewhat. And, while bringing the patient some certain relief, it may yet be a defining difference.'

As he spoke, the young doctor looked, hopeful, in Paulellen's direction: a gesture that, after so much cold, impersonal analysis, brought her to draw some comfort, at last.

'All in all, Doctor McSwiney,' said the older doctor, apparently set to offer an appraisal over the top of his glasses, 'as a method, I'm afraid such a level of involvement would not be practicable in a workhouse environment. But if you achieve the desired result, a pleasing addition might be made to our stock of professional knowledge, with considerable advantage to patients in suffering. Facts are stubborn things, and can only be contradicted by proving their incorrectness. But a more lengthened trial should corroborate this simple statement. I wish you luck with it, Doctor.'

Where Paulellen was concerned, Dr Crooke had seemed honest in his opinion. But she felt disappointed that he had not once commented on her husband. Perhaps he feared the worst and did not wish to upset her.

'Thank you, Doctor Crooke. I appreciate your encouragement,' McSwiney said. 'Shall I walk you to the door?'

'Thank you, Doctor McSwiney. And for your hospitality, Mrs Creed, thank you,' the old doctor said, passing her chair, with Dr McSwiney in tow. 'Please keep me apprised of Mr Creed's progress?'

'Certainly, I will, Doctor Crooke.'

Paulellen heard the doctors' voices fading off, and, discovering Dr McSwiney's journal open upon the chair, began quickly to scour his entries for anything of an honest, if not hopeful, nature.

July 8th – day two. Great turgescence of the integuments. The skin is hot. Tongue dry, flabby.

July 9th – quick and embarrassed respiration. Hydropathic treatment commenced.

10th – violent symptoms – gastric and abdominal irritation. Employed leeches, calomel, opium.

11th – Unfavourable symptoms continuing, patient delirious, worn out from want of sleep, difficulty breathing, excited state of the brain of an inflammatory nature. To delirium succeeded prostration and collapse.

12th – Gastro-alimentary membranes disordered. Unconfined state of the bowels.

Day 7, missed.

Jul 14th – Dry cough and sonorous rales returned. Patient has the fixed glare of unconsciousness.

July 15th – Mr Creed troubled with immoderate thirst.

Results, while encouraging, not curative despite extensive application. Continue 1–2 days more, then decide as to continued utility.

40

Na Galláin

Before he opened his eyes, Pádraig had been convinced of the sensations his body was sending to the dream. With no purpose, sight, or sense of himself, he had simply been a colossal stone: one of the ancient gollanes fallen upon the landscape of Clashmaguire, carved and discarded by the giants of long ago.

There in the sun he had lain for an eon, baked and devoid of moisture or softness, his back so aligned with the flat of the soil that nothing could separate them. But from an existence of numb, granite stone, he had somehow been stirred, and, with opening his eyes, a feeling of familiarity began to emerge at the sight of something taking form above.

Across the span of gathered minutes, long flowing lines became rivers and rivers turned to weaving branches until a mess of knotted wooden limbs holding up the thatch brought Pádraig to remember the picture he had awoken to so many, many times, and something he had watched his family grow to resemble. For, just as twisted, famished and brittle, those below had come to mirror the tangled array of naked branches above that, in the face of all the weather the world could throw at them, clung more desperately to each other for strength and support. As though gazing upon the reflective surface of a lake, some mornings he had recognised his family's likeness among those unhewn roof trusses, intertwined just so precariously that if any one branch were to be removed, the lot might collapse.

With the remembrance of where he was, Pádraig's feeling of numbness was transformed to one of immeasurable thirst, as, involuntarily, he attempted to shout the names of those he sensed were beside him, either alive or dead.

Yet no sound came when he tried to speak, or from anywhere. Was he deaf? he wondered, and attempting to physically locate them felt almost as heavy and immovable as one of the very standing stones he'd dreamed himself to be. But, as though forcing and ripping himself from just such a column of solid matter, by degrees, Pádraig strained until his neck turning confirmed he could move.

As desperate as he was to find water, he had first to discover the condition of his family. *Where are they?* he thought, or shouted in fright within the vacuum, and foresaw himself discovering them at last, one at a piece around him, as dead as the sleeping rock too.

Frantic, he tried to shake them, and realised by the dim light of the windowless cabin he was merely gripping the ground. Finding a limb, he traced the small body to a crop of hair he recognised as Síle's. When grabbing her brought no reaction, Pádraig thought for a moment she was, indeed, dead. But though cold, her body was not frozen or stiff like the corpse of the man he'd awoken beside in the scelp months before, and – hearing again – he understood a sound as being her breath, faint but warm.

Cáit he found next, behind his head. Turned away from him, she was facing the back wall. But as well as cold, she on the other hand *did* feel stiff – until at his probing she winced, reacting to his touch.

But where was Diarmuidín? Sweeping and searching before him, around him, in all the spaces between Síle and Cáit, Pádraig found nothing but straw and flat earth. Propping himself up, despite great pain and cramps, he at last saw Diarmuidín wrapped up between his mother's chest and the wall.

'Please God!' On the back of a moistureless rasp, Pádraig sent forth a whisper that carried a thousand prayers. But extending an arm, he reached the boy's leg and discovered his little Diarmuidín was soft too, and not cold.

Though alive did not mean unscathed; with memory added to instinct Pádraig worried over what he might still discover of their conditions. He recalled the sound of footsteps approaching when, battling fever, he had almost killed himself to get to the door and close it to the insatiable wind.

But by an overwhelming onslaught of physical pain and emotional shock, Pádraig was stunned out of his remembering and allowed himself to collapse back to the floor, if only for a moment.

Driven by a need to find water for his family, with whatever strength was possibly still dormant in the hidden reserves of his limbs, he began an effort to stand.

41

Dark River

'The Union has put to tender again for a new master,' Paulellen said: attempting to lure him out of himself, Creed perceived. But he had seen that notice already, *prior* to this whole vicissitudinous change in his fortune.

'You might be pleased to hear the other Gordon is gone at long last,' she tried after another while. 'With the last of the works dismantled, on the twelfth.'

Still, Creed would not bite.

'Ah, Con, I know you're upset, but you've been brooding for days,' she said, sitting at the end of the bed, clearly exhausted. 'He may come back yet. I've asked all the boys who walked him to keep an eye out. Come now. Aren't you lucky to be alive?' she pleaded, her hand resting upon his foot, for encouragement. But, if anything, the sensation made Creed want to draw his foot away.

Lucky? he thought to say, angrily, pointing out the insensitive use of the dog's name. He was bereft for the animal. 'I'm just tired,' he said, instead, staring up at the window. And that was partly true. But there was so much more.

'Maybe it's not just the dog that has you upset. Has it something to do with that Ua Buachalla fellow, and the shoes?' Paulellen asked, bringing him to meet her eyes at last over a subject he could not resist. 'When you were delirious, in the throes, sometimes it was nonsense. But when it was clear, it was him you talked of most.'

'What did I say?' Creed asked.

'You kept talking to some Hallissey fellow, saying it was too late. 'He is dead! Ua Buachalla is dead!' you kept shouting over and over. That you had failed, and couldn't save him. You cannot blame yourself for the death of every pauper that ever crossed your doorste–'

'Just dreams,' he said, cutting her off.

When Paulellen sighed, hurt, a great part of Creed felt shame and remorse. Why could he not show her his kindness, his gratitude, and his love after all she'd gone through for him? The answer he came up with was that showing such emotions would only encourage her to seek the solace of his affections, and that until he was clear of this malady entirely, he would remain a danger to her. But that made no logical sense, because all through the illness she had evidently washed him, fed him and nursed him devotedly. In reality, he did not know why he felt the way he did: like a magnet, whose energy repelled him away from her. He just knew that sentimentality increased the feeling.

'How long will I remain contagious, did McSwiney say?' Creed asked, contriving a possible escape to Leades.

'If you don't relapse, you may already be clear,' Paulellen answered, 'but he insisted you mustn't exert yourself, Con. Perhaps you *shouldn't* try to walk yet.'

Feeling something akin to an itch, Creed lowered his head, allowing a deep breath to flare his nostrils.

'I know you say it's just a few steps in the corridor, but – listen, I'm going across to check on Dorcas and Samuel,' she said, changing the subject when he fell quiet once more. 'Are you happy there for a half hour, or so?'

'Of course …' Creed said, almost relieved at the idea of being alone for a while. He needed time to think, and to unravel the knot in his mind. 'I'm glad you didn't close the shop,' he added, hearing the gentle murmur of commotion below.

'Well, Thomas was sure he could manage it,' said Paulellen. 'There's a soft egg on the tray beside you there. Try to eat a little, won't you?'

'Thank you.' He nodded, and turned to find a stack of papers also upon the tray. 'Oh, what are –?'

'I brought your post,' she said, rising, as Creed ran the blade of a letter-opener along the flap of one envelope. Hidden amongst the stack, though Paulellen had apparently missed it, ominously stamped 'URGENT' in red ink, it had caught Creed's attention as he'd sifted the pile and now revealed a bill from the Provincial Bank of Cork, proclaiming:

LETTER OF DISTRAINT

'Bye, dear,' he answered, and drew a sharp breath, rapidly stuffing the page back inside, to hide it from his own sight. But with realisation came the sense of a deluge, smothering his body and his mind.

That night, flowing in the breeze of the open window, the wavering curtains seemed to unfurl those distant cries still coming from along the water's edge as Creed lay awake, wrestling his conscience.

For all its purple and white patches, the fever-chewed wreck of his body looked mostly blue in the moonlight. It was a strange thing, he thought, that the mind could not remember pain. The impression of it stood. But, once passed, the intensity of suffering could no more be appreciated than the grandeur of a building, as sketched by an artist long after it had crumbled to ruin. However great the ordeal to his physical body, it was mostly the exhaustion and weakness that remained tangible now. And yet, if what Paulellen had related was true, what had happened to Sam would very likely befall him too, and at a moment's notice.

Suddenly alert, Creed's senses were alive to something in the yard: a rattling of wood, followed by what sounded like quick, light steps.

Someone jumping the fence, he thought, envisaging a thief, or thieves! Whatever cash remained now was ever important, Creed realised, and if some desperate soul were to breach the premises, he and Paulellen would be in mortal danger, held at gunpoint for the safe's combination.

Before he knew it, Creed had rolled himself out of bed and was half way to the kitchen. The steps were much harder than he'd expected, but with the aid of the rail, he at last reached the bottom, where, from the trumpery beneath the stairs, the cold lump of the iron pistol under his hand brought great relief. But what to do next, he wondered in panic. It would be foolhardy to unbolt the door and confront whoever it was, effectively inviting them in. Had he even heard anything at all, he now questioned, surrounded by his own laboured breathing in the dead silence between the stairs and the yard.

Perhaps a light might scare them, he thought, and, resting the gun, took down the lamp hung by the door. With a rip, the glass-bejewelled head of the friction match blazed in the dark, burning the chemical phosphor then dying away as the lamp's wick took the flame. Retrieving the weapon, Creed was about to press his ear to the door when came the steps again, followed by a loud snort at the threshold, then rapid breathing, moving away.

'Lucky!' he whispered, excitedly, and began to undo the bolts.

But, opening the door, Creed felt his heart split to tiny pieces at the sight of the dog, a nocturnal beast, changed in the half-light, the white of its face fouled and besmirched with black rusted blood. It growled, crouching over something as, with wearied footsteps, Creed approached, only to discover it snatching up what appeared to be a child's limb in its mouth.

'Lucky, no!' Creed uttered beneath his breath, broken.

Instinctively, he looked around to make sense of the scene. At a glance, the gate was closed. *How could he have regained access*? But closer inspection revealed it was merely resting closed. In the glow of the lamp, the latch appeared to have been worked by a crowbar. Perhaps the night Lucky vanished, someone had tried to break in, and, frightening them off, the dog had escaped, Creed theorised. Loose, he must have joined the mayhem of those ranks plundering the graveyards and only now returned, having somehow escaped being shot or poisoned.

With a heart-searing grief that seemed to surpass every ache and contortion he had endured in weeks past, Creed now turned to approach the dog through his tears: the one who had saved him; the friend he had thought a guard against such evils that day by the river; sent to protect him from himself and his imagined curse, perhaps even his misdoings, that he might stay to correct them. *That* creature had been just another prop of his own invention, Creed now understood, while the one crouched before him was nothing more than a savage animal, obeying its base nature.

Through the distortion of his tears as he closed in, Creed watched the blur snarling and retreating along its paws, until with nowhere further to go, the spout of iron, heavy in his hand, descended to meet its crown. But with his finger upon the trigger, the unwieldy object began to shake and tremble to the convulsing of his body. Struggling to control his unravelling emotions, with barely the strength to hold the object, he sighted the barrel and tried to steady his breath. Only now, instead of crouching, the dog seemed to cower, and, letting go of its prize, Lucky, the faithful companion who was afraid of guns, whimpered and cried, high pitched, looking up at him with two different-coloured eyes. Clenching his teeth, Creed cried in torment and, to the metal click of the trigger, imagined an explosive belch of fire and sulphur that filled his senses as the gunpowder sent forth a blast of noxious smoke, the force of the discharge jolting his arm back to its socket.

'You damned, silly … creature,' Creed burst out, distraught, chewing his lip, but found himself paralysed, unable to follow through. To shoot the creature that had walked him through his own rebirth? His ally and confidant? Without Lucky, he'd have had no second chance, nor the heart to take it, perhaps.

Grabbing at his eyes, shaking at the core of himself, Creed tried hopelessly to stifle the walls collapsing inside him: walls he had built to shore up the disappointment, horror and anguish at all he had witnessed. But with the guilt, it burst like a quiet dam, pouring out from some untapped pool, to merge with the torrent that, a mere hundred yards or so away, he could hear gushing through the night.

Bending low, Creed took Lucky by the collar and walked him to the other side of the yard where behind the stores he found a rope and tied him to the fence. But what to do with the God-forsaken object that lay dead in the corner of the yard? The sad remains of some poor child. If he buried it the dog would dig it up. The churchyard was too conspicuous. It had to be gone before Paulellen would see it, he was decided.

Reaching the top of the stairs again, with the gun returned to its cupboard below, Creed realised with terror he was sweating profusely. Was this the inevitable re-beginning, he feared? Dressing, he was arrested by the voice of Paulellen, calling from Alicia's old room, sleepy and disturbed. 'Con, are you out of bed?' she moaned.

'It's all right, dear, I'm ... I intend to visit Doctor McSwiney ... I'm feeling rather weak.'

'What?' she answered, 'Doctor –'

'I'll be fine, dear. Sleep,' he reassured her.

Paulellen mumbled something back, then fell silent. She had drifted off again, he realised, listening hard. In the kitchen, Creed doused a cloth in the sink to cool his face and neck, before making for the stairs again. Crouching in the yard, he took the same cloth and, holding Lucky by the snout, cleaned as much of the blood from his fur as he could find in the darkness.

'Now ... she'll never know.' Fondly, Creed thumbed the silk of the dog's ear. 'Begin again,' he whispered, and having met its head with his own briefly, turned away.

Retracing his steps he found the awful morsel, bloodied and mauled, behind the tree. The sight of it made his soul blanch and brought his stomach to churn.

With a heavy heart, he squeezed out the cloth by the wall, then used it like a glove to gather up the thing, and, wrapping it, concealed it beneath his coat, disgusted by the smell.

Finally, to the sound of the dog whining sorrowfully, Creed passed his belt through the lock hole and tied the gate shut.

The town was deserted as Creed skirted the square and headed for Castle Street. If there was no one on the bridge, he would toss the parcel over there, to join with the other bodies lately floating down the river for some unknown destination, the mystery of which somehow lent it a sense of sacredness. Perhaps it would be reunited with loved ones, Creed imagined. Afterward, he could visit the doctor.

But by the time he was nearing the dispensary, slowed by lead-weighted steps, a tired Creed considered whether he should reverse the order of the plan and visit the doctor first, only to discover the futility of his design. For, at almost four in the morning, the dispensary was in complete darkness, and would be for some hours yet, he realised. Next passing the rectory, sounds of whispering and coughing indicated he had disturbed some poor family dropping off the remains of loved ones by the cover of night.

As with every error lately discovered of his own judgement, this too had been badly planned, Creed lamented, when, reaching the bridge, he perceived an urchin, wandering toward him from the other side. What to do with the cargo now, he wondered, already decided to not disturb those poor wretches sheltering under the east side. But he daren't acquaint the child with something so gruesome, either.

'Is the gate to Mr Coppinger's field open?' he asked the boy as they passed.

'Sir?'

'I intend to take a swim,' Creed blurted out, that he might continue advancing and soon rest.

"Tis closed, sir,' the boy said, and slowed, so that Creed felt the child's eyes track him to the last yard of the parapet, where, turning, he rounded the steep bank leading to the dry arches beneath. Sliding on chips of shale and brittle stones, Creed's descent was only aided by his inability to slow himself until, coming to rest at the bottom, he realised he had no way to get back up.

Though surprisingly bright below, shadows lurked still beneath the rounded vaults amid sounds of sad, forlorn life, moaning to survive, or moaning to die. Frightened, stumbling out in search of the riverside walkway, Creed found himself ankle deep in the mud and silt of the alluvial strand.

'Ugh,' he grunted, struggling to free himself, by which time he was exhausted again, and, sitting upon the dry meadow of Coppinger's field, away from the bank, he divested himself of his boots and his coat, whose ends had trailed in the stream.

When he'd gathered his breath, Creed walked back toward the river, and, through a clearing, found the moon had come out to meet him. From behind the silhouette of the castle, it appeared to smile. By now, unable to register much more than the difficulty of remaining upright, he stared back, perplexed. But in lowering his gaze, the face of the moon met him once more upon the glass surface of the dark river. Only this time, it frowned, and Creed looked back and forth between the two until he could no longer tell if either one wore any expression.

At length, Creed held up the terrible cloth-wrapped object, and, steadying himself, lobbed it toward the water. For a moment as it sailed, there was nothing. But with a splash that broke the silence of the night it shattered the moon into a sea of blue and white eels. Devouring their quarry, they tumbled over one another, until, sated, the river regurgitated only the cloth, left drifting away to the south.

Transfixed, Cornelius Creed watched as, like magnetic strands of mercury pulling back together, the ripples reformed, fluid and silver upon the surface, and, erelong, the still face of the moon beheld him once more, hungry and waiting, the human sacrifice deemed insufficient, he perceived.

It was an image that, at once, struck Creed a fitting parable of his life and, suddenly, everything was clear.

The truth, he realised, was that before the shock of the letter, he might well have gone on, even in the wake of Pádraig Ua Buachalla. But so much had changed since that morning alone: first, the letter; then the dog; and finally, being reduced to carrying the seeds of a fever that was now, with certainty, relapsing, for he knew the symptoms well: the flushes of heat; his dripping brow; the sharp pains in his gut. A look to his trembling hands merely confirmed to Creed that he was fast running out of time.

Nothing now but a blazing torch to the brittle staff of his wife's safety and a penniless agent of disease to his poor customers, useful to no one, Creed had ultimately recast himself: an instrument of eleemosynary kindness, turned something as dangerous as the loaded firearm he'd held to the dog's head not one hour before.

With every ounce of wit and intelligence he possessed, he had pitted himself against the crisis and all the cruelty of its parent society, he reflected, the breeze of the night air cool upon his face as it rushed the leaves of the great chestnut on the far bank. But, in place of relative wealth, the sum of his efforts had amounted to virtually nothing. In the face of all his morality and exhausted energies, a devastating, unhearing foe had smiled back, just like the moon, saying *give me more*, until, now, there was nothing left, Creed thought; nothing but himself.

Everything had led him here, whether to the actual river this night, or to this point in his life, along a river of another kind. Either way, he had not the strength to get back, and the flame of the ever-hotter torch he was becoming begged to be doused.

Wide and dark the river planed, still but for the tiny black eddies twisting and swilling upon the surface. Somewhere out of sight, a fish jumped, then reimmersed itself.

It seemed like a long moment that he stood there, appreciating the quiet, inviting peace of it all.

And it seemed, too, that for some time, an eon perhaps, everything else had been the opposite: hunger, devastation and suffering. He had seen so much suffering.

Still smiling, the moon watched on until, like the fish, to feel the cool relief of the silvery depths, Creed summoned what last of his strength remained and leapt from his toes in the direction of the sky.

Try to stay still, he told himself as with a frigid gush he plunged toward the bottom, tetherless and cold. *Wait*, he told himself, calmly, and opening his eyes for a last look at his life in the world, saw nothing but darkness.

Now … breathe, he commanded his body, and opened his mouth to suck back all of his words.

Looking up, Pádraig realised it was the brightness of the moon, shining in, that had disturbed his sleep. In the whole time they'd been in Doire Liath, he could not recall it ever being visible through the hole in the roof, or even crossing that part of the sky before. Yet there it was looking straight down at him in all its glory. The old people would speculate on what its appearance might augur for the coming harvest, he supposed. But superstition and such fancies had saved no one from the unrelenting hardship of the last years, and Pádraig, for one, would put no faith in a moon that looked as blue and cold now as it had done in the numbing depths of frozen winter.

Though wrapped up in the overcoat, another fit of coughing was brought on by the bite in the air, and convulsing in the shadows, Pádraig contemplated that, typical of nature's cruelty in recent times, even the summer nights were cold. Maybe that was why, weeks after recovering from their desperate bout with fever, they were, all four of them, still struggling to shake off the lingering symptoms of the malady.

How they had managed to survive it was a mystery to Pádraig, when even people with riches and access to medicine in the towns were dying all over, sometimes as quickly as the poor who had nothing. From discussions afterward it seemed he and Cáit had each shared the same inexplicable impression that the other one had nursed them through it.

'Then who went for water, if it wasn't you or me?' Cáit had said. 'We must have been days like that, incapable of fending for ourselves.'

It made no sense. Síle had no memory of going for water either, and they had ruled the neighbours out.

'Had you sickness in there?' Micilín shouted down from the corner of the ridge one day, after they'd come to, when Pádraig was outside with the bucket. 'One of the children saw someone banging, but said they got no answer.'

'Unless it was Diarmuid Ua Laoghaire, or one of his clan,' Cáit suggested.

But whoever or whatever it was got them through it, be it God or man, as he watched his wife and children curled up asleep beside him now, Pádraig was eternally grateful that they had been given another chance to get past all of this; perhaps the one that mattered most of all.

Already he was hearing reports that the blight had lost its potency; that this year's crop had escaped it. Could they really have survived it all? Was it really over? Come October, he himself would have very little to dig. But if they could get through just one more winter, maybe they'd have come through the worst of it, Pádraig thought, as, racking his body, another fit of coughing came on.

With God's help, next year he could go working for Taidghí and Con Críodáin again. Then they might finally have equilibrium. In the meantime they'd be reliant upon the outdoor relief in Clondrohid and Cáit's place over Mountcross at the sewing school. Before falling asleep this night she had insisted she felt well enough to attempt the journey again soon. Pádraig just hoped they would still have a place for her there as, tired again, he noticed the moon had almost passed over. Tomorrow would answer.

42

Felo De Se

Silent and benumbed, Paulellen sat staring at her husband's remains. That he was not moving was incomprehensible; that his lips were blue; the scratches and cuts on his bloated face; his glasses missing, lost.

He looked so cold. She was compelled to go to him and warm him. But something was preventing her: Dorcas, her sister, curling an arm through hers, she remembered. How could this have happened, she questioned, utterly confused by it all; a kind of singing in her ears, like noise, with no noise, together. This was not how she had imagined it. How had they ended up separated like this? She, held back by her sister; and he, by some invisible force restraining him, never to communicate again, she realised, after all those years of sharing everything. He was here, but gone, dressed as though ready to go somewhere, but lying mute upon the table of a disgusting taproom floor commandeered for the purpose, to be gawped at and speculated upon.

After Dr McSwiney had finished his 'work' with him at the dispensary, she had finally been allowed to see Cornelius and had sat by his side all the previous night there. Finding him upon the doctor's table, uncared for and only partially covered with a sheet, she had brushed his hair and dressed him once more, this time without protest and in silence, though with no help from his stiffened remains. But the scar along his chest where he'd been stitched back up: Paulellen was struggling greatly to purge that from her mind now and found that all fondness and admiration she'd had for the young doctor was turned to resentment and a sense of betrayal at such an unforgivable act.

'Are you sure you're up to this?' Dorcas whispered, clasping her arm a little tighter, at which, though her eyes did not leave him, Paulellen slowly raised and lowered her head, sensing it was about to begin. There was *some* peace upon her husband's face now, she thought, looking hard at his waxen, pale skin. Though at what cost to her? Perhaps most of all, Paulellen had an abiding sense of his being, somehow, just out of reach.

'We are two bodies short,' said a well-dressed gentleman crossing Paulellen's line of sight. 'Fetch me two tales outside; whoever's passing will do,' he pressed, apparently the superior of the other officious-looking gentlemen he was addressing, and perhaps of the whole legal contingent.

'Yes, Mr Baldwin.'

Though she was largely disconnected from the goings-on and their purpose in that moment, there seemed to Paulellen an air of authority and efficiency about Mr Baldwin, a slightly bow-legged man whose hair was still quite black for one of such a vintage.

'In fact, grab one or two more, to ensure we reach *some* conclusion,' he added, then turned to finish his drink as more and more people filed in. It was all so very strange, Paulellen lamented.

'Franklin Baldwin,' a voice whispered, nearby, 'grand thing we got him so quickly. Could be anywhere the county over. Busy man this weather.'

'I was hoping for the People's Hall,' a more familiar voice said. 'Something more befitting than this den of slobber and grime.'

'They insisted upon the nearest tavern,' the first voice returned.

'The poor divil, look at him,' the familiar voice spoke again, and, to the sounds of liquid being poured freely on the other side, Paulellen found it was Fr Lee, who had already come to her upon arrival, she remembered.

'Mrs Creed?' the woman with tea offered.

'Thank you. She is fine,' Dorcas answered for Paulellen, then encouraged her to sip the tonic Matthias Ryan had prepared her.

'Can we get underway?' Mr Baldwin asked his assistant, when, at the appearance of a dishevelled old pauper ushered in leaning on a stick, it seemed the complement was complete.

'Well, I heard of being called to the bar?' the old man quipped, halting in the doorway, before spying Cornelius, laid out. 'Ah … 'tis yourself, Mr Creed,' he called to him in affectionate tones.

Being made to wait, Mr Baldwin looked to his pocket-watch as, taking his time, the old man approached the table and spoke aloud, removing his hat: ''Tis a sad day when such a fine and virtuous man is struck down along with all of this covetousness.'

'Very good. Very good,' Mr Baldwin said, escorting the old pauper away, blessing himself, to a chair. 'You'll all have time to pay your respects later,' he announced, then turned to address all assembled.

'Gentlemen, relatives and friends of the deceased, good day to you all,' he began, with a tone of stateliness. 'As coroner to the district of the west division of the County of Cork, in a case of sudden or suspicious death – which drowning is surely deemed, be it accidental or otherwise – in accordance with the Coroner's (Ireland) Act of Eighteen Forty-Six, I am charged to empanel *you*, the jury, to consider the evidence.' In her peripheral vision, Paulellen here perceived the speaker motioning to those gentlemen assembled on her right. 'Upon hearing that evidence, you will, ultimately, certify the cause of death. Twelve of you must come to agreement on the verdict as, together, you will act as an essential cog in the machinery of Ireland's justice system, representing and preserving harmony between the action of the law and the sentiment of the people.'

Amid the listening silence as the coroner spoke, another sound seemed to catch Paulellen's attention, irritating her at first. But on tracking it to a young man's pen, scratching furiously upon the page, she found that, instead, it brought her some comfort. For, while it was strange to learn that, still motionless upon the table, Cornelius was not the source of the skitter she was so used to hearing by his hand, for the first time since the awful event of two nights since, the sound that came from the young man and his satchel of writing equipments made her somehow feel that Cornelius was there.

'Now,' the coroner continued, as the pen and his voice marched on in union, 'to avoid any pre-emptive conclusion, I must insist you *disregard* any report already in circulation on this matter. I refer, specifically, to the *Examiner* article of Wednesday the twenty-first, announcing a *Melancholy Suicide*,' Baldwin forewarned, much to Paulellen's shock. 'But as this is likely in your mind ... in case it *is* concluded that the deceased intentionally forfeited and extinguished his life from himself, I will remind you that the law has much changed with regard to how such events are considered. Gone are the days of burying suicided corpses at the crossroads and other such measures of punitiveness.

'I acquaint you with the Suicide Burial Act of Eighteen Twenty-Three: "Whereas it is expedient, that the laws relating to the interment of the remains of persons, against whom a finding of *felo de se* shall be had: be it henceforth enacted by the king's most excellent majesty, with the advice and consent of the lords spiritual and temporal and commons, and by the present parliament assembled, that from the passing of this Act it shall not be lawful for any coroner holding inquests to direct the interment of the remains in any public highway ..."'

Though Paulellen's greatest concern regarding this proceeding was that Cornelius would get a proper burial, at the monotony of the coroner's reading, she felt herself lose any sense of his meaning, until, by some terrible words, her attention was firmly gripped anew: '"But that such coroner *shall* give directions for the private interment of the remains, *without any stake being driven through the body,* in the churchyard *or* burial ground in which the remains might, by Law or Custom, be interred, if the verdict of *felo de se* had *not* been found; with such interment to be made within twenty-four hours from the finding of the inquisition, and to take place between the hours of nine and twelve at night,"' he concluded.

'And yet, gentlemen, I must remind you, that, in spite of those changes, what is still at stake by your deliberation is not only the memory and reputation of the deceased and his family – for the law has not completely changed. But in the case of a verdict of *felo de se*, i.e. that, of sound mind, a "Felon of himself" took his own life with clear knowledge and understanding of his actions and their consequences, punitive measures may still be enacted, and the hand of the law felt upon his estates, goods and chattels. Therefore, you must each personally adjudge and weigh every factor and consequence of the evidence presented, and look with great attention to the testimony brought forward.

'Acting together, as a jury, you should deliberate with great caution the case presented. Ultimately, if you do not reach a strong conclusion of guilt, you *must* acquit the deceased, Mr Creed, of a crime the most detestable and ignominious to contemplate.

'On the shortness of time by which you have been summoned, I offer my regrets: as you might expect, an inquest should be held and the body viewed before it be altered by decomposition or otherwise. I now hand over to the Clerk of the Peace, Mr Noble Johnson, to proceed the swearing-in.'

'Thank you, Mr Baldwin,' a tall gentleman said, who looked to wish himself as noble as his name suggested. Holding out a blue Bible, he wasted no time addressing the band of mismatched men, among whom Paulellen recognised only some.

'You shall diligently inquire and true presentment make', he began the unmusical vow, 'of all such matters and things as shall be given you, in charge, on behalf of our sovereign lady the Queen, touching the death of Cornelius Creed, now lying dead, whose body you must view. You shall present no man from hatred, malice, or ill-will; nor spare any through fear, favour, or affection, but a true verdict give according to the evidence and the best of your skill and knowledge. So help you God.

'Crier of the court, would you count the jury, please?' Mr Johnson demanded, handing the book to another, rather rougher specimen, equally tall, giving Paulellen the impression they were somehow related, even if their features did not match.

'When you hear your name called, you will come forward, kiss the Bible, and proceed in turn to this area. Robert Harned, Esquire; Patrick Riordan; Cornelius Murphy; Henry Swanzy.'

One at a time they filed past Paulellen to the spot where her lifeless husband lay. It was so very comforting to see James Welply called next among the group, while not so comforting to see was an unusually deferential Massy Warren, who, earlier, had arrived in a sweat, clearly anxious to insert himself amongst the proceedings.

'Henry Minhear; William Garde Browne; John Pearson; Edward Ashe; Robert Warren; James Twohig; Talesmen: John Cronin and William Shanahan.'

The last called was the old man with the stick, Paulellen noticed, who refused to kiss the Bible, insisting on the 'kissing of his thumb' instead, which the coroner accepted with some frustration.

'Have you all been sworn?' the crier asked sharply, to which those assembled gave a general murmur of agreement.

'Twelve good men and true. Stand together and hear your evidence,' the third official announced, as though giving a military order, then nodded to the coroner.

'Now that you have been sworn, you will please view the body,' Mr Baldwin said. 'Bearing in mind that ofttimes much of the evidence ariseth upon the viewing, I'll remind you to not touch the deceased.'

Paulellen greatly struggled with the fussing that followed as, forming a kind of pack, the twelve men swarmed around Cornelius to ogle and gawk. Feeling protective, she tried to keep her eyes on her husband but, trying to find him through the crowd, could not help looking to some of the men's expressions. Patrick Riordan, for one, shook his head and moved away almost as quickly as he'd stepped up, while, as though upon the back of an involuntary cough, James uttered something that seemed almost a word, but one that perhaps could not find its meaning. Even Massy Warren looked almost to be in shock by his widened eyes. Once again, the old man was the last to leave the body, returning to stand at the front of the group.

'We shall attempt first to establish the cause of death,' the coroner resumed. 'Doctor McSwiney, you will be called separately as a witness, but as the nominated Doctor of *Post Mortem*, could you first ascertain the medical facts for the court?'

'Of course,' the doctor said, quietly.

'Do come forward, Doctor McSwiney.'

'Yes, sir,' McSwiney said, for the first time seeming as young and inexperienced, to Paulellen, as his years ought to have made him, but had not before this moment: perhaps this was his first such grave experience, she thought. Yet although it most certainly was hers, she could not sympathise with nor pity his pain.

'To begin, Doctor,' Mr Baldwin spoke gently, as though understanding of his nervousness, 'what, by your findings, did you establish as causing death to the deceased?'

'Drowning, sir.'

'And, factually speaking, can you say what particulars of either the autopsy or your examination confirm that ascertainment?'

'The *post-mortem* examination revealed fluid aspirated into the windpipe and its branches; water in the lungs; I found evidence of foam, escaped from the mouth and nostrils, which some time after death becomes bloody; some water in the stomach; and cerebral oedema.'

'Cerebral oedema … could you explain such a term for the laypersons among us, Doctor?'

'Oedema is a condition characterised by an excess of watery fluid collecting in the cavities or tissues of the body, most noticeable *here*, in the face and the neck,' McSwiney said, pointing to Cornelius, which brought Paulellen to close her eyes, feeling quite disturbed.

'Very well. Carry on.'

'There was also evidence of *post-mortem* lacerations, or abrasions, ahem, due to scraping along rough surfaces in the water.'

'I see, such as this mark here?' the coroner asked, pointing to Cornelius' cheek, Paulellen saw briefly.

'Correct, sir.'

'So, we can safely say drowning was the absolute cause of death?'

'That is correct, sir, yes.'

'Thank you, doctor. Now, in your capacity as a *witness* to the events *leading* to the death of the deceased, are you happy to continue?'

'Certainly,' McSwiney answered.

'Very good. I am informed you had lately been treating the deceased for a considerable illness. Could you briefly state the nature of this treatment?'

'From the seventh instant until a matter of three days ago, I was daily visiting Mr Creed at his home, to treat him for typhus fever.'

'I see. And when you concluded your treatment, was that because the deceased had recovered?'

'At that time, I was satisfied the patient was convalescing sufficiently, having suffered a great ordeal. Though given the nature of the condition, relapse was both possible and likely.'

'How likely?'

'I'm not an expert on the disease, but –'

'If you were a betting man, Doctor McSwiney, would you wager on his *not* relapsing?'

'I would not, sir.'

'Well enough. Now let us move forward to events of the night before last. Can you recount them as you remember?'

'Of course, sir. I was awoken from my sleep by some loud knocking, and upon answering the door found a boy upon the step, who said someone was in the river.'

'Did the child say how the person had entered the river?'

'Not that I recall.'

'I see. Perhaps we should move to the boy witness now. Thank you, Doctor. We'll recommence anon. Young man, would you approach, please? Don't be afraid.'

'Isn't that one of the boys who gave the dog his exercise while Cornelius was unwell?' Dorcas whispered.

'Is it?' Paulellen replied, unclear in her memory. 'I can't remember,' she said, looking at the ragged child, whom she imagined an orphan.

'Gentlemen, we have established the cause of death,' the coroner announced, as the boy got settled. 'I wish now to ascertain *how* this event came to occur, so that, ultimately, you can decide if death be ruled accidental, intentional, or steered by other causes such as temporary insanity, or matters extemporaneous. To equip you, I will draw the testimony of witnesses to the events, and call some witnesses to the character of the deceased. Now, young man, can you state your name, and place of residence?'

'Patrick Sullivan, of Pound Lane, sir,' the boy answered, downcast.

'Thank you, Master Sullivan. What is your recollection of the events you witnessed two nights ago?'

'I was coming over the bridge, sir, in the late night, and saw a man coming toward me from the town side.'

'This man, did you know or recognise him?' Baldwin asked, at which, though she could not be sure, Paulellen thought she perceived the boy to look to Massy, as though afeared of his presence, before answering.

'I did not, sir.'

'But the man you met *is* the very same as the deceased before you now, correct?' the coroner inquired.

'Yes, sir,' the boy said, staring hard at Cornelius.

'Did he speak to you?'

'He inquired if the gate to Mr Coppinger's field was open, sir. I told him it was not, having only passed it.'

'And how did he seem, to you?'

'Not fully well, sir.'

'I understand. Did he say anything else?'

'That he intended, sir … to take a swim.'

The boy's answer created a stir among those present, Paulellen noticed, feeling herself shocked by it, too.

'Quiet, please. Thank you. What happened next, Master Sullivan?'

'The man got under the bridge and into the field that way. He then removed his boots and his coat, and, without taking off any other portion of his dress, sir, he walked towards the river.'

'I see. And what transpired?'

Drifting in and out with exhaustion, Paulellen's sense of hearing became absorbed by the young reporter's writing and, vacantly, her eyes followed the pen's movement.

Boy witness deposed: by gentleman's appearance and the unseasonable hour, on seeing deceased go toward the river, went immediately to raise the alarm. Returning to bridge found gentleman had disappeared; pointed out the spot he had last seen deceased to gentleman present; did not see deceased actually enter the water; was not present when the body was recovered as sent by gentleman to fetch constable Hadnett and Fr Lee.

Disturbed, but thrilled at the excitement of what he was recording for the *Examiner*, Justin McCarthy scribbled hurriedly in his notebook.

'And you did not know the deceased?' Mr Baldwin asked.

'I did not, sir,' the boy said, but again seemed slightly hesitant and looked to the men of the jury, Paulellen noticed, returned to her senses.

'And just to reconfirm, young man – this is most important – you feel certain you did not actually see Mr Creed enter the water?'

'I am certain, sir. He was walking toward the river when I ran to raise the alarm.'

'Thank you, Master Sullivan. You may return to your seat,' the coroner said, then turned to address the room. 'Did *anyone* actually see the deceased enter the river?'

Paulellen surveyed the faces of both jury and witnesses, though no answer came.

'Mrs Creed, would you be happy to answer some questions?'

Surprised at how quickly her turn had come, Paulellen arose with her sister's aid and took herself forward.

'Perhaps we can utilise a chair in this instance,' Baldwin suggested as she crossed the floor to sit by her husband, from whom still came the smell of some strong chemical she guessed as formaldehyde. Once more, Paulellen could not help but notice the stitching beneath the top of his blouse, so that, quite dizzy and upset, she felt greatly relieved at gaining the chair.

'Mrs Creed, you had lately nursed your husband through a fever, is that correct?'

Paulellen nodded and made a sound of affirmation, though her lips did not wish to talk.

'I'm sorry, Mrs Creed, you'll have to speak a little louder for the court. Are you able?'

'Yes,' she answered reluctantly.

'Thank you, Mrs Creed. This won't take long.'

Sworn, wife of deceased deposed husband had been regaining his strength; did not think her husband unhappy generally but conceded to his being despondent since recovering; heard him stirring in the adjoining room on night in question, her habit being to sleep in separate quarters throughout his illness; by the height of the moon, witness thought it around half past three when deceased declared he felt weak and intended seeing Dr McSwiney.

'I thought, perhaps … I was dreaming,' Paulellen said, with tears in her eyes.

'Quite, Mrs Creed. Given you had nursed your husband day and night through a bout of severe fever over a period of weeks, while also assisting other relatives through the same dire malady, it is quite understandable you would fall back asleep and, under the circumstances, believe you were dreaming. May I ask did your husband ever swim in the river before?'

At this Paulellen wavered, calling to mind the revelation of the shoes, the dog and the river, when Cornelius had divulged all. But that had been something different, she believed. He had not intended to throw *himself* in then. 'No, not that I am aware of,' she finally replied. 'Perhaps as a child?'

'Indeed, could he swim at all, to anyone's knowledge?' Baldwin asked, opening an arm to the court once more.

His childhood friend would probably know best, Paulellen thought, and looked for James, but instead found Massy Warren, who, staring hard at the floor, appeared to be contemplating much.

'Most interesting,' the coroner remarked. 'Mrs Creed, thank you for bearing with us, and for sharing your testimony. My deepest condolences on your loss. Doctor McSwiney?'

The doctor came forward once more, and, pulling in his lips, made a solemn face of commiseration as Paulellen passed him.

'Doctor, when last we spoke, you had just been awoken by loud knocking and told there was someone in the river. Can you recollect what happened from there?'

'Yes, sir. Having ascertained the location from the boy –'

'That being?'

'The west side of the river, in Mr Coppinger's field, facing the castle, or thereabouts. I told the boy to head back there, but to gather as many as he could along the way, and bring them to the spot; that I would follow with my equipment.'

'What such equipment?'

'Eh … a blanket; scissors to remove the wet clothes; a lamp; also a strong hartshorn, or some stimulating embrocation, but mostly just the rudiments, given the urgency. While dressing, I asked my wife to put together as many hot articles as could be found, with the help of neighbours, and to meet me at the dispensary, which I would have to open, in preparation.'

'Hot articles, Doctor McSwiney?'

'Bottles or bladders of water; socks filled with warm ashes or sand, heated by pan; hot bricks or oven racks. Anything that could be utilised to bring heat back to the body.'

'I see. So, at that stage, you considered restoration of life was possible?'

'Certainly possible, however unlikely, Mr Baldwin.'

'Why so unlikely, Doctor?'

Loath to hear such details, Paulellen observed Val McSwiney blowing out his lips, as though struggling with the questions.

'Though there are many examples of successful resuscitation after longer periods, being under water continuously for three minutes and a half, sometimes even less, is sufficient to cause death,' McSwiney answered. 'With each passing minute the silver cord is loosened, and my estimation bade me prepare for the worst.'

'I'm curious about this estimation, Doctor? Please humour me. How long did you perceive the deceased had been in the water by then?'

'Well … *if* he had entered the water as the boy ran to my door: from the bridge, along Castle Street, then across the square – a distance of approximately three hundred yards – I suppose about two minutes might have passed. It might have been another minute before I answered the door and I venture a minute more, perhaps two, for the boy to alert me and receive my instruction back. More minutes would have lapsed by the time the boy returned to the bridge, not allowing for the time required to wake others along the way, of course.'

'So, in total?' the coroner inquired.

'By the time the boy returned with the help he'd gathered, a period of some eleven minutes, at minimum, should have elapsed. But even then, I'm afraid the body had yet to be located and recovered at the expense of more precious time.'

'Suffice to say, there was very little hope of reviving the deceased by then?'

'I'm afraid so, Mr Baldwin.'

'Thank you, Doctor. To the scene then. When did you arrive and what was taking place?'

'The body had just been recovered. I was …'

Witness deposed to not knowing whose body he had been called to attend to; was very surprised to discovered deceased was Mr Creed; whilst water was being made hot, and bags of hot salt got ready, witness had deceased stripped and desired four men to commence rubbing the body with dry flannel; despite protracted efforts found all attempts to resuscitate the unfortunate gentleman unavailing; had not detected anything of deceased's personal circumstances to feel he was unhappy with his lot generally; could not be sure if relapse had begun but certainly thought it possible, even likely, given deceased had wished to seek medical attention; admitted the prospect of such an occurrence would be very frightening given severity of deceased's recent symptoms.

'Thank you, Doctor McSwiney. One last question: to your mind, could there be any reasonable circumstance by which a person in Mr Creed's position might logically wish to "take a swim" at such an hour, in twelve to sixteen feet of water, other than to commit the act of *mors voluntaria?*'

'If his fever *was* relapsing,' McSwiney proposed, 'by the tendency of the body to extreme heat – at the height of summer, it must be remembered – Mr Creed could quite reasonably have felt compelled to visit the dispensary. This he would have found closed, however, having by then excited his condition even more through exertion. I would suspect, Mr Coroner, that, finding himself already close to the river with no other way to lessen the symptoms, swimming, or immersing himself in the water, would conceivably have been a very tempting solution, however dangerous.'

Realising the extent of panic and torture her poor husband must have endured, Paulellen came undone at the thought, and realised Dorcas was weeping too.

'Thank you, Doctor. You may stand down. I wonder if we can hear from one of the men who fished the body from the water?' Mr Baldwin said.

At length, John Horgan, a carpenter from Castle Street, was called forward and on being handed the Gospels attested to joining with three others after being awoken by commotion. Upon reaching the river, having broken through Mr Coppinger's gate, Horgan testified to not being able to locate the body for some time, until eventually something had been spotted floating among the reeds of the near bank.

'We had great trouble retrieving him on account of the deficiency of the hook,' Horgan said, gravely. 'His body was face down when we discovered him. I did not fancy the damage could be reversed by then, but we assisted Doctor McSwiney at rubbing the body for an hour at least. I never saw any change.'

Having thanked Mr Horgan, the coroner told the court they would then hear some character references, 'beginning with Thomas French, who worked as clerk to the deceased at his pawnbroker's establishment … Mr French, will you come forward, please?'

With pity, Paulellen watched Tom French ambling forward, his head low, slumped in sadness.

'Mr French, how long were you in the employ of the deceased?'

'Almost three years,' Mr French said, beginning to sob almost immediately.

'Can you continue?' Mr Baldwin prompted, with a gentle firmness that led Mr French somewhat to straighten up. Nodding, he took a handkerchief to his eyes.

'Did you find your employer to be unhappy in himself of late?'

'I did not, sir. On the contrary, he recently reopened the shop and took great pride in helping his customers,' French said, his voice meek and breaking as he spoke, continuing to dab at his puffy eyes.

'How would you sum up your employer as a person, Mr French?'

'Mr Creed was a very kind man … with a great intellect. I found him to be a man capable of great calculation, but one who counted his morals quicker than his profits.'

Moving his head in such a way as one might say yes and no at the same time, the coroner seemed to feel wonder. 'Is that so?' he asked, walking away from Mr French, hands clasped behind his back, as if processing the statement. 'What a nice way to be remembered,' he concluded. 'You may stand down, Mr French, thank you. Father Lee, would you like to offer an appraisal of Mr Creed?'

'I would,' answered Thomas Lee, who, arising to approach the makeshift bench, seemed proud but burdened.

'In your own time, Father, did you know the deceased well?'

'I was his priest; I married him and Paulellen many years ago not long after taking up the parish here. I have been friends with them since and had occasion to work with Cornelius often, through the Relief Committee, Guardians' meetings, the Church, and so on.'

'I understand. When did you last see the deceased alive, Father Lee?'

'Oh … only days ago. On the evening of the seventeenth instant I conferred last rites over Cornelius in preparation for death.

Priest deposed to believing deceased severely affected; had not foreseen that he would survive; found himself surprised to learn deceased had recovered; by the delirium deceased had exhibited in his presence, supposed he had not fully emerged from it, despite the doctor's statement.

'How would you sum up your friend, Father Lee?'

'If you're asking whether I think he took his own life, sir, I confess to knowing no more of the circumstances of the night in question than any other here. What I *can* say is that Cornelius Creed was a poor tormented creature, who could not do enough good in the world. And whatever evils he found himself responsible for – an amount most people would not blink at – he found that hard to live with.'

'Thank you, Mr Lee,' Baldwin said with raised eyebrows, seemingly as surprised at the priest's candour as Paulellen was.

'Gentlemen of the jury, we have gone minutely into the circumstances surrounding the decease of the body before you, being that of Cornelius Creed. I avouch it is quite unnecessary for me to add a single word in explanation of the evidence.

'We have established, as fact, that death was caused by drowning. What is *unclear*, and left for you to decide, is if the act of *felo de se* was committed. The deceased was found floating, but did he *jump*, *fall*, or even *immerse* himself in the cool water out of desperation, unwittingly losing his life in the process? Nobody can say for sure. But his exact words, according to the boy, were that "he intended to take a swim", an act that might prove fatal even for an active person in the fullness of his health. Mr Creed was not active in the athletic sense and was certainly not at the peak of his health for some time prior to his death. *But*, as the doctor has so intuitively pointed out, Mr Creed might well have felt compelled to alleviate his symptoms at *any cost*, despite those facts.

'I remind you that a verdict of self-destruction, exhibited in all its heinous shape, would brand any man in the ordinary circles of society with a deep stain, as decreed by law, *and* sentence his *widow* to a beggarly life of wretchedness,' the coroner said earnestly, to Paulellen's great shock, while gesturing, with an open hand, for all to perceive her. 'And while such an impropriety we could never sanction,' he went on, 'I say you should ask yourself still, do the many acts of kindness and civic duty attributed to the deceased bear out with any similitude to the serious charge you have to try?

'The result will, I trust, prove of infinite service, or indeed bring infinite grief, not alone to those close to the deceased, but to your community at large. I now leave you to your conclusion.'

The jury having reached an unanimous decision, Mr William Shanahan, elderly pauper turned foreman of the group, stepped forward to deliver its qualification: 'We, the jury, find that the said Cornelius Creed, on the 21st of July, in the year aforesaid, died of accidental drowning, brought on by derangement, having suffered great debilitation and delirium through fever, likely acquired in the action of performing his many benevolent, selfless, and community-minded endeavours.'

The jury having signed the inquisition, the court separated.

43

SNUFF

To collect the hat he'd forgotten when leaving the inquest, Thomas French re-entered the tavern that evening, still utterly shaken and outside of himself. Much to his surprise he there found a drunk coroner slumped upon a stool, his head resting on the bar; Mr McCarthy, the young reporter to the *Examiner,* asleep on another; and an upright Mr Shanahan between them, clearly in much better shape, holding court.

'Ah, Mr French, my heart flew up to you today. I commend you on a fine tribute to your dearly departed employer,' said he, inviting the clerk to join his circle.

'Thank you, Mr Shanahan.'

'Shannie, to you, Mr French. Hard pressed for company, I am. Would you look at this lot? I am but a lump of sugar round which these queer fellows, like so many blue-bottle flies, settle all at once. This gentleman is much partaken of the whiskey punch; the young lad is not schooled at all; and behold those mullakins in the corner,' he said, pointing out the gangly Crier of the Court and Clerk of the Peace, both asleep halfway under a table down the room. ''Tis all owing to the grape, and none of them able to handle it. Barkeep, two jars of porter on my good fellow, the coroner, here.'

'Certainly, Mr Shanahan,' the man answered, coming to his tap.

'I don't often imbibe, Mr French. But I'll drink to the honour of a good man this day, in Mr Creed. Many's a day we did battle across that counter,' he reminisced, 'but always we concluded our business with respect and dacency, having consigned some item into the careful safe-keeping of "my uncle", for the benefit of the poor.'

'The deceased was your *uncle*?' asked the barkeep, a slovenly type with a huge moustache.

'*That* is a technical phrase,' Shannie answered, with some contempt.

Suddenly sitting up, the coroner shouted, 'Talesman!' then flaked again, returning to his dream.

'Mr Baldwin! As you love me, don't speak,' the old pauper recited over the ear of the unconscious gentleman, as though acting in some drunkard's pantomime, 'as your bail, let me defend you. Leave it all to me. That's a good fellow,' he said, patting his back, mockingly.

'Mr Shanahan, I'm afraid I won't be staying. I no longer partake –'

'Nonsense, Mr French. Let us pore over the memory of a tireless friend to the poor,' insisted the bushy-eyed Shannie, as, after a while fumbling in his pockets, he produced a snuff canister. 'Allow me to descant upon the excellent quality of what I refer, the real, immortal, memory stuff,' he said, unveiling the cacao-brown tobacco dust in earnest. Taking a load upon his little finger, he shot it up one nostril, then held out the box. 'Manufactured by the respectable firm of Lambkin,' he grinned, as French moved a small pinch to the back of his hand.

In place of a drink, Thomas decided. For, in all probability, this was as close to a wake as Mr Creed was going to have under the circumstances. Drawing it up his nose with a quickened snort, French felt instantly dizzy and blocked, until, compelled to clear it, he took out his handkerchief and blew fervently in.

'I should like to apologise to the bench for not offering them a snuff,' Shannie announced. 'I fancy this too pungent for their redundant olfactories, Mr French. But I'll stand a sneezer for me auld rummy,' said he, then, holding high another load, as though an offering to the absent Mr Creed, shot one more himself. 'Oh, and one for Mr Baldwin here, to rouse his pluck,' Shannie added, at the coroner's coming to. But the wily old pauper returned the canister to his pocket before Mr Baldwin apparently understood. 'Barkeep!' He slapped the counter, at which the young reporter jumped to life.

'Thank you Mr, Shanahan. I have my hat,' French said, much too uncomfortable to stay longer, both out of respect for Mr Creed, who'd helped him to outgrow such places, and at the memory of the day's events.

'Right enough, Mr French. Well, whatever about the bad end, here's to you and your dear employer both, on a well-played hand of cards.' Shannie winked knowingly, and, with that, raised his glass to eye level, drained its contents, and stuck it to the counter.

LÚNASA

AUGUST

44

A Whisper from Oblivion

With a shunt, the sliding bottom of the coffin dropped its beshrouded cargo into the large open pit, where, scattered with lime, it was committed to dissolve and entwine with those countless other souls, brimming to the edges.

'I wish to be buried with the ignominious poor,' Cornelius had whispered to Fr Lee during the illness preceding his death, and thus were his wishes being respected.

But in the act of observing them, Paulellen felt only horror: at the indignant thump of his body, as, creaking, the burial cart was pulled away to begin its task anew amid an endless procession of the day's dead; the idle caw of a churchyard crow; the eerie taunt of the wind blowing through her shawl.

By her side were Dorcas and Samuel, James and Mary. But the children had been forbidden to come. For Samuel, it was the first step forth out of his sickbed, and, though Paulellen worried about the fragility of his health, she greatly appreciated his being there. Con's sister, Alicia, had come with Denis. But they remained at a distance.

'A simple prayer but say over me, Father Thomas,' Paulellen had heard Cornelius to say during a moment of lucidity then. But, so disconsolate at his final resting place, in thrall to the last glimpse she would have of him in this life, she could scarce hear a word of what the priest said now. Instead, Paulellen stared, bereft, at her husband's linen-wrapped remains, laid over a sunken ground, broken here and there by something protruding. At complete odds with summer, the pit conjured a sea of frozen waves covered over by a blanket of snow: its carpet of lime preserving one last vestige of dignity for the owners of those putrefying remains beneath, while protecting the eyes of the living from what they perhaps could not withstand into the bargain.

When, leaving the cemetery, Paulellen felt herself held upright beneath James' shoulder, the verse of the blind beggar at the gate seemed a fitting capstone upon the bitterness of the whole event.

'Out of my family I am the last. My poor wife and children before me have passed,' he recited artlessly, shaking his tin, a lonely penny or pebble bouncing inside. 'The Queen, Peel, and Russell have weaned us from life, with the longest, and slowest, and bluntest of knives. Rattle my bones over the stones. I'm a poor pauper that nobody owns.'

But now it was Paulellen's turn, and by the flickering candles of night and the blinding glimmer of sunlight that split the curtains by day, she battled the insatiable malady her husband had been made to suffer.

For some interminable shift of the hours, helpless in its grasp, she lay defenceless and as crippled as a rabbit in a snare. Further and further from hope with each new awakening, Paulellen sensed she was losing herself, and might have given up were it not for Dorcas, Charlotte, and Marie caring for her so tenderly: for who else had she left to live for now?

Through her illness, the memory of the burial scene weeks before at St Colman's haunted Paulellen: only now in her dreams, it was *her* falling through the coffin; *her* breath punctured with a thump as her back met the bones of those below; *her* gasping, unable to move for the linen shroud that bound her; all the while burning up and freezing cold, unable to speak.

When, sometimes, Con's words circulated in her mind, Paulellen did not know whether she was hearing them or if she herself was speaking them: *bury me with the ignominious poor,* came her own voice, but Con's too; Fr Lee above her, chanting his prayers, rubbing the balm on her lips, head, and feet.

'*Cuimhnigh …*' she heard Cornelius say, tortured, in the throes of his fever, as over and over he conversed with the mysterious Mr Hallissey. '"*Cuimhnigh,*" Mr Hallissey, Pádraig Ua Buachalla whispered it to me, dying. What does it mean?' her husband had called aloud repeatedly in his delirium, yet never seemed either to get an answer or to conclude the conversation. But whether her husband was dreaming, or recalling some real event, *Paulellen* had known what the word meant.

'Remember,' she poured softly into his ear, whenever he'd fixated on the question, 'it means *remember*, Connie.'

In her own fever, Paulellen woke up, crying for him, unsure if he was alive or dead, wondering if it was all just some frightful dream she was having. Perhaps *she* was sick, hallucinating, and *he* was caring for *her? But why then doesn't he come?*

'Cornelius?' she cried weakly in the darkness, blind to her surroundings, when Dorcas was not there, easing her fever and cooling her down. She felt better when her sister or one of the children was with her.

But it was at reaching the point when, as though floating under water, Paulellen could no longer tell if anyone was there or not and, save for the distant sound of muted voices, no answer came at all – that was when she felt most alone.

Am I dying? she asked.
Am I dying, Con?

———

'The shoes! The shoes!' Paulellen panicked, trying desperately to rise from the bed.

'Paulellen, what are you doing to yourself? You must stay lying down!' Dorcas insisted.

'The shoes! I have to …' Paulellen cried aloud, struggling for breath.

'What shoes? We can get one of the boys to fetch them,' her sister reasoned. But by her eyes it was clear Dorcas thought it was the fever talking;

that maybe Paulellen was relapsing now too. It being the first time she was coherent and strong enough to talk, Dorcas had just broken the news that, during her unconsciousness, the bank's agents had come to enforce the distraint, and had cleared out the shop.

'Pat Riordan saw "A Pawnbroker's Lot" advertised as going up for auction at the Cork Bazaar, on Saturday.' Samuel added.

'Which Saturday?' Paull wheezed, in her weakened state. 'What day is it today?'

"Tis Sunday,' Samuel answered, when Paulellen realised with horror that the whole contents of the shop had most likely been already sold, and were probably being broken up already.

'I have to …' she repeated, attempting to rise again.

'Everything is gone, Paull,' Dorcas insisted, sounding equally upset. 'John was there for the distraint and said there wasn't a hair left in the place. They took everything, he said.'

'No … it can't be!' Paulellen broke down, at last, crying hysterically.

'Oh, my poor sister,' Dorcas said, as Paulellen flailed her arms in despair, 'you poor thing … you poor thing. Oh, you have a lot to cry for,' she said, consoling her, stifling Paulellen's sobs in her chest, like a mother. Paulellen sobbed openly for a while, until, eventually quiet, she rested, spent, in her sister's embrace.

'Now, tell me … what is so special about these shoes?' Dorcas asked.

'Cornelius feared they were cursed,' Paulellen began, free to dry her eyes with the corner of the bed sheet. 'His greatest anxiety was that they'd be passed on to someone else and that the curse would go along with them … I know, 'tis ridiculous,' she went on, weeping softly, 'but real or imagined, that was his fear and for the sake of his memory if nothing else I have to retrieve them … that he might rest at peace, God help him.'

'We'll find them somehow. Don't worry,' Dorcas said, embracing her again.

But the auction had already passed, Paulellen knew, and a pin in a field of hay would be easier to find than a pair of old shoes amongst all the paupers in Cork city.

That night, frightened at feeling feverish again, Paulellen could not sleep.

By the morning, her condition had intensified and once more, in her delirium, she recognised the voice of Dr McSwiney.

'We can only hope she has strength enough left to endure a second bout,' he said as, bound and shrouded, out through the door of the coffin Paulellen landed with a slump, her wind punctured amongst the lime-caked remains of the overflowing pit.

And were the haunting images of her husband's interment not enough: as she slipped in and out of lucidity, those other grief-stricken questions came repeatedly to the surface too.

Didn't you love me, Connie? How could you have left me like this?

Desperate for solace, in a moment of clarity, Paulellen cast her mind back to the morning, days after the burial, when she had run to James and Mary's house …

45

Balancing the Books

Frantic, Paulellen had arrived with every worst thought in her mind and banged upon the door. Despite the verdict of the inquest, which had brought her great comfort, she now believed Cornelius had ended his own life, after all. There could be no other explanation, she thought, horrified.

'Paulellen, welcome. Come in, come in,' Mary said, evidently surprised at the unannounced visit, and Paulellen's demeanour.

'I'm sorry for calling so sudden, Mary. Is James at home? I'd very much like to take his counsel,' Paulellen pleaded.

'Of course,' she answered, gazing at the letter Paulellen was clutching. 'He's in his study, come through.'

'James!' Paulellen called out as he arose from his desk. 'James, I went back to the house today for the first time, and, where I'd last brought Cornelius food and his post, I found this letter which he clearly opened. I don't know what to think. Surely there must be some mistake?'

'Paull, have a seat,' James said, donning his glasses. 'Let me look at this carefully. Mary, could you bring some tea, for Paulellen?' he called abroad.

'On the hob,' Mary shouted back from the kitchen.

'"Letter of distraint,"' James read, and held the glasses at his temple, as though doing so might reveal more of the document's meaning. Sitting back, he began, silently, to examine what Paulellen had already tried numerous times to decipher on her way there:

By the 39th section, it is provided that if any proprietor or lessee of the premises, or any other person, shall at any time after sunset on Saturday, or between that time and the rising of the sun on the following Monday morning, buy, sell, loan, transfer, or aid or assist in the buying, selling, trading or removal of any assets or monies, material or otherwise, from any part of the property to prevent same from being distrained against any rent, loan, or mortgage, defaulted upon or payable thereout, every such tenant, proprietor, or person so offending shall be deemed guilty of a criminal act and shall be imprisoned, with or without hard labour, for such period not exceeding twelve months, as the court shall direct.

And by the 40th section, it is provided that if proprietors, lessees, or any others fraudulently carry off, or attempt to carry off from the premises any goods or chattels to prevent a distraint, the bank or other person so entitled to make a distraint may seize such good and chattels, and the horses and carriages employed for carrying them off; and parties concerned in such actual or attempted carrying off shall be guilty of misdemeanour and liable to the penalties recited in the preceding section.

Governors of the Provincial Bank of Cork.
Monday, July 19th, 1847.

'What do you think, James? I'm praying it was sent by mistake,' Paulellen said, as, removing his glasses once more, he lowered the letter. Still considering the document, James did not answer at first.

'I have business on tomorrow, in Cork,' he said eventually. 'Let me have a word with the governor. See what we can learn. I know him ... But Paulellen,' he inquired, cautiously, 'was Cornelius in any ... difficulty, that you are aware?'

By the earnestness in his voice, Paulellen felt such a question did not bode well.

'No,' she answered, unequivocally, 'but you would know quicker than I, James.'

Shaking his head gravely, James seemed to infer it was as much a surprise to him.

'Let's see what tomorrow brings,' he said.

The following evening, returned from Cork, James found Paulellen, Mary, Dorcas and Samuel around the table, all anxious to discover whatever he had learned.

'I've talked with the bank,' he said, removing his coat, 'and have also been to the shop with Mr French, whom I called upon to show me the books, so that I might make sense of it all, and, well … it seems Cornelius had defaulted on some recent borrowings, that –'

'Borrowings?' Paulellen repeated, clearly shocked.

'I'm afraid he had overextended his credit and was seemingly unable to make good on the repayments.'

'James, what does "overextended" mean? Can you talk in plain terms?' Mary requested, as James considered how he might explain such technical circumstances as he was still trying to unravel for himself.

'Apologies. As I understand it, long before Cornelius reopened the shop; after the losses of Forty-Five; in fact, a year or more before he even *closed*, he was already in debt and operating at a loss.'

'But the same was surely true of most businesses?' Sam suggested, still weak in his speaking.

'True, at least to some extent,' James answered. 'However, I expect a person in the business of loaning money, or giving credit, would be more exposed than the average trader: perhaps left with a surplus of unsold stock. Yet Cornelius would have *hoped* to balance this out, with a good harvest in Forty-Six.'

'Yes, I heard him say things of that nature, around then,' Paulellen interjected.

'But when that, of course, did not come, well, closing the shop would appear to have been an attempt to limit the damage. His next decision, however …' James said, stopping to pass a heavy sigh, '*reopening,* at the great risk of borrowing against his assets, I can only presume, must have been a knowing gesture of charity.'

'Charity?' Mary repeated. 'With all respect, is that possible in such a business?'

'I don't understand either,' Paulellen added, 'and how could he have lost so much in just *three months* since reopening? I never knew the shop to be busier!'

Though he wished he were not the envoy of such tidings, James realised it *had* fallen to him to represent the situation, and, as Con's oldest friend, to take great care in doing so.

'It may be painful to hear this,' he began, 'but according to the books, and corroborated by Mr French, it seems as though not a single payment was taken across the counter from the day the shop reopened, and that at Con's specific instruction. It is as much as I can establish that in all the time since, he simply ... gave out money, and gave people back their goods.'

At the conclusion of this statement the room fell silent and, for a long moment, there was dead stillness. But by degrees, Paulellen's expression turned to one of torment or despair.

'To what end?' she blurted out. 'What has changed? The poor are still dying in their droves! And whether knowingly or not, he has killed himself in the process!'

No one dared to answer, James sensed, perceiving the atmosphere of disbelief around the table.

'Did he plan to leave me a pauper, altogether?' Paulellen asked, as, gripping her hair, staring blankly, she seemed to direct her question inward.

Who could answer or attempt to console a person left in such agonising grief, James reflected. Such a depth of privacy was a sacred province reserved alone for the partners in a marriage, whose lives it concerned so deeply and intimately. And yet, here were they – he, Mary, Samuel and Dorcas – thrust by fate, and perhaps the negligence of one derelict in his usual intellectual capacities, to fill the breach in his absence.

Though he worried it might be out of place to say it, what James wished *most* to express to Paulellen was his growing admiration for what, morally, he more and more considered to be a noble stance on her husband's part; at least when separated from all its futility and disregard for the ultimate consequences. For his friend's actions had surely changed much, and for a very great many if the books were accurate, just not in a way that was readily visible to anyone present.

'If I know Cornelius, he would have had some plan.' Dorcas broke the silence, intervening before Paulellen broke down, James supposed. 'He would never knowingly put Paulellen in this position,' she said, and stroked her sister's hair.

'I tend to agree,' James put up. 'I had all the journey home to reflect upon it, and I suspect he must have planned to right himself whenever the crisis ended. I know he believed it would, and surely *must*, end sometime. But, Paulellen, I must apologise … I have only just now remembered; it seems there was one thing Cornelius safeguarded through all of this.'

'Oh?' Paulellen replied, appearing hopeful.

'At some point last December, the proprietorship of the building itself, or its lease, was transferred to your name. The caveat, however, is that while the bank would not disclose to me in any detail – being that I hold no actual interest in the matter – they did make clear that a large part of its value would need to be expended to cover the outstanding debt: also inherited by you. But what is left, I suspect, will allow you a reasonable living, and I'm quite sure I speak for all here when I say that Dorcas and Samuel, Mary and I, will not see you wanting for anything.'

As he spoke, Dorcas and Mary rallied around Paulellen, squeezing her hands.

'We are family,' James added, knowing full well he and Mary were not actual relatives. But by a lifelong friendship, and by extension through Dorcas and Sam, he felt adamant it was true nonetheless.

'That's right, James,' Mary agreed, leading a chorus of endearments and affections.

When, finally, Paulellen was brought to the point of tears, Mary and Dorcas jumped to embrace her.

'Thank you all. Thank you … I just … how could I have missed it?' Paulellen asked, broken.

'I am ashamed to say, I had a feeling at one point he might be in unusual territory,' James admitted, 'but it being Cornelius, I questioned my intuition and reasoned that, of all people, he would have it worked out and finely projected, plotted on a graph. I was wrong … and I regret not questioning.'

'No, James, don't blame yourself,' Paulellen said, touching his hand.

But, feeling encouraged, James decided to attempt his reasoning: 'For all his logic, it seems to me a wish to do something noble and altruistic became Con's priority. But at some point he either lost sight of, or simply abandoned, any notion of balancing the books. In fact … huh …' Realising how much easier it was to see in retrospect, James mocked himself under his breath. 'The clerk, who I must say is terribly upset and feeling greatly responsible at having been taken into Cornelius' confidence, confessed to me that when he questioned the new system, and whether or not Con thought the poor would ever repay his kindnesses or not, the reply he got was essentially that "it would all balance out", or, that "he was sure they would some day", is how Mr French put it.'

'I expect we may never know the full extent of his actions, nor understand them,' Sam proposed, 'but I think we have to acknowledge that our Cornelius was deeply troubled, if an equally well-intentioned soul, perhaps not cut out for the horror of our times. Not that any of us are, mind. But what we are picking over here, I believe, are the results of his trying to reconcile with the extraordinary events still unfolding around us, as best *he* could, by his own compass. And what I think *you* are saying, James, is that on the presumption that he and Paulellen could outlast the crisis intact, Cornelius perhaps reasoned that the business would right itself … but that in the meantime, he was compelled to give whatever he could of himself in service to the poor,' Sam finished emphatically.

'Exactly,' James responded, bringing his fist to the table, grateful at his brother's finding the words that he himself could not.

'And with the shop consigned to Paulellen's name,' Sam continued, 'he likely thought he had safeguarded against the worst, but –'

'Yes?' James encouraged him.

'But he just realised too late – with the receipt of that *bill*, that it all had happened much faster than he'd expected, dishing out money like that. I think poor Cornelius must have got such a shock …'

James did not answer this time, but nodded slowly in agreement, as though for all, when Paulellen too seemed at last to be taking heart from the reasoning of those around her.

After a time, when there were no new questions, Dorcas suggested they had likely absorbed enough for one day. 'Perhaps we should all get a good rest.'

'Paull,' James called to her, leaving, 'as Mary's father is very unwell, we must go to Skibbereen a few days. But I will write to the bank beforehand, urging them with whatever influence I have, to hold off.'

'Thank you, James,' Paulellen replied, looking very tired.

46

Clondrohid

'Clondrohid,' the voice said.

Startled, Pádraig stood back at the sudden appearance of the ghost before him. For there on the doorstep, leaning on the same nobbled stick, was the old man who, so many moons before, had guided him through the streets of Macroom to the pawnbroker's establishment and represented him there over the transaction of the shoes.

The man's face had left an indelible mark upon Pádraig's memory that day, and, while surely more weatherbeaten and aged by hardship now, there was no mistaking it. Unless Pádraig was dreaming, Cáit had heard the knock too, he reflected. It just made no sense that the man was here, at the door, in Doire Liath.

'Won't you invite the man in?' Cáit said, when the visitor, removing his tattered old hat, held it to his heart, politely reminding them of the old custom, perhaps, of always offering the passing stranger a morsel, or a seat by the fire.

'Forgive me,' Pádraig said, remembering his manners. '*Bail ó Dhia ort*. The blessings of God upon you.' He gestured a welcome.

The old man returned the blessing, then greeted Cáit, the woman of the house, and smiled down upon the children. They were unused to visitors, and Pádraig was surprised to discover in their faces something long absent, a glow of joy.

'Oh – these are for your pot,' the visitor said, and all eyes lit up at his producing a small handful of potatoes from his pockets, the first they'd seen all year.

'Beyond generous, Mr –' Pádraig said, only to realise he could not recall the man's name.

'Shannie,' the guest said with a gentle bow, and Pádraig remembered, *Ua Seanacháin*.

'Are ye all recovered?' Shannie asked, settling himself upon the stool offered while, at such a question, Pádraig and Cáit swapped a look of confusion.

'We are faring as we are faring,' Pádraig answered, unwilling to pretend they were in good health, but impatient, too, to learn what strange sequence of events had led to this moment.

Seeming to sense his host's impatience, the old pauper got to his meaning. 'Do you remember the pawnbroker?' Shannie asked.

Ah, thought Pádraig, understanding at last: the broker had discovered his whereabouts and sent the old man to do his bidding, who had 'the tongue' to speak to him. Ready to offer his visitor the door, Pádraig arose.

'He is dead,' the old man said, hat still over his heart, with his eyes rolling up to follow Pádraig, now standing above him.

Sensing now there was more to this visit than the mere collection of a debt, Pádraig retreated and, sitting, invited the old man's talk.

'He was looking for you, you know? But not for the reason you think,' Shannie said, lowering the hat, and once more implying, to Pádraig's bemusement, a strange knowledge of his recent concerns.

From there, by the glow of the fire, the old man explained how he had lately observed the pawnbroker to reopen his shop and, how, thereafter, Mr Creed had given everything of himself in service to the poor, only to die by drowning himself in the river after a bout of fever.

Though moved by the tragic tale, Pádraig was at a loss to understand his part in it all. But the old pauper was not finished, saying it had only been after the distraint had taken place, in full public view, that with great sadness, the poor of the town had come to realise that in his efforts to help them, Mr Creed had ruined himself, emptying his coffers entirely while at the same time giving back everything he had in pledge to any poor person who returned to claim it: clothes; blankets; coats; bowls; hats; or whatever could be used to barter for food. With some delight, Shannie described a contraption in the newly reopened shop that flung those freely redeemed items back out through the counter wall to the desperate souls on the waiting side, while the coin chute delivered money, like manna from heaven, for whatever items they could lay their hands on to offer in pledge. There was little discussion of when they should pay it back, or even requirement to place the items in his keeping, Shannie said.

His two hands resting over the stick, Ua Seanacháin related the tale he had heard on the wind, of Mr Creed's having visited the pestilent hut of a dying man all but days before his own reckoning with the dire malady had begun, which Shannie supposed was how he had contracted the disease.

But it had not been until he'd overheard the tale of the horseman in the public tavern just two nights before that Shannie had begun to put two and two together; for there, as he'd listened in, the horseman had divulged to his company that, as the driver, *he* had taken 'the pawnbroker' out to the realm of Gurranenagappul that night, where a customer of Mr Creed's had insisted they would find one 'Pádraig Ua Buachalla', the man the pawnbroker was so desperate to find.

But, alas! They had there arrived only in time for Mr Creed to behold the man taking his dying breath, his poor dead family stretched in fever and poverty all around him.

The horseman had thereafter driven the pawnbroker back to Macroom, forlorn and likely pregnant with the seeds of his own demise upon his person, for the trouble.

'And what did he want of the man; this other Ua Buachalla?' Pádraig asked, 'or are you going to say it was me he was seeking?'

'*'Twas* you he was looking for,' Shannie insisted. 'I wasn't sure, myself, until the driver remarked that throughout the journey there and back, the pawnbroker had closely guarded one specific item in his possession,'

Ua Seanacháin recounted colourfully. 'Loud enough for the driver to hear, shouting over the horses' hooves and the bouncing of the carriage, Mr Creed told Hallissey, his guide, that the pair of shoes in his lap once belonged to the father of Pádraig Ua Buachalla, the man from Clondrohid, who'd pledged them to him some eighteen months before. Sure, when I heard the part about the shoes, I knew the poor divil had found the wrong man,' Shannie said, lifting, and poking the stick into the floor, his eyes sparkling with the flicker of the light as a yellow glow of warmth enclosed his face. 'And wasn't it lucky for you he had the wrong man?' he said, with a quick twist of his neck.

'What did he want with me?'

'That I do not know,' Shannie answered, his arms opened out for a moment, 'just that he wished to return you them.'

Frustrated, trying to understand, Pádraig lowered his head and scratched violently through the dense mat of his hair. 'How did you know where to find me? Or even that I was still alive, tell me?'

'Oh, I knew you weren't dead,' Shannie countered, assuredly.

'How?'

'Sure, I've been keeping an eye on you,' the old man announced, as if this should be something already known to Pádraig, who shook his head. 'From time to time,' Shannie added, quieter, seemingly with a hint of shame. It was the gentlest shrug of his shoulders, gave that impression to Pádraig, who could hardly believe his ears.

Was he ashamed at watching after him, or guilty at only doing so from time to time, though, Pádraig wondered, somehow suspecting the latter. Either way, the whole idea was becoming more fanciful and harder to accept by the minute.

'Didn't I find you lost in the square that day, and bring you to where you needed to go?' said Ua Seanacháin, as if sensing his doubt.

'You did,' Pádraig answered, though that still did not explain how, one year and a half later, with no apparent idea of where they lived, the old man had landed at their door.

'On last Christmas Day, didn't you find a cake of bread upon the step?' Shannie asked, to a long silence, when – though he did not know how – Pádraig began to believe him.

'And how do you suppose the four of you survived the ravages of fever, practically unconscious, with no way to feed or bring water to yourselves, six weeks ago and more?'

Feeling something dripping onto his hand, Pádraig looked down to realise the ball of a tear had fallen off his cheek and, looking to Cáit, found she was crying too. But more unexpected was the surprise of turning back to find Shannie, a supposed stranger, with his eyes also filled, glistening with the vulnerability of a soft soul that, though Pádraig had sensed before, now showed in his face too.

Learning that, at the lowest of low times, when, broken, Pádraig had been unable to carry the burden himself, this lonesome pauper, a wiry old man, had stepped in like some mysterious guardian to save him and his family, was too disarming and, throwing his hands up, it was all he could manage to get the word 'why?' out, as instinctively he swiped at the tears with the back of his hand.

'Because one act of kindness can change the world,' Shannie replied, out from under the be-charred eyebrows of an earnest frown, 'and you, as a boy, taught me that.'

Desperately trusting, but unable to find anything in his memory that spoke to the claim, Pádraig squinted, forcing more tears, so that the picture distorted before him, when, of a sudden, the image grew to resemble a moment from so long ago: at the fair in Clondrohid, where he had cried at seeing a travelling wiseman scorned and mocked by a crowd of those looking on, who had not believed what he had to say.

'You remember, don't you?' Shannie said. 'When everyone else laughed and jeered, you stood up, a boy, and shamed men amongst them, until they walked away, quietened. Where was their kindness for a stranger, you asked them.'

Unable to speak, Pádraig nodded his understanding and, pushing his tears away once more, now recognised the face of the much older man in a new light. 'Clondrohid,' he coughed out, on a stifle of laughter, feeling his children draw close to comfort him.

'Clondrohid,' Shannie returned, smiling back but deathly serious, locking eyes with Pádraig, as though one soul to another. 'That's why,' he added.

Just then, realising Cáit could not have followed the conversation, Pádraig turned to explain. 'Mind how I told you of the old man who took me to the pawnbroker's?'

'I remember,' Cáit said, smiling as though her heart had been warmed.

'How he'd greeted me with that word, as though he somehow knew where I'd come from, and I standing in the middle of the town?' Pádraig continued, even though Cáit had already acknowledged his meaning, 'and you insisted on calling me Clondrohid, which vexed me,' he told the old man with a light-hearted reprimand. 'So why come now, after all that time?'

'Because … in Mr Creed, I lately saw the same kind of magic that I saw in you that day, in the eyes of a child. And I thought you of all people, capable of the same wonder, would wish to know the regard he had for you, a like soul. You asked me *why*, and I said I don't know. That is true. But it occurred to me perhaps your spirits were drawn to one another; linked somehow, by such magic, and such deeds.

'Because kindness like his, and like yours, deserves not to be kept secret. It ought to be shared, instead. Realising that gave me to understand I should thank you,' the old man continued. 'But lastly, and perhaps most of all, because I am old, and won't always be here to look in on you,' Shannie said, water glistening in his eyes once more, 'and before I'm done, I would wish you to know the effect your kindness had on me.'

Reaching out, Pádraig clasped the old man's hand with a force he had no longer thought he possessed. 'If any of this is true,' he said, squeezing firmly, 'then I say you have well repaid any kindness I showed you, Ua Seanacháin, and I free you of the need to offer any more. Besides that …

if the pawnbroker and I *are* linked, then 'tis you connected us, with the eyes to see such magic,' Pádraig added and watched, as, at last, a tear brimmed from the old man's eye and rolled slowly down his cheek.

MEÁN FÓMHAIR

SEPTEMBER

47

THE SILENT BELL

At Codrum, by the grand fire, Massy Warren was observing his late routine of going through petitions for aid from his tenants and consigning each one to the flames, when the next, written in a crude hand, stood out as no petition at all.

> Massy Warren I know youd that dog brung to the bodies
> but will YOUR hounds com back I wonder
>
> sined
> the widow creed

Propped up in bed, Paulellen stared at the wall, reliving the conversation they'd been having before Dorcas had left the room.

'Am I well again?' Paulellen had asked.

'Thank God, it seems you're through it,' Dorcas had answered and, taking Paulellen's hand, had brought her own head to rest where their fingers entwined. 'Oh, Paull, I thought you were gone. I don't know what I would do if … We're all that's left of the Crones now, you and I.'

'I know,' Paulellen replied. 'Thank you for looking after me, sister.'

'It hardly needs saying, Paull, but Sam and I want you to stay here with us now. We have the room, and the children will not hear otherwise. They love you being here.'

'Even sick?' Paulellen laughed, then began to cough.

'Even sick,' Dorcas said.

That was when her sister had left the room, to answer the door.

As she blinked slowly, with heavy eyes, the question of the shoes and what had become of them was still in Paulellen's mind; though something she would simply have to let go of, she was quietly accepting. Being in no state to go finding them herself, it would be rude and ungrateful to ask any more of Dorcas and her family.

'Paull, you have a visitor. Agnes Fowler?' Dorcas said, returned with a questioning look. It was a name Paulellen did not recognise either, but, too tired for most any other expression, she accepted with a beckoning motion. Shown in was a red-haired woman, who was not wealthy, but cared for, Paulellen imagined.

'Forgive me Mrs Creed, I think we have not met. Fowler is my married name. I am Agnes French, a sister of Tomasín.'

'Ah, how is Thomas? He might come and see me?' Paulellen said, full of affection for the clerk.

'I'm afraid he passed, a few days since, ma'am,' the woman answered, tilting her head in sadness.

'Oh no … what happened?' Paulellen asked, grief-stricken.

'Fever 'twas, ma'am,' said the woman, clutching a handkerchief, pitifully. 'Anyway, I see you're convalescing, ma'am, I don't want to keep you – his last request before he got bad was that if he did not recover, I was to bring you these, for safekeeping.'

As the woman unveiled the old leather brogues from beneath her shawl, Paulellen drew back her breath and gazed in awe, as though a miracle had occurred.

'He saved them from the distraint, ma'am, said he knew what they would mean to you.'

———

'It's so lovely to share to this day with you all,' Dorcas said, taking Paulellen's hand on one side and Sam's on the other as, seated at the dinner table, they prepared to mark Charlotte's twelfth birthday.

Almost a week since she had recovered this time, though cheerful, smiling as she stroked the roseate skin of her niece's cheek, Paulellen found she was struggling to adjust to her new life.

'Did you hear the Guardians' meeting had to be held at the courthouse, Saturday?' Sam remarked later, when the children had left the table. ''Twas deemed ill-advisable to resume at the boardroom, for fear of infection at the workhouse.'

'They could meet anywhere and they'd still bicker at every nuance,' Dorcas answered, 'but mostly about their precious rates – and the Union in a bankrupt state.'

Dorcas rolled her eyes playfully when Sam looked away. Paulellen knew her sister just wanted everything to be right for her. But where she was concerned, it was a comfort to see the Sam of old back to his portly self, apron on, in from the bakery.

'We might have survived this harvest, but we are far from out of the woods,' he continued, picking up his paper. 'Listen to this: "Out of an estimated three and a half *million* acres *usually* planted across Ireland, England and Scotland, which under normal circumstances would yield just over thirty million tons of potatoes, an average of one-half the entire crop failed in Forty-Six, with up to two-thirds of Ireland's portion lost. But to think that in the present year, the entire surface planted was barely one million. If even the whole of the seed planted was to yield nine tons to the acre, they could not hope to produce more than nine million tons of the usual *thirty*."' Sam shook his head inside the paper, as he finished reading. 'And winter coming soon – the third in a row with hardly any food, for those worst off. In reality the crisis is going from bad to worse,' he said, turning the page, 'and the official line, rather ridiculously, is that the famine is over! I'm not sure how much you have still to catch up on, Paull,' he added, looking over his glasses, 'but with the first glimmer of light on the horizon, the government announced all measures of relief were to be dismantled immediately. Perhaps it's as well poor Cornelius is not alive to see this. I think this would –'

'Samuel! Dear God –' Dorcas intervened, her voice awash with disbelief.

It was the first time Paulellen had heard anyone speak his name since she'd recovered, she realised. Not that she had resented the silence. Rather, she'd understood the sensitivity. But how nice it was to hear it now, she thought, missing him so terribly.

'Forgive me, Paull. I'm sorry,' Sam said, frowning.

'No, Sam, I miss hearing his name. We should say it more often, in fact.'

At this, Dorcas clapped a hand upon her heart as though her mind had been eased.

'I'm going to visit the shop tomorrow,' Paulellen announced, when the atmosphere seemed stunned to silence.

'Are you sure you're ready?' Dorcas asked, tentatively.

'I need to get out and take the air anyway, while the weather is good,' Paulellen replied. ''Tis just across the square, besides.'

'I think it's a good idea,' Samuel said, smartly.

'Of course,' Dorcas said, with some hesitance, 'what I mean is, are you ready to face the shop?'

'I think so,' Paull answered, consulting herself. If only to gather her thoughts and have some time in familiar surroundings, she decided. 'I want to see it one last time, before 'tis sold … and make my peace with it,' she said, smiling gently to reassure them both.

'I suppose you have to face it some time,' Dorcas relented. 'I can accompany you, if –?'

'No,' Paull said, and took her hand, assuredly, 'I need to do this on my own.'

Reaching the far side of the square the following afternoon, Paulellen felt more like she had climbed a mountain than walked a few yards, so short was her breath. At one point, she'd had to stop, and bought a small basket of eggs in case Dorcas might be watching from the upstairs window.

But seeing the footpath outside the shop had made all the effort worthwhile. There, laid carefully beneath the window, were boughs of laurel and evergreen twigs by the pile. With the late September sun behind her, the sight brought a great feeling of warmth to Paulellen's heart and, moved by such an outpouring of grief at her husband's death, she closed her eyes, inviting the sharp tonic of the freshly cut offerings into her senses.

Once inside, the empty shop had never seemed so quiet, and, remembering Lucky, Paulellen hoped that James and Mary's children were as happy to have him back as Dorcas had promised they were.

For the briefest of moments when, behind the counter, she drew back and released the contraption that squealed and thumped as the springs pulled it back into place, Paulellen caught a glimpse of the grim scene with the coffin and the churchyard once more, but reasoned that the harder memories would loosen in time. A brighter thought was the understanding, from the drawer's function, that Cornelius *had* tried to protect her.

Stepping through to the shop floor again, Paulellen looked back to the empty counter, nevermore to ring with the voice of either her poor Cornelius or Thomas French, two of the gentlest souls a pauper could hope to meet, she imagined, both gone and lost in a blink. How cruel a purse for their untiring efforts to save the poor from such needless tragedy; while many more, inspired to senseless indifference, walked amongst them still.

As though in a dream, Paulellen saw them working together behind the counter amidst the throng, ferrying goods back out to the poor, the ring of coins landing down the chute.

'Oh Connie, what am I to do without you?' she asked. At the sound or the shadow of something almost imperceptible, Paulellen turned to behold a pauper stopping outside to lay down a wand of laurel that, in shape at least, closely resembled the man presenting it: a long, gaunt figure, in tattered short trousers and a hole-ridden vest. But, though careworn and poor, his hair and beard neglected, the way he stood upright and held himself as she approached to watch the ceremony of his actions revealed a noble being, his cap removed as he considered the shrine.

Forgetting herself, Paulellen was surprised when, looking up, the man met her eyes directly, and, after a moment, gently nodded his respects.

Paulellen felt proud in that moment of the regard her husband had earned of the people and, feeling herself his representation, returned the gentle bow.

Having held his gaze a while, Paulellen smiled and was preparing to turn away when the mourner, with a gesture, pointed to the door of the shop: a request of her to meet him there, she understood.

Remembering she had locked it, Paulellen went to unbolt the door and wondered, as it opened, at the absence of the bell overhead: something she had not missed on the way in, she realised.

'Hello,' she greeted the stranger, inviting him to stand in.

But, though clearly ready to accept, the man first asked a question.

'Bhfuil Gaelainn agat?' he asked. *Do you have Irish?*

'Some,' Paulellen replied, at which point he obliged and, lowering his head, crossed the doorstep.

'I learned of your husband's death, and of all he did for the poor,' the visitor announced, as, listening, Paulellen thanked him by gesture. 'I am told he looked for me,' the man said, to her surprise.

'Ua Buachalla?' Paulellen said aloud, and perceived the stranger to nod once.

'*Pádraig* Ua Buachalla?' she asked, making certain, when the man repeated the gesture.

'But you were dead … my husband said he saw it with his own eyes.'

'I am not dead,' Ua Buachalla replied with a knowing but gentle smile, before looking to his toes a moment, for embarrassment, but met her eyes once more with the same expression.

'Well, of course,' Paulellen corrected herself, relieved, 'but he *was* looking for you. There's a pair of shoes – I have them, I can –' Speaking excitedly, she reached, as though to retrieve them from across the square, neatly placed in the light of her bedroom window at the Welplys'.

'No need,' Pádraig Ua Buachalla said, raising a hand, 'I was well looked after for the shoes. Anyway, I'd give them no use ... God's shoes,' he said, directing her eyes to the toughened, worn skin of two naked feet that looked to have carried him through many miles, Paulellen imagined.

'I came only to pay my respects,' he said. 'But whatever comes of me, or any of those whose lives he affected, let it be known your husband deserves to be remembered well.'

Solemnly, Pádraig Ua Buachalla extended his hand.

Paulellen cried and shook it lightly, then, watching as he left the shop, smiled at the realisation that Cornelius had got it all wrong ...

The shoes were not cursed at all, she thought, but merely a symbol of the nature in the best of people to do whatever they could to help one another, regardless of the cost to themselves; that life is resilient and carries on, however uncaring the powers that be, or unimaginable the struggle; and that there was honour yet for those who, through their deeds, gave life such value, even if, in doing so, they themselves had lost their way.

Suddenly, Paulellen remembered the basket of eggs she'd left resting on the counter and, grabbing them up, raced to the door. Blinded by the glint of the sun outside, Paulellen searched the square and the mouths of the lanes, ready to shout the name of the tall man and give him the eggs to bring to his family.

'Pádraig Ua Buachalla,' she whispered. But as quickly as he had appeared, the elusive pauper had vanished, and was gone once more.

Acknowledgements

Before I list and thank those who had a direct bearing upon the writing of this book, I would like to acknowledge that the path to writing *A Whisper From Oblivion*, and indeed *The Pawnbroker's Reward*, has been one carved and cleared by many others without whose efforts and/or encouragement my own work on this subject would not have been possible. Gratitude to all of those, unseen, whose efforts have contributed to my understanding of this period and its inhabitants.

The unnamed aside, there are a number of people I must thank individually. John O'Connor inspired me to this subject and his book remains a thorough and dependable touchstone of reference and fascination. Though deceased, I'd like to acknowledge *an t-Athar* Peadar Ua Laoghaire, who, in his memoir, recorded his boyhood recollection of the Ua Buachalla family and provided many vivid and insightful local accounts.

Without the initiative of Nicki Howard at Gill Books, neither of these books would exist. I extend my sincere gratitude to Nicki and her team for their continued faith in my ability to tell this story and commitment to helping me do so.

The first soul I report back to returning from the 1840s – Conor Kostick – has been a nurturing and enthusiastic editor. He has been a friend to these writings and I can hardly believe the chemistry we've shared so far. Thank you, Conor.

My appreciation to those whom I've had cause to communicate and work with directly at Gill Books: Esther Ní Dhonnacha, Aoibheann Molumby, Fiona Murphy, Paul Neilan and Charlie Lawlor.

Mo mhíle buíochas to poet and *gaeilgeoir* Ben McCaoilte, who helped greatly with the Irish-language element of this volume. Down many rabbit holes we have fallen together, the shovels abandoned.

A thousand thanks to Georgina Laragy, of TCD, for her generous guidance in the realm of nineteenth-century suicide, cemeteries, and burials; and Niamh Howlin for expertise in nineteenth-century law, juries, and inquests.

Warmest gratitude to the following people for local knowledge and hospitality in the region of Macroom and its bounds: the late Máire MacSuíbhne; Jim Cooney at Cooney's Bookshop, Macroom; Fr Michael Kelleher; Maura O'Flynn; John Kelleher; Tadhg Creedon; Margaret Murphy; Dr Con Kelleher; Catherine Lynch; Geraldine Powell; Majella Flynn; Martin Fitzgerald; Jack Buckley.

Buíochas le hUachtarán na hÉireann Micheál D. Ó hUigínn agus a bhean chéile, Sabina.

To friends of *The Pawnbroker's Reward* whose help carried through to *A Whisper From Oblivion*: Edward O'Rourke; Prof. Christine Kinealy; Prof. Joseph O'Connor; Michael Harding; James Harrold; Dearbhla Walsh; Dominic Sherlock; David Rooney; Joe and Deirdre Hayes; Roz Kachchhi and Anu Halonen; Martin Meyler and Archibald Simpson; Marianne Kennedy; Maeve Kelly; Grainne Fox; Cathal Póirtéir; Caroilin Callery; Kieron Tuohy; Mark McGowan; Dr Jason King; John O'Driscoll; Martin Fagan; Sheila Nicholas; Colm Mac Con Iomaire; Brendan Graham; the late Shay Healy; Edwin Garland; Joe Lancaster; John Sheahan; John Dolan, features editor and assistant editor at *The Echo*; Jane Davies, curator, Lancashire Infantry Museum; Charles Reid, Gordon Highlanders Museum; Dr Jonny Geber, University of Edinburgh; Marion Acreman; Will de Búrca of De Búrca Rare Books; Dominique Ellickson; Daragh Bohan; Patrick Maher; Caitríona Frost; Liadain O'Donovan; Hugh Comerford; Nik Quaife; Dr. Yael Danieli and all at ICMGLT; Irish Arts Center, New York.

Finally, all my love in appreciation of the source, my family: Eimear, Londubh and Jonah. Tammy, Niamh and Ed. O'Rourkes. Killeens. Brennans. In-laws and outlaws.

Recommended Reading

Some authors and works that aided the researching of this book, to list a few:

Black Blight, Michael Galvin – Litho Press, 1995.

'Mortality among institutionalised children during the Great Famine in Ireland: bio-archaeological contextualisation of non-adult mortality rates in the Kilkenny Union Workhouse, 1846–1851', Jonny Geber – from *Continuity and Change*, Vol 31. Cambridge University Press, 2016, 351.

'Scurvy in the Great Irish Famine: Evidence of Vitamin C Deficiency From a Mid-19th Century Skeletal Population', Jonny Geber and Eileen Murphy – *American Journal of Physical Anthropology*, 2012.

Tales from Victorian Cork, Roger Herlihy – Red Abbey Publications, 2012.

Juries in Ireland: Laypersons and Law in the Long Nineteenth Century, Niamh Howlin – Four Courts Press, 2017.

Macroom Union Workhouse 1843–1921, Dr Con Kelleher – Con Kelleher, 2019.

This Great Calamity, Christine Kinealy – Gill & Macmillan, 1994, 2006.

'Items in the sum of that great calamity: suicide in Dublin during the Great Famine', Georgina Laragy – from *Dublin and the Great Irish Famine*, UCD Press, 2022.

Famine in Muskerry: An Drochshaol, Máire MacSuíbhne – Cúilín Gréine Press, 1997.

Grim Bastilles of Despair: The Poor Law Union Workhouses in Ireland, Paschal Mahoney – Quinnipiac University Press, 2016.

'What do people die of during famines: the Great Irish Famine in comparative perspective', Joel Mokyr and Cormac Ó Gráda – from *European Review of Economic History*. Cambridge University Press, 2002.

The Workhouses of Ireland: the fate of Ireland's poor, John O'Connor – Anvil Books, 1995.

My Own Story, An tAthair Peadar O'Laoghaire, translated by Sheila O'Sullivan – Gill & Macmillan, 1973.

A Want of Inhabitants: The Famine in Bantry Union, Geraldine Powell – Eastwood Books, 2021.

Macroom Through the Mists of Time, Denis Paul Ring – Castle House Publications, 1995.

Mo Sgéal Féin, Peadar Ua Laoghaire – Browne & Nolan, 1915.